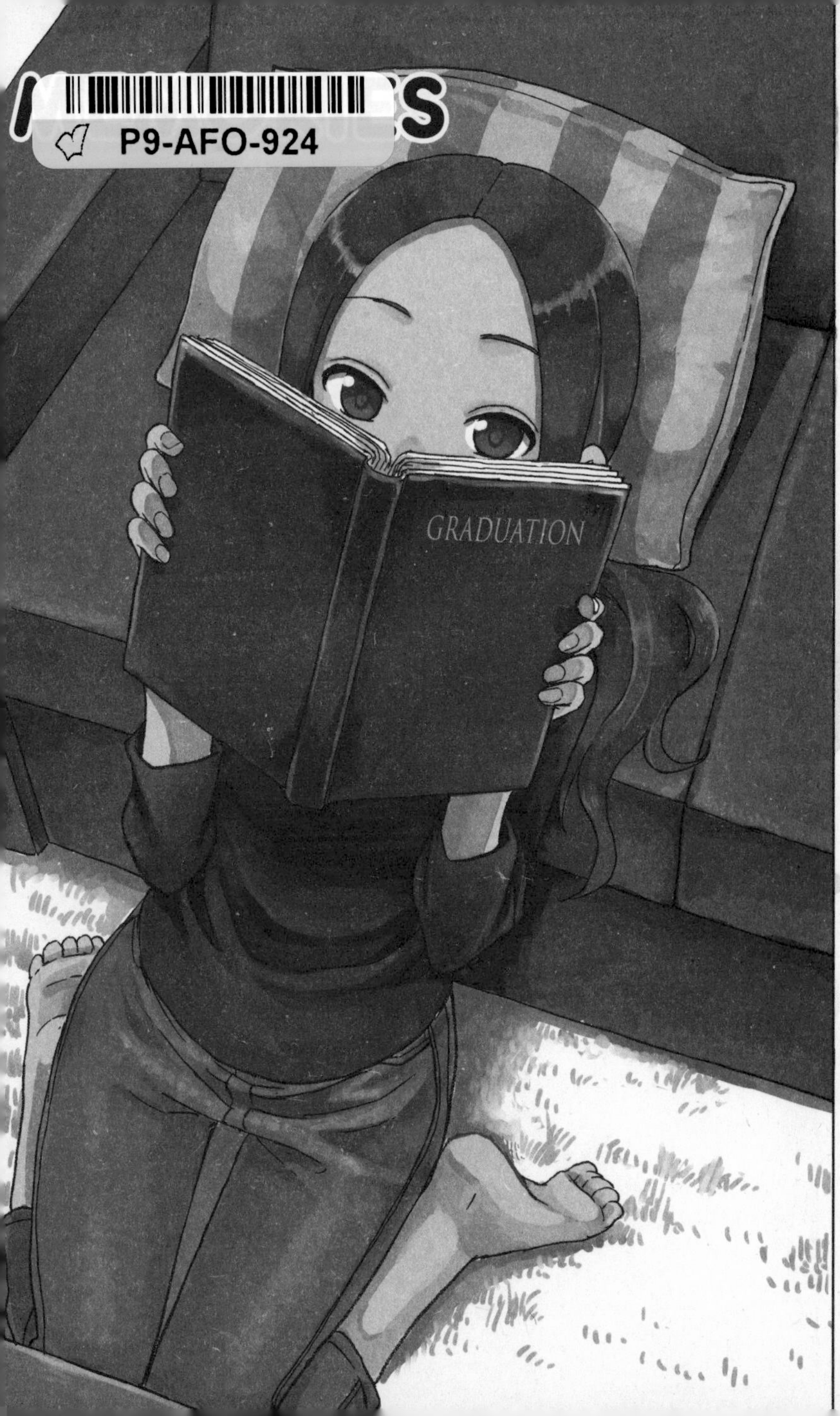
GRADUATION

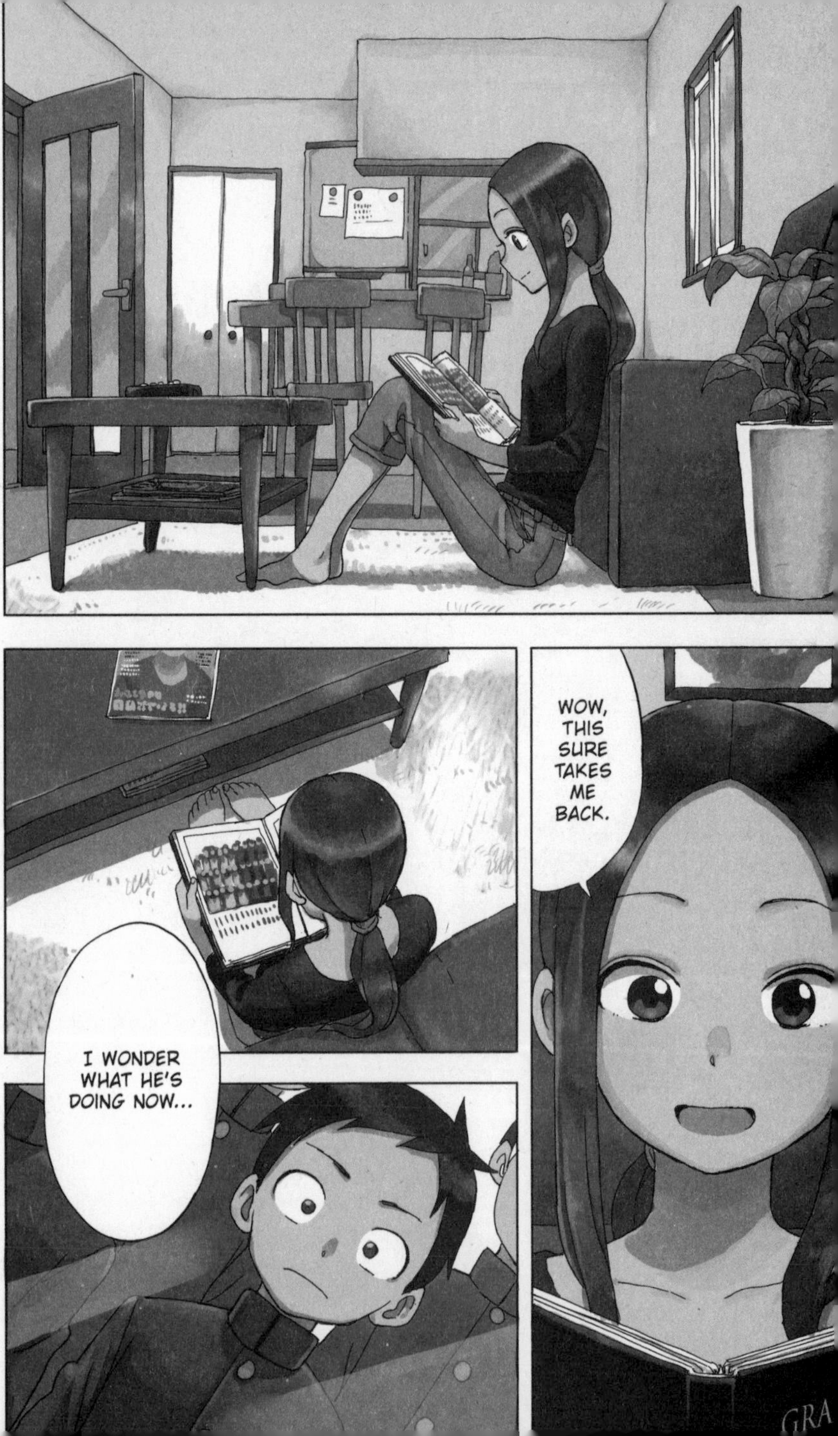
WOW, THIS SURE TAKES ME BACK.
I WONDER WHAT HE'S DOING NOW...

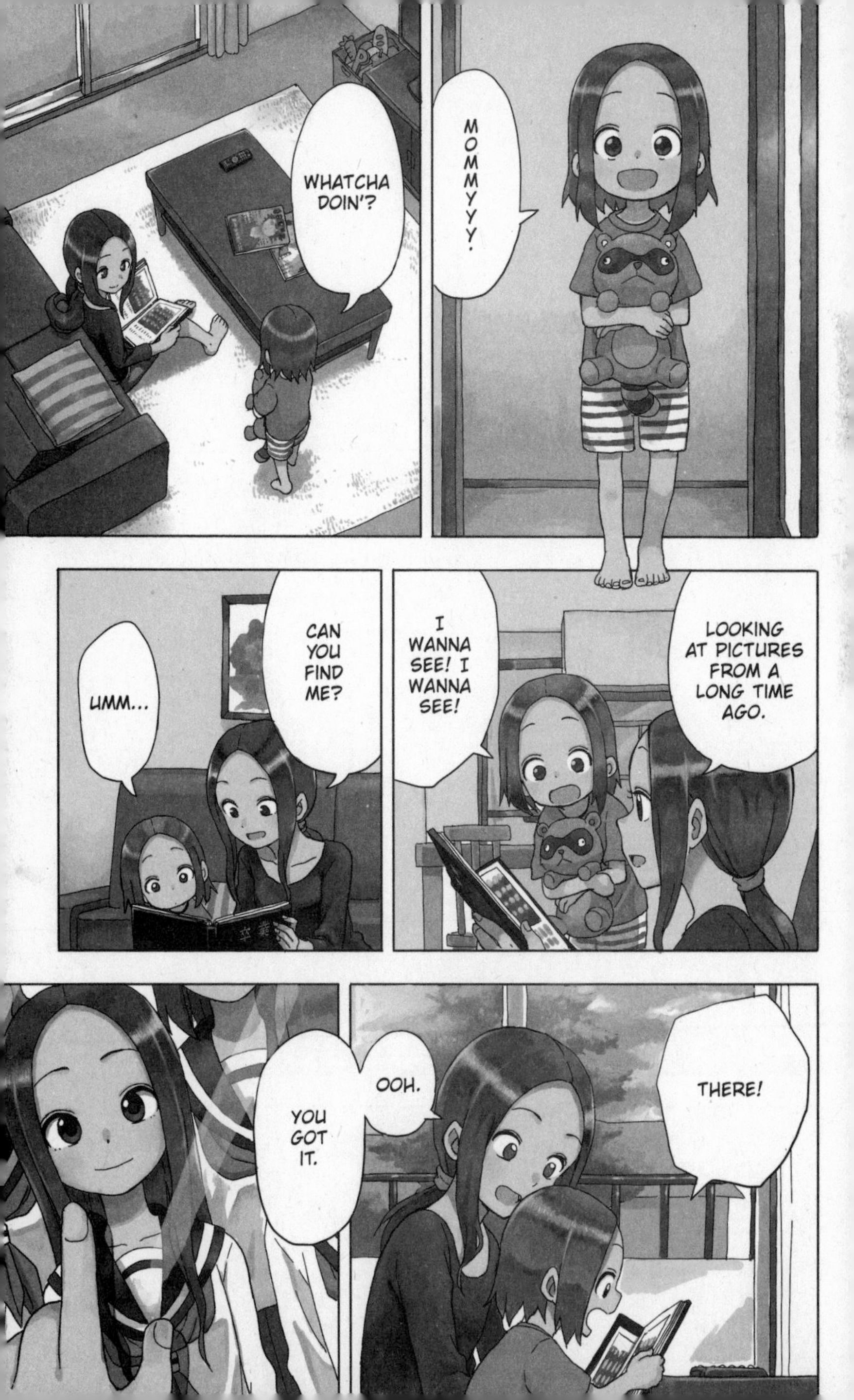
MOMMYYY.
WHATCHA DOIN'?
LOOKING AT PICTURES FROM A LONG TIME AGO.
I WANNA SEE! I WANNA SEE!
CAN YOU FIND ME?
UMM...
THERE!
OOH.
YOU GOT IT.

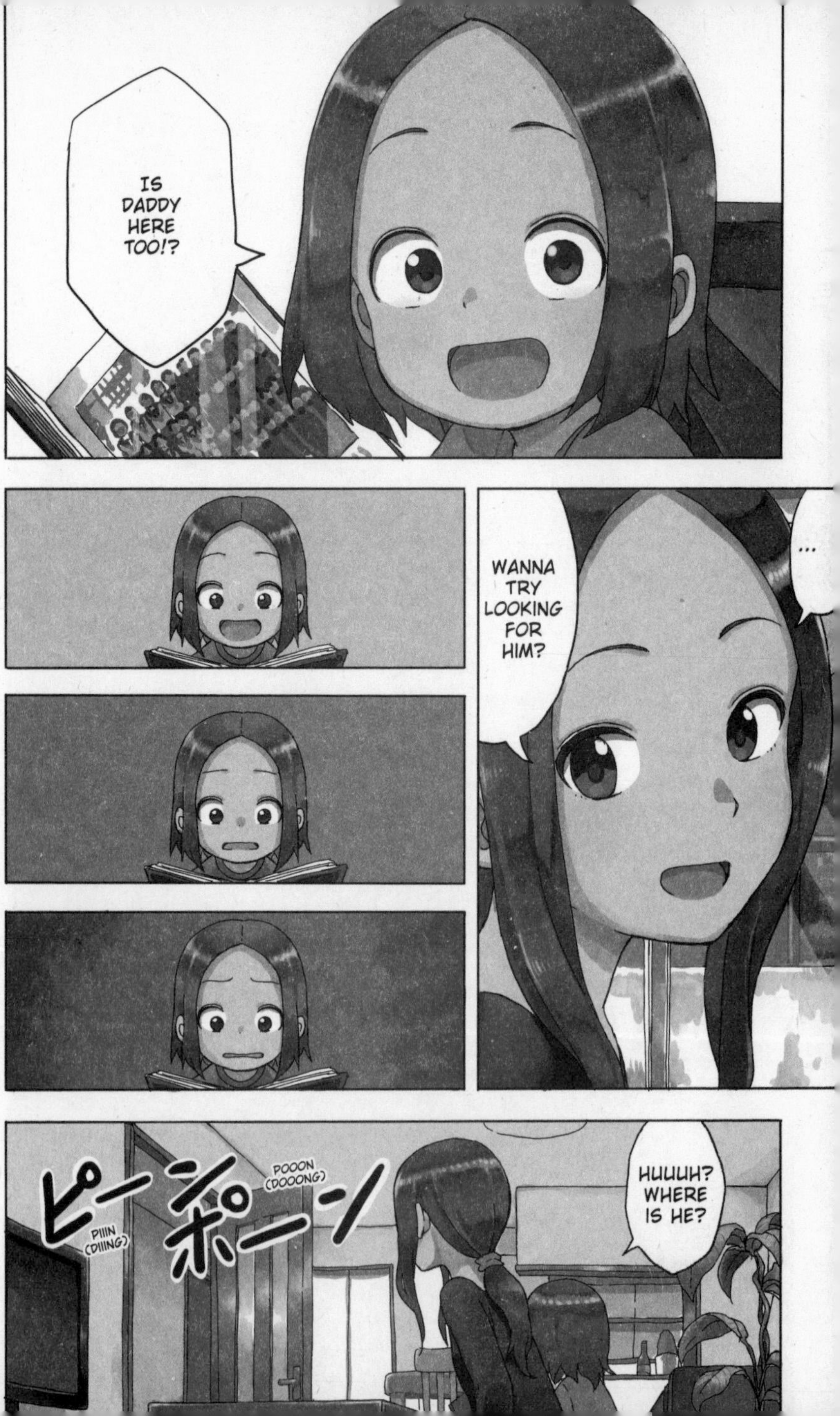
IS DADDY HERE TOO!?
...
WANNA TRY LOOKING FOR HIM?
HUUUH? WHERE IS HE?
ピーンポーン
PIIIN (DIIING)
POOON (DOOONG)

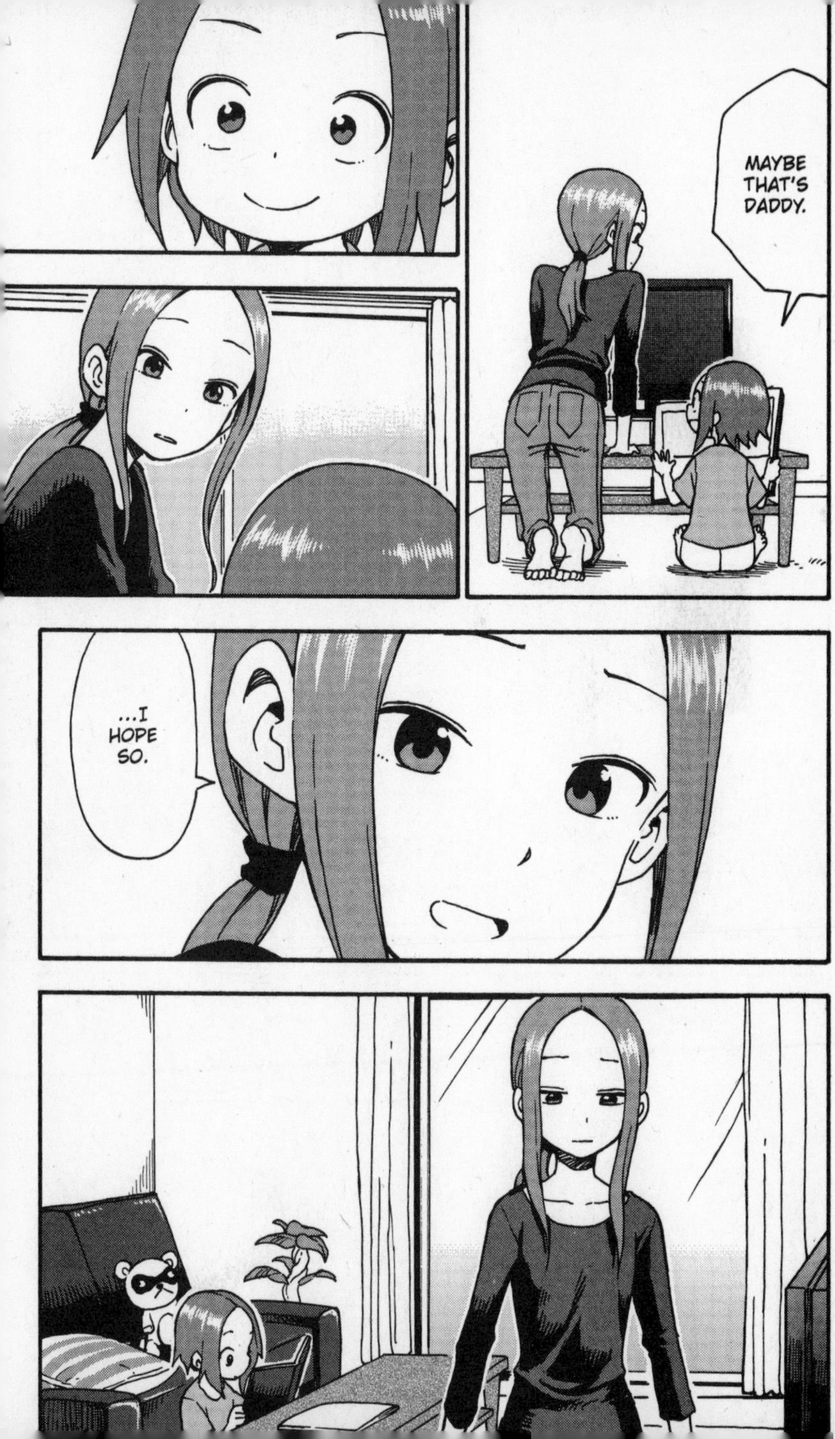
MAYBE THAT'S DADDY.
...I HOPE SO.

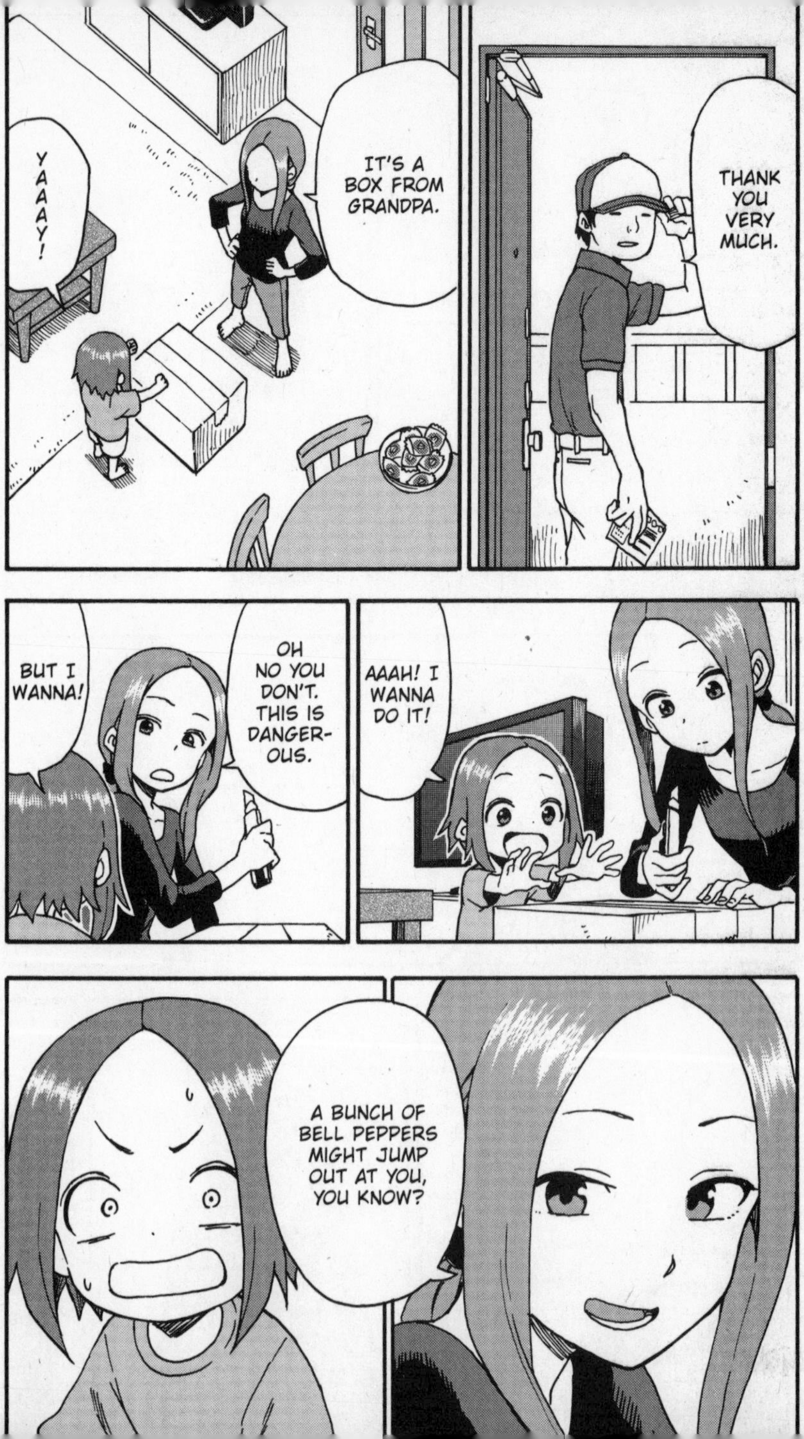
THANK YOU VERY MUCH.
IT'S A BOX FROM GRANDPA.
YAAAAY!
AAAH! I WANNA DO IT!
OH NO YOU DON'T. THIS IS DANGER-OUS.
BUT I WANNA!
A BUNCH OF BELL PEPPERS MIGHT JUMP OUT AT YOU, YOU KNOW?

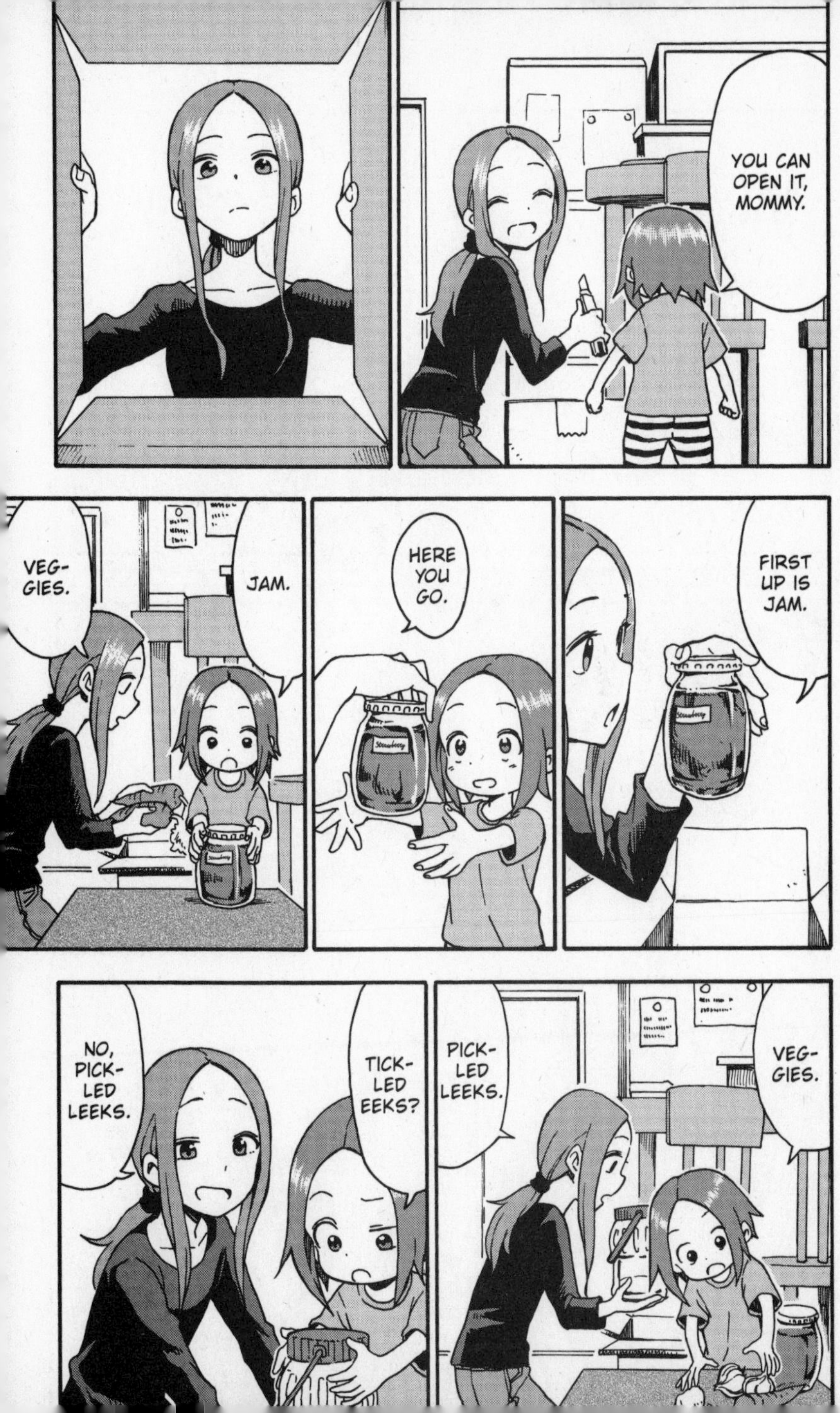
YOU CAN OPEN IT, MOMMY.
FIRST UP IS JAM.
HERE YOU GO.
JAM.
VEG-GIES.
VEG-GIES.
PICK-LED LEEKS.
TICK-LED EEKS?
NO, PICK-LED LEEKS.

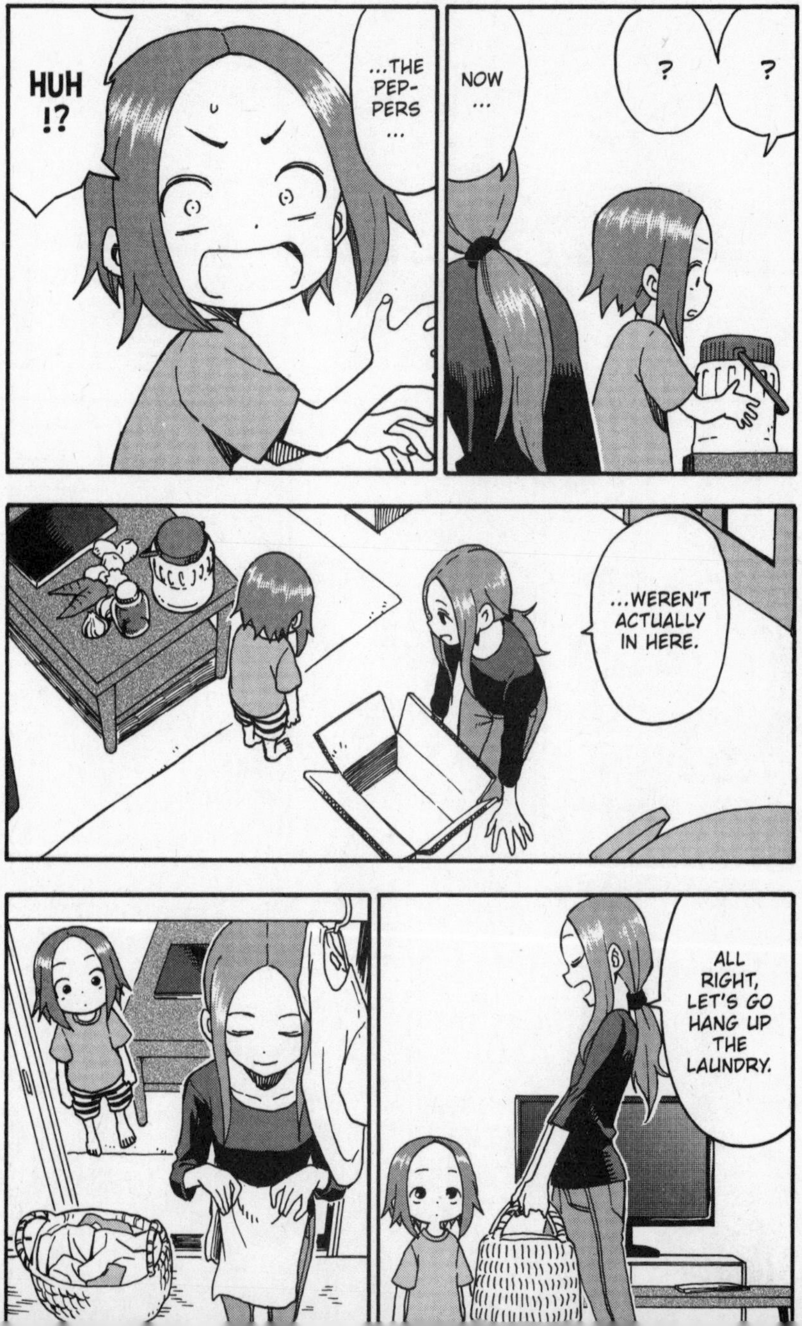
?
?
NOW ...
...THE PEP-PERS ...
HUH !?
...WEREN'T ACTUALLY IN HERE.
ALL RIGHT, LET'S GO HANG UP THE LAUNDRY.

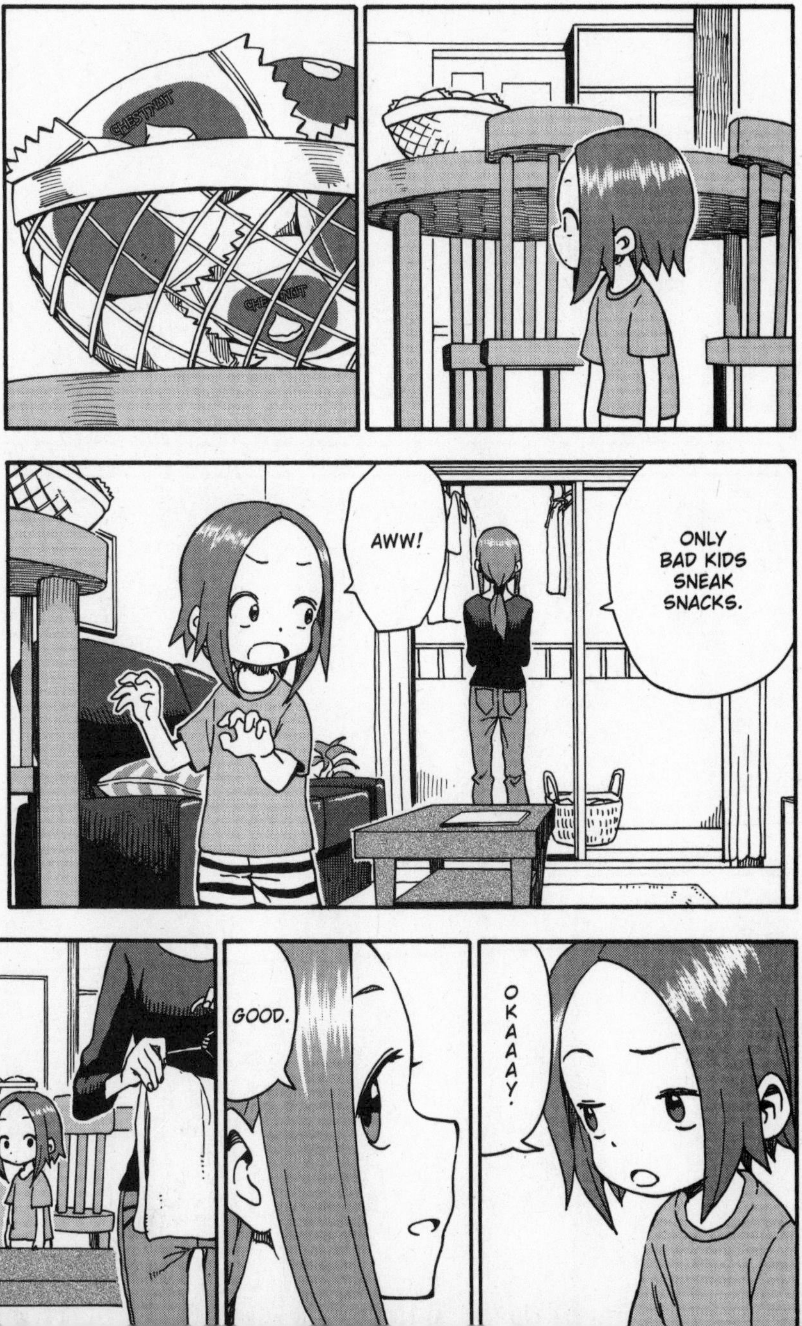
CHESTNUT
CHESTNUT
ONLY BAD KIDS SNEAK SNACKS.
AWW!
OKAAAY.
GOOD.

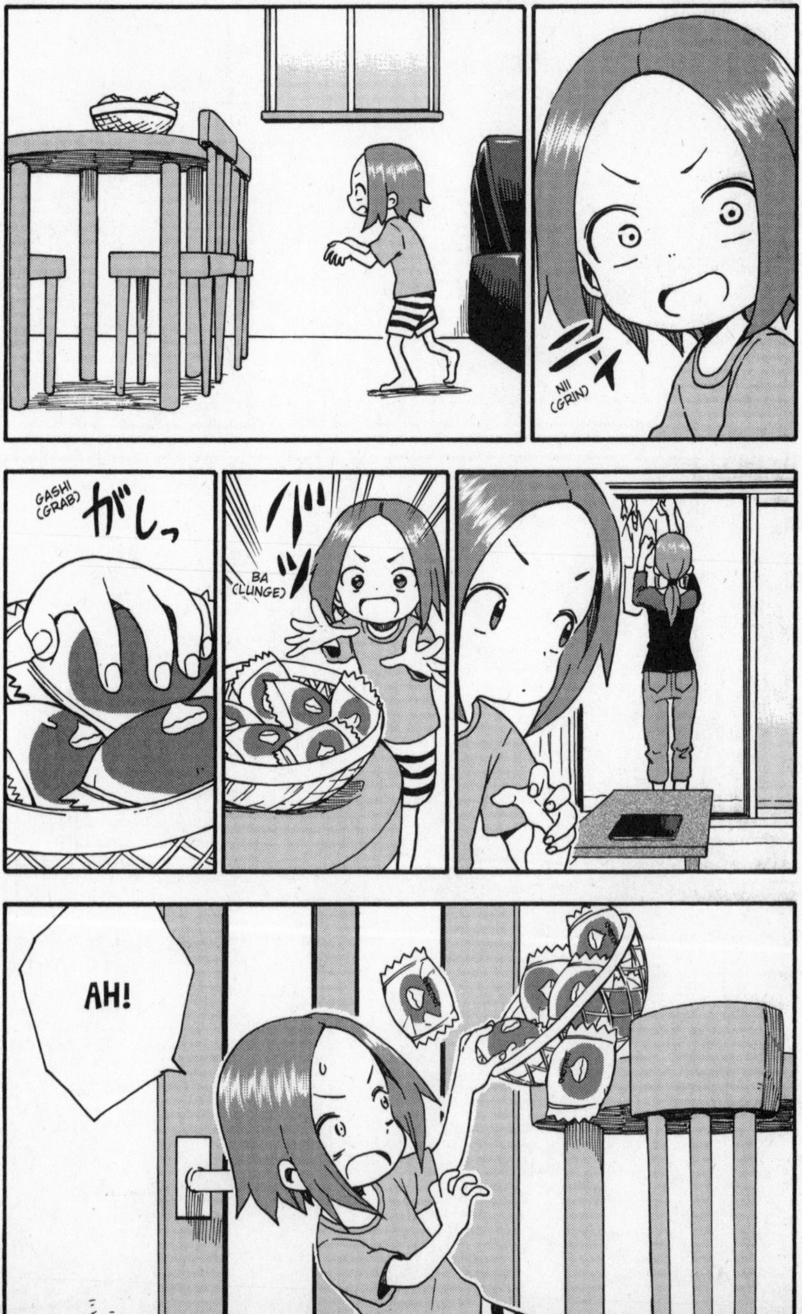
NII (GRIN)
BA (LUNGE)
GASHI (GRAB)
AH!

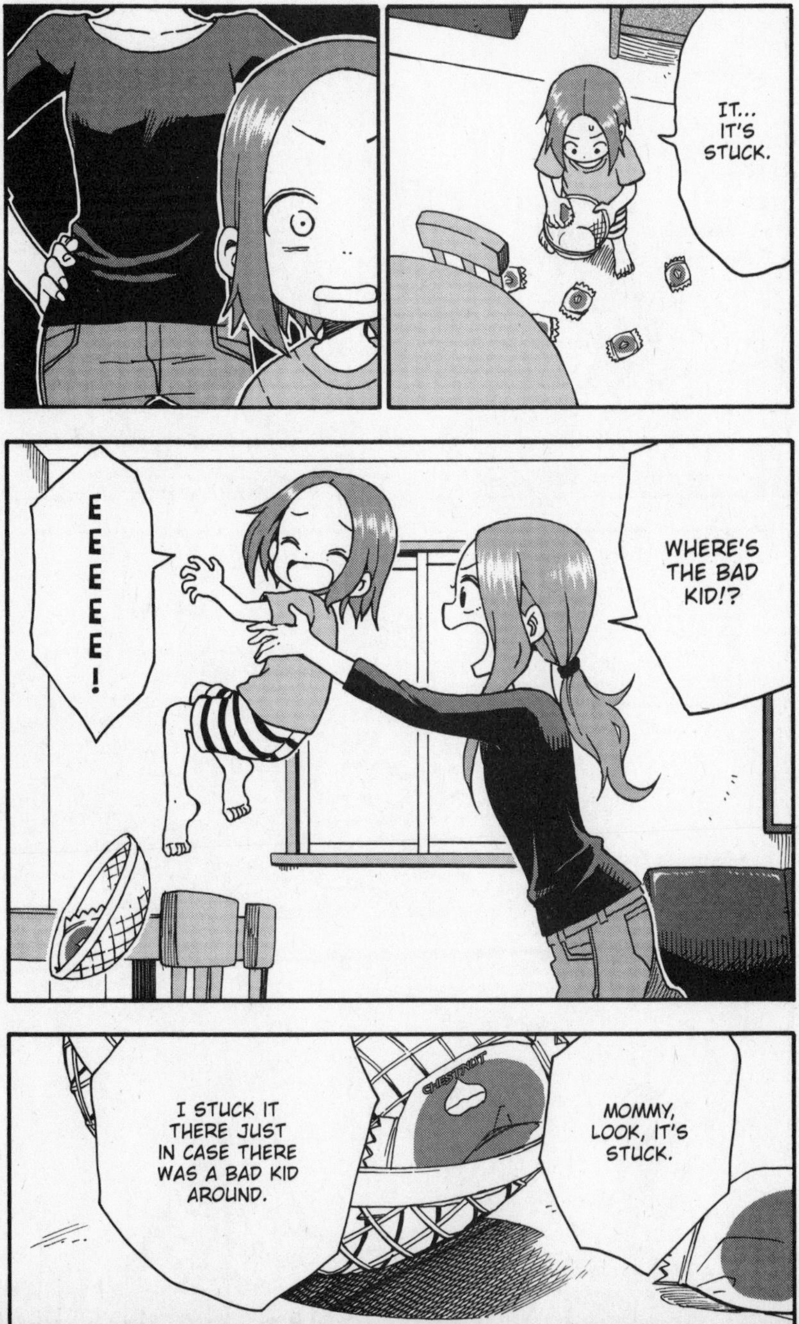
IT... IT'S STUCK.
WHERE'S THE BAD KID!?
EEEEEE!
MOMMY, LOOK, IT'S STUCK.
CHESTNUT
I STUCK IT THERE JUST IN CASE THERE WAS A BAD KID AROUND.

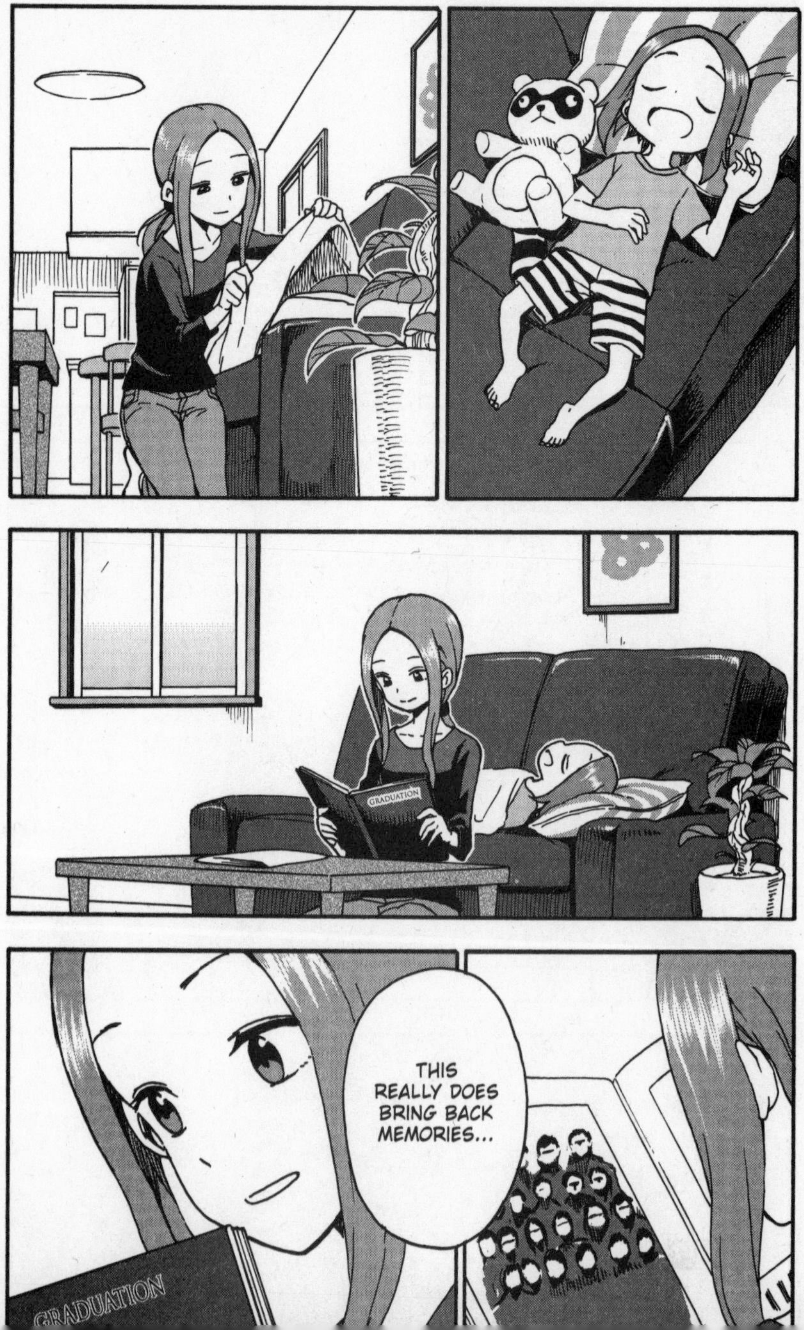
GRADUATION
THIS REALLY DOES BRING BACK MEMORIES...
GRADUATION

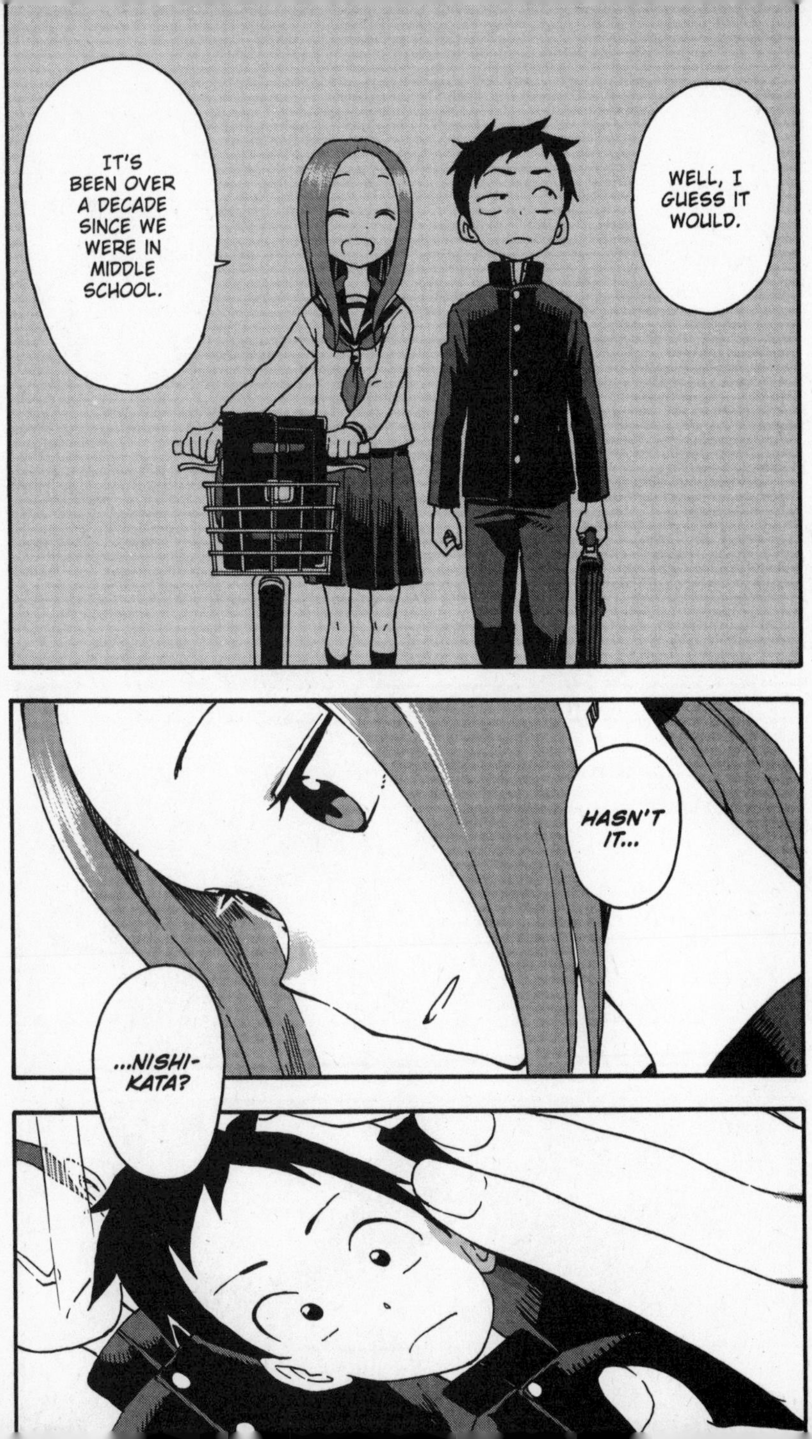
WELL, I GUESS IT WOULD.
IT'S BEEN OVER A DECADE SINCE WE WERE IN MIDDLE SCHOOL.
HASN'T IT...
...NISHI-KATA?

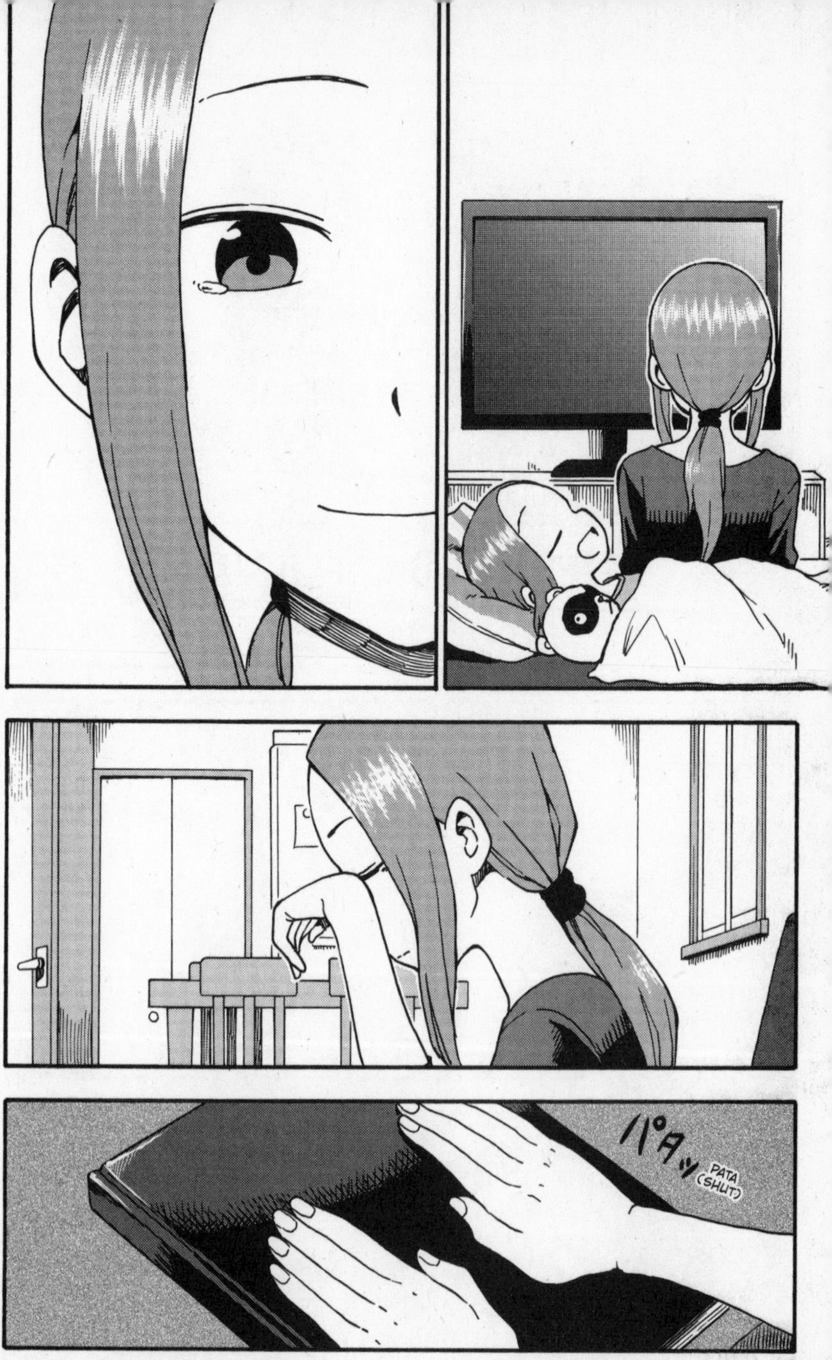
パタッ
PATA (SHUT)

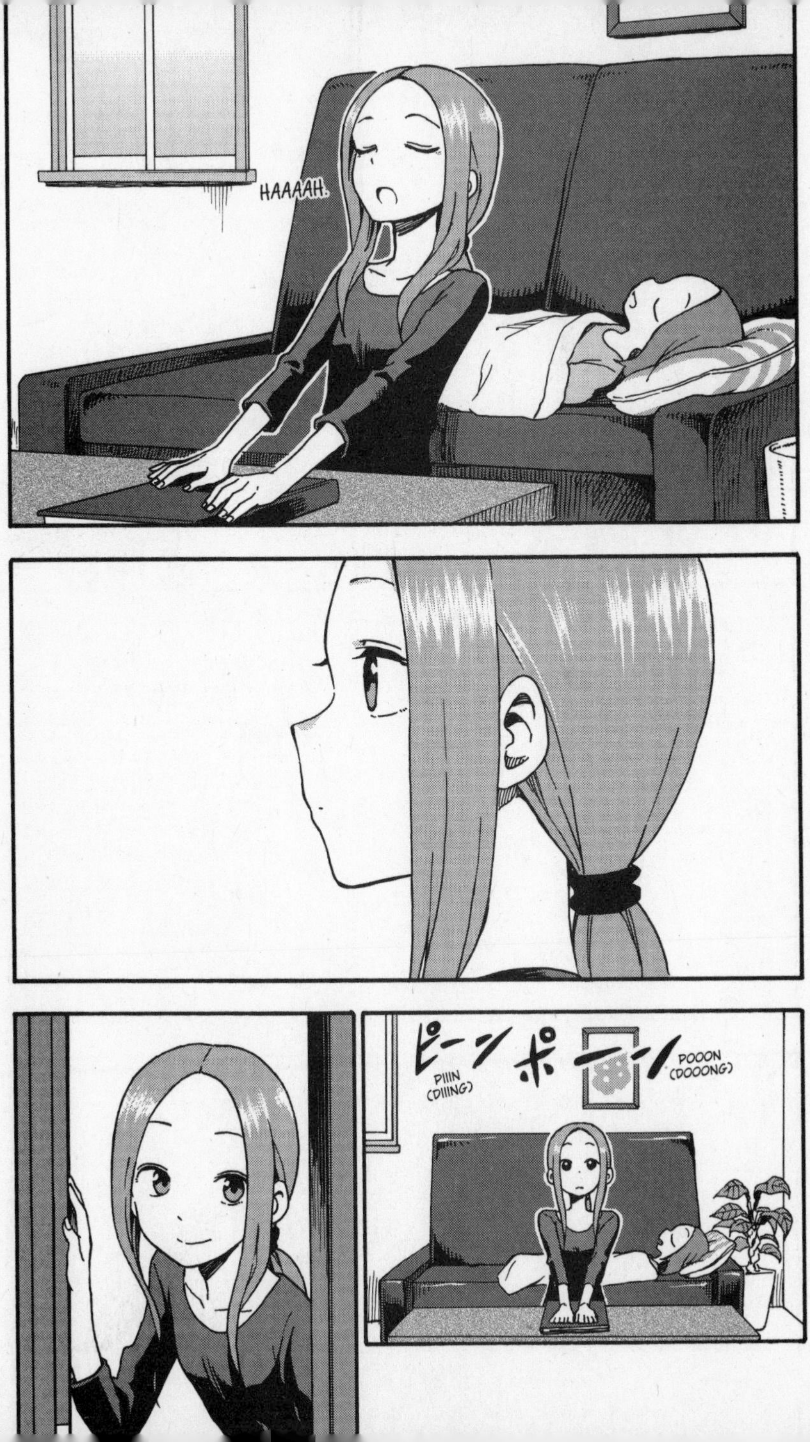
HAAAAH.
ピーン
PIIN (DIIING)
ポーン
POOON (DOOONG)

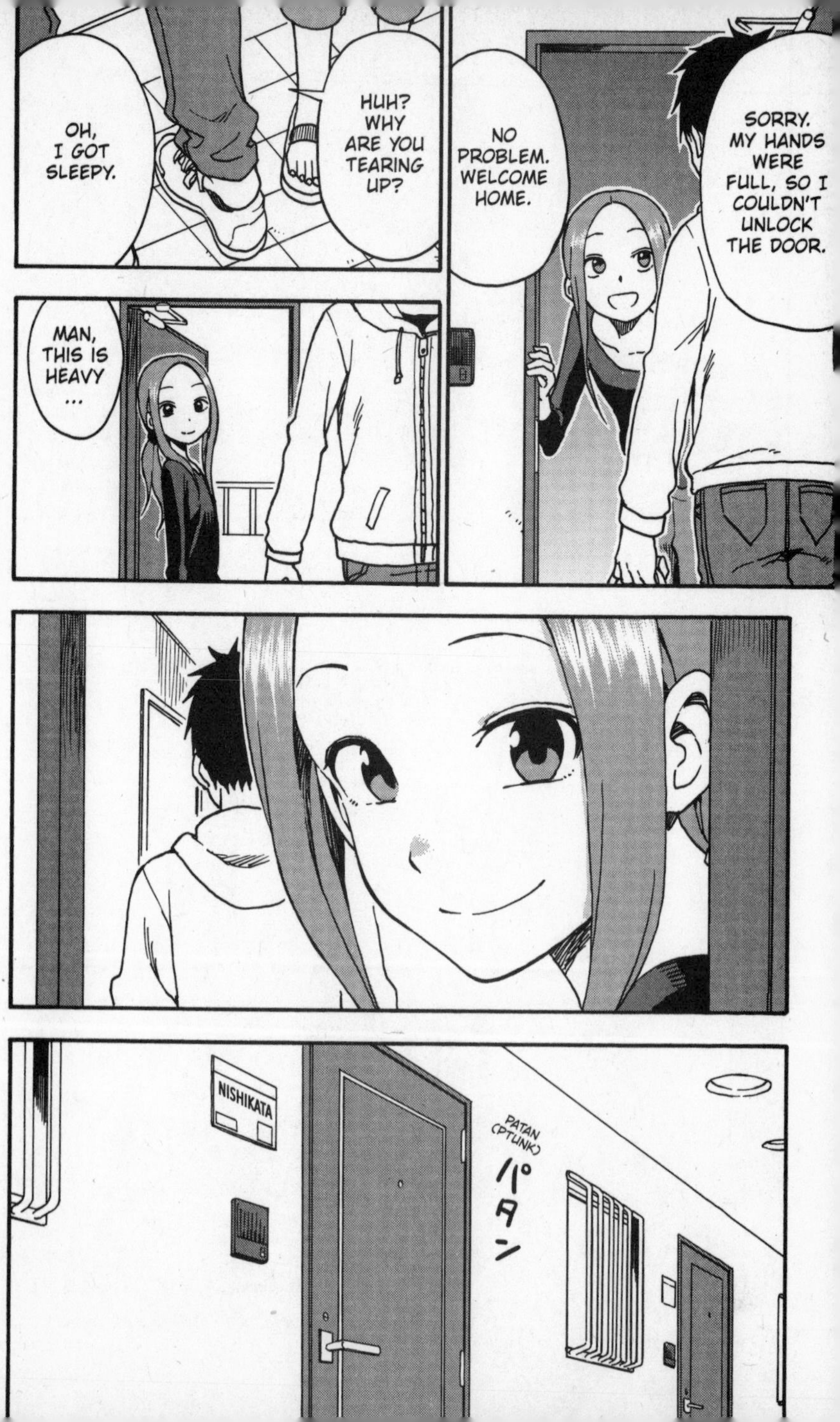
SORRY. MY HANDS WERE FULL, SO I COULDN'T UNLOCK THE DOOR.
NO PROBLEM. WELCOME HOME.
HUH? WHY ARE YOU TEARING UP?
OH, I GOT SLEEPY.
MAN, THIS IS HEAVY ...
NISHIKATA
PATAN (PTUNK)
パタン

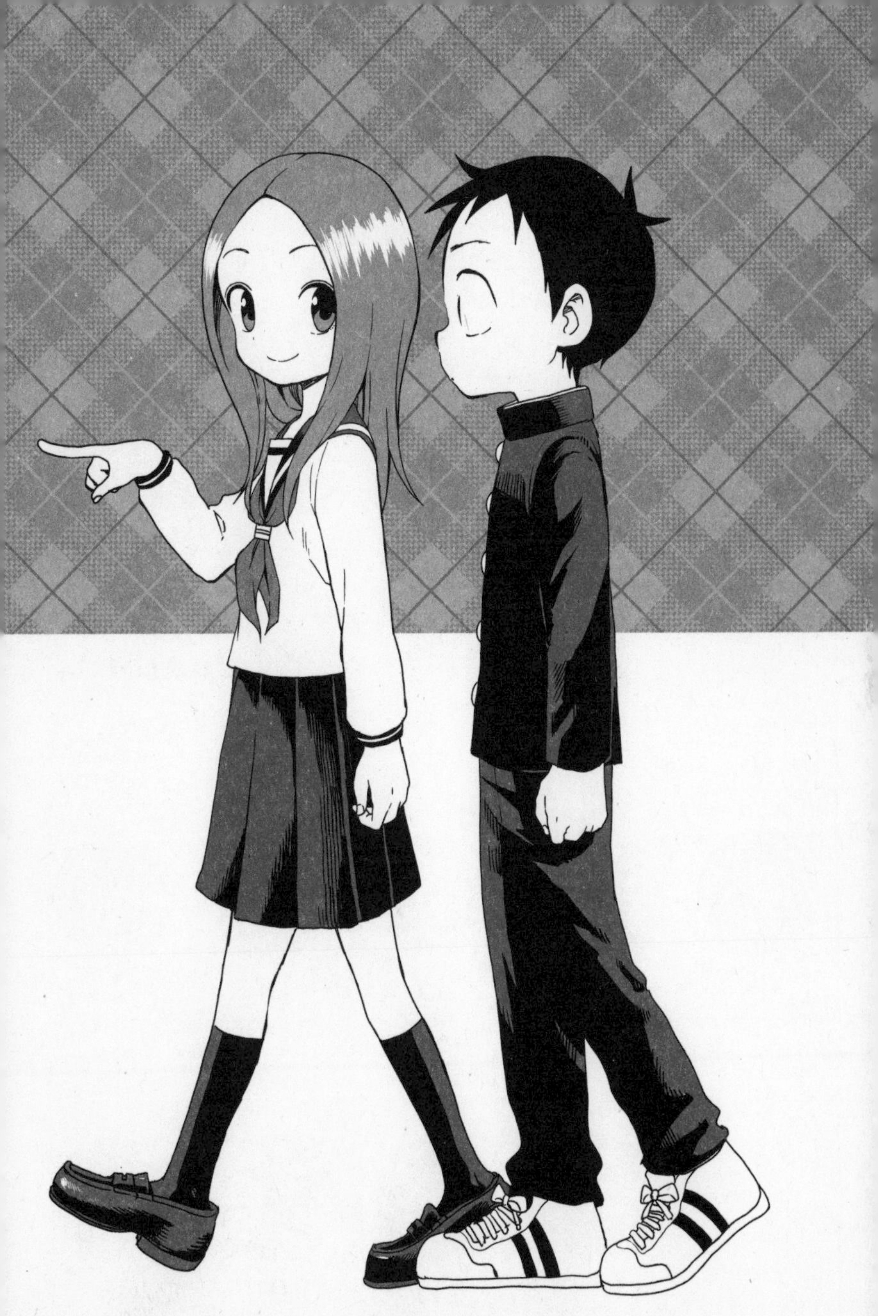

Teasing Master Takagi-san 5 Soichiro Yamamoto

Contents

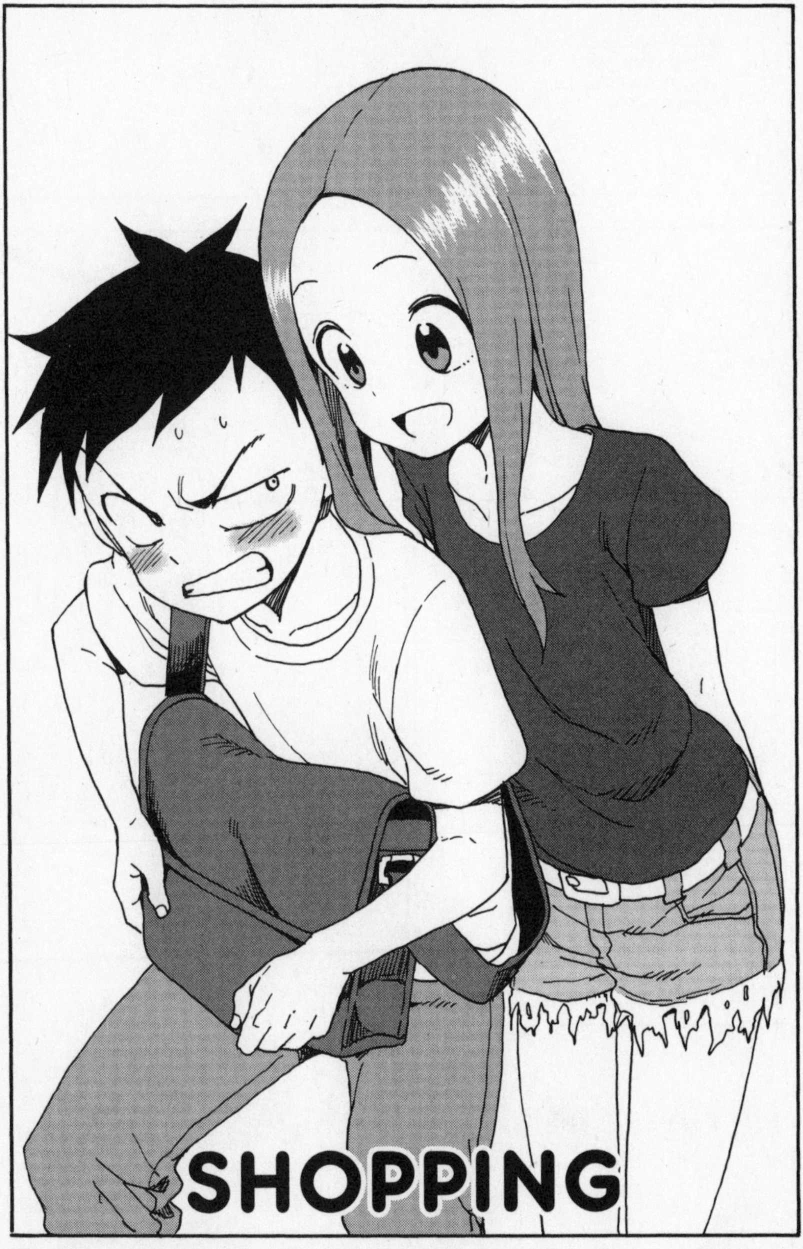
SHOPPING

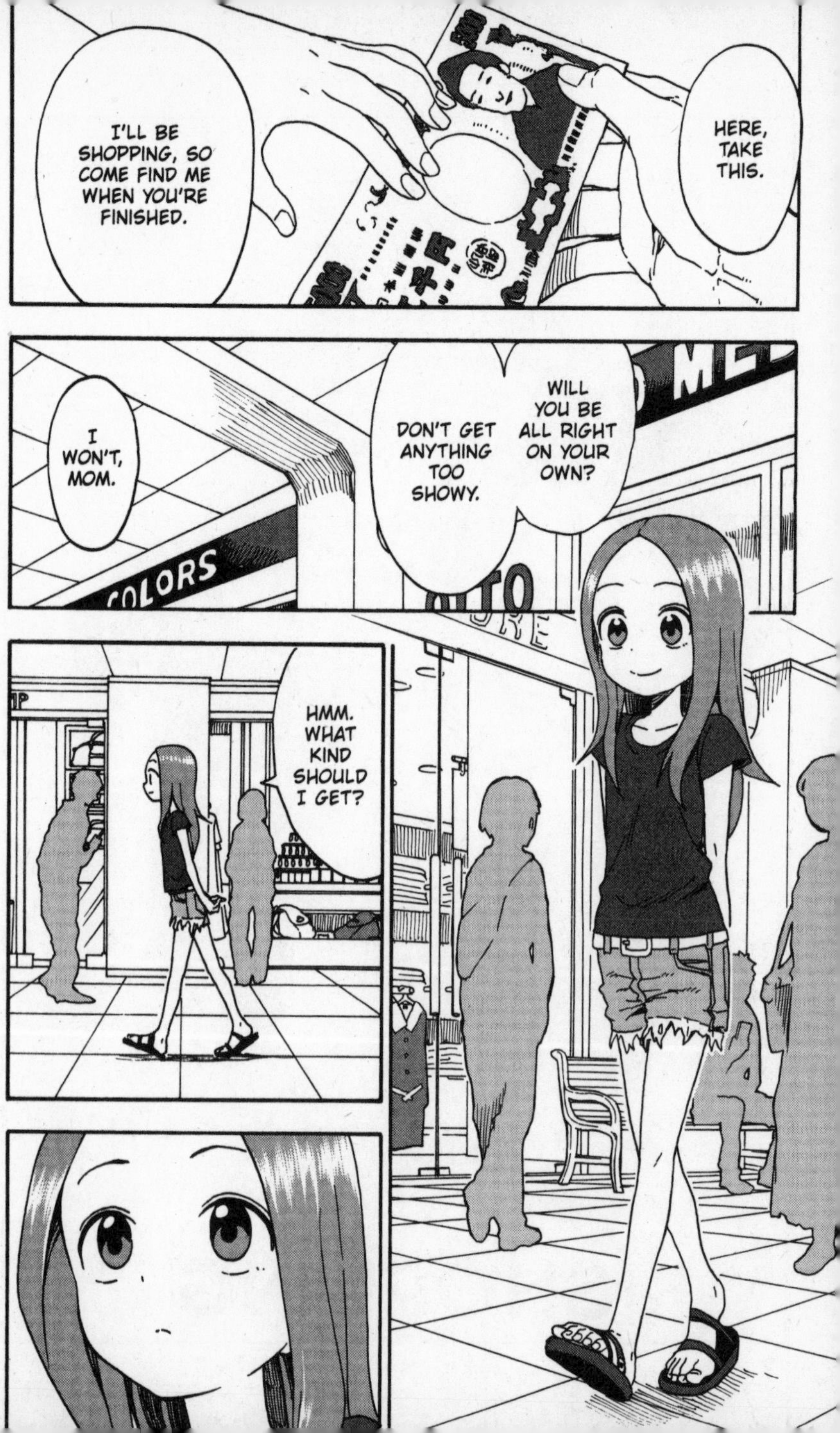
HERE, TAKE THIS.
I'LL BE SHOPPING, SO COME FIND ME WHEN YOU'RE FINISHED.
WILL YOU BE ALL RIGHT ON YOUR OWN?
DON'T GET ANYTHING TOO SHOWY.
I WON'T, MOM.
COLORS
HMM. WHAT KIND SHOULD I GET?

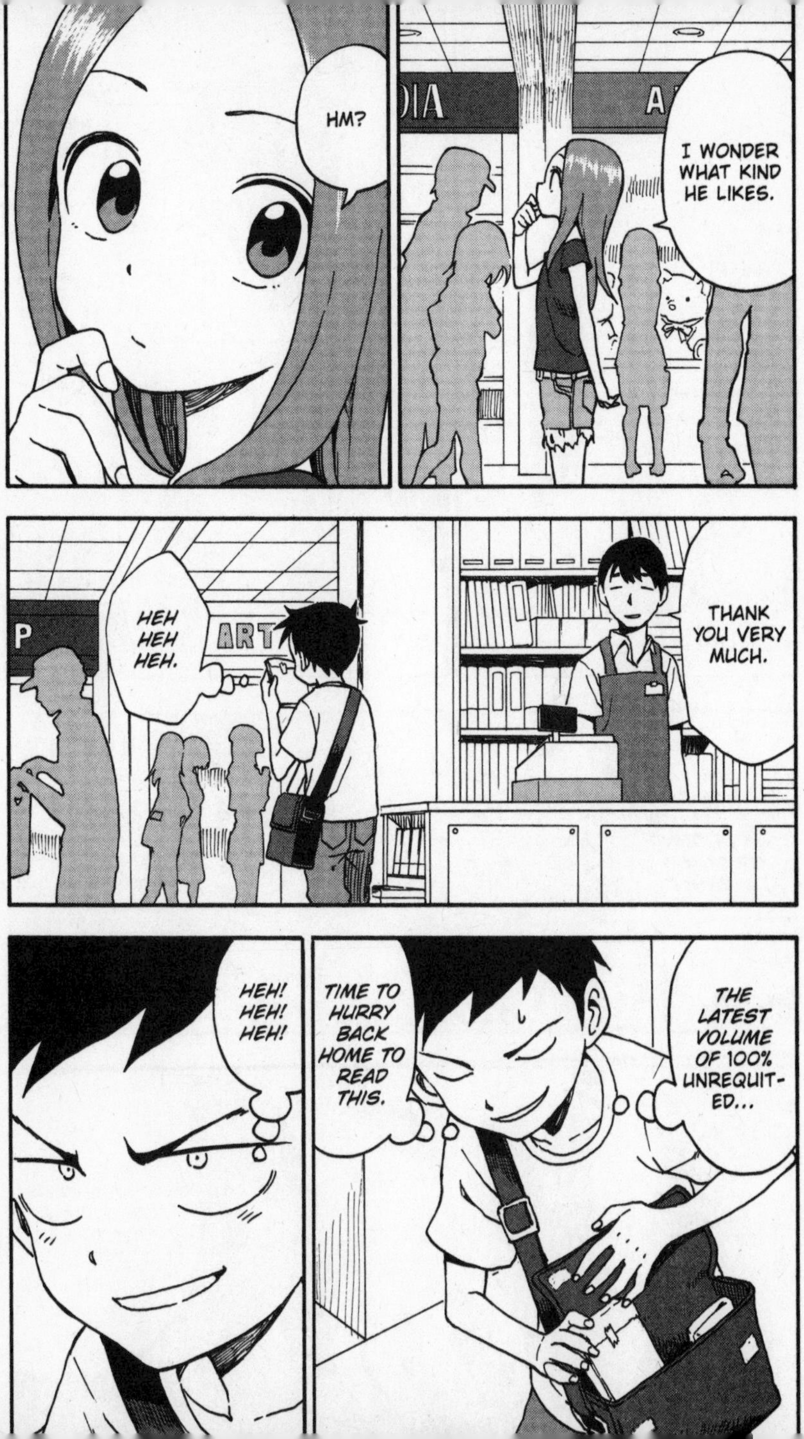
I WONDER WHAT KIND HE LIKES.
HM?
THANK YOU VERY MUCH.
HEH HEH HEH.
ART
THE LATEST VOLUME OF 100% UNREQUIT-ED...
TIME TO HURRY BACK HOME TO READ THIS.
HEH! HEH! HEH!

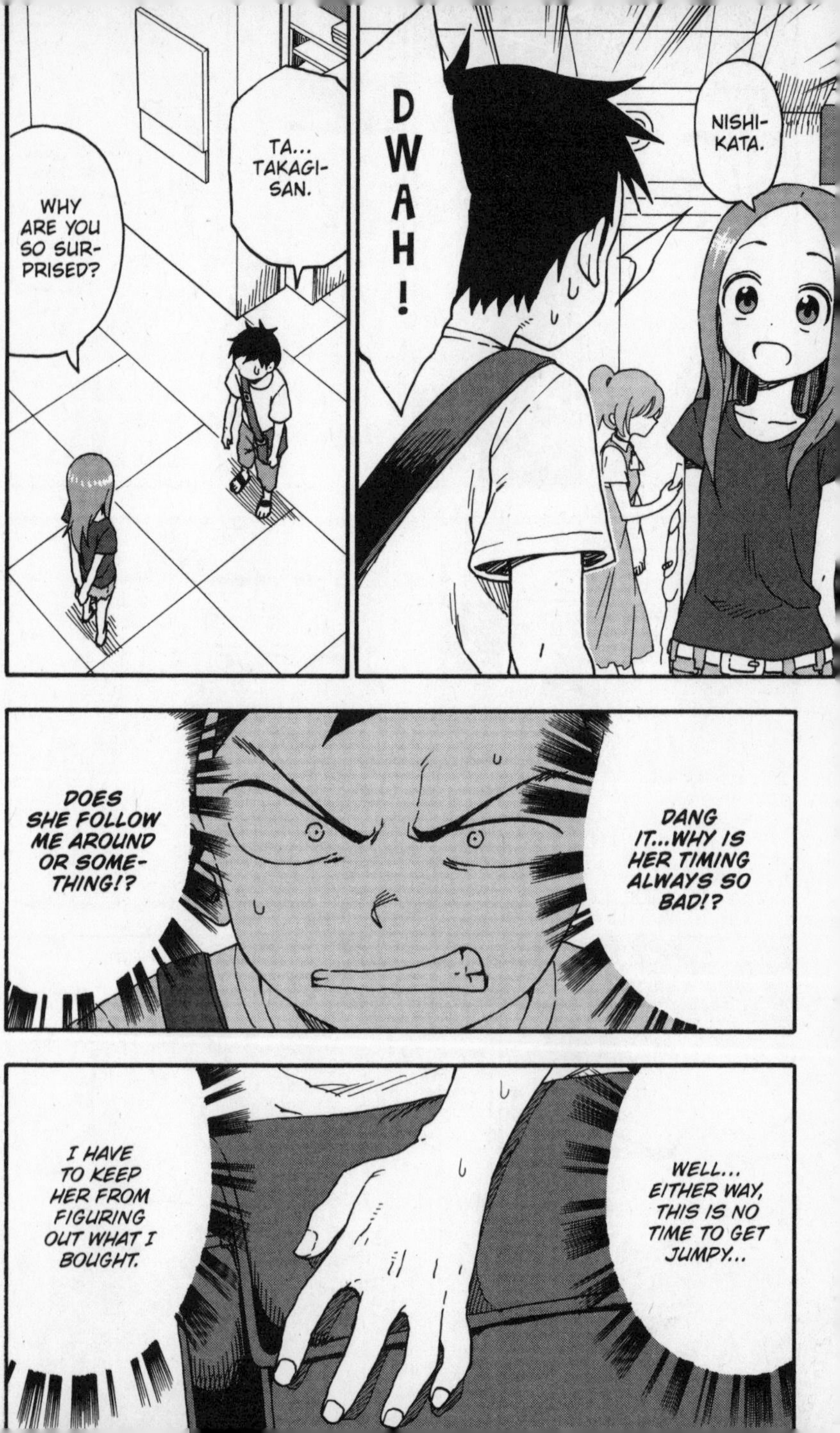
NISHI-KATA.
DWAH!
TA... TAKAGI-SAN.
WHY ARE YOU SO SUR-PRISED?
DANG IT...WHY IS HER TIMING ALWAYS SO BAD!?
DOES SHE FOLLOW ME AROUND OR SOME-THING!?
WELL... EITHER WAY, THIS IS NO TIME TO GET JUMPY...
I HAVE TO KEEP HER FROM FIGURING OUT WHAT I BOUGHT.

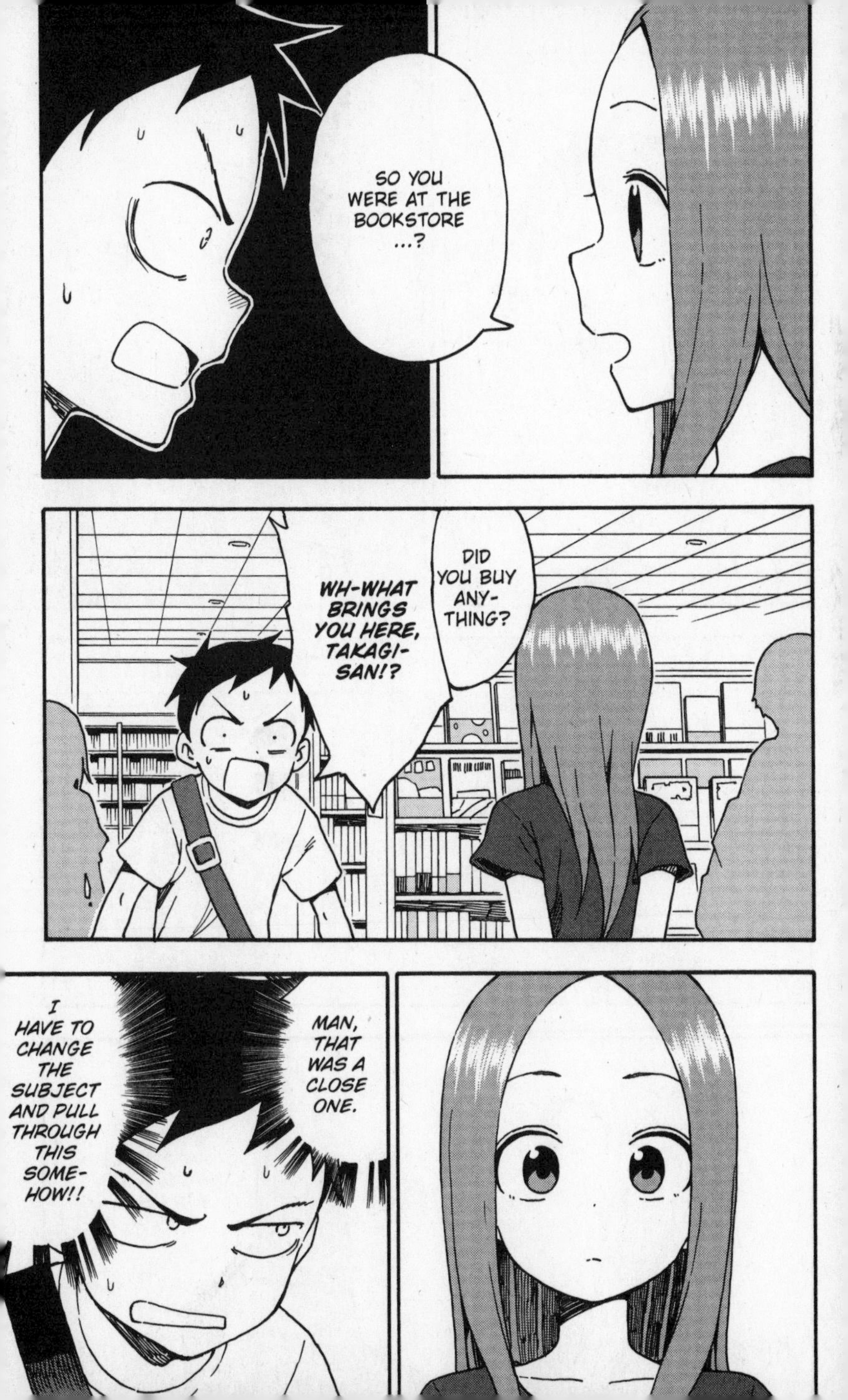
SO YOU WERE AT THE BOOKSTORE ...?
DID YOU BUY ANY-THING?
WH-WHAT BRINGS YOU HERE, TAKAGI-SAN!?
MAN, THAT WAS A CLOSE ONE.
I HAVE TO CHANGE THE SUBJECT AND PULL THROUGH THIS SOME-HOW!!

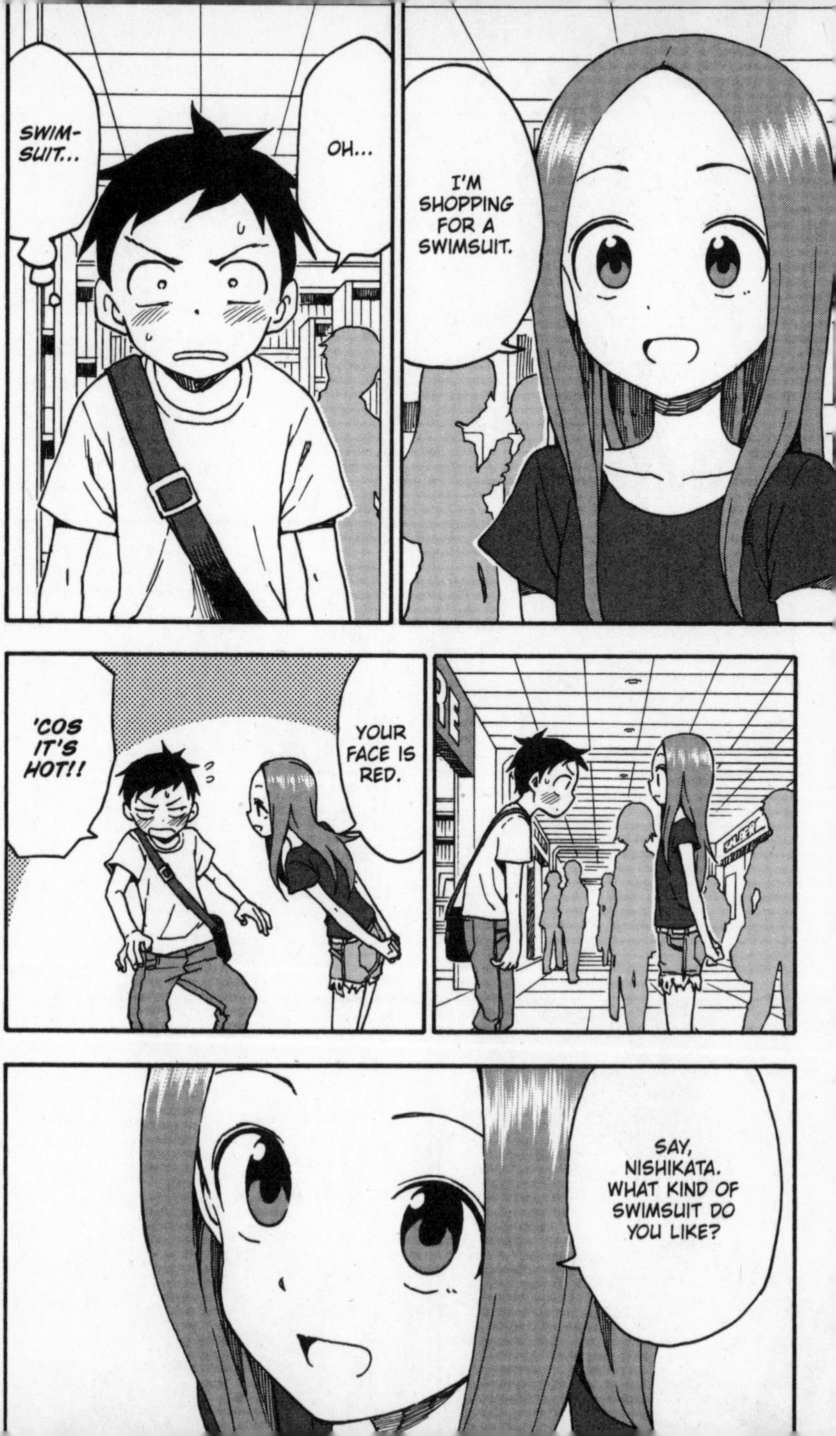
I'M SHOPPING FOR A SWIMSUIT.
OH...
SWIM-SUIT...
YOUR FACE IS RED.
'COS IT'S HOT!!
SAY, NISHIKATA. WHAT KIND OF SWIMSUIT DO YOU LIKE?

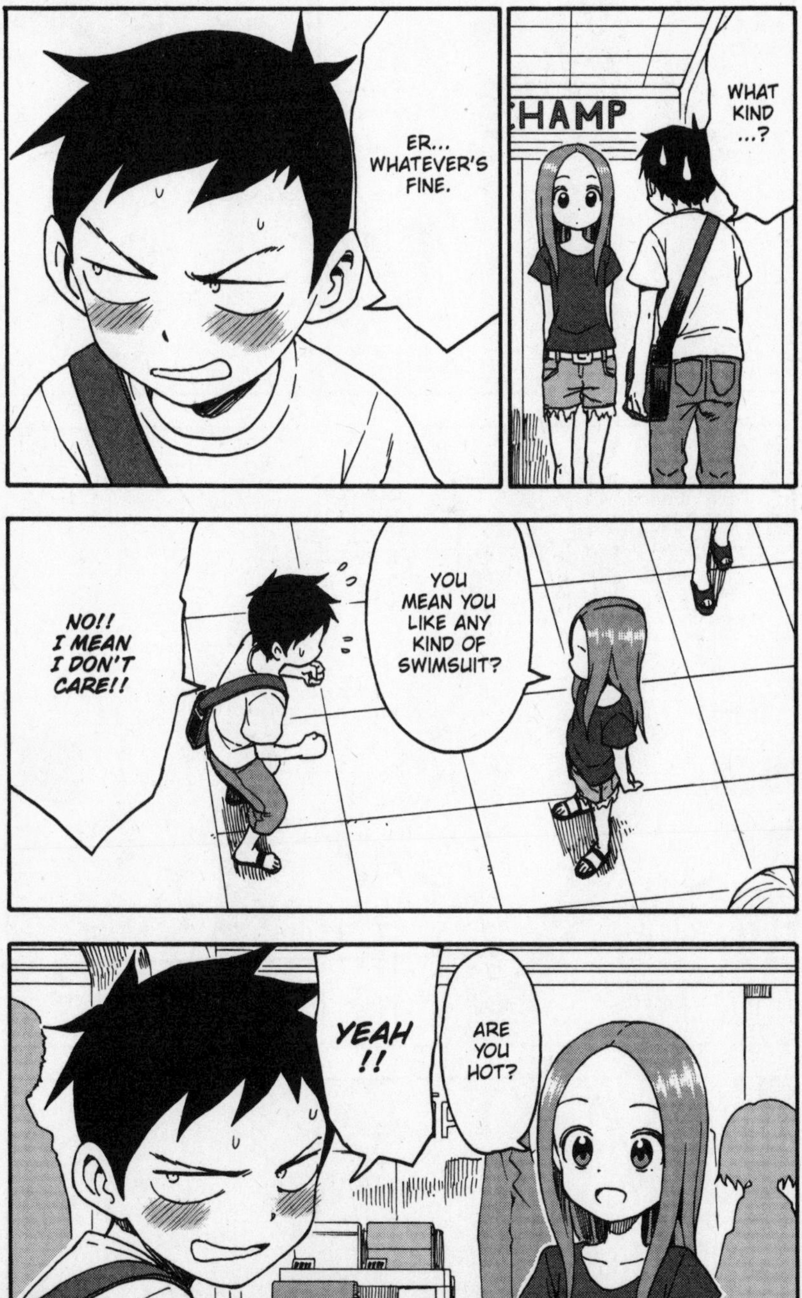
WHAT KIND ...?
ER... WHATEVER'S FINE.
YOU MEAN YOU LIKE ANY KIND OF SWIMSUIT?
NO!! I MEAN I DON'T CARE!!
ARE YOU HOT?
YEAH !!

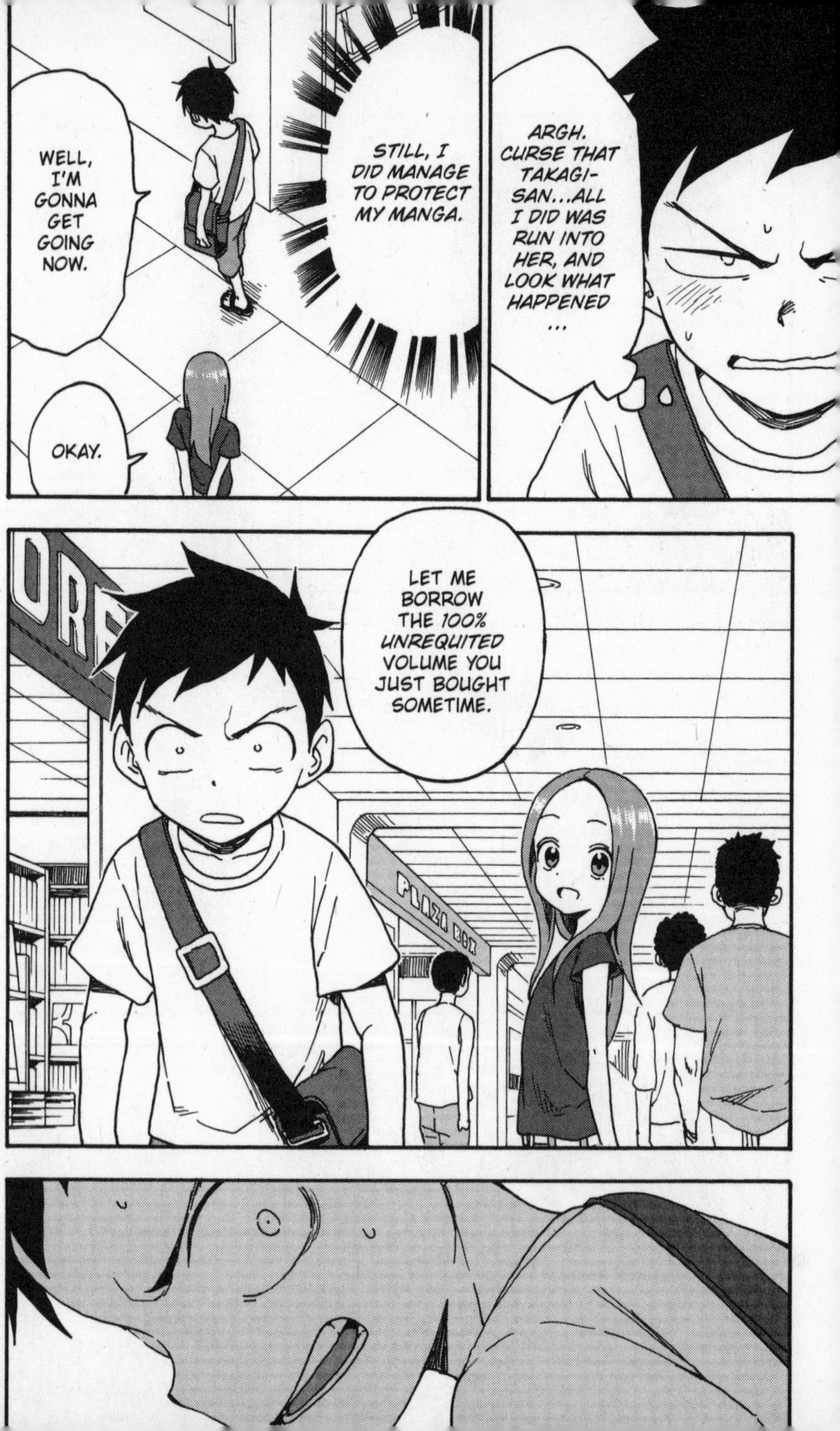
ARGH. CURSE THAT TAKAGI-SAN...ALL I DID WAS RUN INTO HER, AND LOOK WHAT HAPPENED...
STILL, I DID MANAGE TO PROTECT MY MANGA.
WELL, I'M GONNA GET GOING NOW.
OKAY.
LET ME BORROW THE 100% UNREQUITED VOLUME YOU JUST BOUGHT SOMETIME.
PLAZA BOX

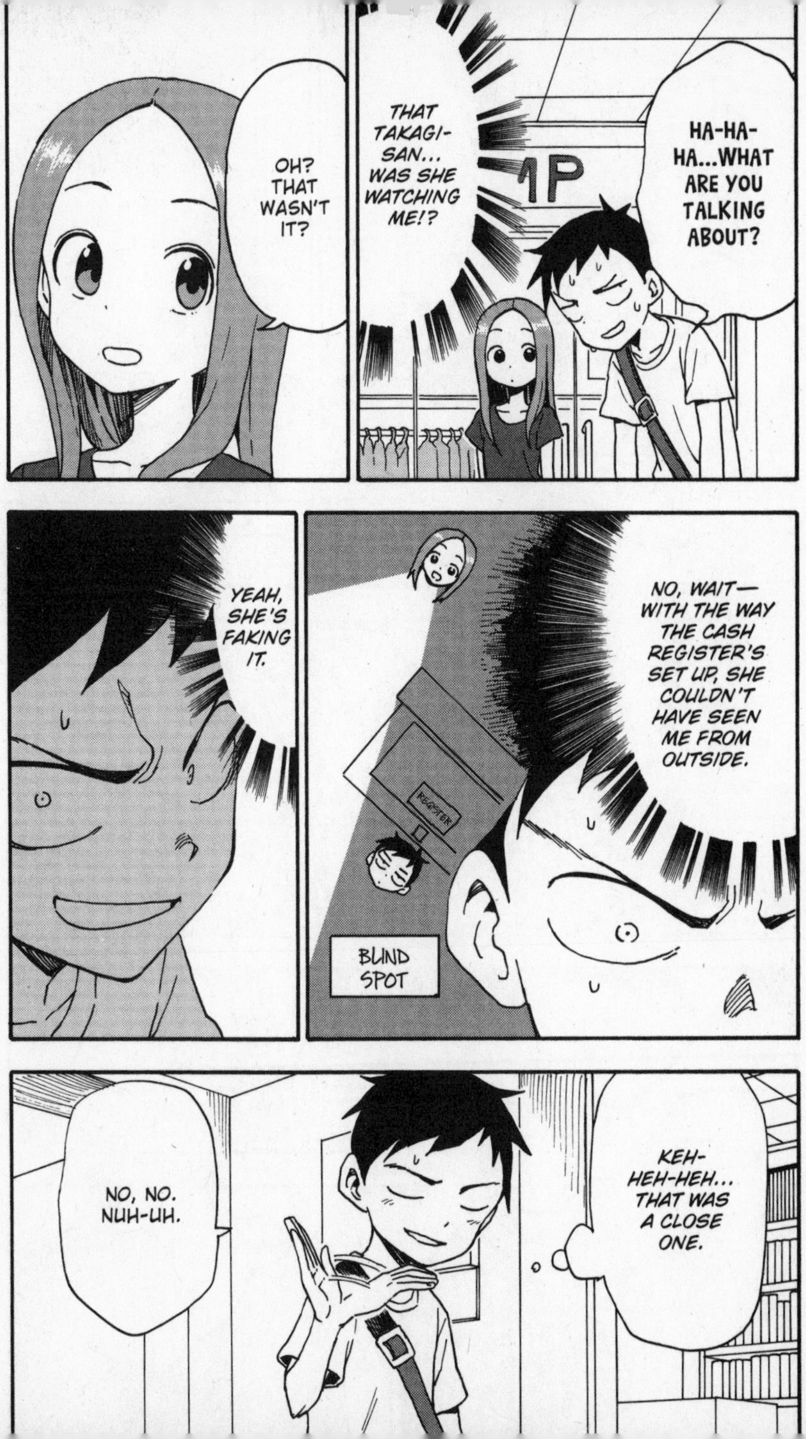
HA-HA-HA...WHAT ARE YOU TALKING ABOUT?
1P
THAT TAKAGI-SAN... WAS SHE WATCHING ME!?
OH? THAT WASN'T IT?
NO, WAIT— WITH THE WAY THE CASH REGISTER'S SET UP, SHE COULDN'T HAVE SEEN ME FROM OUTSIDE.
REGISTER
BLIND SPOT
YEAH, SHE'S FAKING IT.
KEH-HEH-HEH... THAT WAS A CLOSE ONE.
NO, NO. NUH-UH.

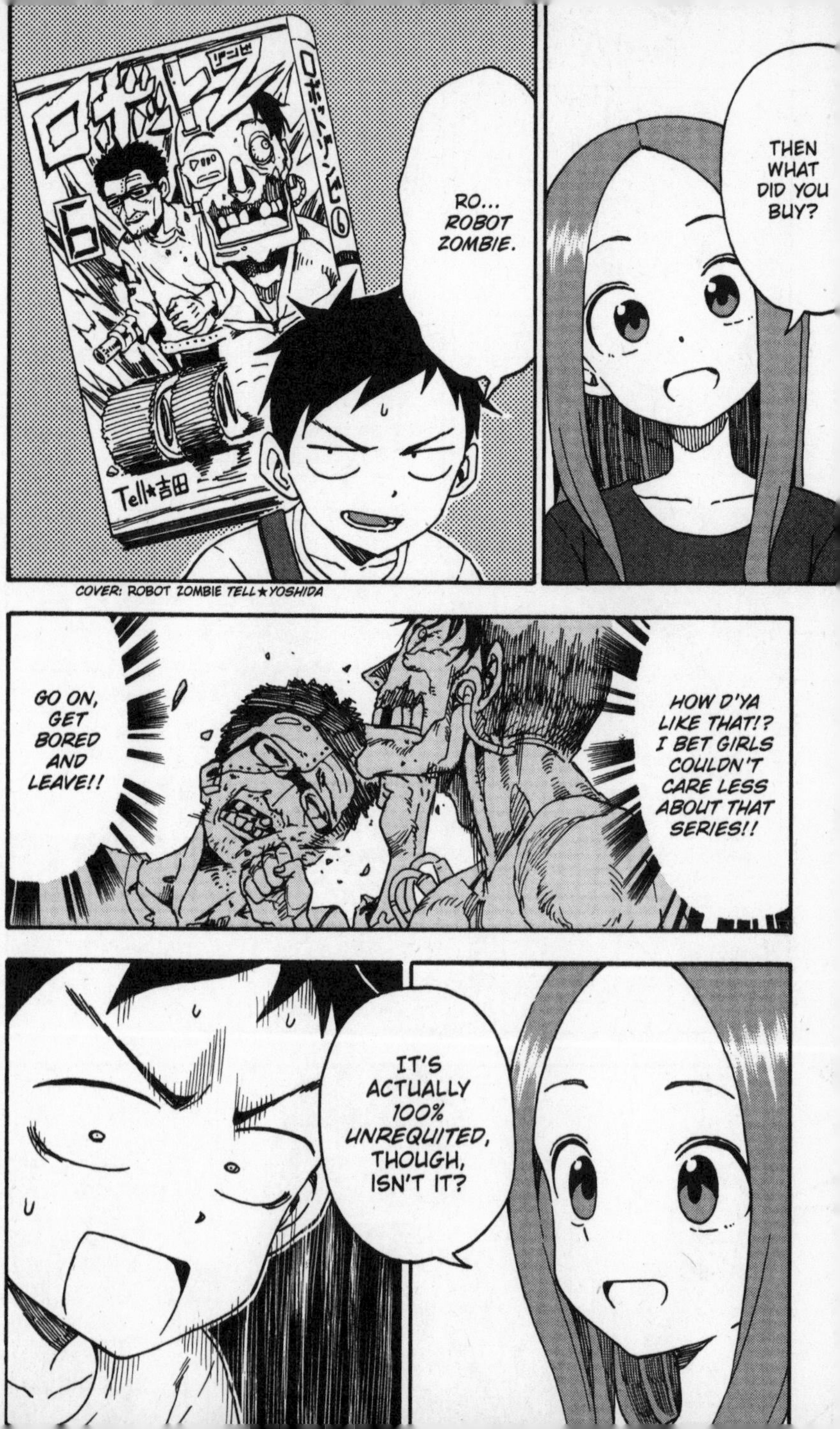
THEN WHAT DID YOU BUY?
RO... ROBOT ZOMBIE.
Tell★吉田
COVER: ROBOT ZOMBIE TELL★YOSHIDA
HOW D'YA LIKE THAT!? I BET GIRLS COULDN'T CARE LESS ABOUT THAT SERIES!!
GO ON, GET BORED AND LEAVE!!
IT'S ACTUALLY 100% UNREQUITED, THOUGH, ISN'T IT?

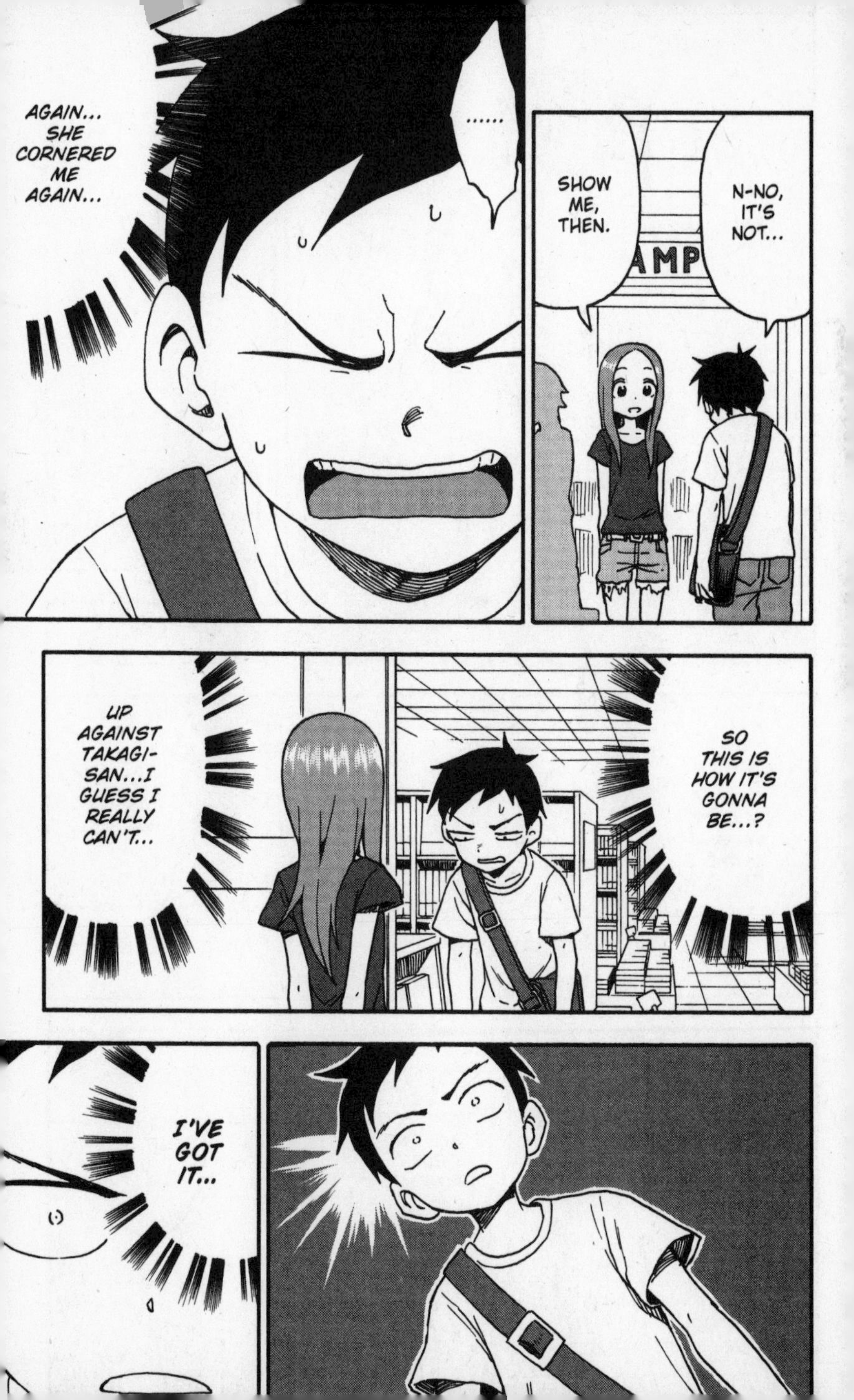
N-NO, IT'S NOT...
SHOW ME, THEN.
......
AGAIN... SHE CORNERED ME AGAIN...
SO THIS IS HOW IT'S GONNA BE...?
UP AGAINST TAKAGI-SAN...I GUESS I REALLY CAN'T...
I'VE GOT IT...

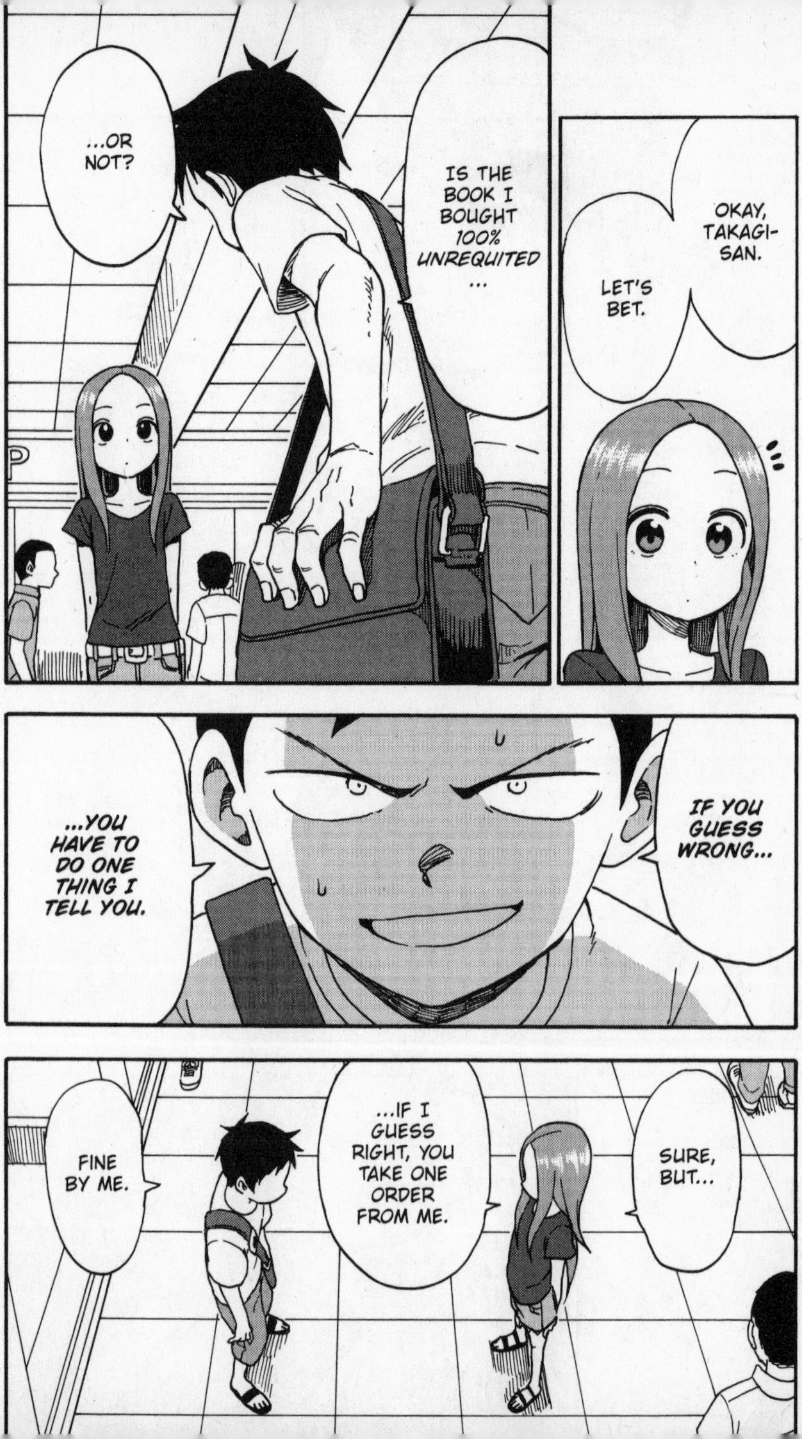
OKAY, TAKAGI-SAN.
LET'S BET.
IS THE BOOK I BOUGHT 100% UNREQUITED...
...OR NOT?
IF YOU GUESS WRONG...
...YOU HAVE TO DO ONE THING I TELL YOU.
SURE, BUT...
...IF I GUESS RIGHT, YOU TAKE ONE ORDER FROM ME.
FINE BY ME.

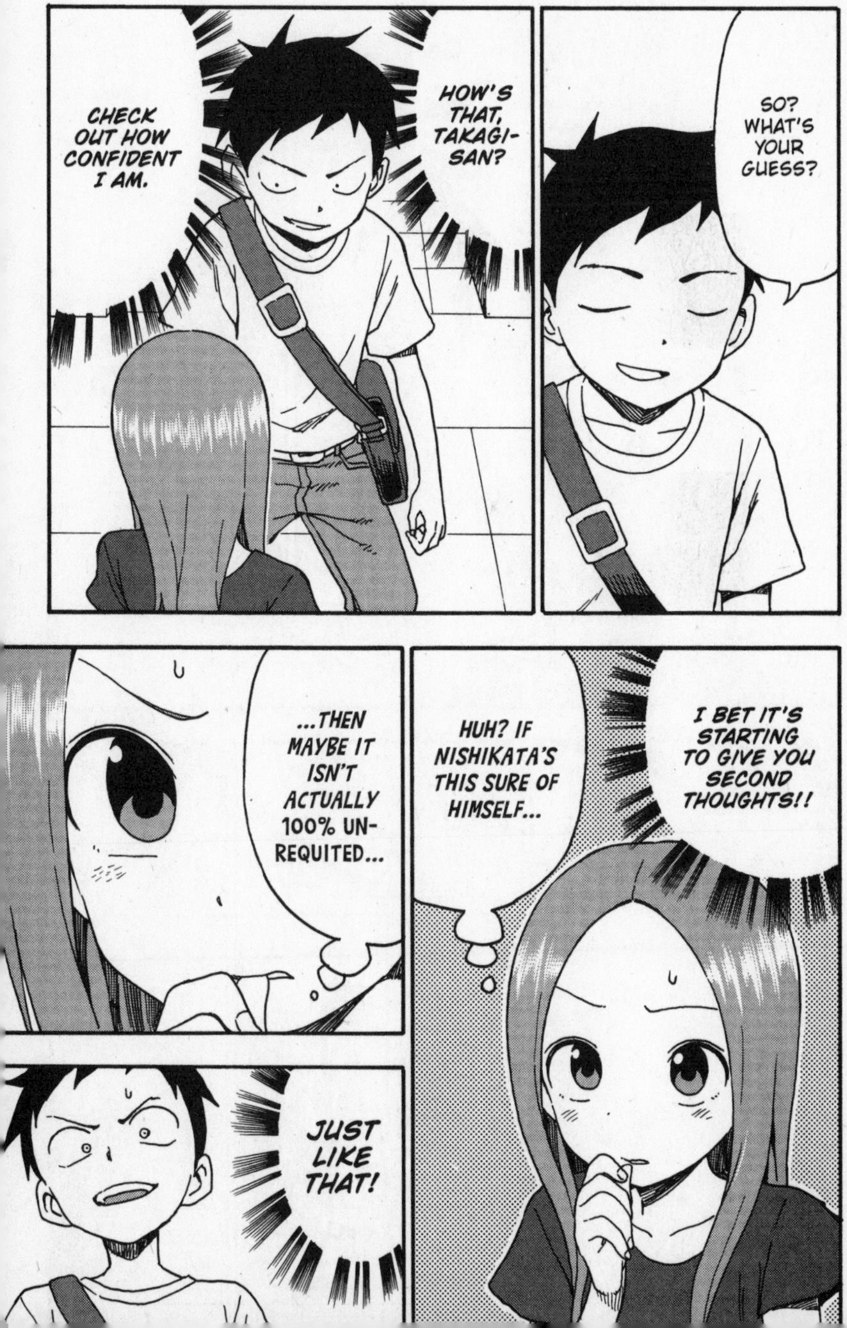
SO? WHAT'S YOUR GUESS?
HOW'S THAT, TAKAGI-SAN?
CHECK OUT HOW CONFIDENT I AM.
I BET IT'S STARTING TO GIVE YOU SECOND THOUGHTS!!
HUH? IF NISHIKATA'S THIS SURE OF HIMSELF...
...THEN MAYBE IT ISN'T ACTUALLY 100% UN-REQUITED...
JUST LIKE THAT!

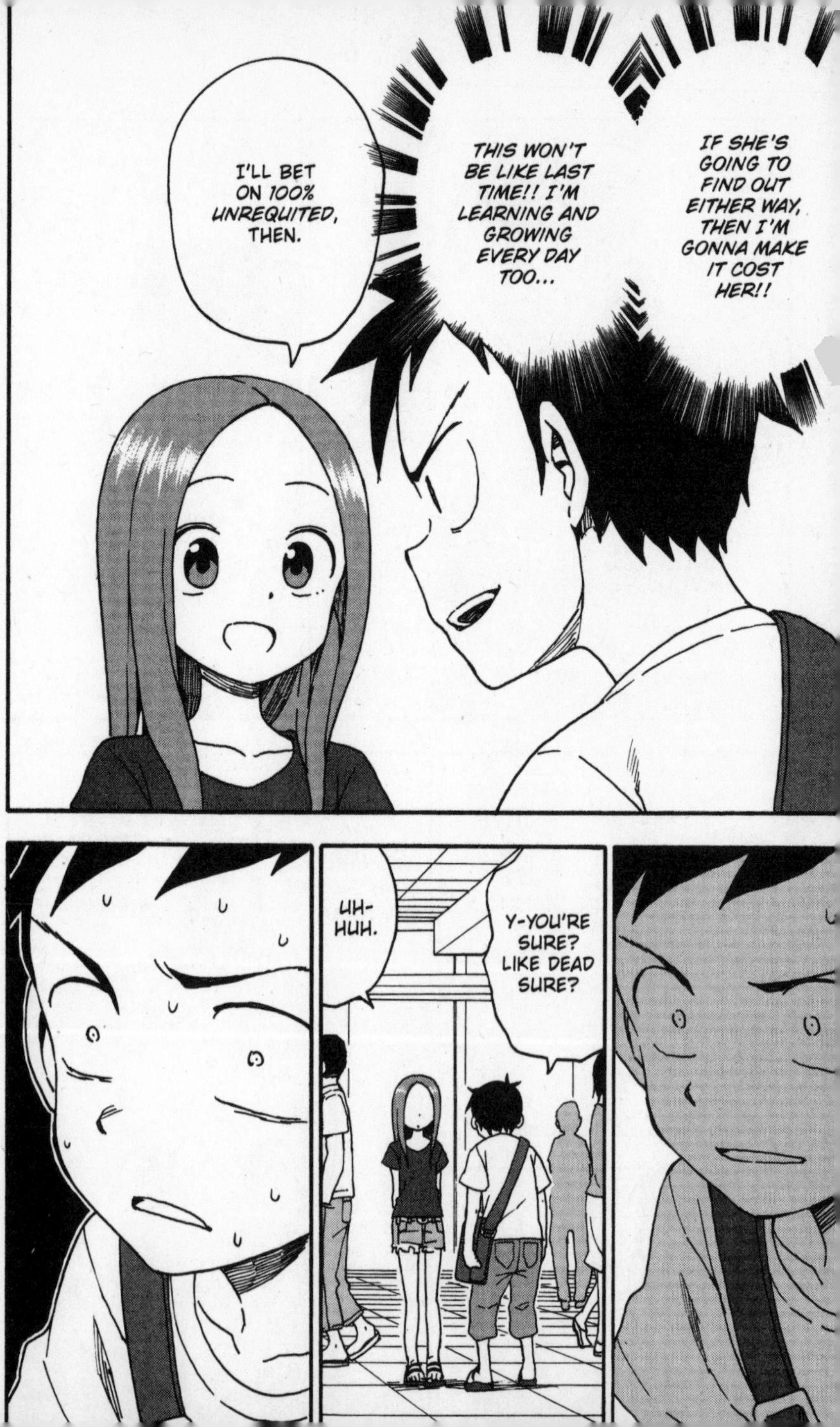
IF SHE'S GOING TO FIND OUT EITHER WAY, THEN I'M GONNA MAKE IT COST HER!!
THIS WON'T BE LIKE LAST TIME!! I'M LEARNING AND GROWING EVERY DAY TOO...
I'LL BET ON 100% UNREQUITED, THEN.
Y-YOU'RE SURE? LIKE DEAD SURE?
UH-HUH.

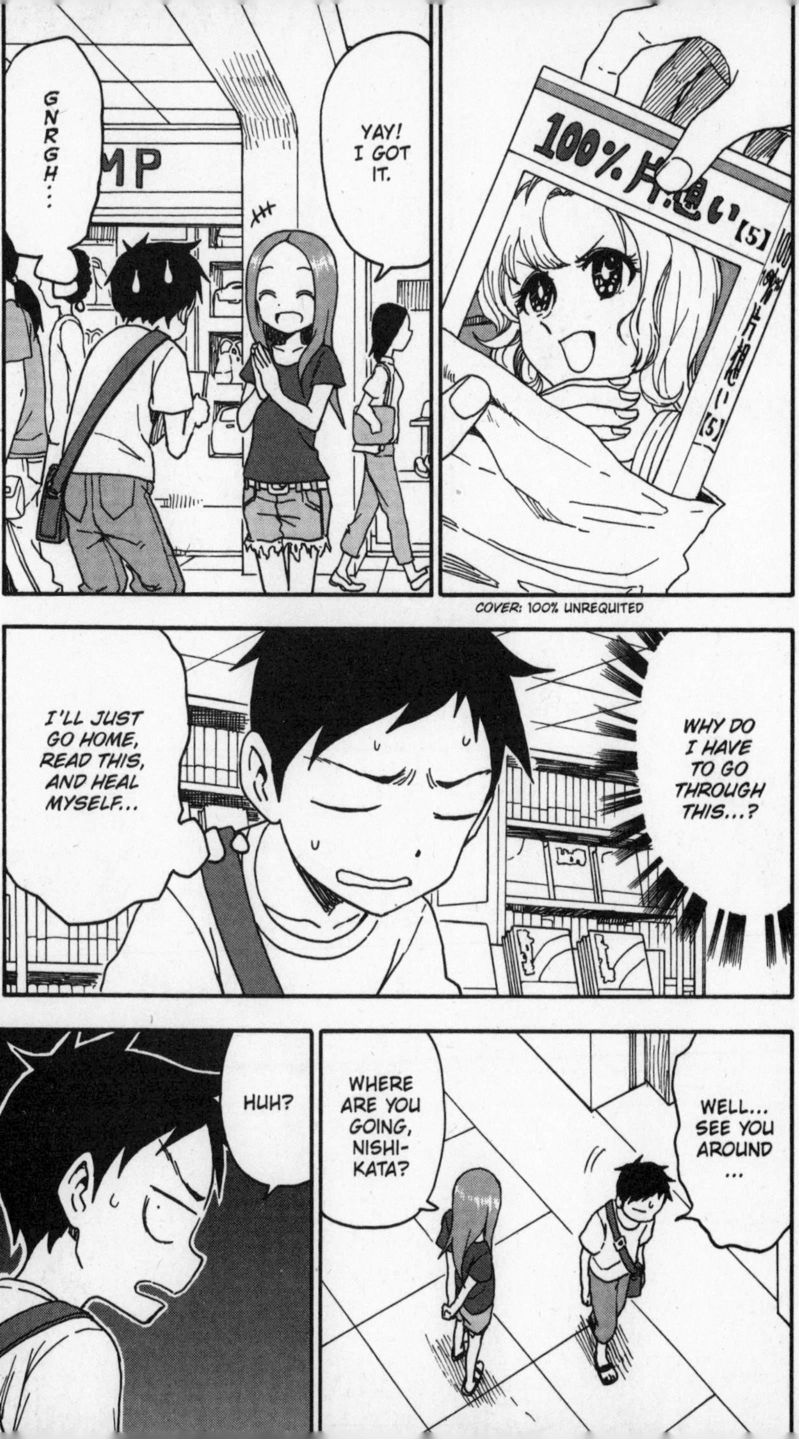
100%片想い【5】
COVER: 100% UNREQUITED
YAY! I GOT IT.
GNRGH...
WHY DO I HAVE TO GO THROUGH THIS...?
I'LL JUST GO HOME, READ THIS, AND HEAL MYSELF...
WELL... SEE YOU AROUND...
WHERE ARE YOU GOING, NISHI-KATA?
HUH?

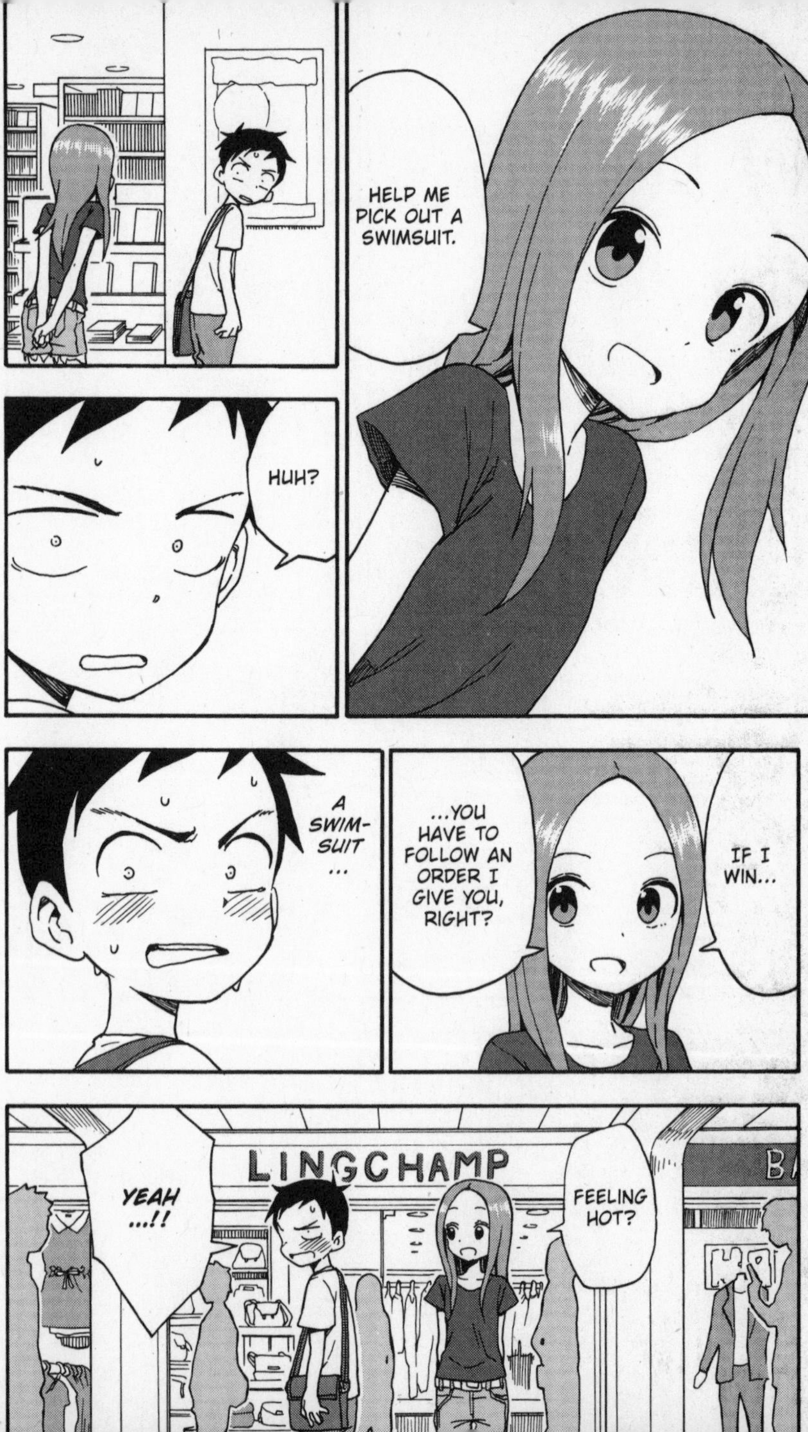
HELP ME PICK OUT A SWIMSUIT.
HUH?
IF I WIN...
...YOU HAVE TO FOLLOW AN ORDER I GIVE YOU, RIGHT?
A SWIM-SUIT ...
LINGCHAMP
FEELING HOT?
YEAH ...!!

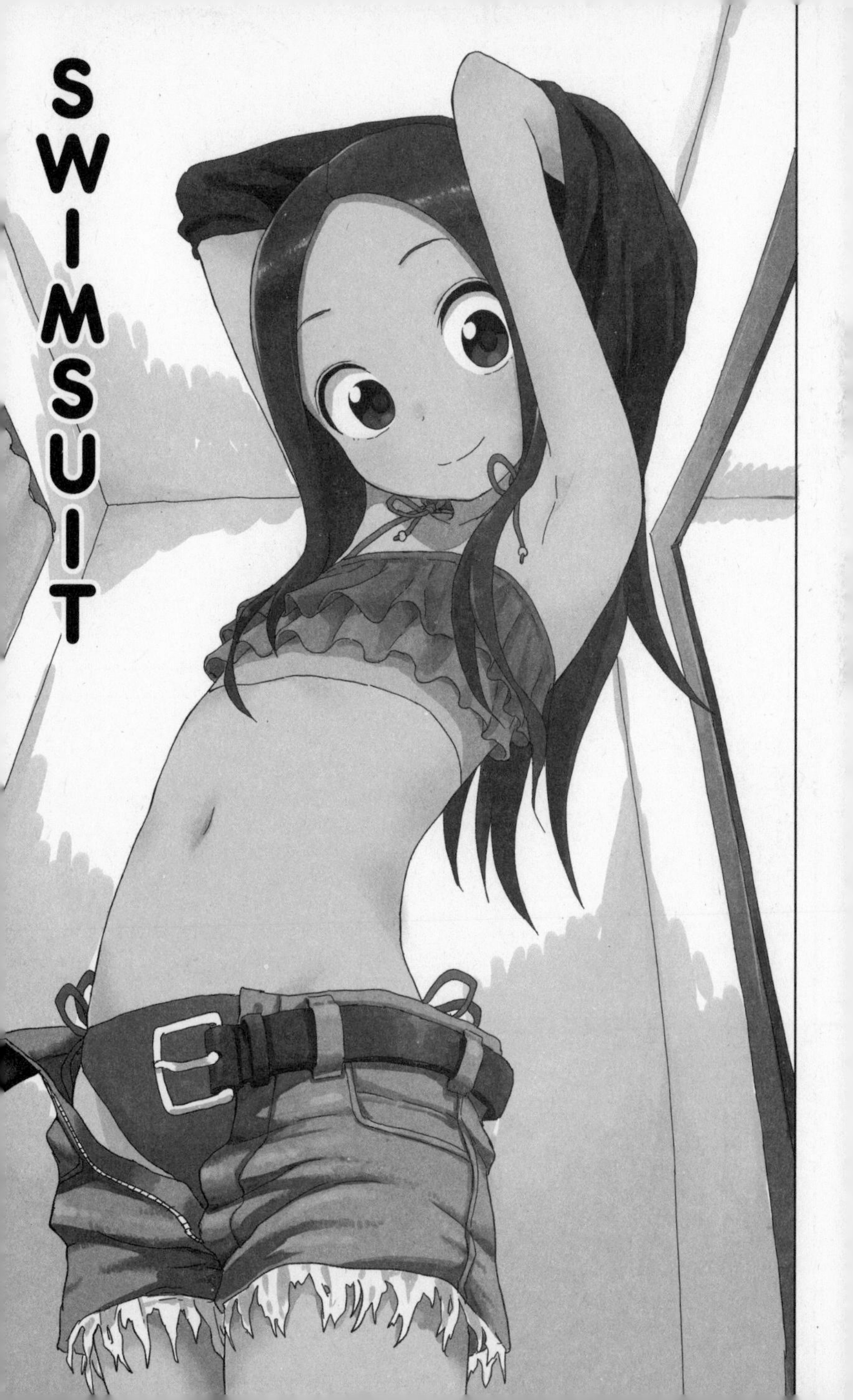
SWIMSUIT

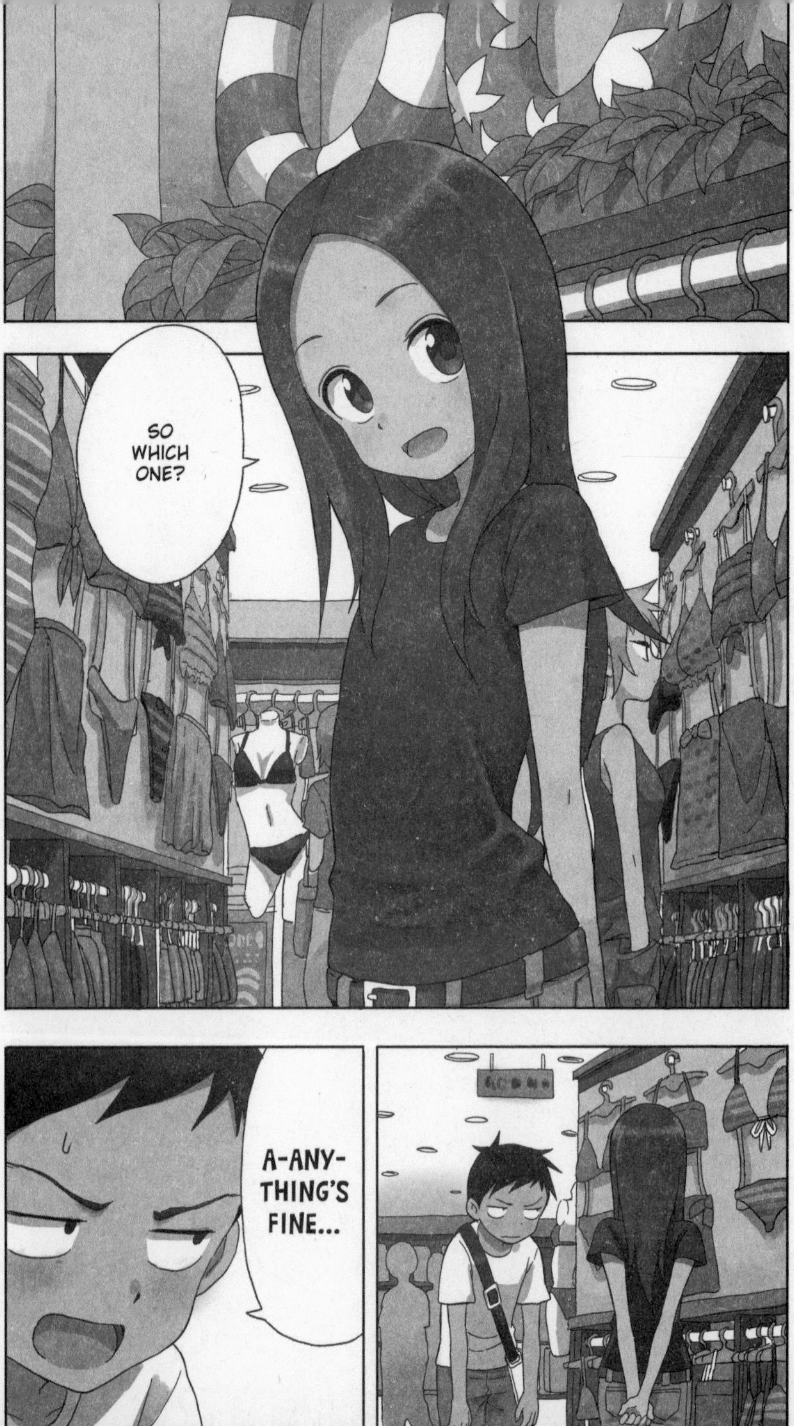
SO WHICH ONE?
A-ANY-THING'S FINE...

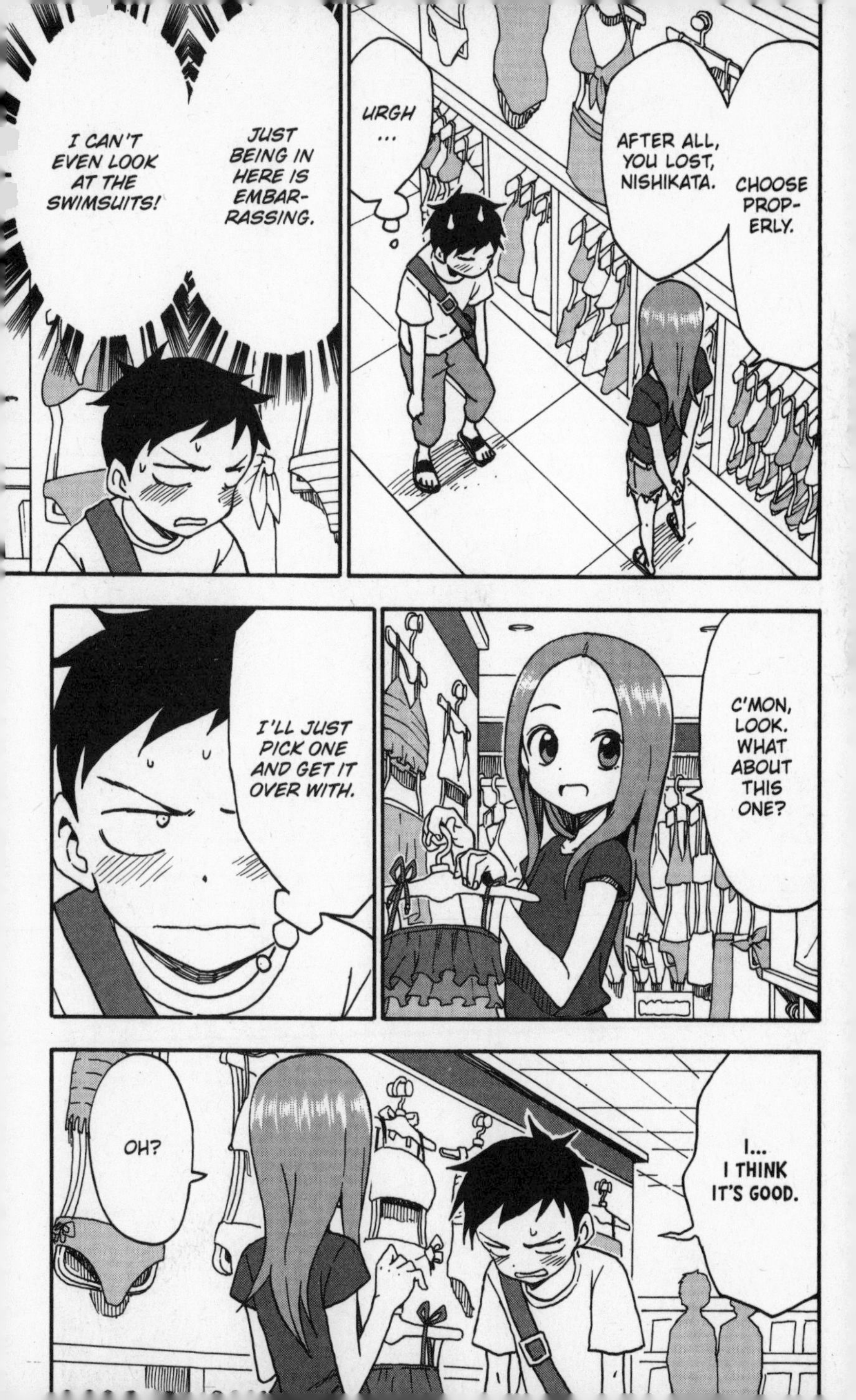
CHOOSE PROPERLY.
AFTER ALL, YOU LOST, NISHIKATA.
URGH ...
JUST BEING IN HERE IS EMBARRASSING.
I CAN'T EVEN LOOK AT THE SWIMSUITS!
C'MON, LOOK. WHAT ABOUT THIS ONE?
I'LL JUST PICK ONE AND GET IT OVER WITH.
I... I THINK IT'S GOOD.
OH?

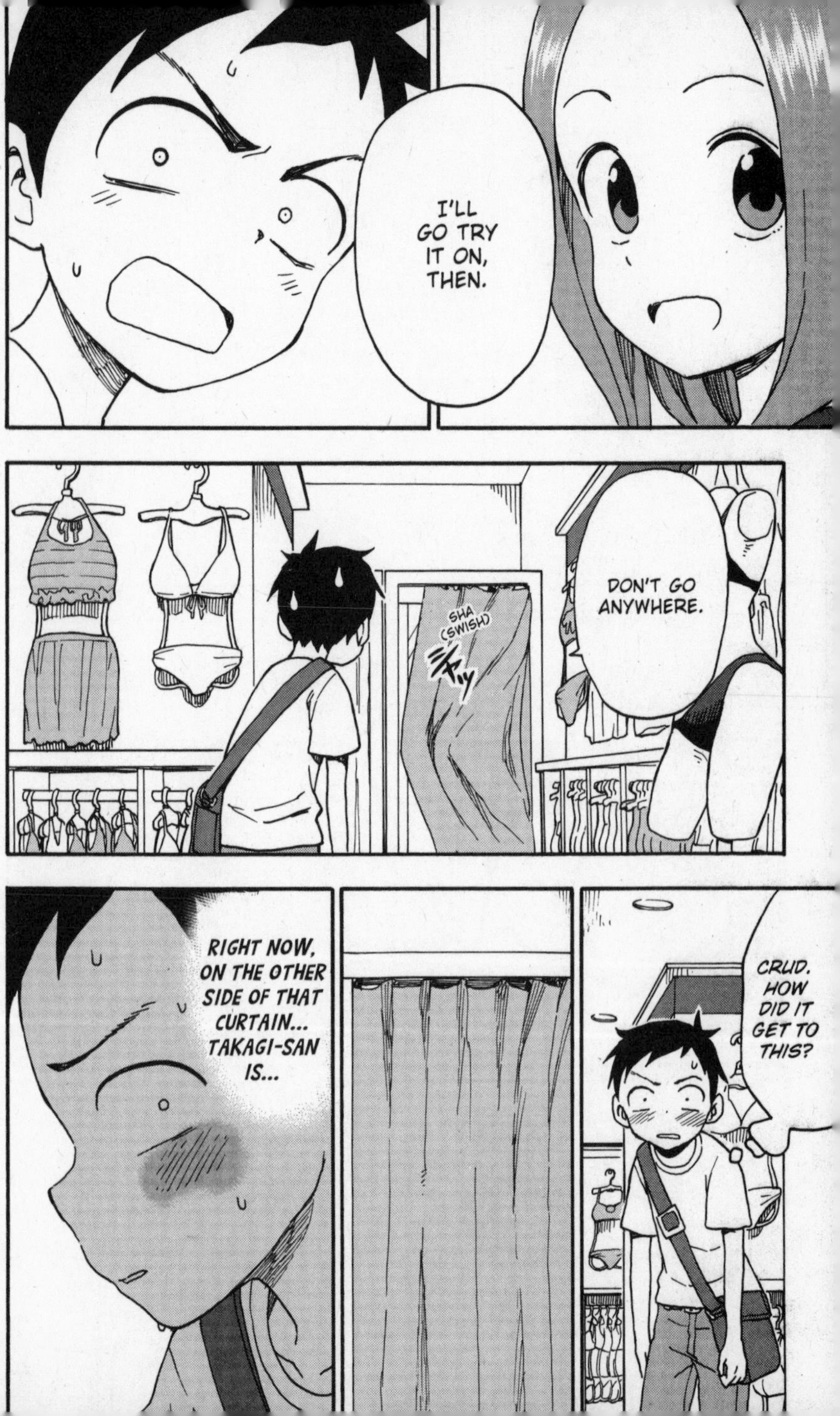
I'LL GO TRY IT ON, THEN.
DON'T GO ANYWHERE.
SHA (SWISH)
CRUD. HOW DID IT GET TO THIS?
RIGHT NOW, ON THE OTHER SIDE OF THAT CURTAIN... TAKAGI-SAN IS...

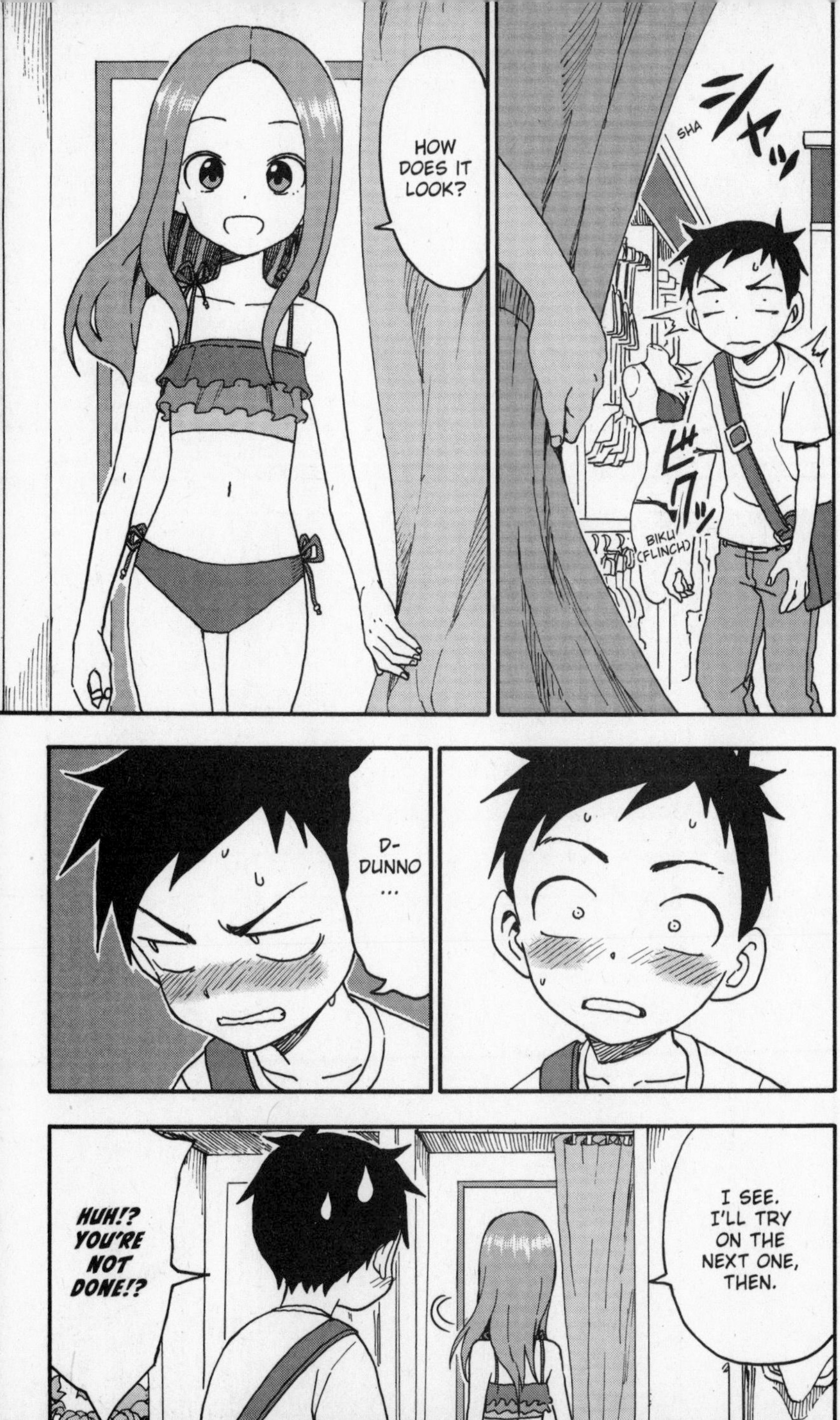
SHA
BIKU (FLINCH)
HOW DOES IT LOOK?
D-DUNNO...
I SEE. I'LL TRY ON THE NEXT ONE, THEN.
HUH!? YOU'RE NOT DONE!?

SAY WHAAAT...?

SHA (SWISH)

I MIGHT KEEP GOING UNTIL YOU TELL ME IT LOOKS GOOD ON ME.

THERE'S NO WAY I COULD SAY SOMETHING THAT CORNY!!

COULD YOU GRAB ME A SWIMSUIT?

SORRY.

!

NISHIKATA.

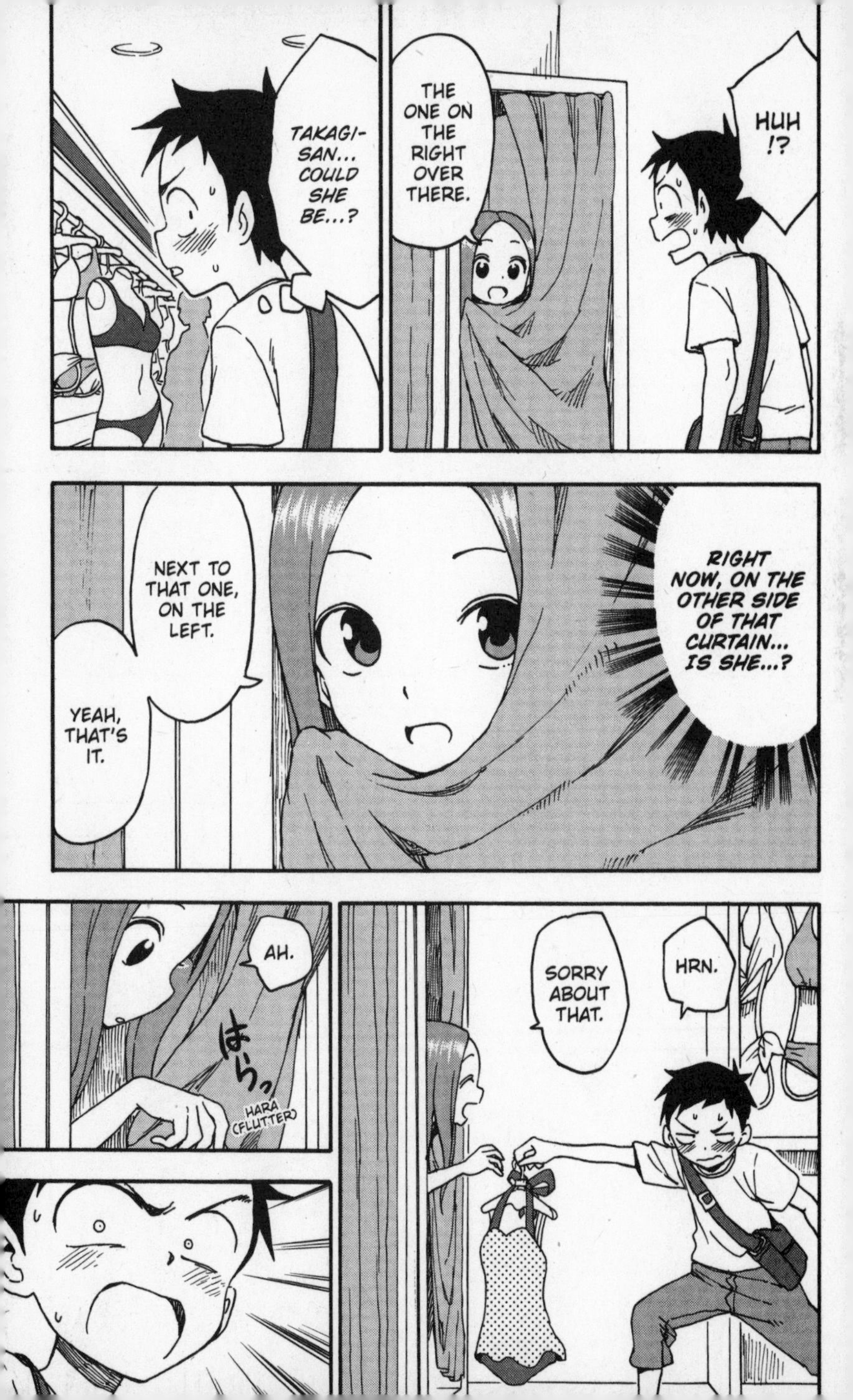
HUH !?
THE ONE ON THE RIGHT OVER THERE.
TAKAGI-SAN... COULD SHE BE...?
RIGHT NOW, ON THE OTHER SIDE OF THAT CURTAIN... IS SHE...?
NEXT TO THAT ONE, ON THE LEFT.
YEAH, THAT'S IT.
HRN.
SORRY ABOUT THAT.
AH.
はらっ
HARA (FLUTTER)

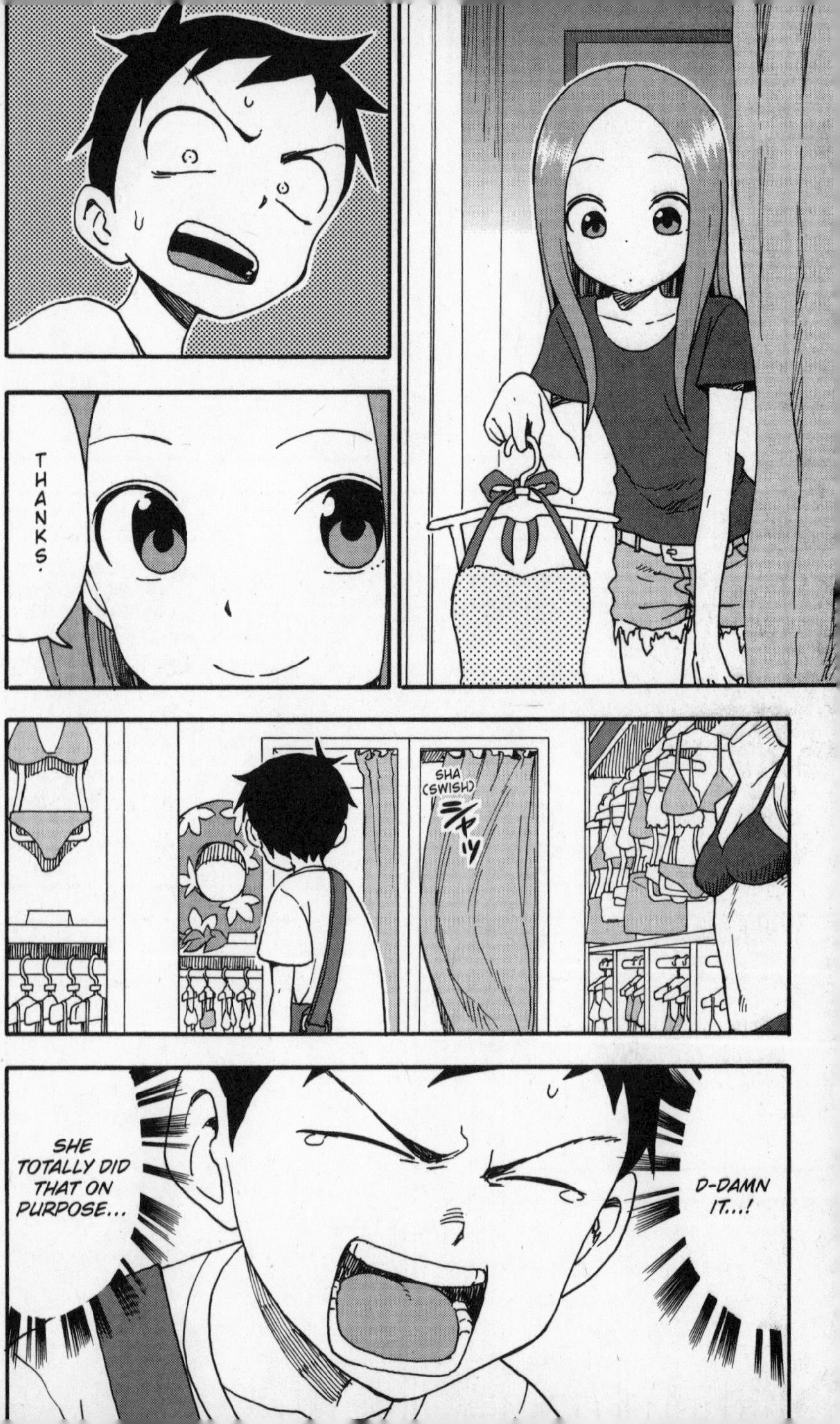
THANKS.
SHA (SWISH)
シャッ
D-DAMN IT...!
SHE TOTALLY DID THAT ON PURPOSE...

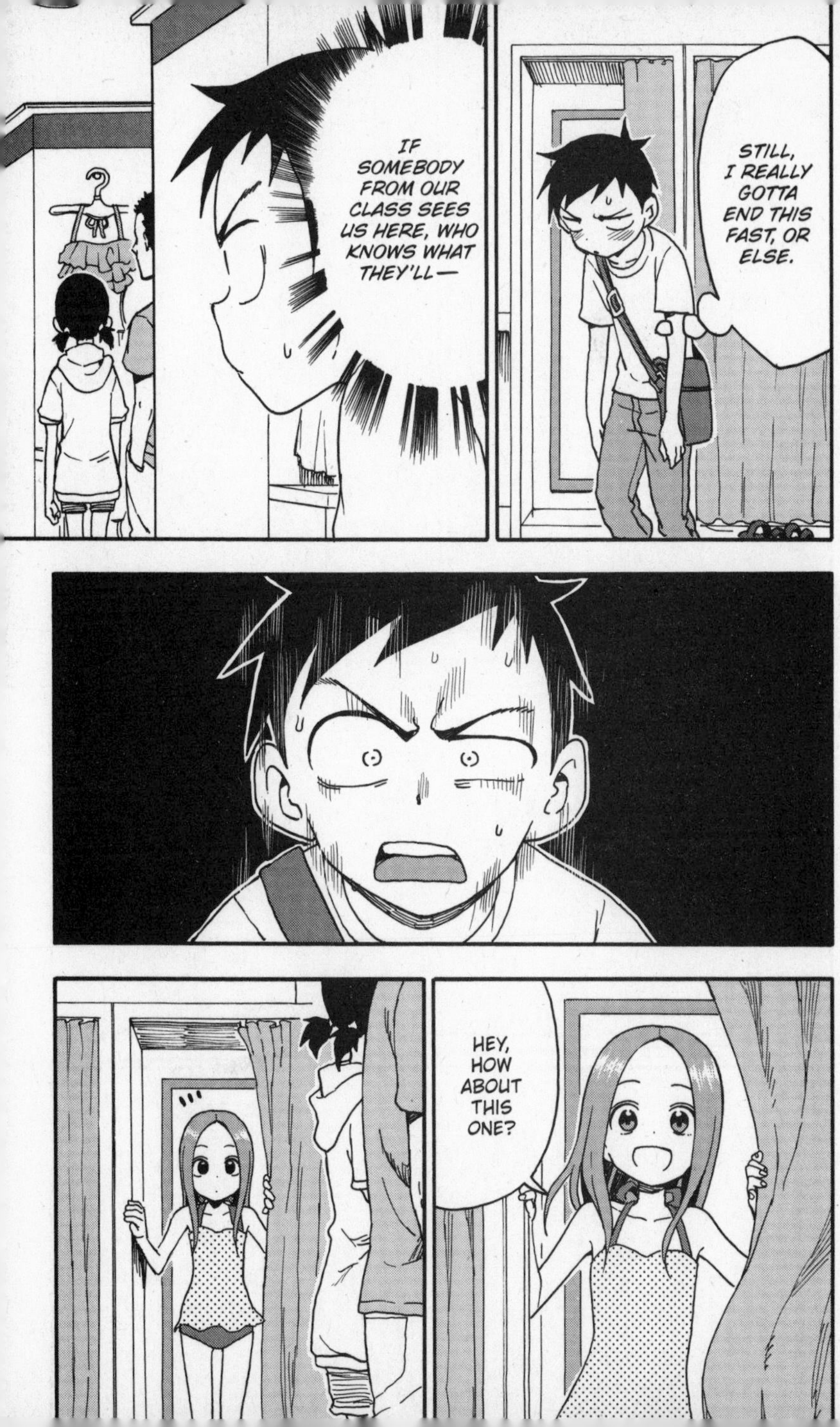
STILL, I REALLY GOTTA END THIS FAST, OR ELSE.
IF SOMEBODY FROM OUR CLASS SEES US HERE, WHO KNOWS WHAT THEY'LL—
HEY, HOW ABOUT THIS ONE?

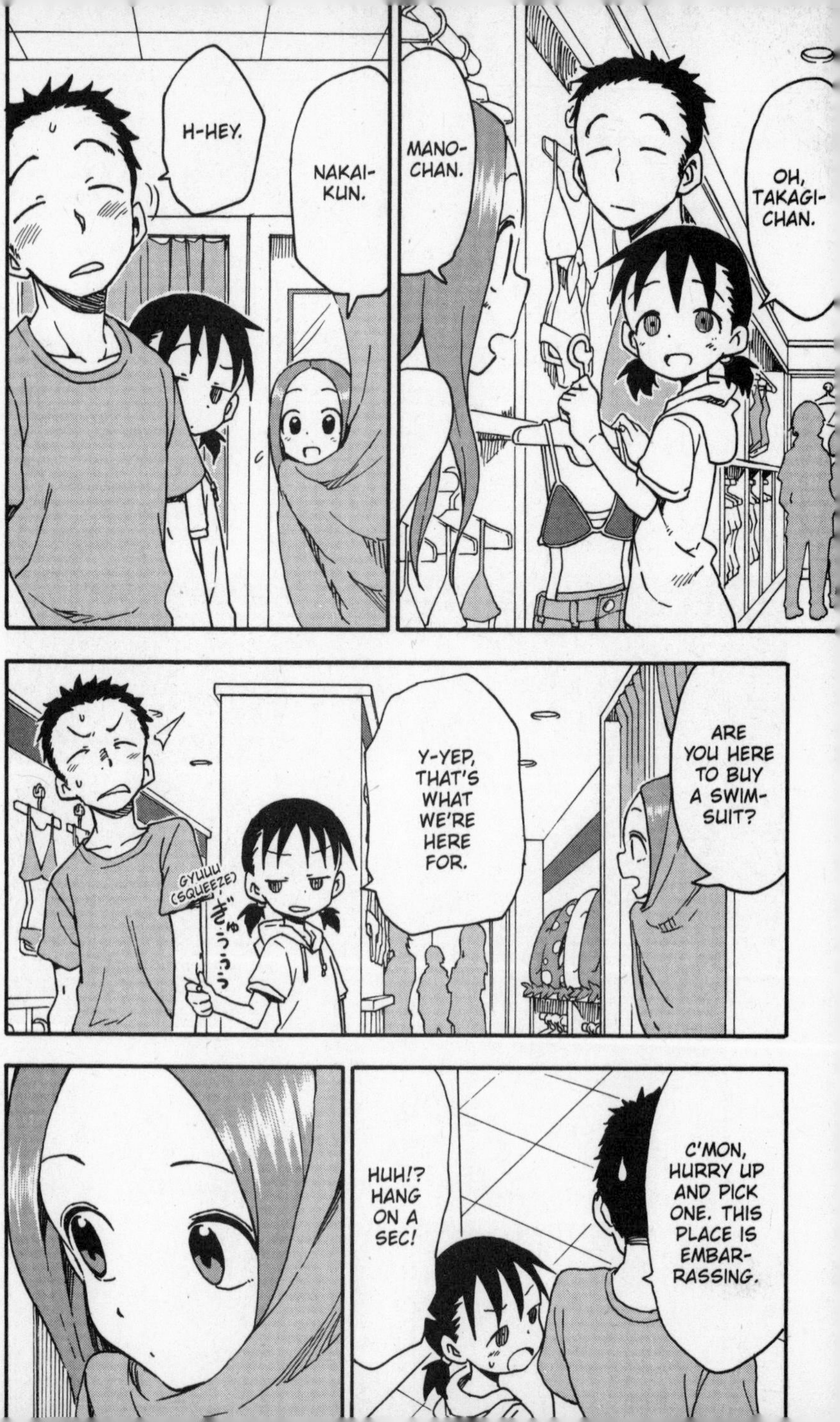
OH, TAKAGI-CHAN.
MANO-CHAN.
NAKAI-KUN.
H-HEY.
ARE YOU HERE TO BUY A SWIM-SUIT?
Y-YEP, THAT'S WHAT WE'RE HERE FOR.
GYUUU (SQUEEZE)
C'MON, HURRY UP AND PICK ONE. THIS PLACE IS EMBARRASSING.
HUH!? HANG ON A SEC!

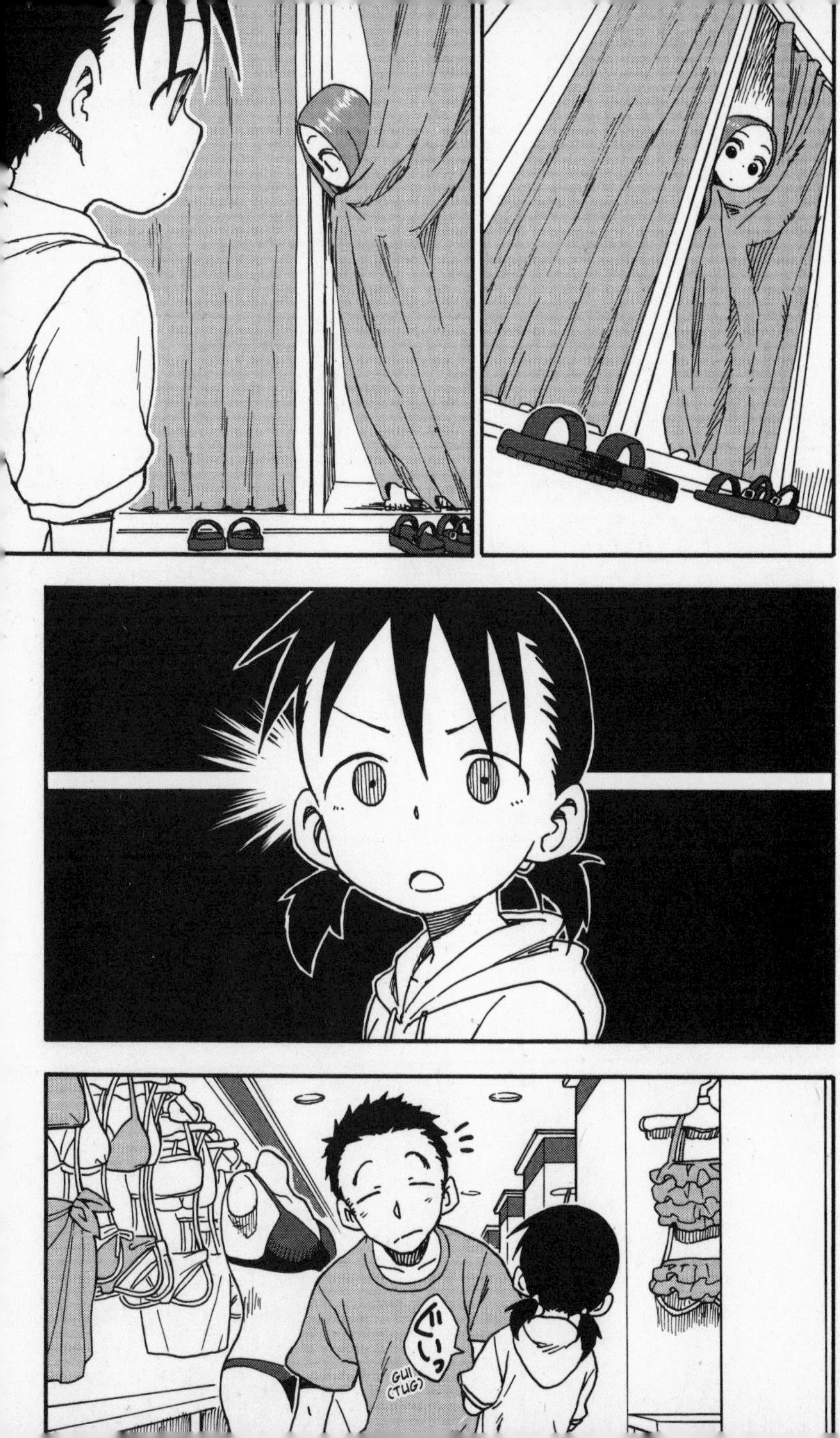
ぐいっ
GUI
(TUG)

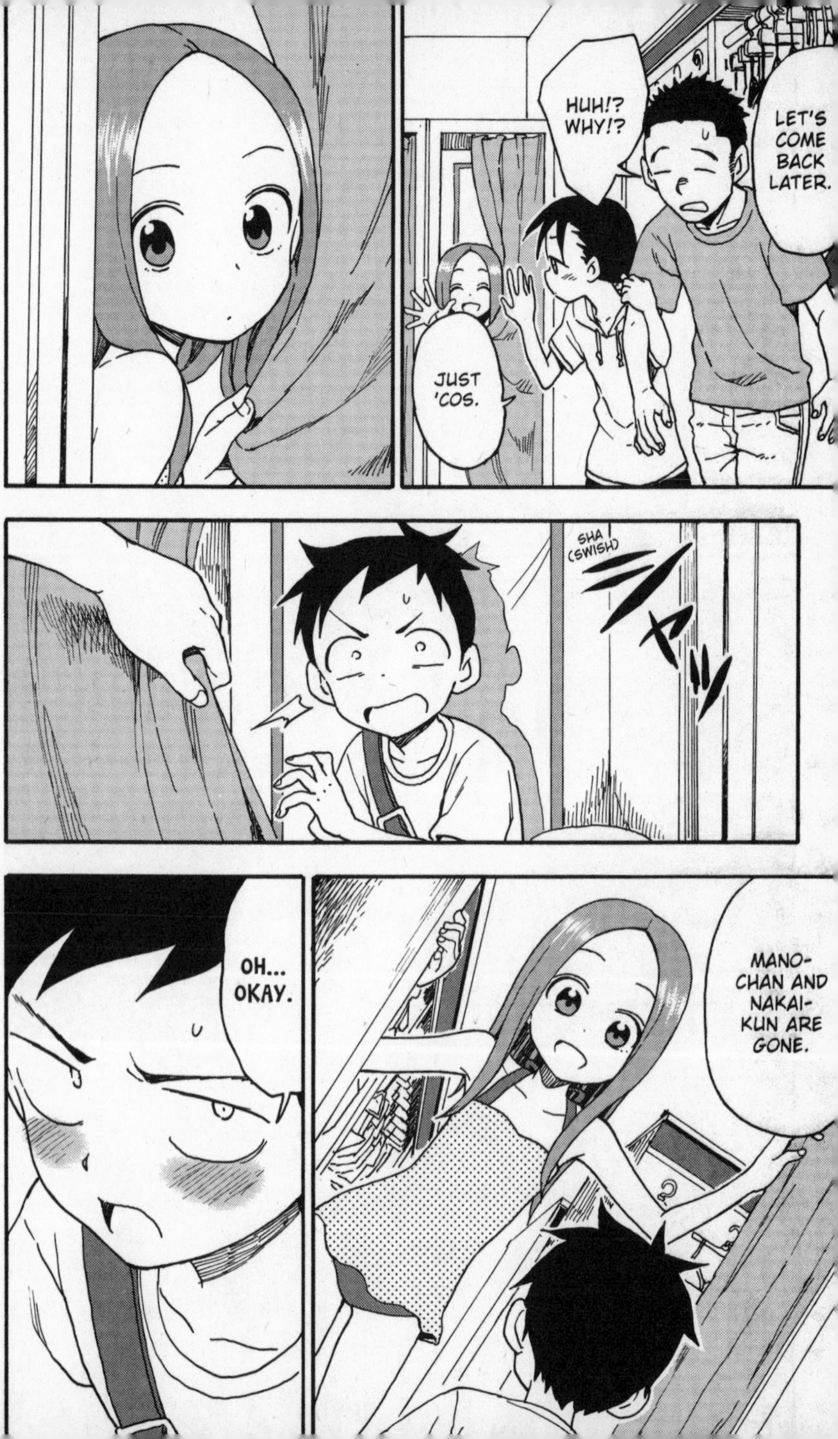
LET'S COME BACK LATER.
HUH!? WHY!?
JUST 'COS.
SHA (SWISH)
MANO-CHAN AND NAKAI-KUN ARE GONE.
OH... OKAY.

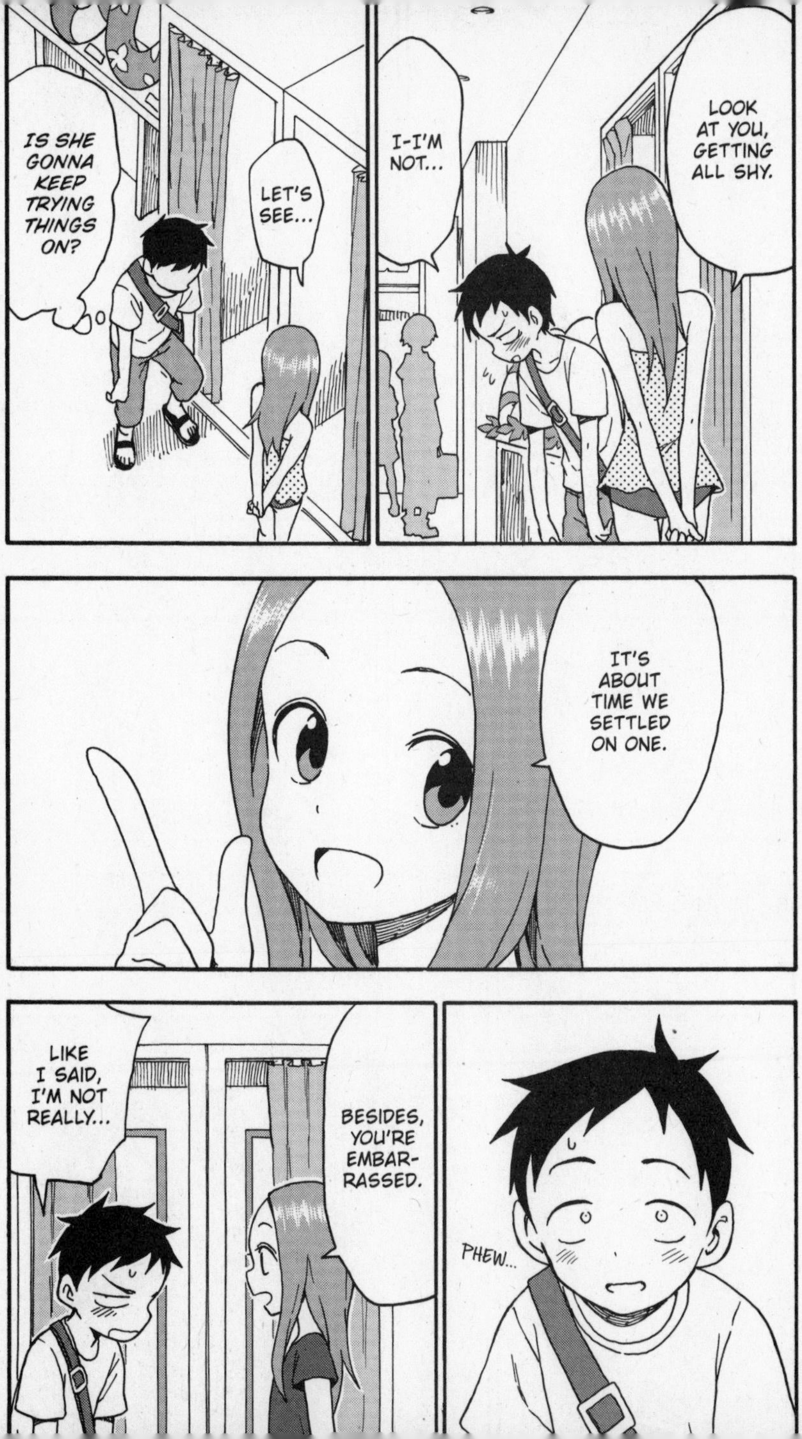
LOOK AT YOU, GETTING ALL SHY.
I-I'M NOT...
LET'S SEE...
IS SHE GONNA KEEP TRYING THINGS ON?
IT'S ABOUT TIME WE SETTLED ON ONE.
PHEW...
BESIDES, YOU'RE EMBARRASSED.
LIKE I SAID, I'M NOT REALLY...

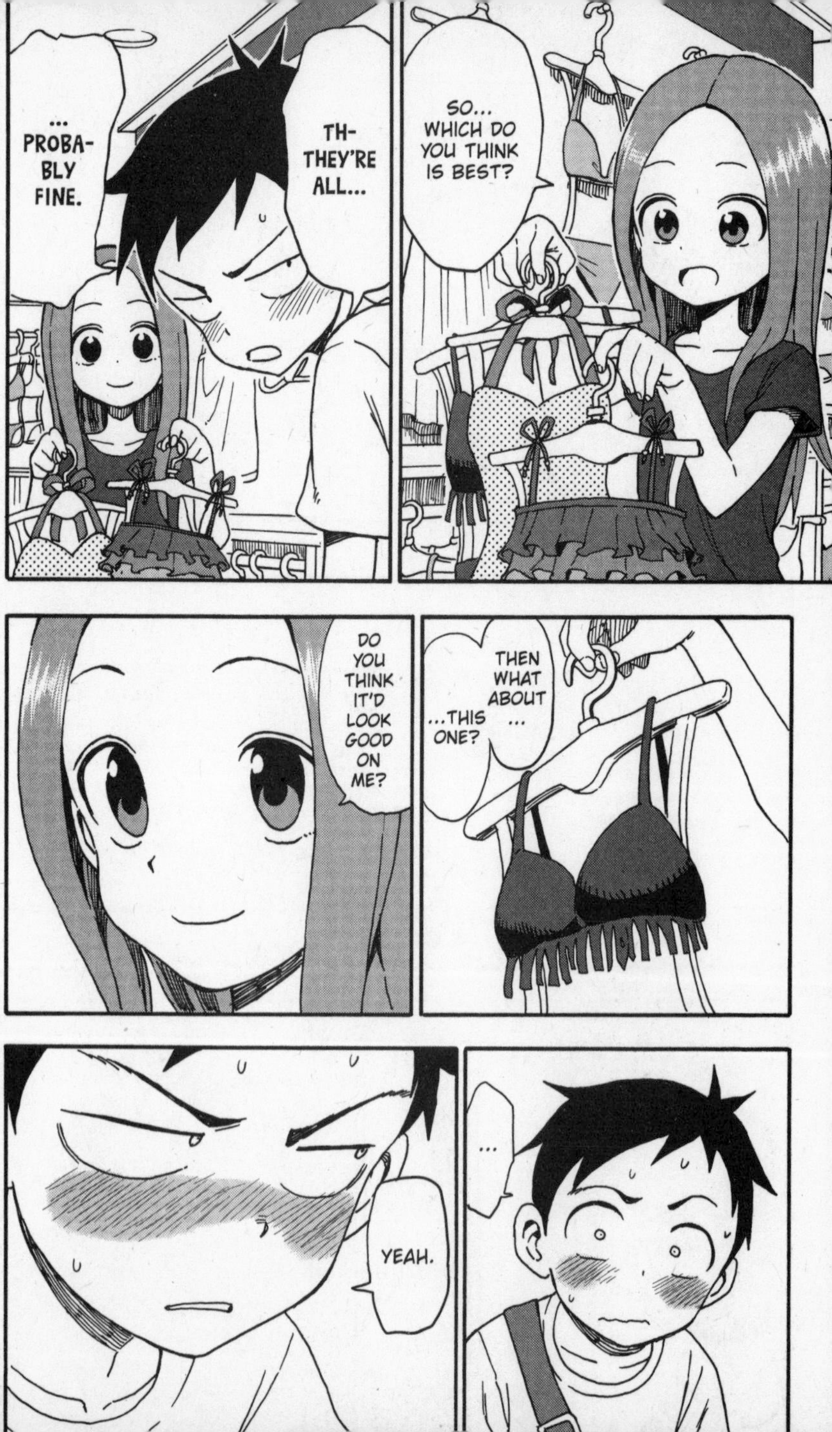
SO... WHICH DO YOU THINK IS BEST?
TH- THEY'RE ALL...
... PROBA-BLY FINE.
THEN WHAT ABOUT ...
...THIS ONE?
DO YOU THINK IT'D LOOK GOOD ON ME?
...
YEAH.

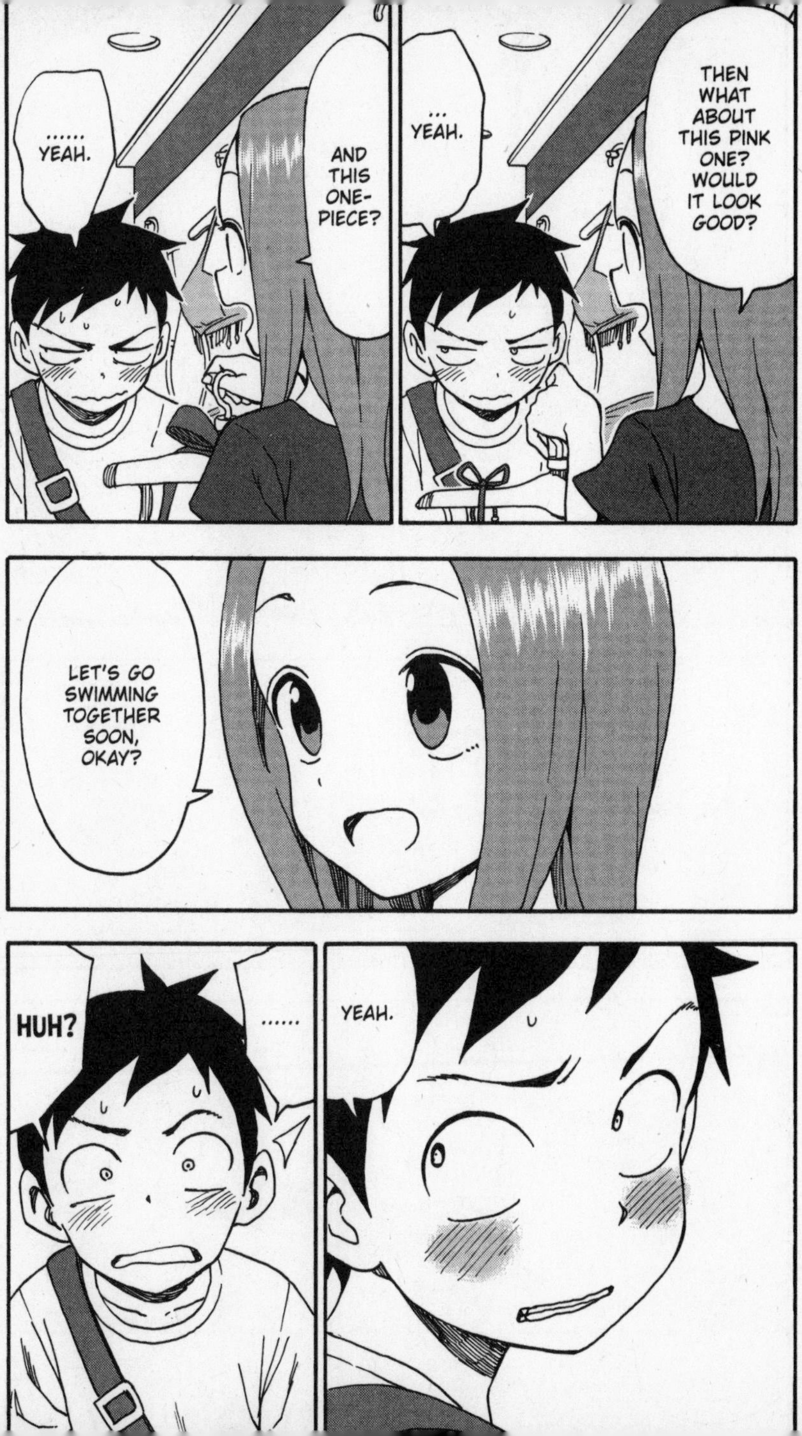

......
YEAH.
AND THIS ONE-PIECE?
...
YEAH.
THEN WHAT ABOUT THIS PINK ONE? WOULD IT LOOK GOOD?
LET'S GO SWIMMING TOGETHER SOON, OKAY?
HUH?
......
YEAH.

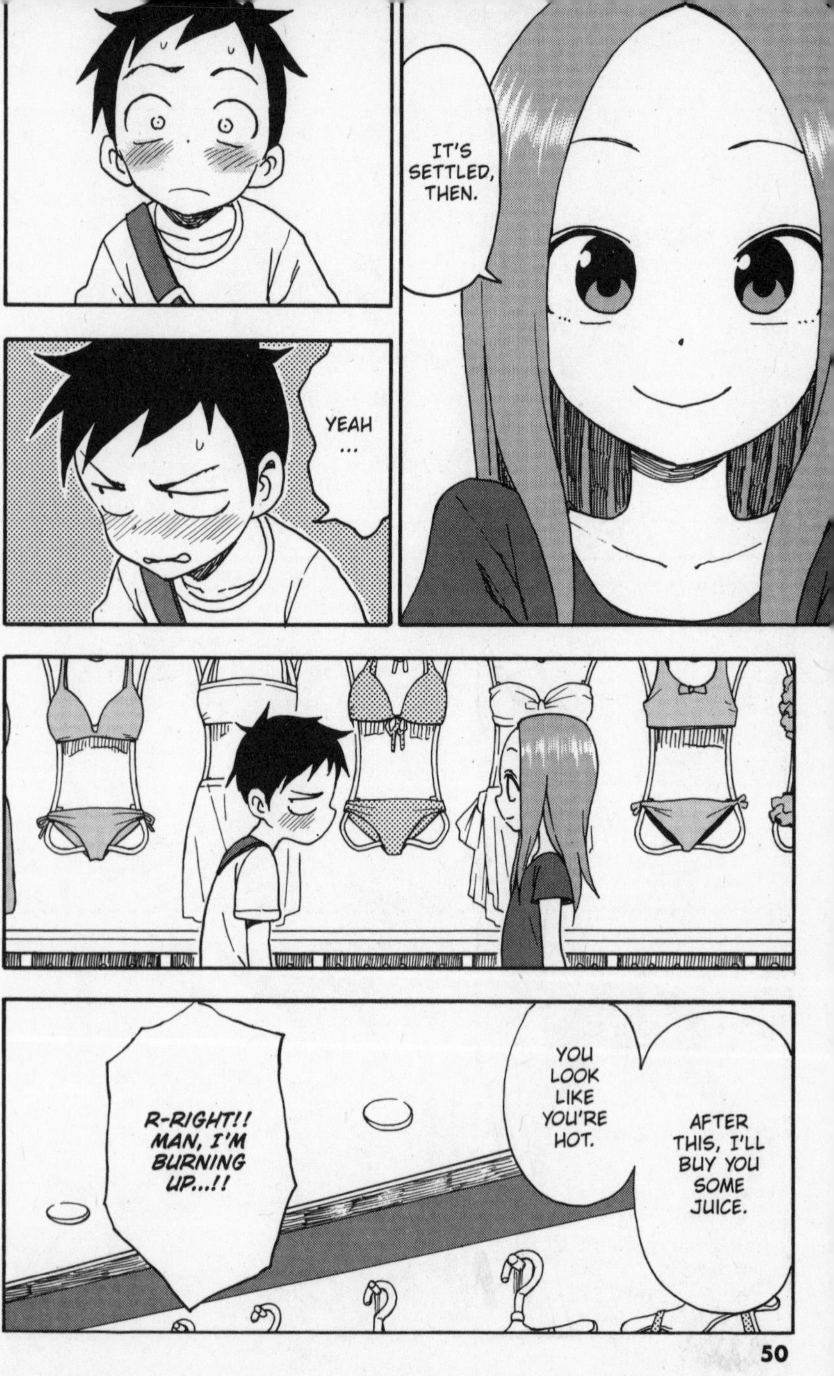
IT'S SETTLED, THEN.
YEAH ...
YOU LOOK LIKE YOU'RE HOT.
AFTER THIS, I'LL BUY YOU SOME JUICE.
R-RIGHT!! MAN, I'M BURNING UP...!!

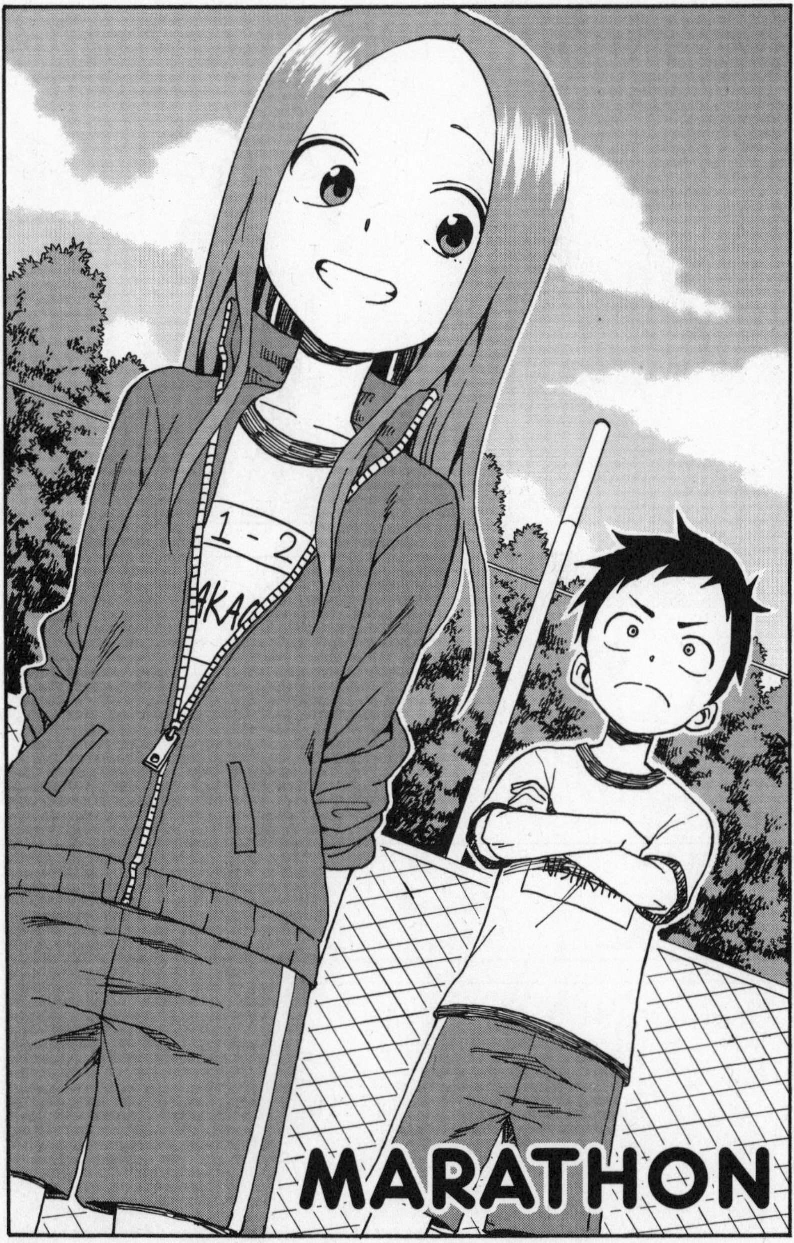
1-2
MARATHON

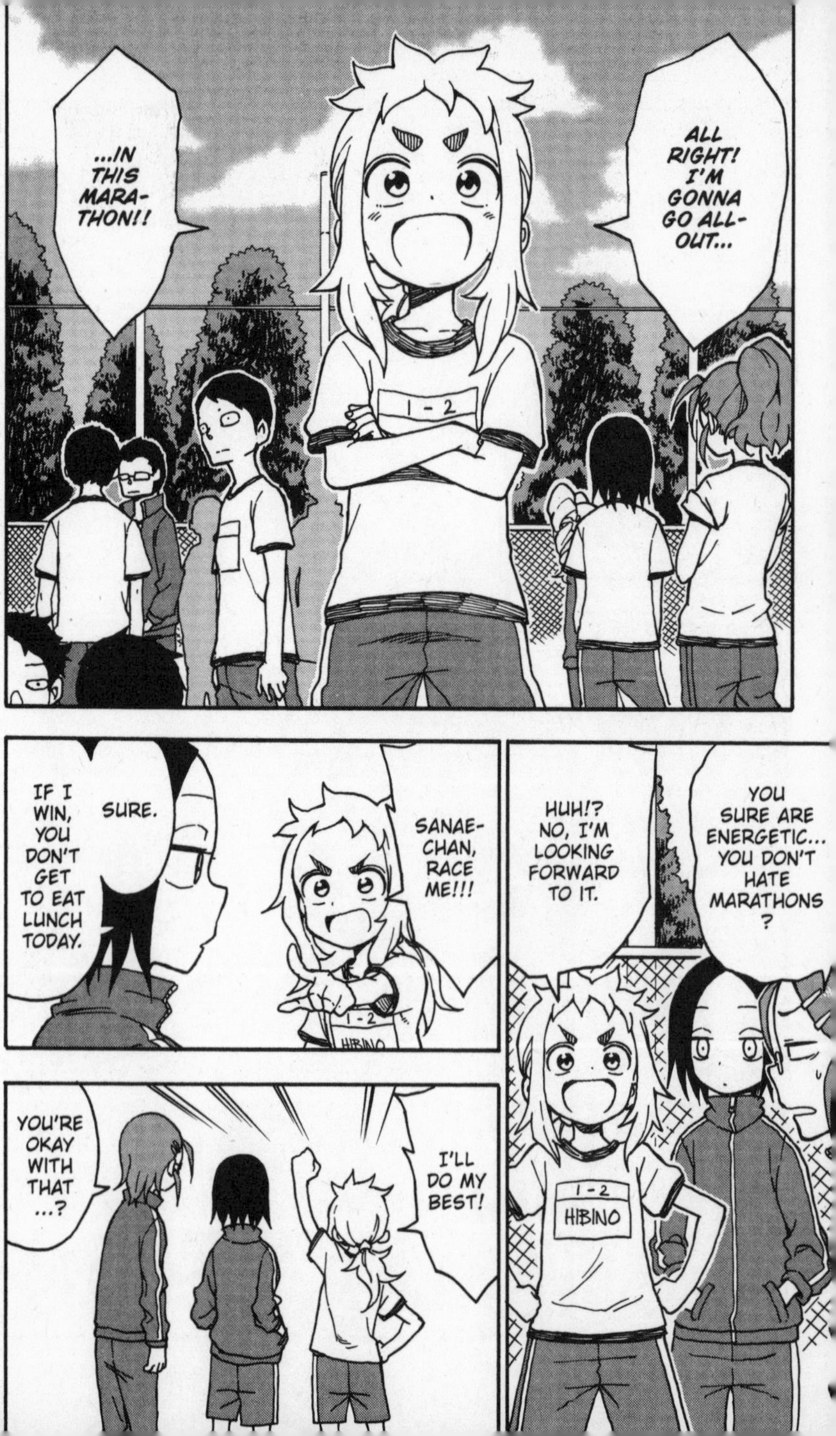
ALL RIGHT! I'M GONNA GO ALL-OUT...
...IN THIS MARATHON!!
1-2
YOU SURE ARE ENERGETIC... YOU DON'T HATE MARATHONS?
HUH!? NO, I'M LOOKING FORWARD TO IT.
1-2
HIBINO
SANAE-CHAN, RACE ME!!!
1-2
HIBINO
SURE.
IF I WIN, YOU DON'T GET TO EAT LUNCH TODAY.
I'LL DO MY BEST!
YOU'RE OKAY WITH THAT ...?

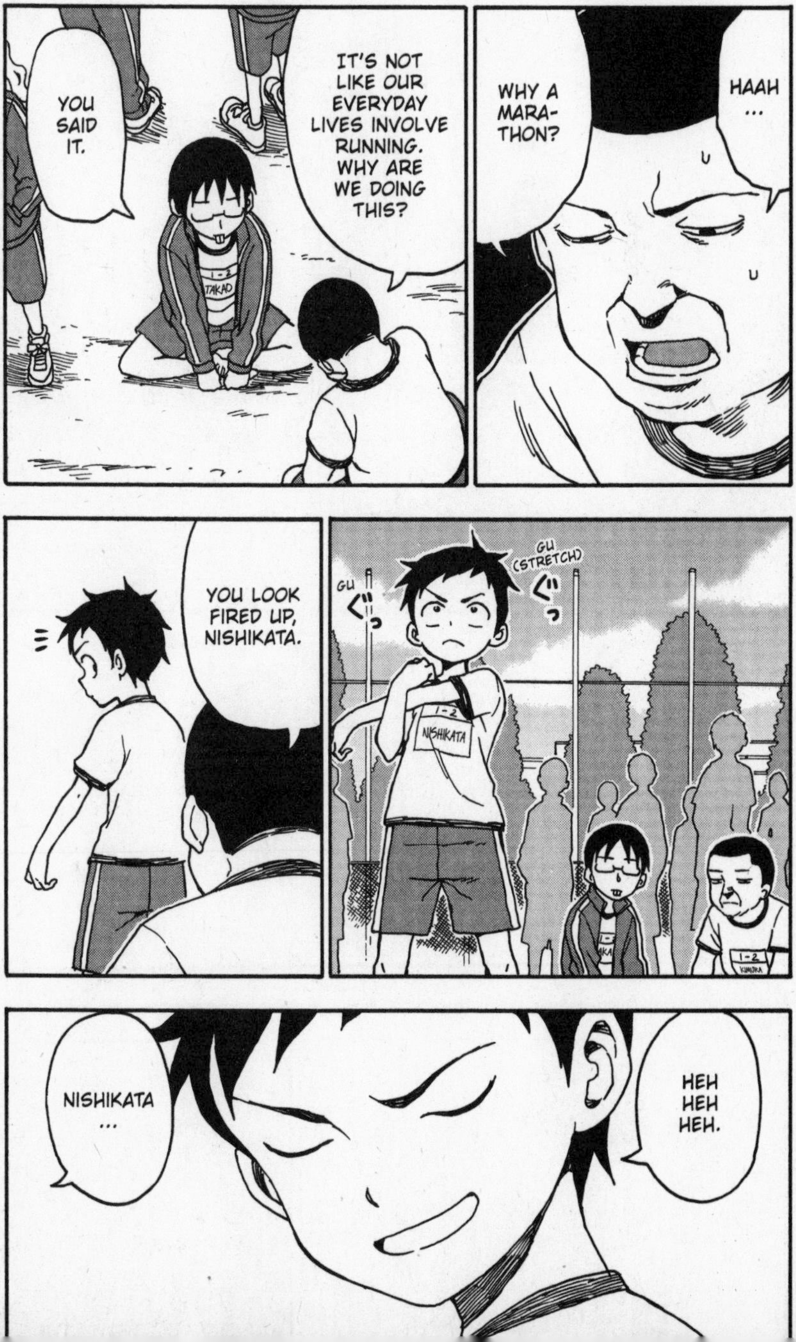
HAAH ...
WHY A MARA- THON?
IT'S NOT LIKE OUR EVERYDAY LIVES INVOLVE RUNNING. WHY ARE WE DOING THIS?
YOU SAID IT.
GU (STRETCH)
ぐっ
GU
ぐっ
YOU LOOK FIRED UP, NISHIKATA.
HEH HEH HEH.
NISHIKATA ...

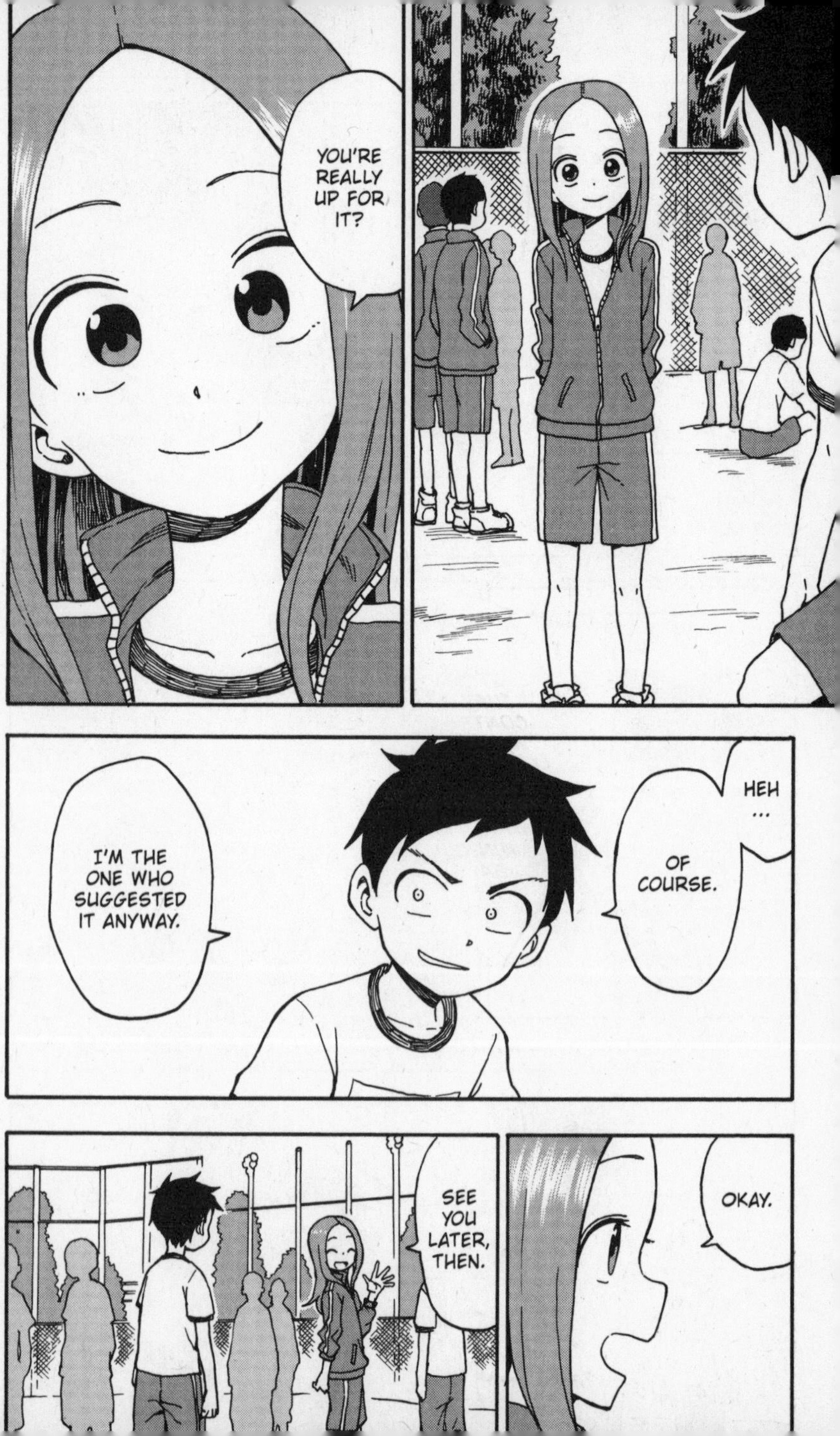
YOU'RE REALLY UP FOR IT?
HEH... OF COURSE.
I'M THE ONE WHO SUGGESTED IT ANYWAY.
OKAY.
SEE YOU LATER, THEN.

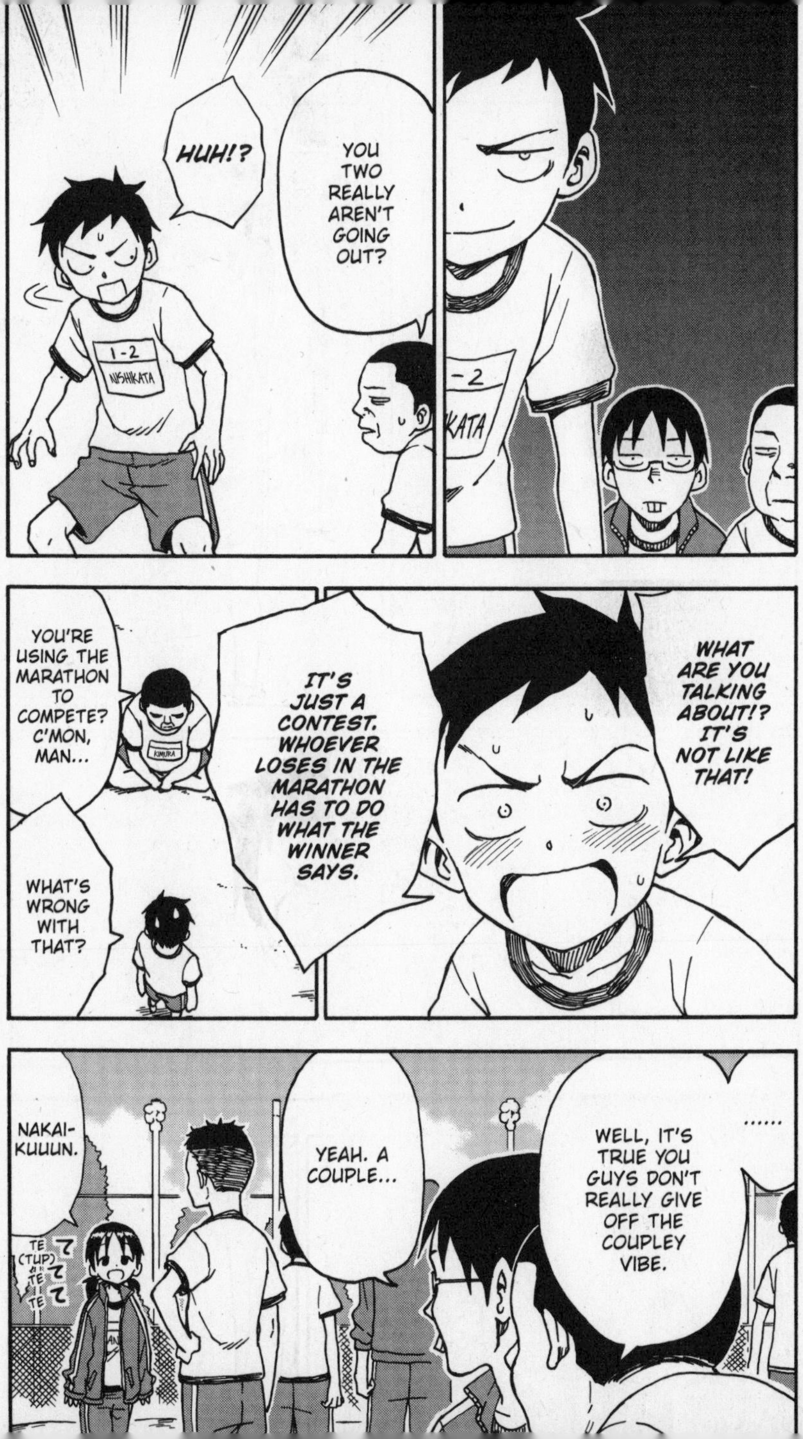
YOU TWO REALLY AREN'T GOING OUT?
HUH!?
WHAT ARE YOU TALKING ABOUT!? IT'S NOT LIKE THAT!
IT'S JUST A CONTEST. WHOEVER LOSES IN THE MARATHON HAS TO DO WHAT THE WINNER SAYS.
YOU'RE USING THE MARATHON TO COMPETE? C'MON, MAN...
WHAT'S WRONG WITH THAT?
......
WELL, IT'S TRUE YOU GUYS DON'T REALLY GIVE OFF THE COUPLEY VIBE.
YEAH. A COUPLE...
NAKAI-KUUUN.
TE TE TE TE (TUP)

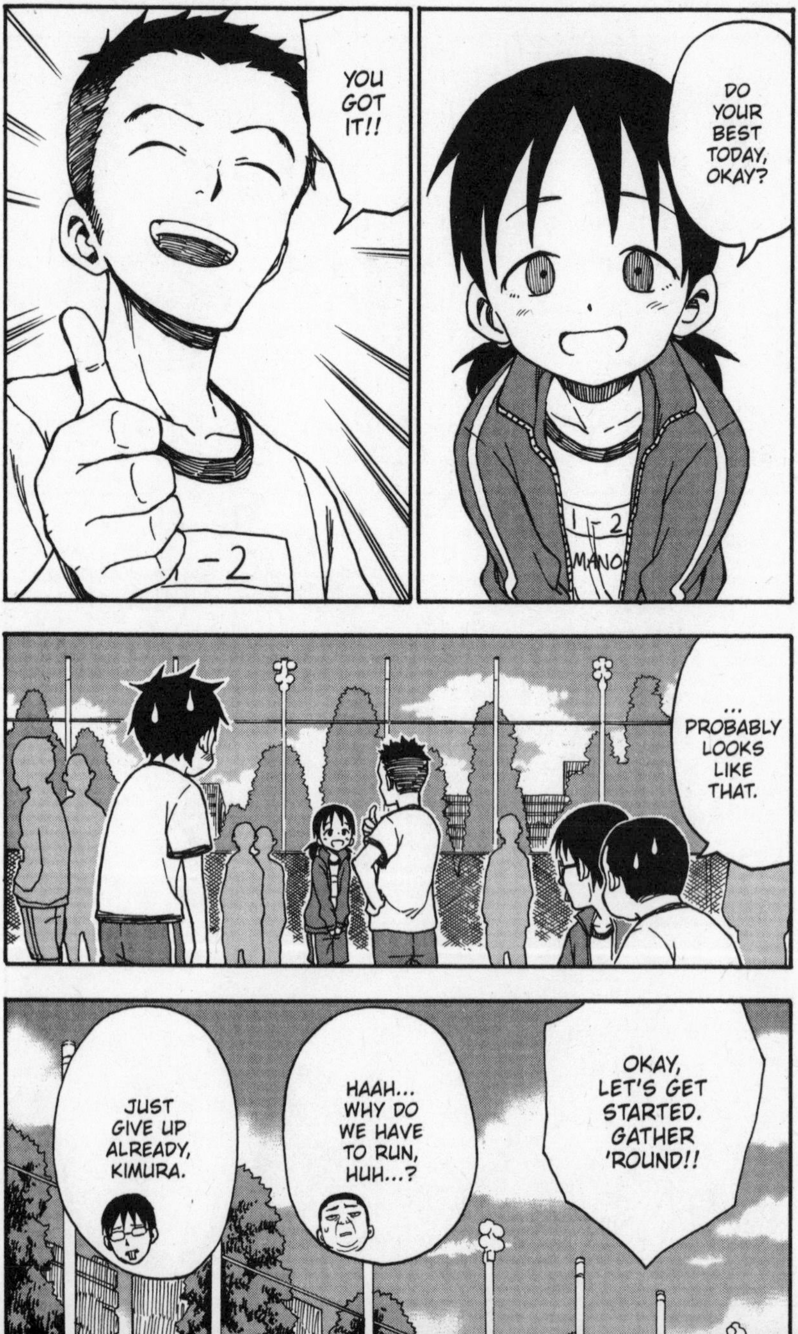
DO YOUR BEST TODAY, OKAY?
1-2
MANO
YOU GOT IT!!
1-2
...PROBABLY LOOKS LIKE THAT.
OKAY, LET'S GET STARTED. GATHER 'ROUND!!
HAAH... WHY DO WE HAVE TO RUN, HUH...?
JUST GIVE UP ALREADY, KIMURA.

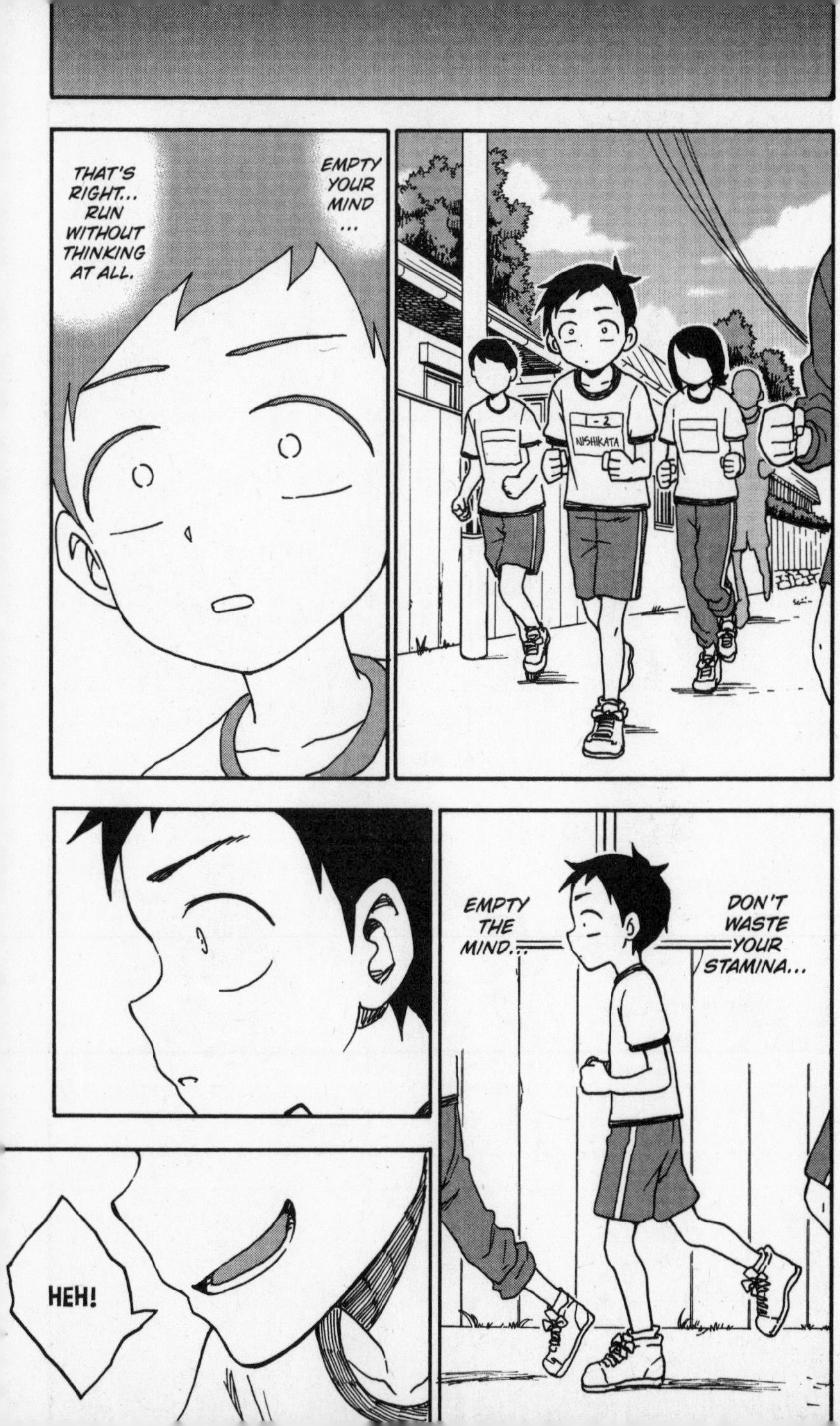
EMPTY YOUR MIND ...
THAT'S RIGHT... RUN WITHOUT THINKING AT ALL.
DON'T WASTE YOUR STAMINA...
EMPTY THE MIND...
HEH!

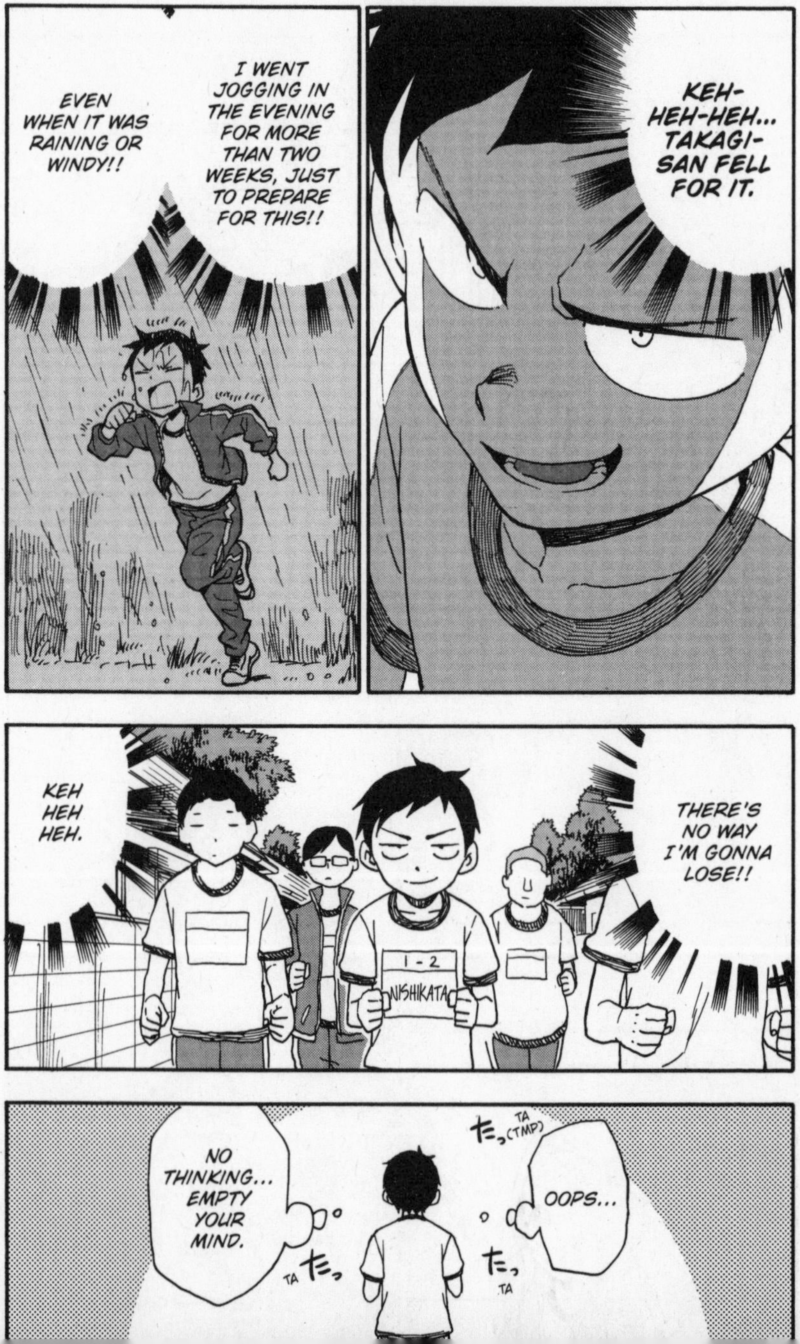
KEH-HEH-HEH... TAKAGI-SAN FELL FOR IT.
I WENT JOGGING IN THE EVENING FOR MORE THAN TWO WEEKS, JUST TO PREPARE FOR THIS!!
EVEN WHEN IT WAS RAINING OR WINDY!!
THERE'S NO WAY I'M GONNA LOSE!!
KEH HEH HEH.
1-2
NISHIKATA
たっ TA (TMP)
OOPS...
NO THINKING... EMPTY YOUR MIND.
たっ TA
たっ TA

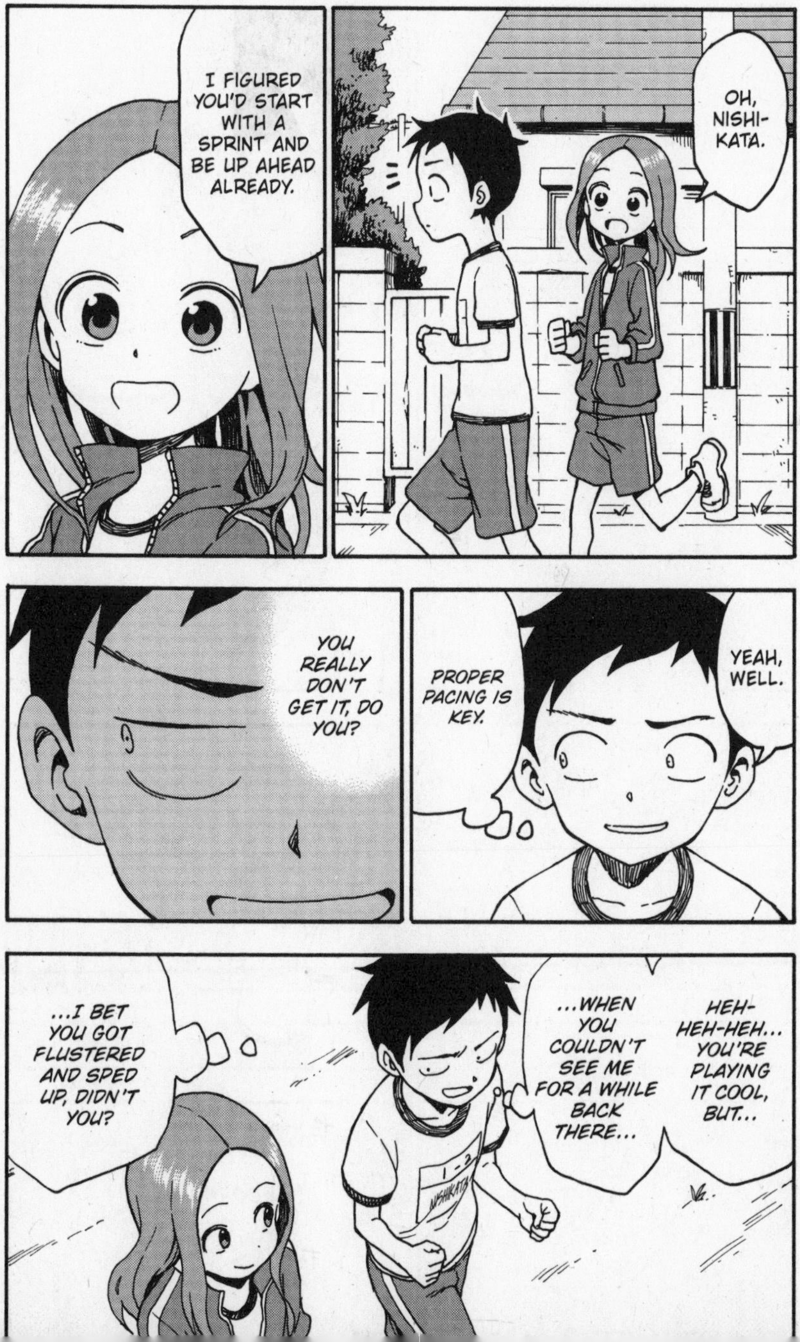
OH, NISHI-KATA.
I FIGURED YOU'D START WITH A SPRINT AND BE UP AHEAD ALREADY.
YEAH, WELL.
PROPER PACING IS KEY.
YOU REALLY DON'T GET IT, DO YOU?
HEH-HEH-HEH... YOU'RE PLAYING IT COOL, BUT...
...WHEN YOU COULDN'T SEE ME FOR A WHILE BACK THERE...
...I BET YOU GOT FLUSTERED AND SPED UP, DIDN'T YOU?

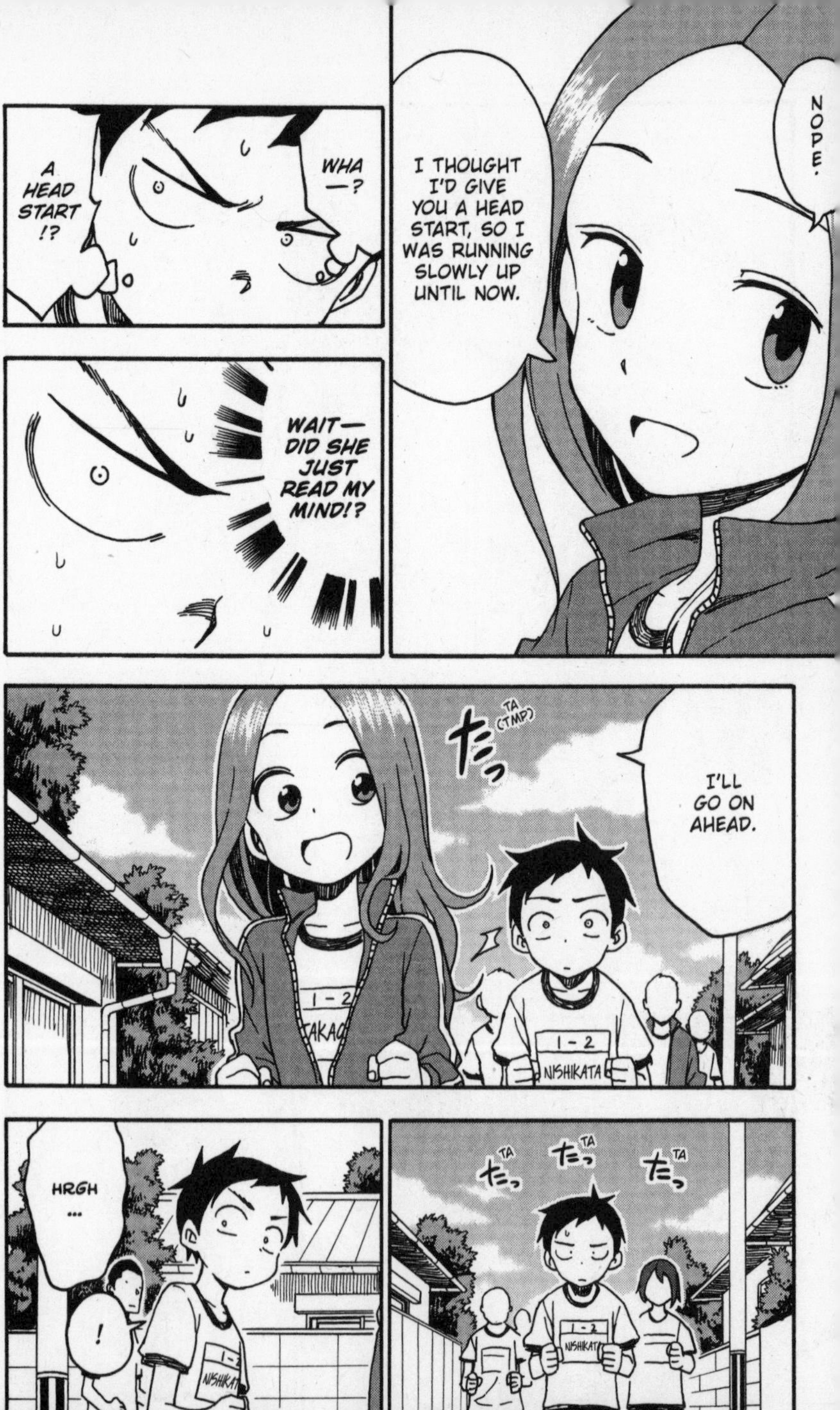
NOPE.
I THOUGHT I'D GIVE YOU A HEAD START, SO I WAS RUNNING SLOWLY UP UNTIL NOW.
WHA—?
A HEAD START!?
WAIT—DID SHE JUST READ MY MIND!?
I'LL GO ON AHEAD.
たっ
TA (TMP)
たっ TA
たっ TA
たっ TA
HRGH ...
!

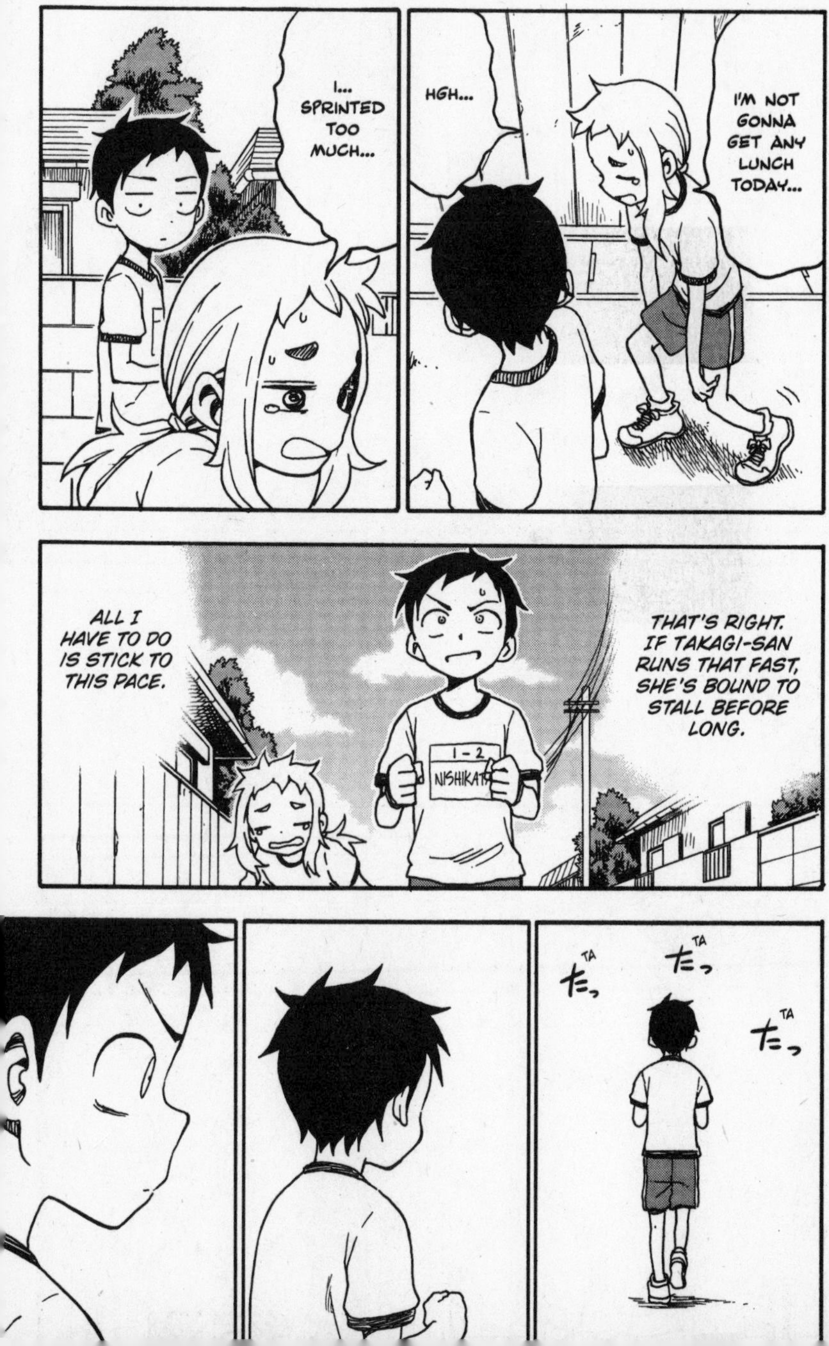
I'M NOT GONNA GET ANY LUNCH TODAY...
HGH...
I... SPRINTED TOO MUCH...
THAT'S RIGHT. IF TAKAGI-SAN RUNS THAT FAST, SHE'S BOUND TO STALL BEFORE LONG.
1-2 NISHIKATA
ALL I HAVE TO DO IS STICK TO THIS PACE.
TA
TA
TA

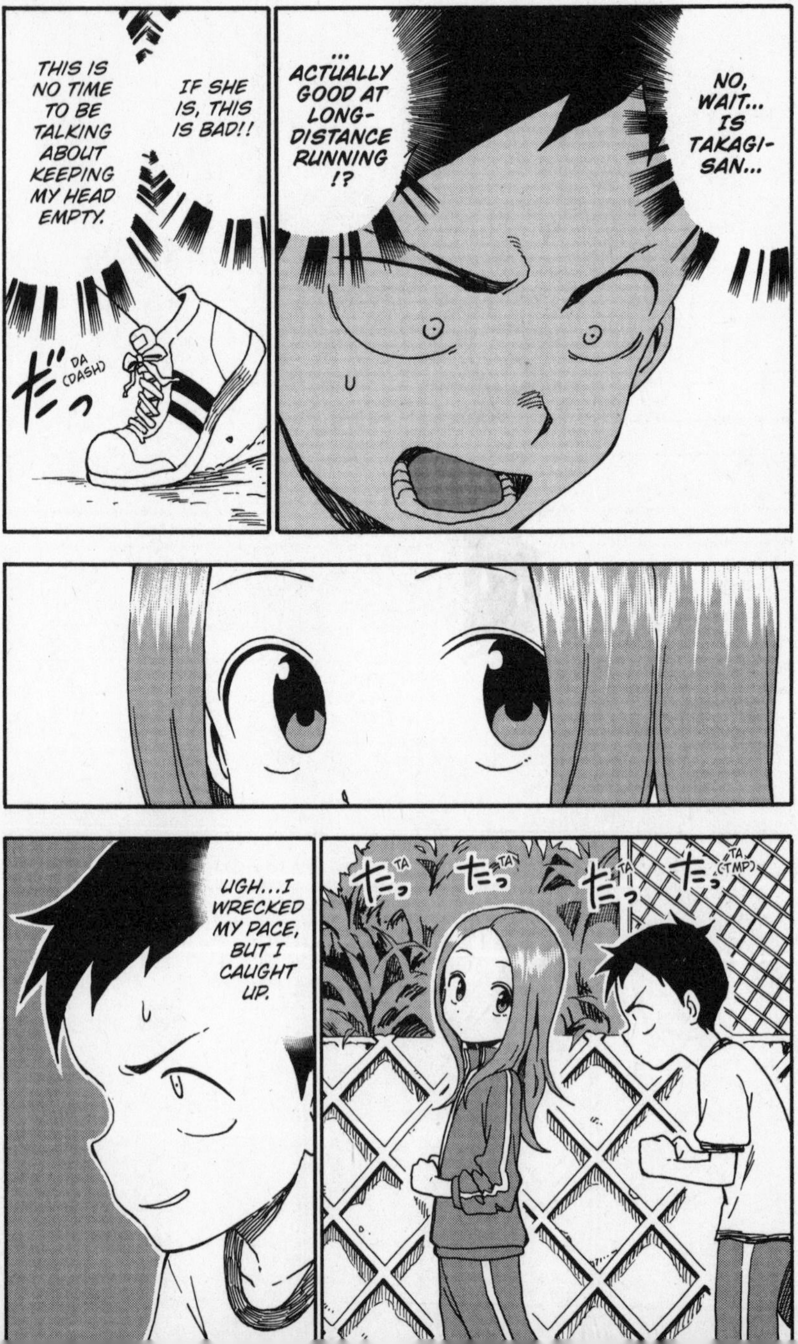
NO, WAIT... IS TAKAGI-SAN...
...ACTUALLY GOOD AT LONG-DISTANCE RUNNING!?
IF SHE IS, THIS IS BAD!!
THIS IS NO TIME TO BE TALKING ABOUT KEEPING MY HEAD EMPTY.
DA (DASH)
TA TA TA TA (TMP)
UGH...I WRECKED MY PACE, BUT I CAUGHT UP.

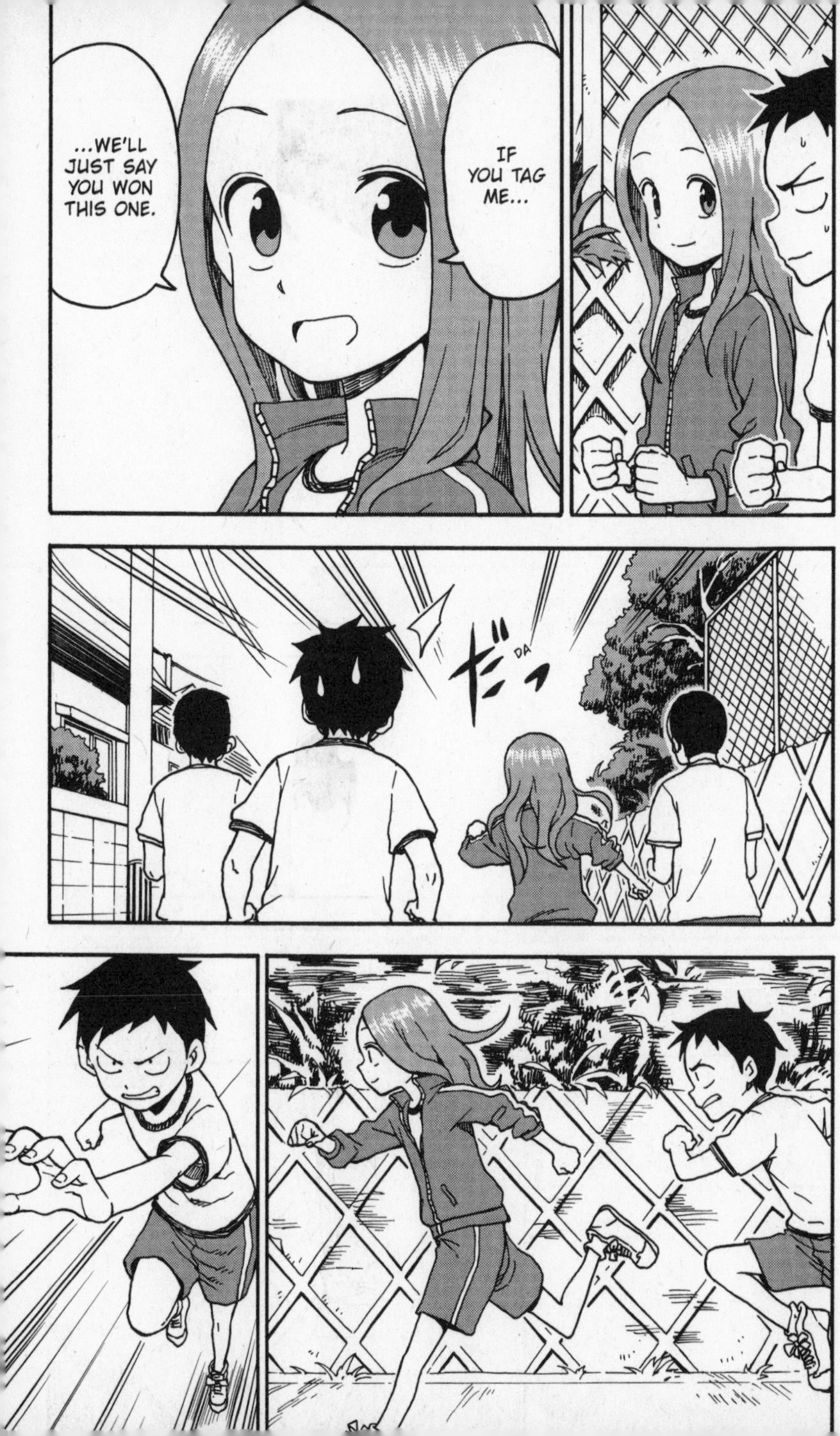
IF YOU TAG ME...
...WE'LL JUST SAY YOU WON THIS ONE.
ダッ
DA

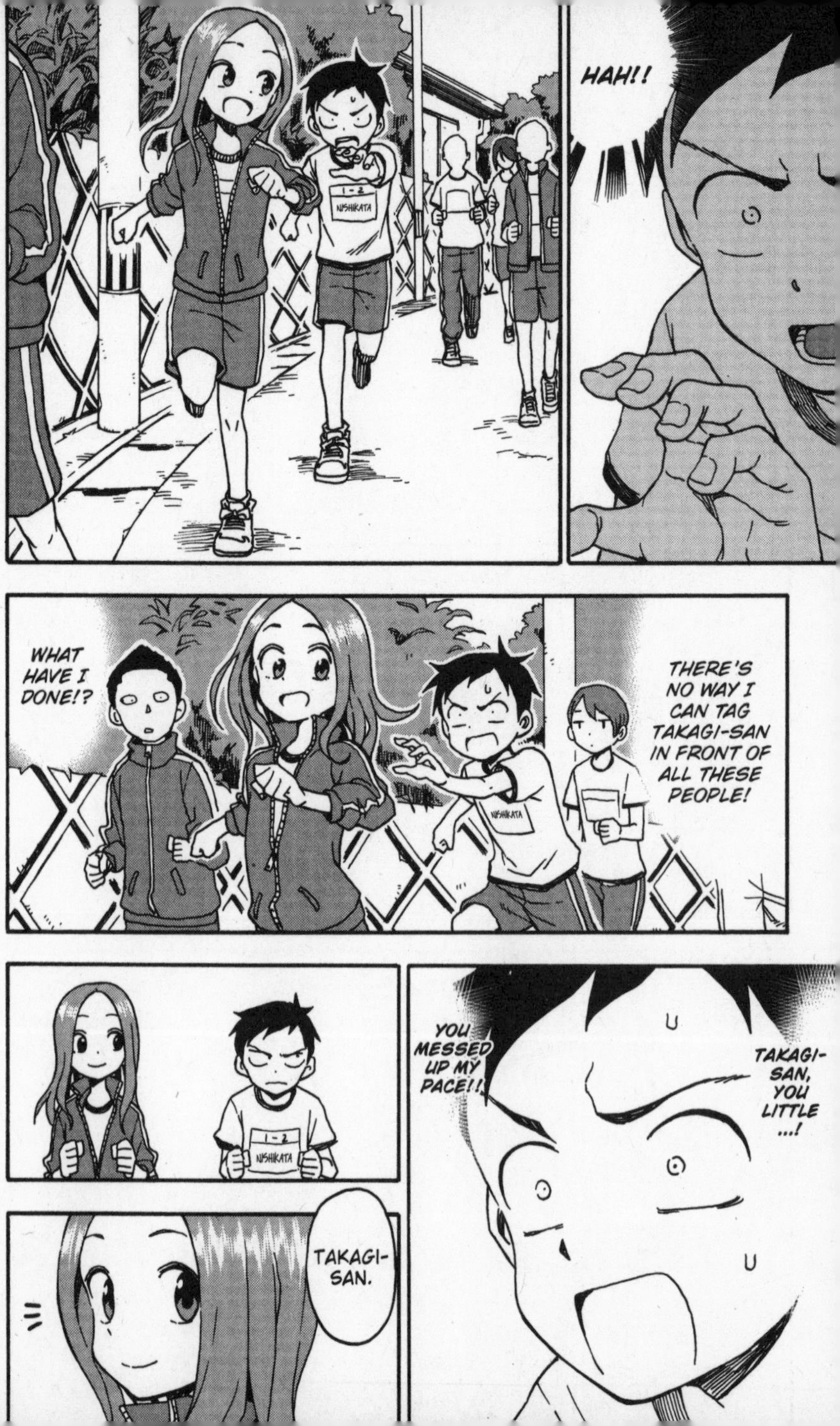
HAH!!
1-2
NISHIKATA
THERE'S NO WAY I CAN TAG TAKAGI-SAN IN FRONT OF ALL THESE PEOPLE!
NISHIKATA
WHAT HAVE I DONE!?
TAKAGI-SAN, YOU LITTLE ...!
YOU MESSED UP MY PACE!!
1-2
NISHIKATA
TAKAGI-SAN.

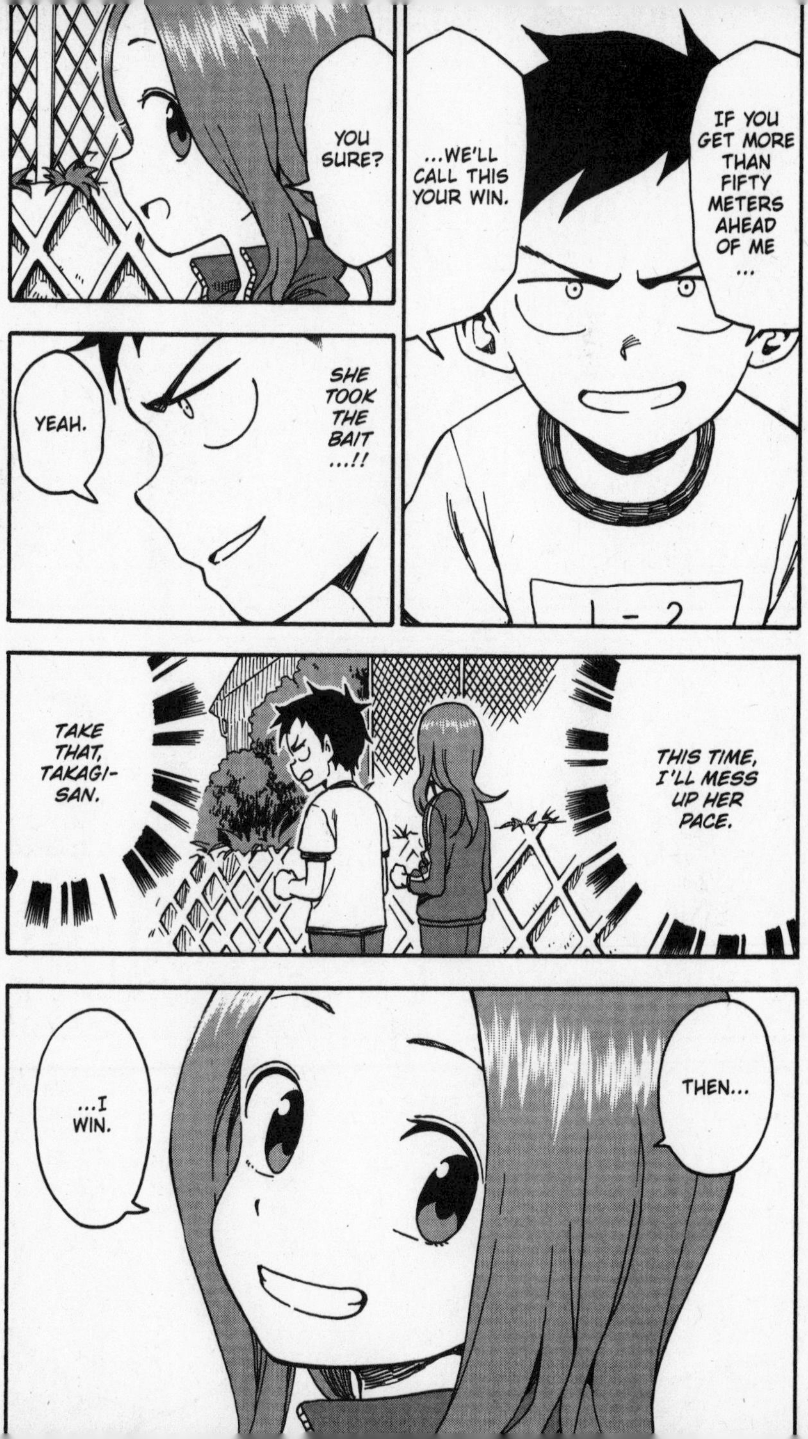
IF YOU GET MORE THAN FIFTY METERS AHEAD OF ME ...
...WE'LL CALL THIS YOUR WIN.
YOU SURE?
SHE TOOK THE BAIT ...!!
YEAH.
THIS TIME, I'LL MESS UP HER PACE.
TAKE THAT, TAKAGI-SAN.
THEN...
...I WIN.

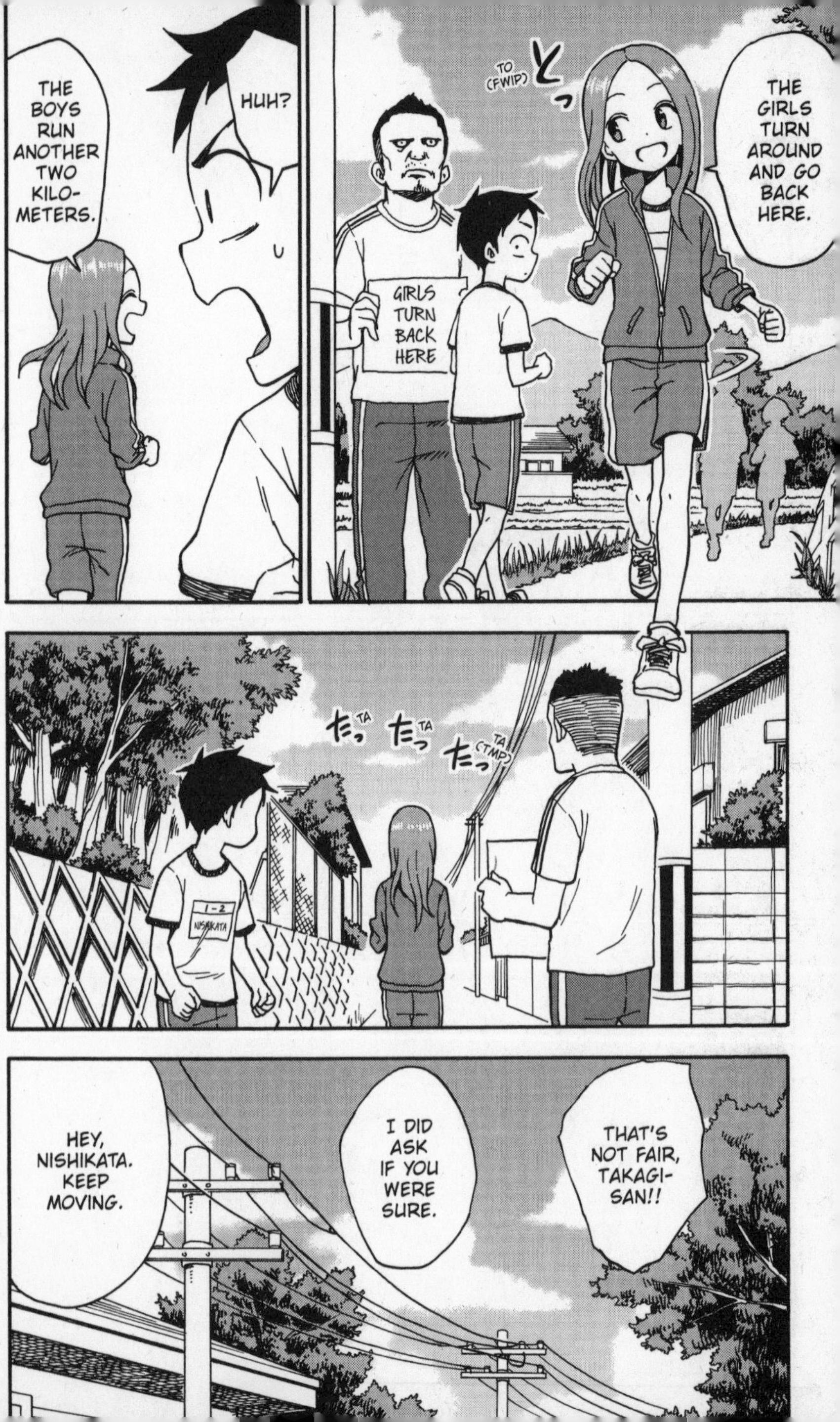
THE GIRLS TURN AROUND AND GO BACK HERE.
TO (FWIP)
GIRLS TURN BACK HERE
HUH?
THE BOYS RUN ANOTHER TWO KILO-METERS.
TA TA TA (TMP)
1-2 NISHIKATA
THAT'S NOT FAIR, TAKAGI-SAN!!
I DID ASK IF YOU WERE SURE.
HEY, NISHIKATA. KEEP MOVING.

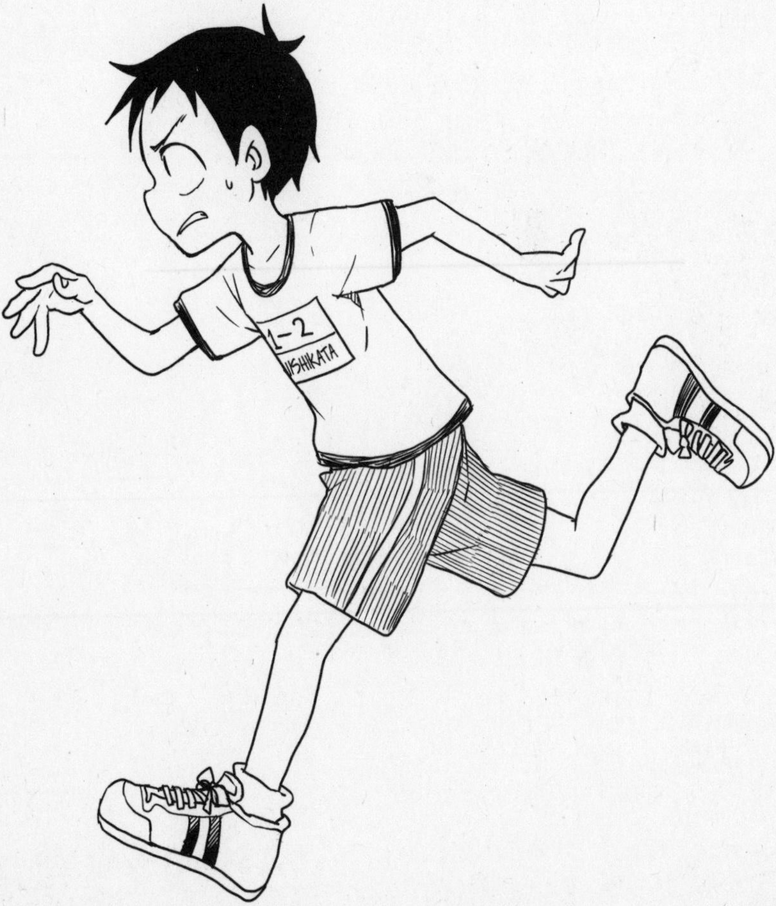
1–2
ISHIKATA

Teasing Master
Takagi-san

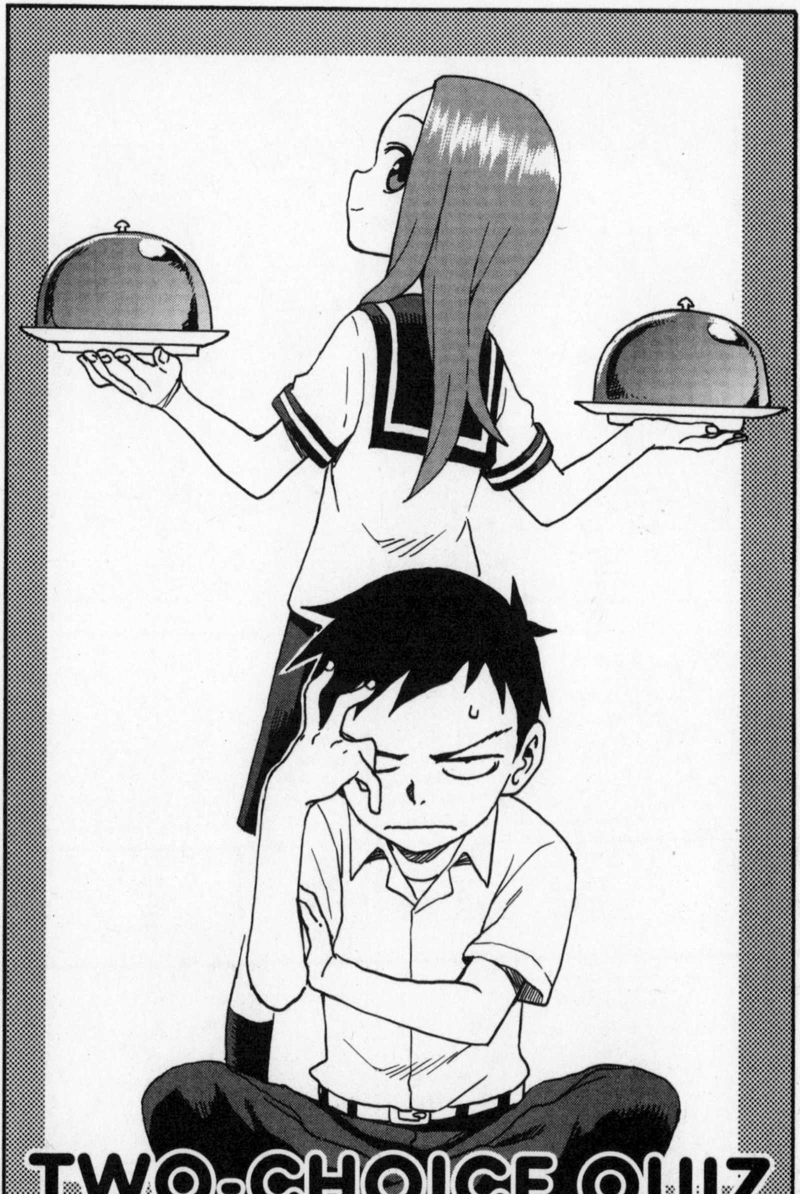
TWO-CHOICE QUIZ

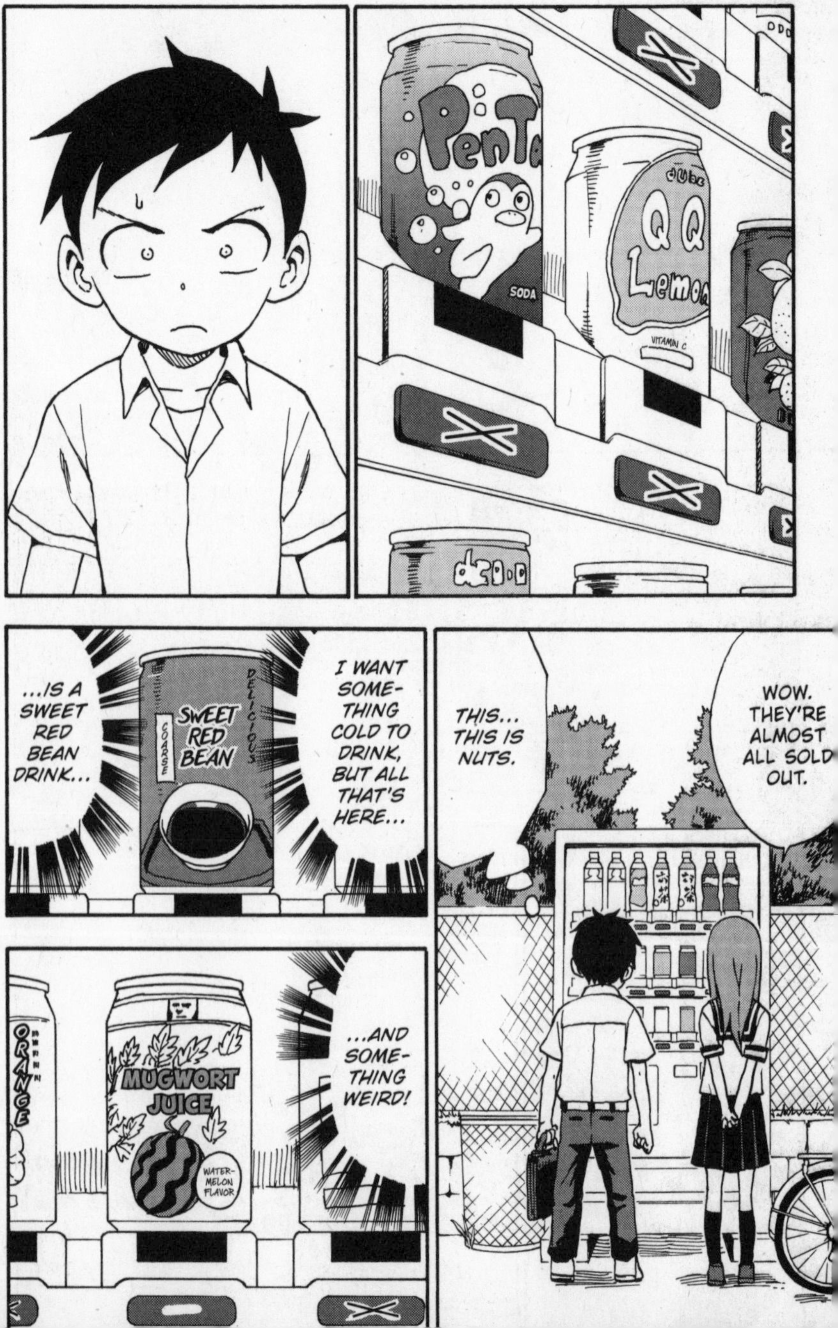
SODA
VITAMIN C
WOW. THEY'RE ALMOST ALL SOLD OUT.
THIS... THIS IS NUTS.
I WANT SOME-THING COLD TO DRINK, BUT ALL THAT'S HERE...
DELICIOUS
SWEET RED BEAN
COARSE
...IS A SWEET RED BEAN DRINK...
...AND SOME-THING WEIRD!
MUGWORT JUICE
WATER-MELON FLAVOR
ORANGE

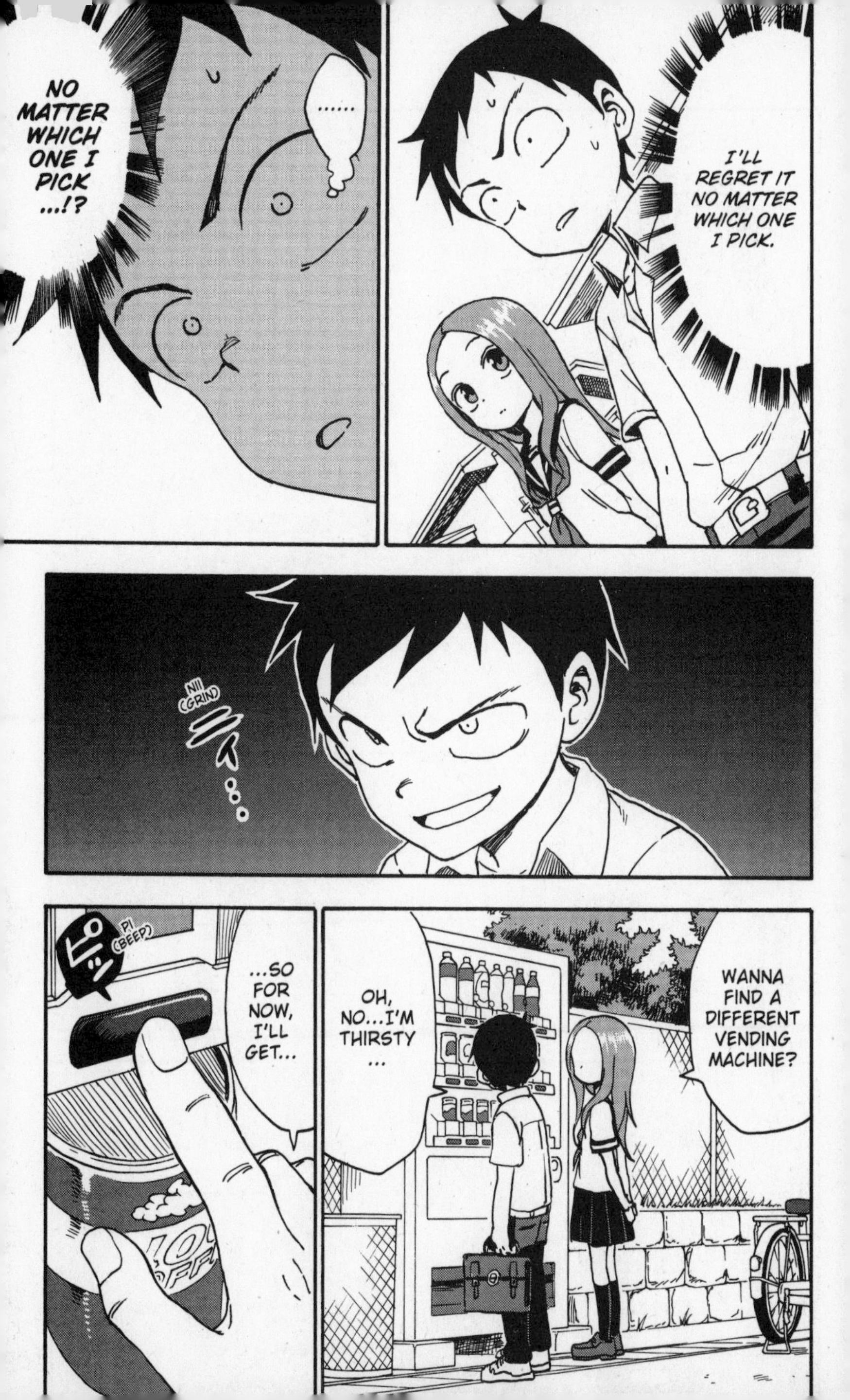
I'LL REGRET IT NO MATTER WHICH ONE I PICK.
......
NO MATTER WHICH ONE I PICK ...!?
NII (GRIN)
WANNA FIND A DIFFERENT VENDING MACHINE?
OH, NO...I'M THIRSTY ...
...SO FOR NOW, I'LL GET...
PI (BEEP)

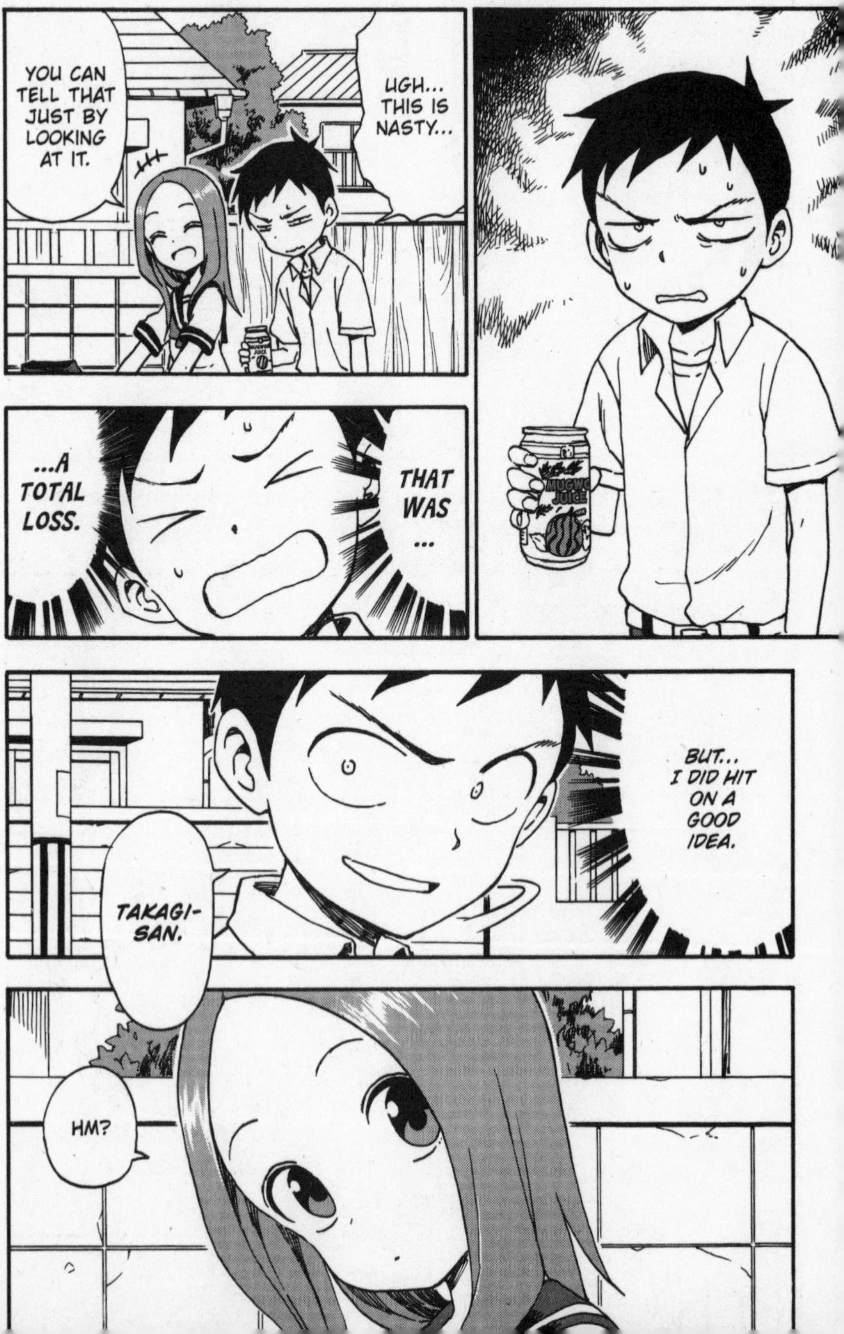
UGH... THIS IS NASTY...
YOU CAN TELL THAT JUST BY LOOKING AT IT.
THAT WAS ...
...A TOTAL LOSS.
BUT... I DID HIT ON A GOOD IDEA.
TAKAGI-SAN.
HM?

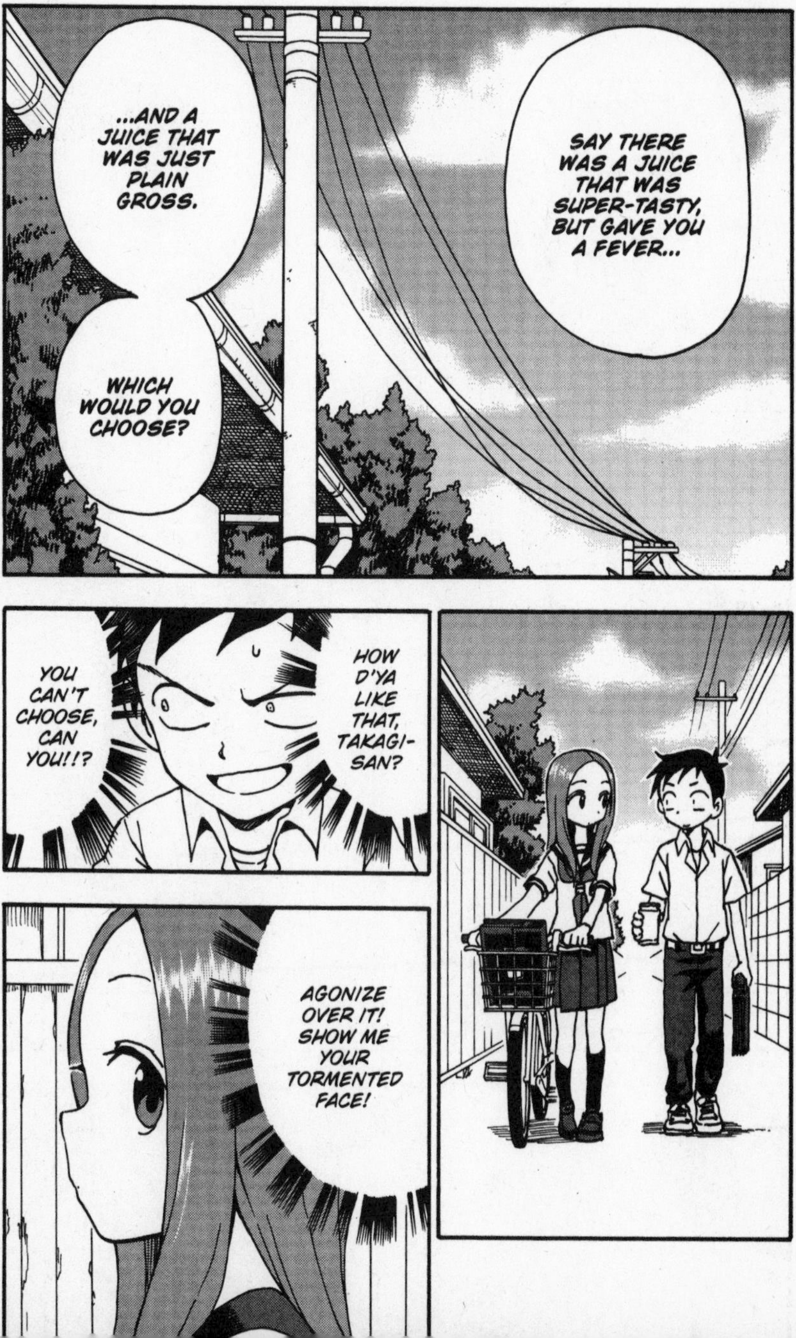
SAY THERE WAS A JUICE THAT WAS SUPER-TASTY, BUT GAVE YOU A FEVER...
...AND A JUICE THAT WAS JUST PLAIN GROSS.
WHICH WOULD YOU CHOOSE?
HOW D'YA LIKE THAT, TAKAGI-SAN?
YOU CAN'T CHOOSE, CAN YOU!!?
AGONIZE OVER IT! SHOW ME YOUR TORMENTED FACE!

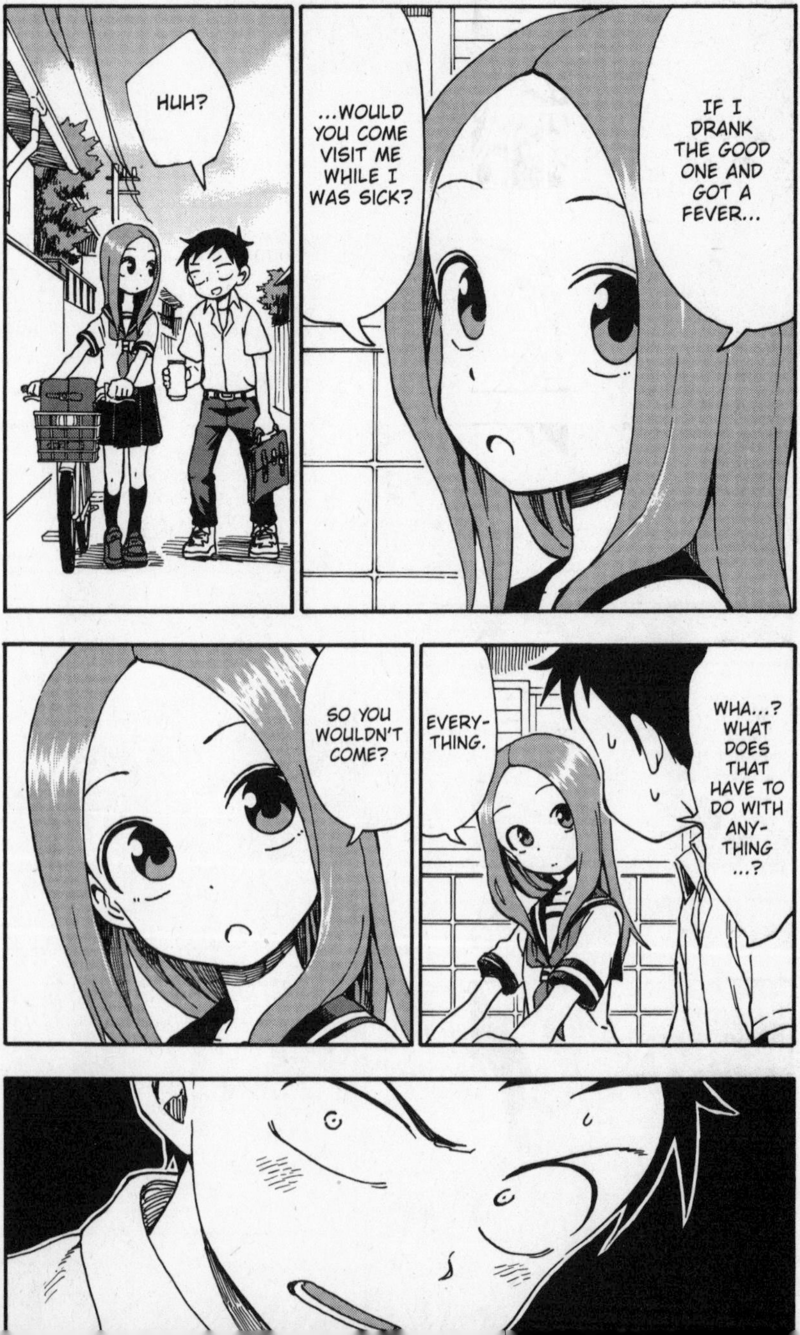
IF I DRANK THE GOOD ONE AND GOT A FEVER...
...WOULD YOU COME VISIT ME WHILE I WAS SICK?
HUH?
WHA...? WHAT DOES THAT HAVE TO DO WITH ANYTHING...?
EVERYTHING.
SO YOU WOULDN'T COME?

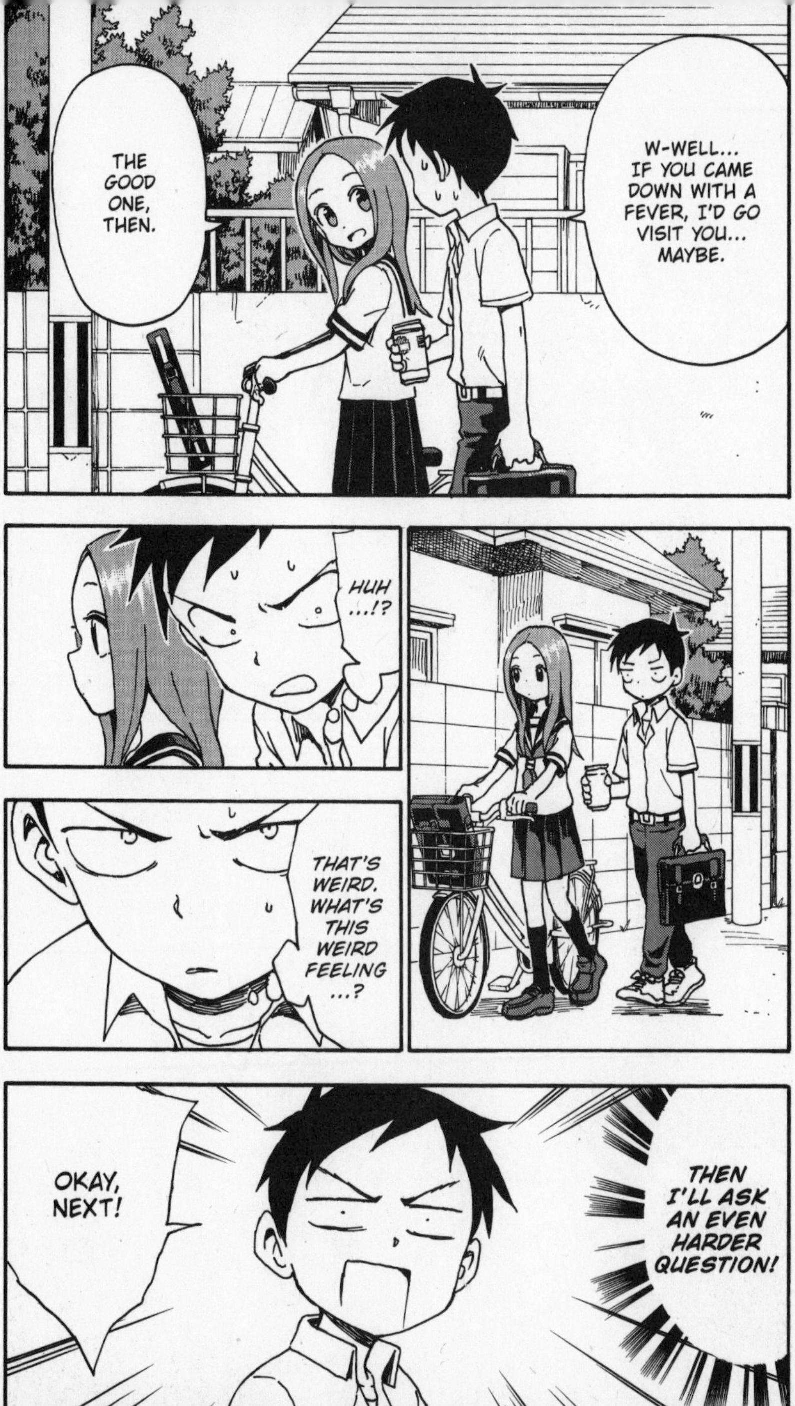
W-WELL... IF YOU CAME DOWN WITH A FEVER, I'D GO VISIT YOU... MAYBE.
THE GOOD ONE, THEN.
HUH ...!?
THAT'S WEIRD. WHAT'S THIS WEIRD FEELING ...?
THEN I'LL ASK AN EVEN HARDER QUESTION!
OKAY, NEXT!

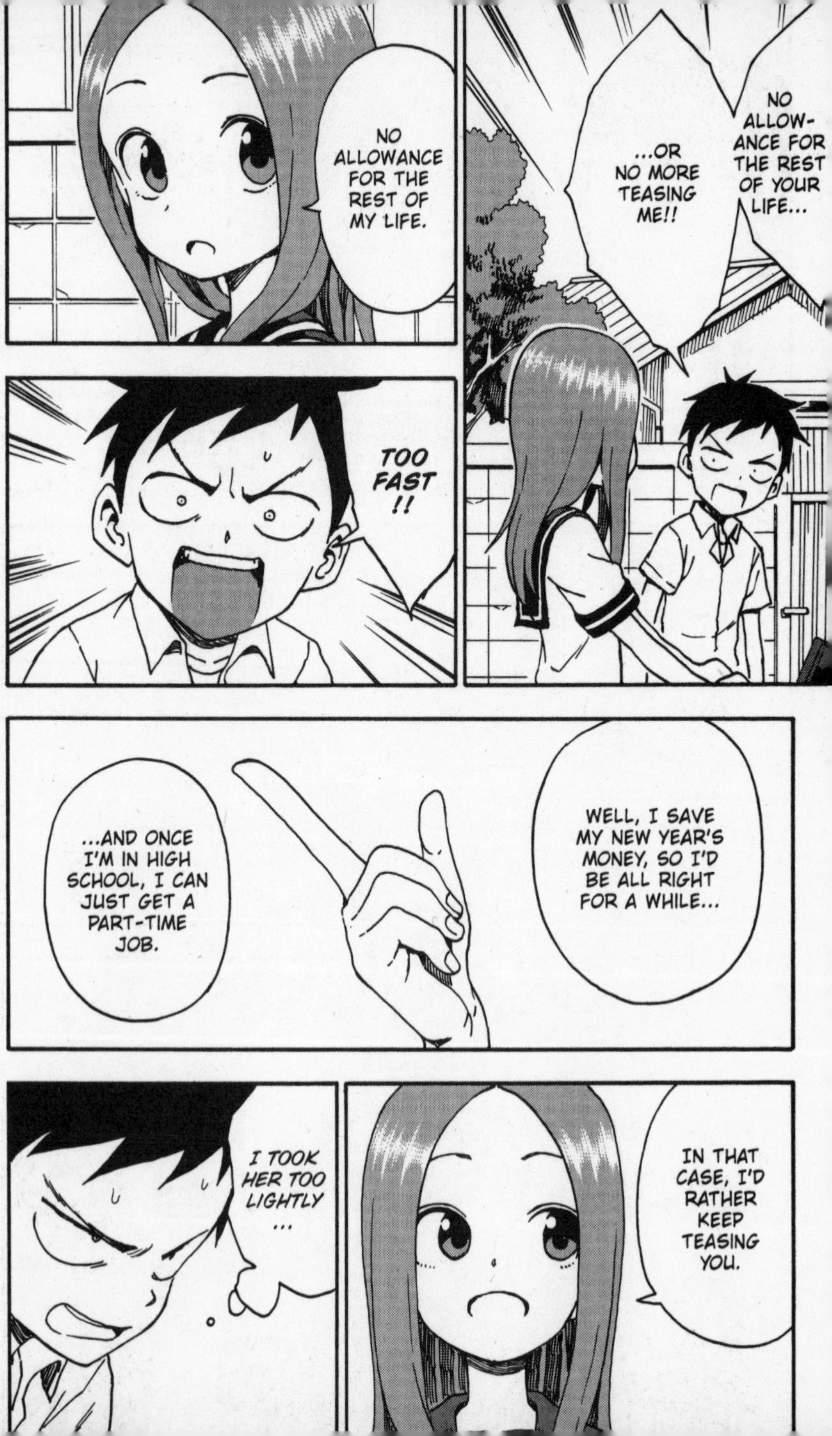
NO ALLOWANCE FOR THE REST OF YOUR LIFE...
...OR NO MORE TEASING ME!!
NO ALLOWANCE FOR THE REST OF MY LIFE.
TOO FAST!!
WELL, I SAVE MY NEW YEAR'S MONEY, SO I'D BE ALL RIGHT FOR A WHILE...
...AND ONCE I'M IN HIGH SCHOOL, I CAN JUST GET A PART-TIME JOB.
IN THAT CASE, I'D RATHER KEEP TEASING YOU.
I TOOK HER TOO LIGHTLY...

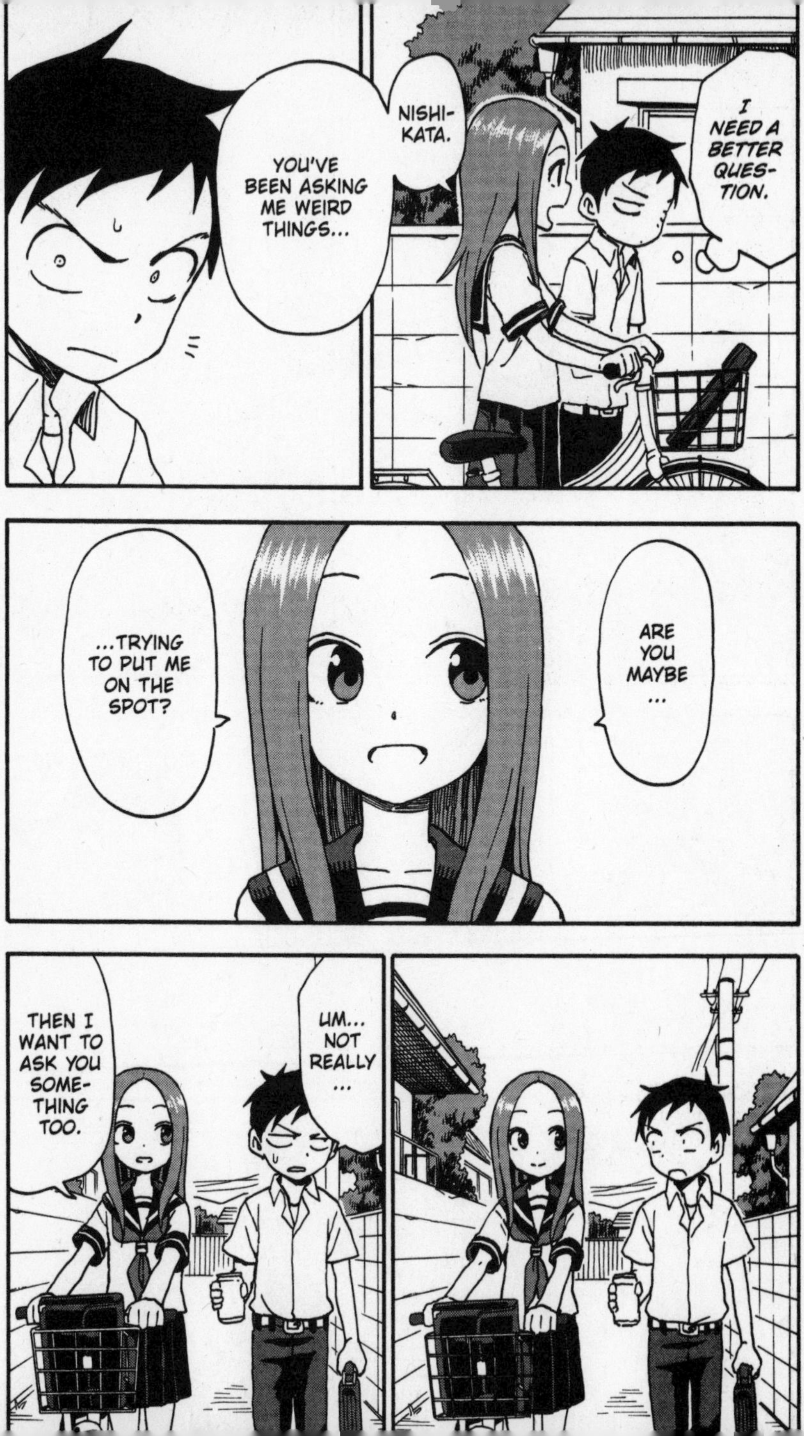
I NEED A BETTER QUESTION.
NISHI-KATA.
YOU'VE BEEN ASKING ME WEIRD THINGS...
ARE YOU MAYBE ...
...TRYING TO PUT ME ON THE SPOT?
UM... NOT REALLY ...
THEN I WANT TO ASK YOU SOME-THING TOO.

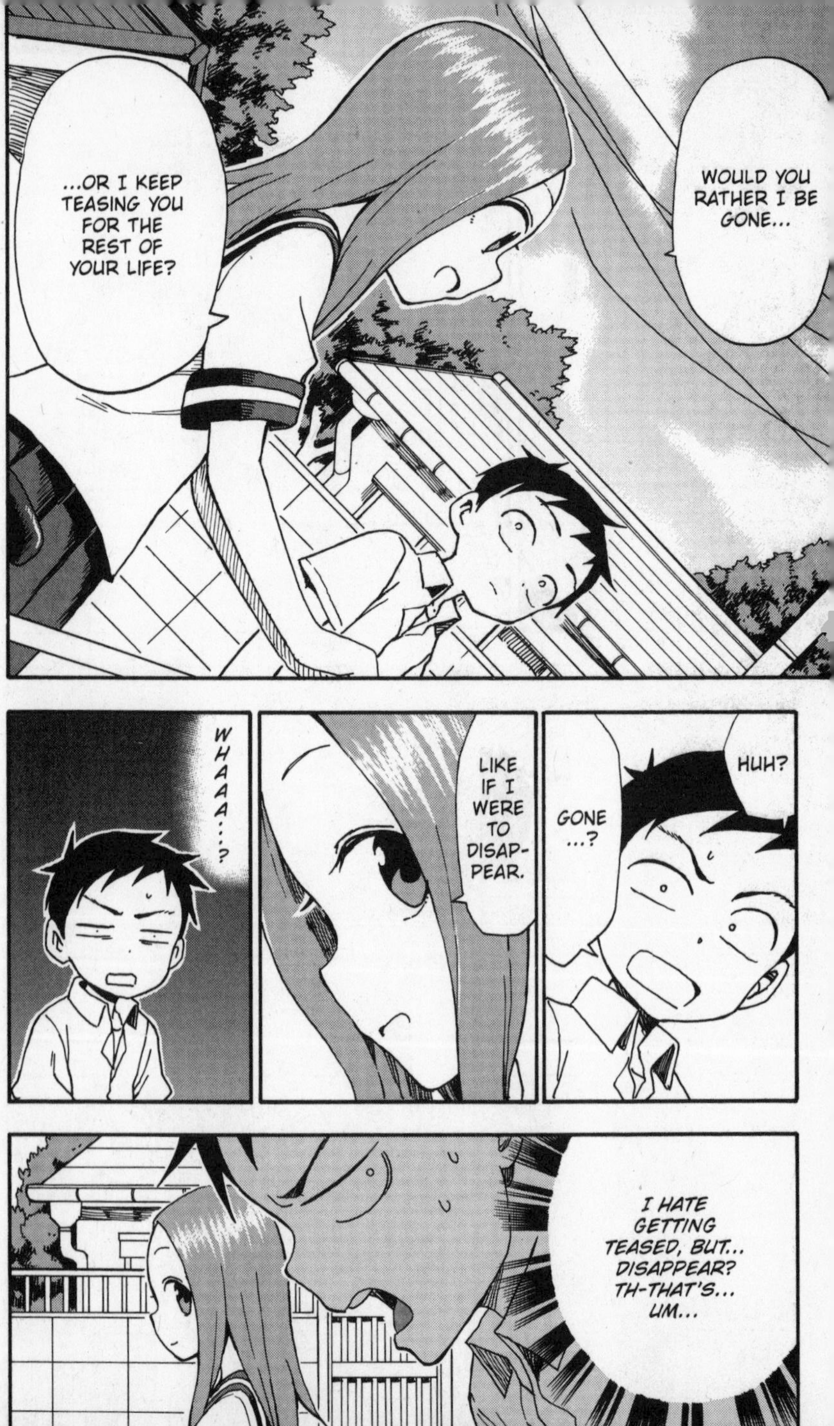
WOULD YOU RATHER I BE GONE...
...OR I KEEP TEASING YOU FOR THE REST OF YOUR LIFE?
HUH?
GONE ...?
LIKE IF I WERE TO DISAPPEAR.
WHAAAA...?
I HATE GETTING TEASED, BUT... DISAPPEAR? TH-THAT'S... UM...

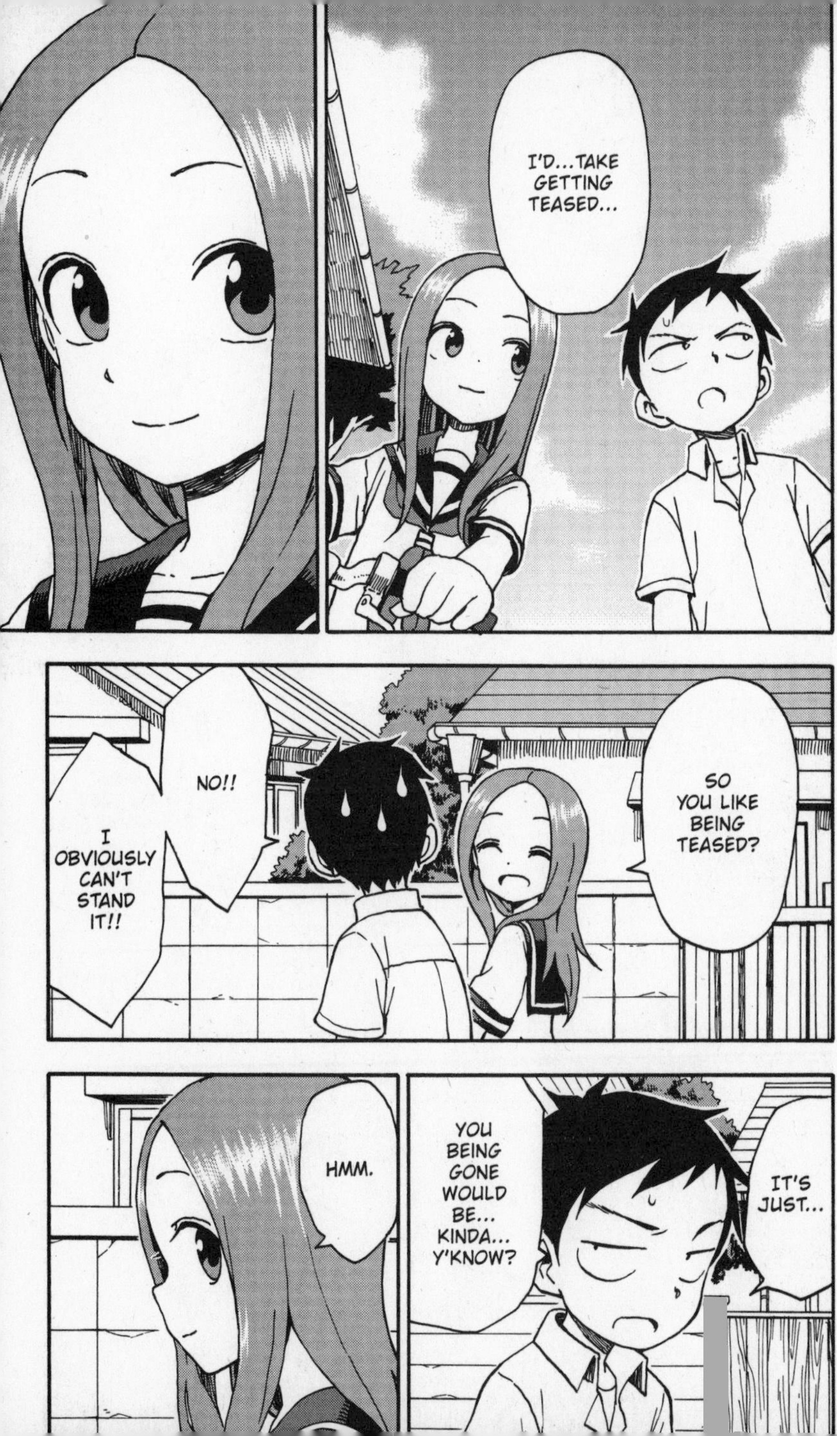
I'D...TAKE GETTING TEASED...
SO YOU LIKE BEING TEASED?
NO!!
I OBVIOUSLY CAN'T STAND IT!!
IT'S JUST...
YOU BEING GONE WOULD BE... KINDA... Y'KNOW?
HMM.

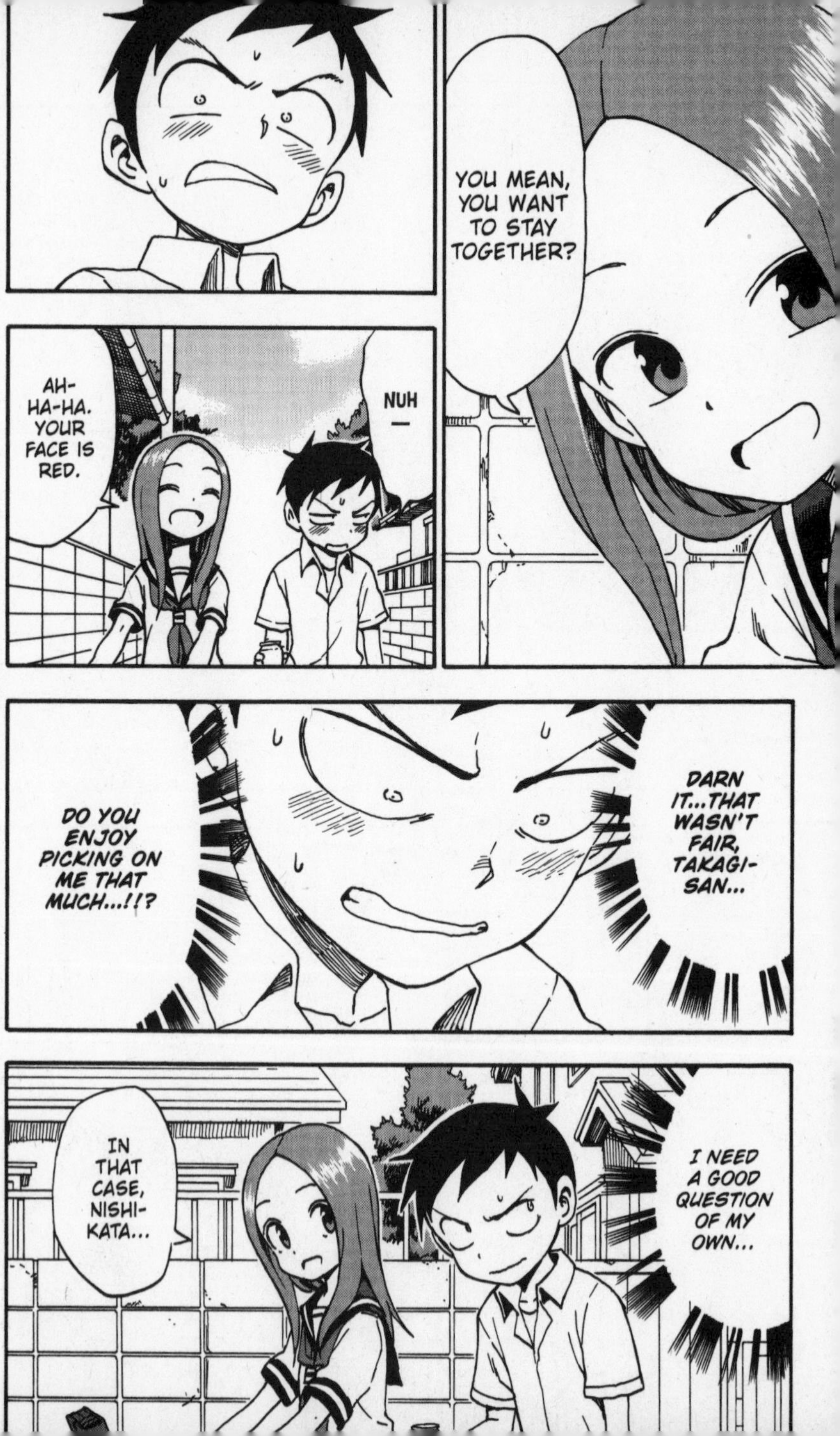
YOU MEAN, YOU WANT TO STAY TOGETHER?
NUH —
AH-HA-HA. YOUR FACE IS RED.
DARN IT...THAT WASN'T FAIR, TAKAGI-SAN...
DO YOU ENJOY PICKING ON ME THAT MUCH...!!?
I NEED A GOOD QUESTION OF MY OWN...
IN THAT CASE, NISHIKATA...

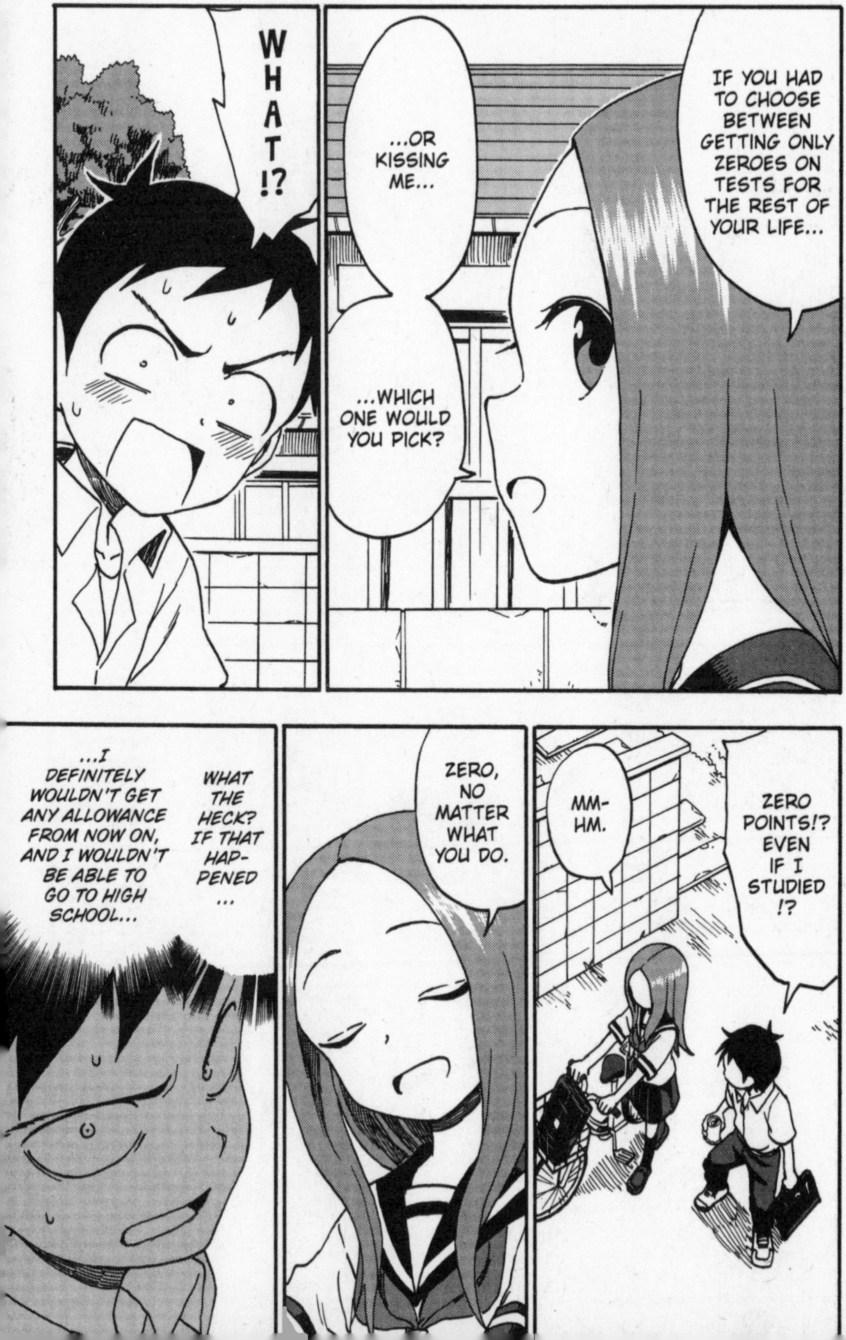
IF YOU HAD TO CHOOSE BETWEEN GETTING ONLY ZEROES ON TESTS FOR THE REST OF YOUR LIFE...
...OR KISSING ME...
...WHICH ONE WOULD YOU PICK?
WHAT!?
ZERO POINTS!? EVEN IF I STUDIED!?
MM-HM.
ZERO, NO MATTER WHAT YOU DO.
WHAT THE HECK? IF THAT HAP-PENED...
...I DEFINITELY WOULDN'T GET ANY ALLOWANCE FROM NOW ON, AND I WOULDN'T BE ABLE TO GO TO HIGH SCHOOL...

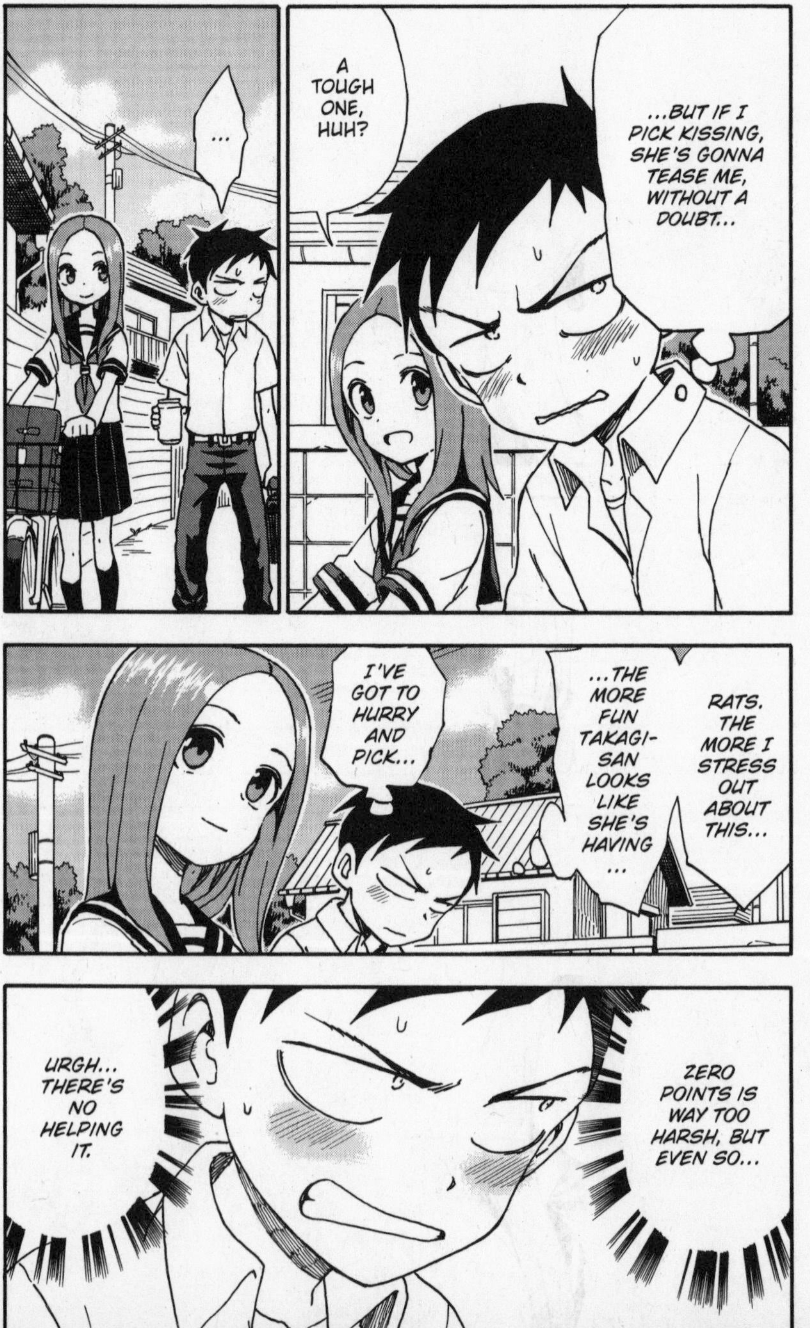
...BUT IF I PICK KISSING, SHE'S GONNA TEASE ME, WITHOUT A DOUBT...
A TOUGH ONE, HUH?
...
RATS. THE MORE I STRESS OUT ABOUT THIS...
...THE MORE FUN TAKAGI-SAN LOOKS LIKE SHE'S HAVING...
I'VE GOT TO HURRY AND PICK...
ZERO POINTS IS WAY TOO HARSH, BUT EVEN SO...
URGH... THERE'S NO HELPING IT.

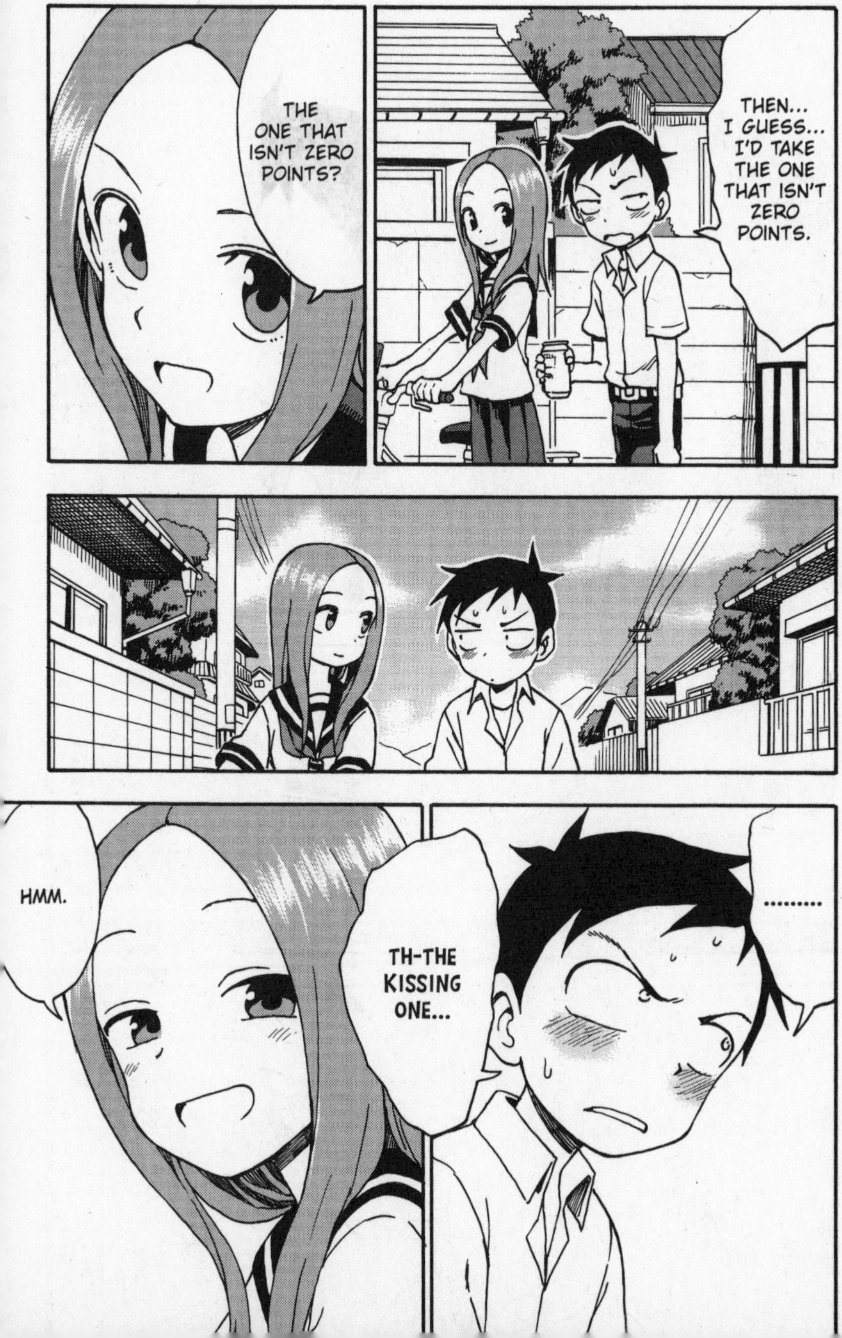
THEN... I GUESS... I'D TAKE THE ONE THAT ISN'T ZERO POINTS.
THE ONE THAT ISN'T ZERO POINTS?
....
TH-THE KISSING ONE...
HMM.

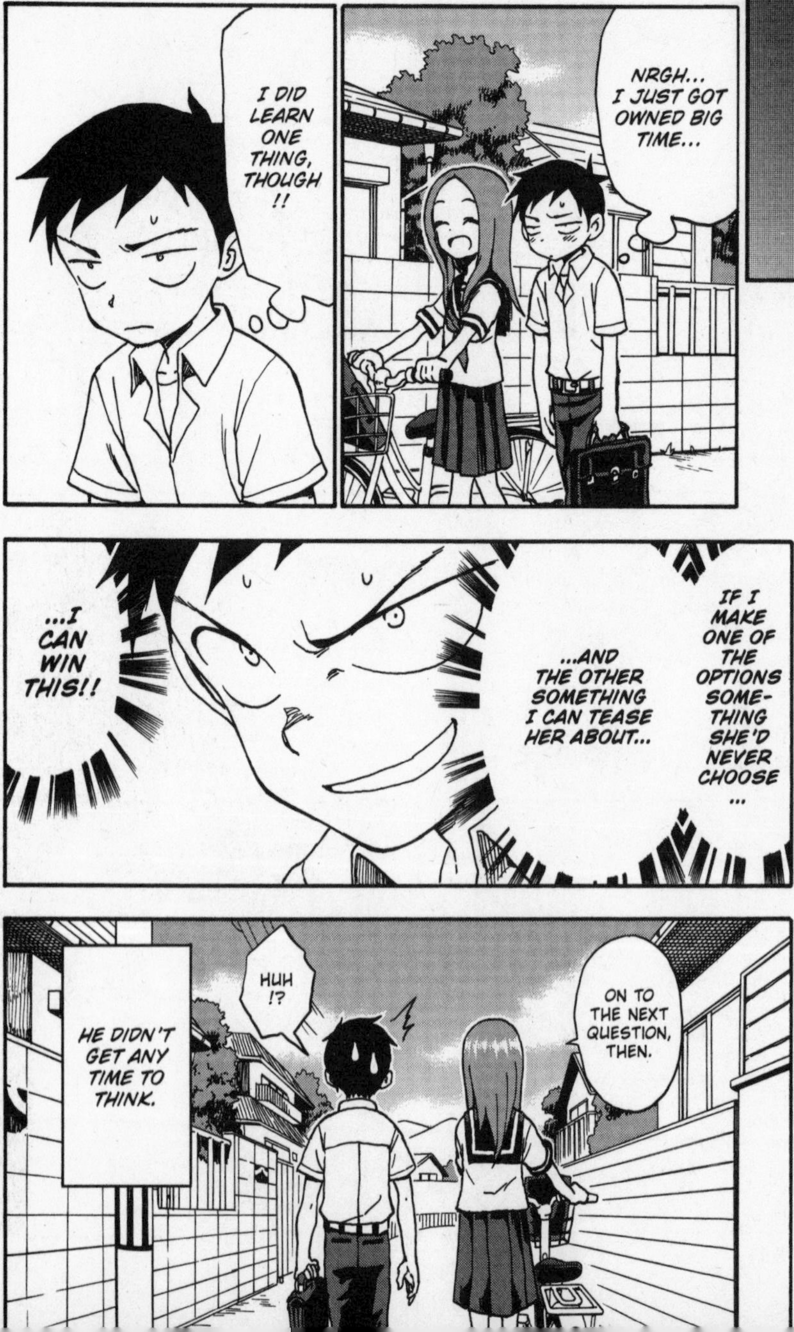
NRGH... I JUST GOT OWNED BIG TIME...
I DID LEARN ONE THING, THOUGH!!
IF I MAKE ONE OF THE OPTIONS SOME-THING SHE'D NEVER CHOOSE...
...AND THE OTHER SOMETHING I CAN TEASE HER ABOUT...
...I CAN WIN THIS!!
ON TO THE NEXT QUESTION, THEN.
HUH!?
HE DIDN'T GET ANY TIME TO THINK.

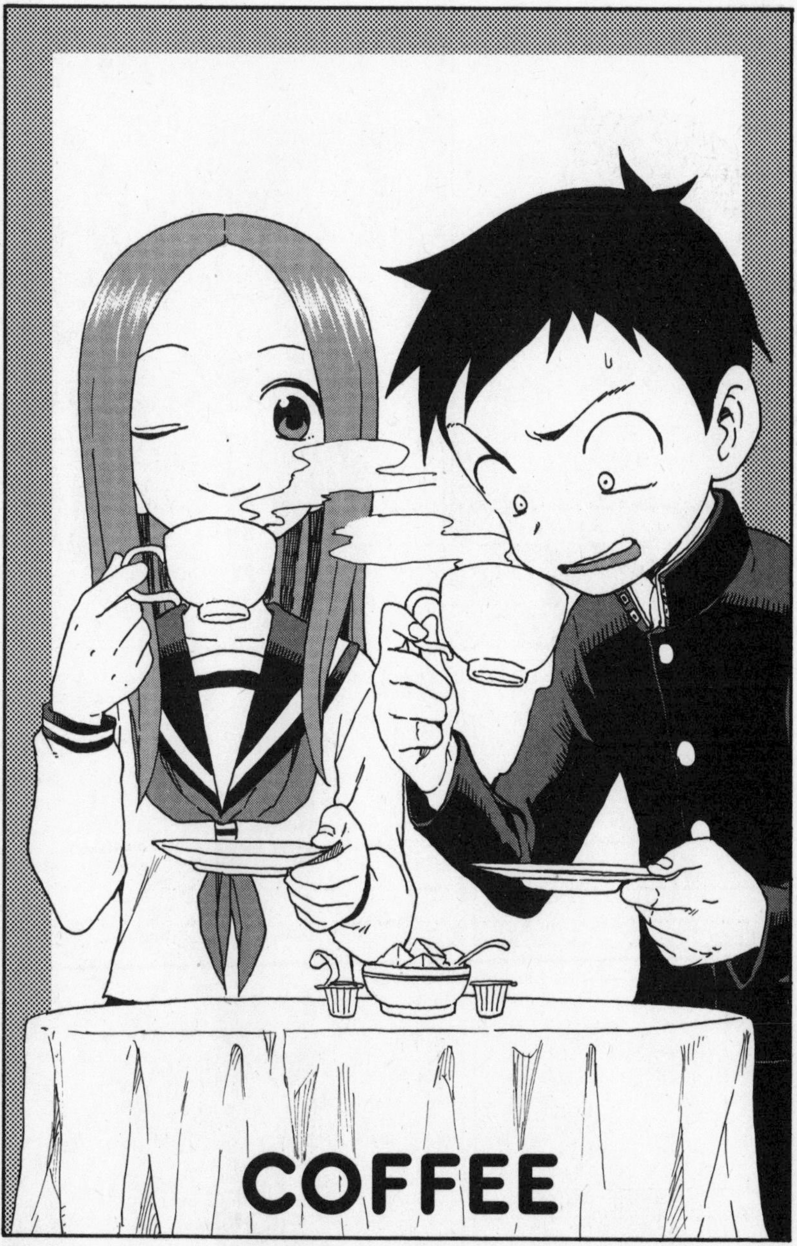
COFFEE

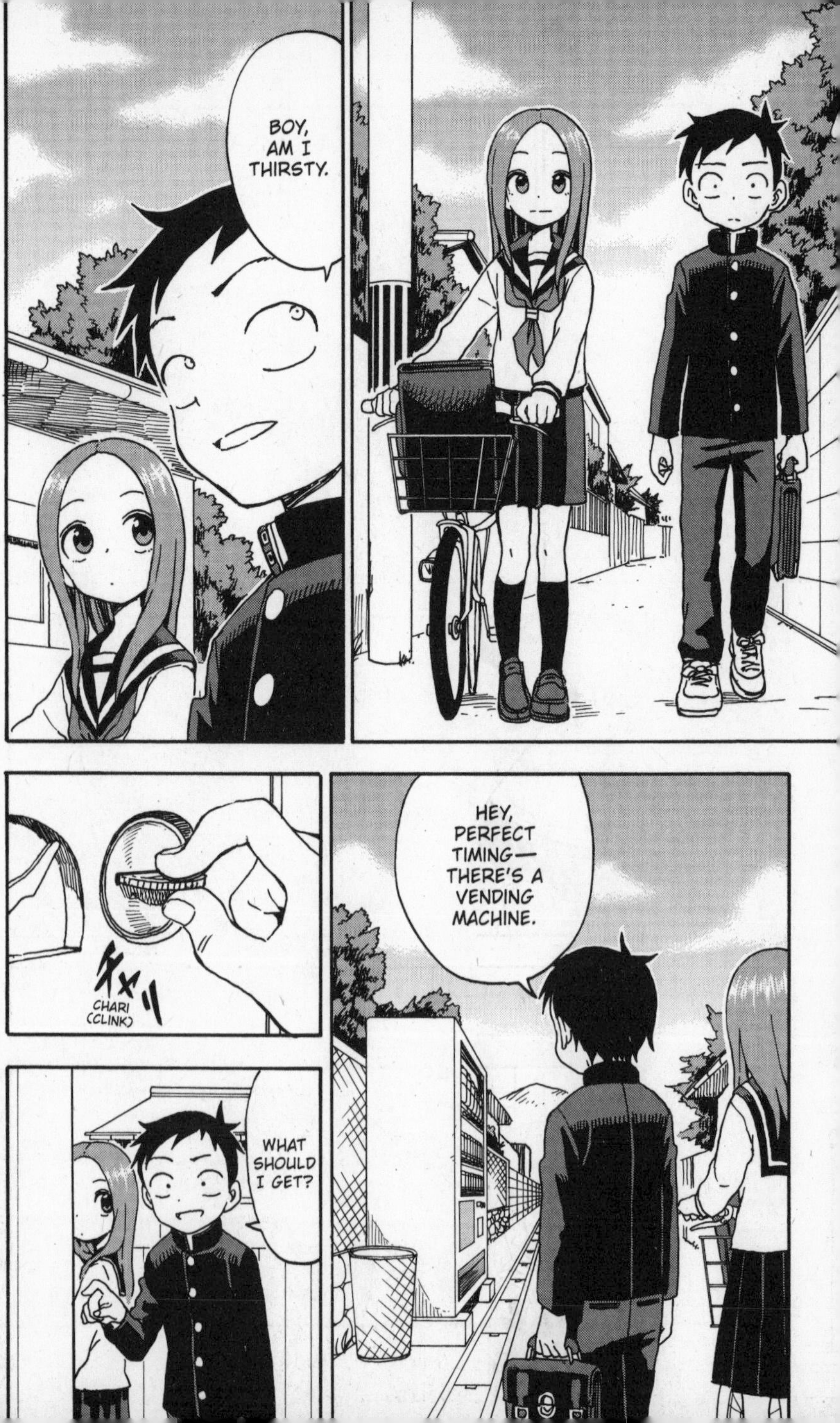
BOY, AM I THIRSTY.
HEY, PERFECT TIMING— THERE'S A VENDING MACHINE.
チャリ
CHARI (CLINK)
WHAT SHOULD I GET?

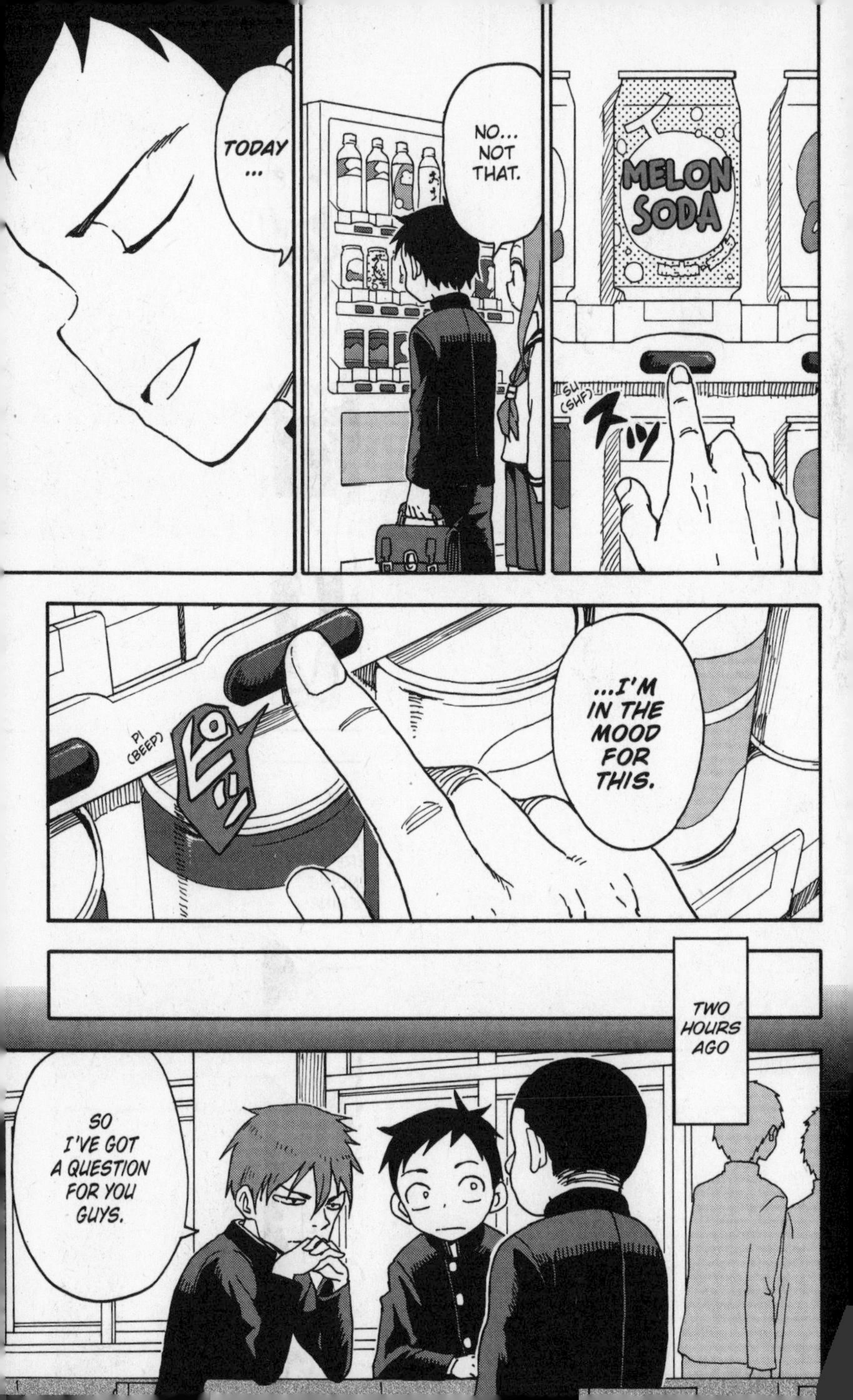
MELON SODA
SU (SHF)
NO... NOT THAT.
TODAY ...
PI (BEEP)
...I'M IN THE MOOD FOR THIS.
TWO HOURS AGO
SO I'VE GOT A QUESTION FOR YOU GUYS.

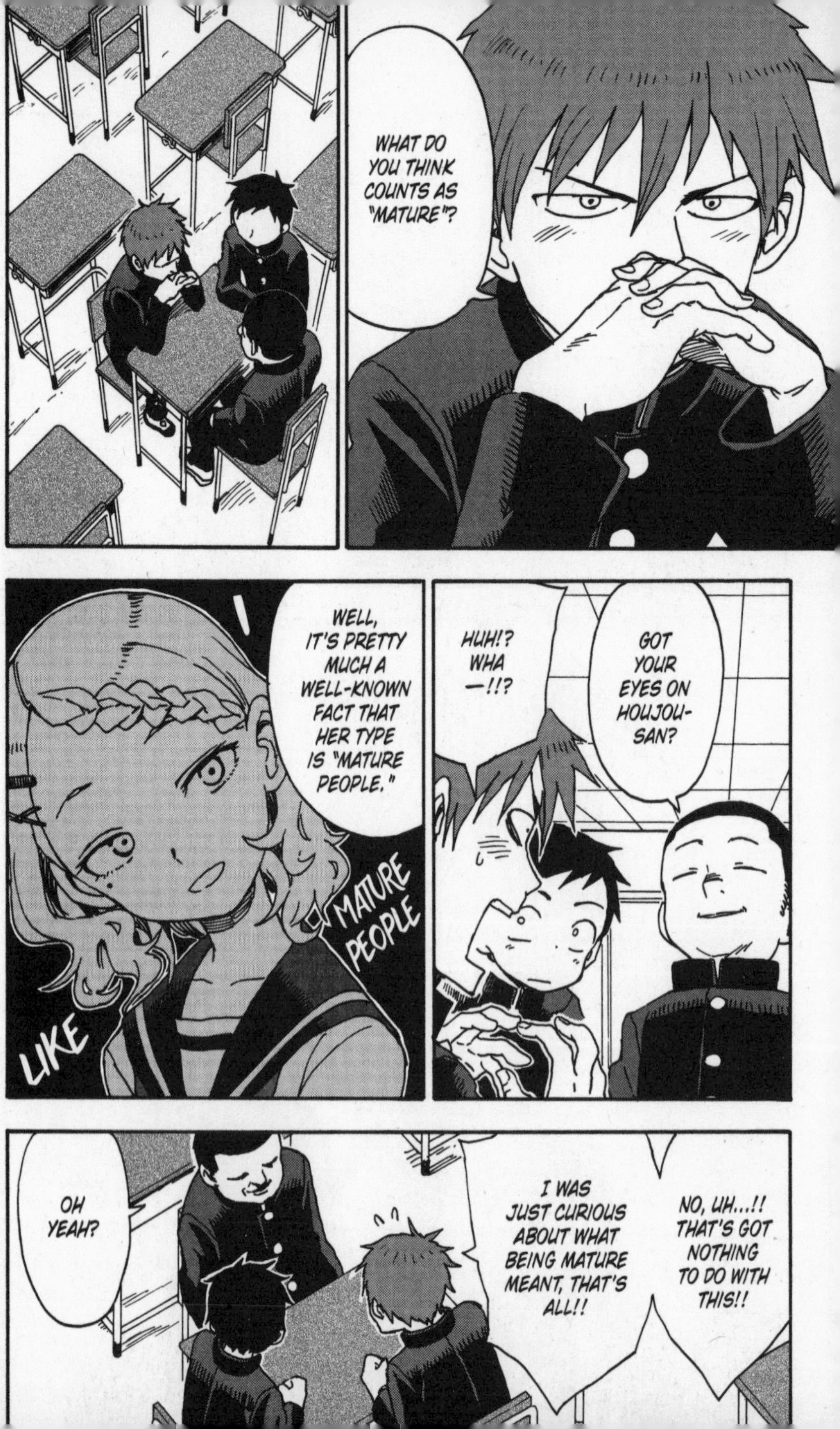
WHAT DO YOU THINK COUNTS AS "MATURE"?
GOT YOUR EYES ON HOUJOU-SAN?
HUH!? WHA—!!?
WELL, IT'S PRETTY MUCH A WELL-KNOWN FACT THAT HER TYPE IS "MATURE PEOPLE."
MATURE PEOPLE
LIKE
NO, UH...!! THAT'S GOT NOTHING TO DO WITH THIS!!
I WAS JUST CURIOUS ABOUT WHAT BEING MATURE MEANT, THAT'S ALL!!
OH YEAH?

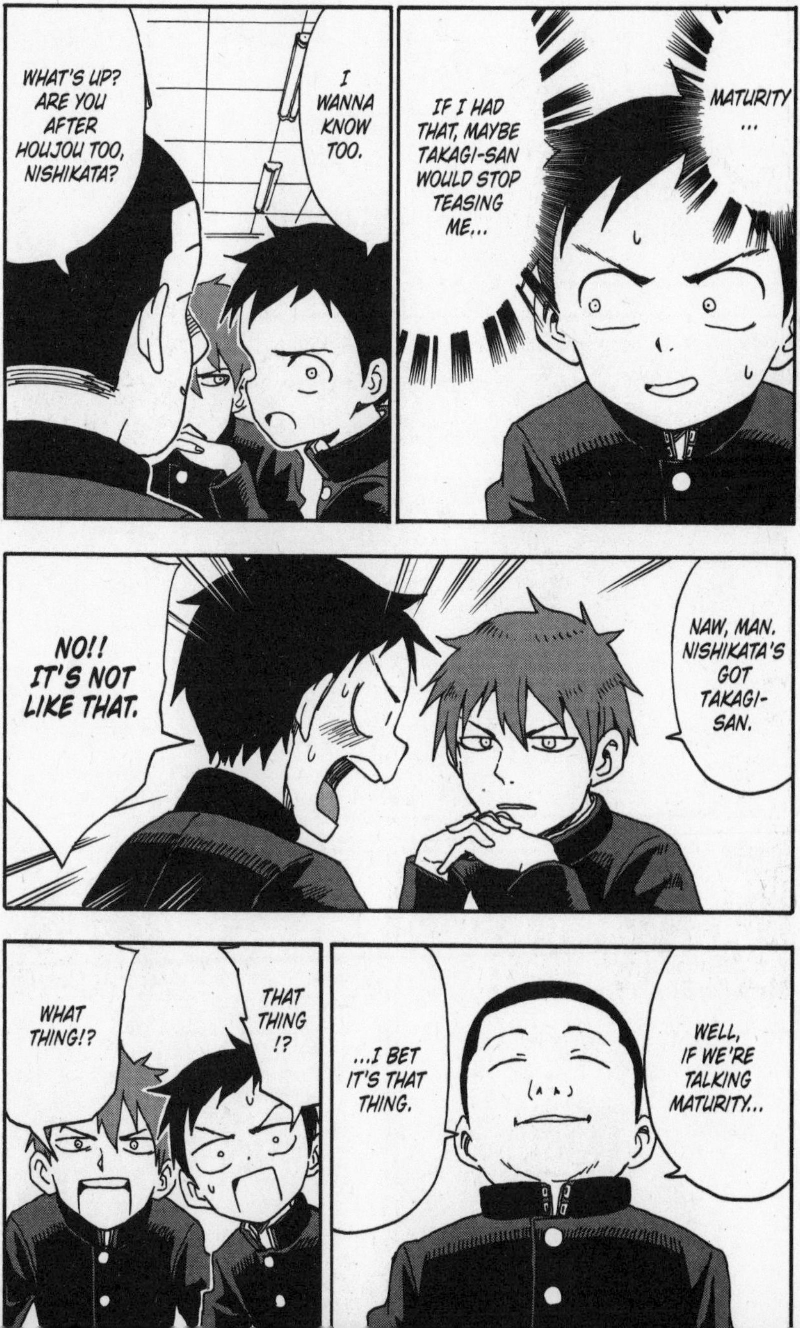
MATURITY...
IF I HAD THAT, MAYBE TAKAGI-SAN WOULD STOP TEASING ME...
I WANNA KNOW TOO.
WHAT'S UP? ARE YOU AFTER HOUJOU TOO, NISHIKATA?
NAW, MAN. NISHIKATA'S GOT TAKAGI-SAN.
NO!! IT'S NOT LIKE THAT.
WELL, IF WE'RE TALKING MATURITY...
...I BET IT'S THAT THING.
THAT THING!?
WHAT THING!?

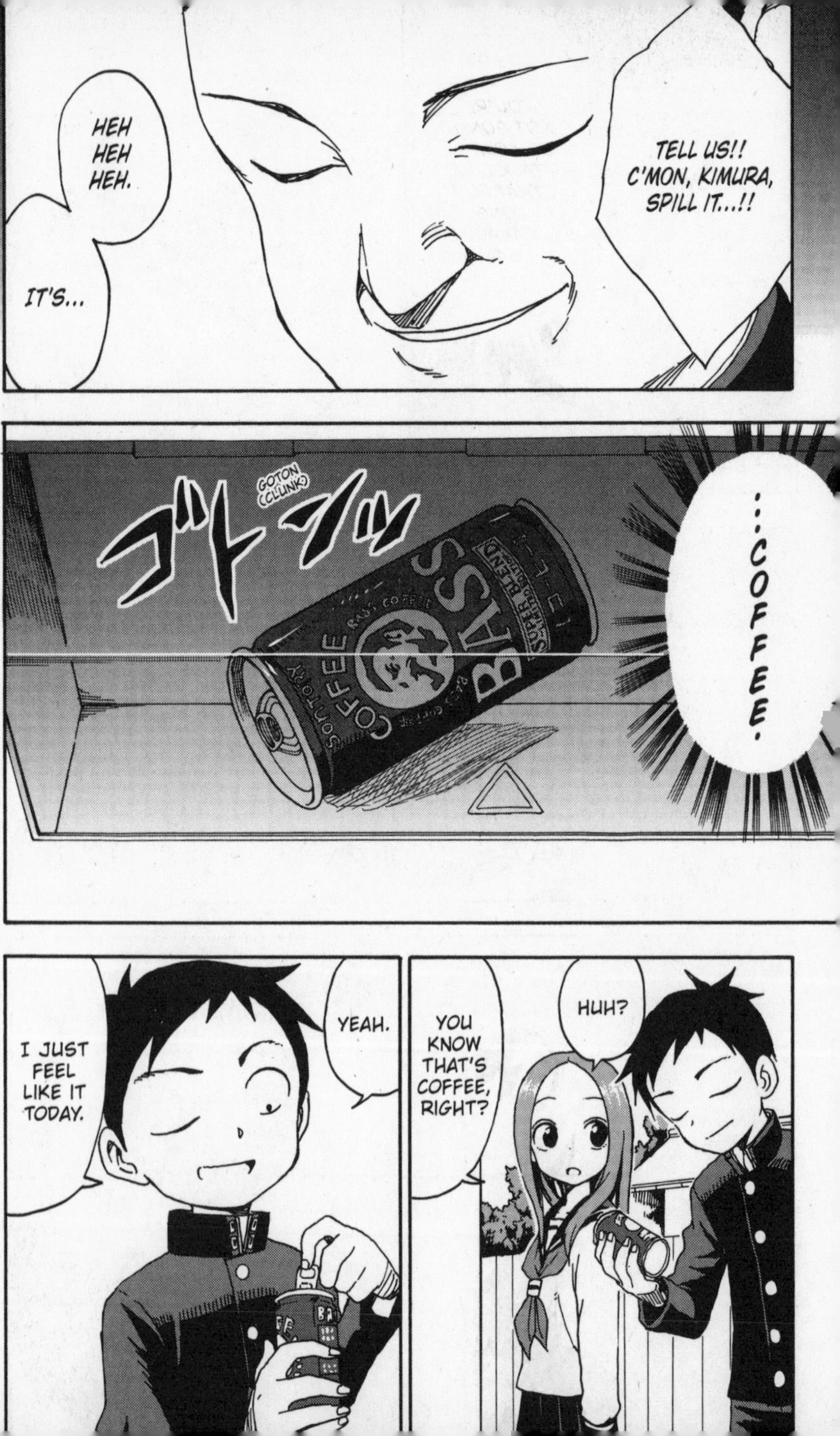
TELL US!! C'MON, KIMURA, SPILL IT...!!
HEH HEH HEH.
IT'S...
...COFFEE.
GOTON (CLUNK)
BASS
SUPER BLEND
COFFEE
SONTORY
HUH?
YOU KNOW THAT'S COFFEE, RIGHT?
YEAH.
I JUST FEEL LIKE IT TODAY.

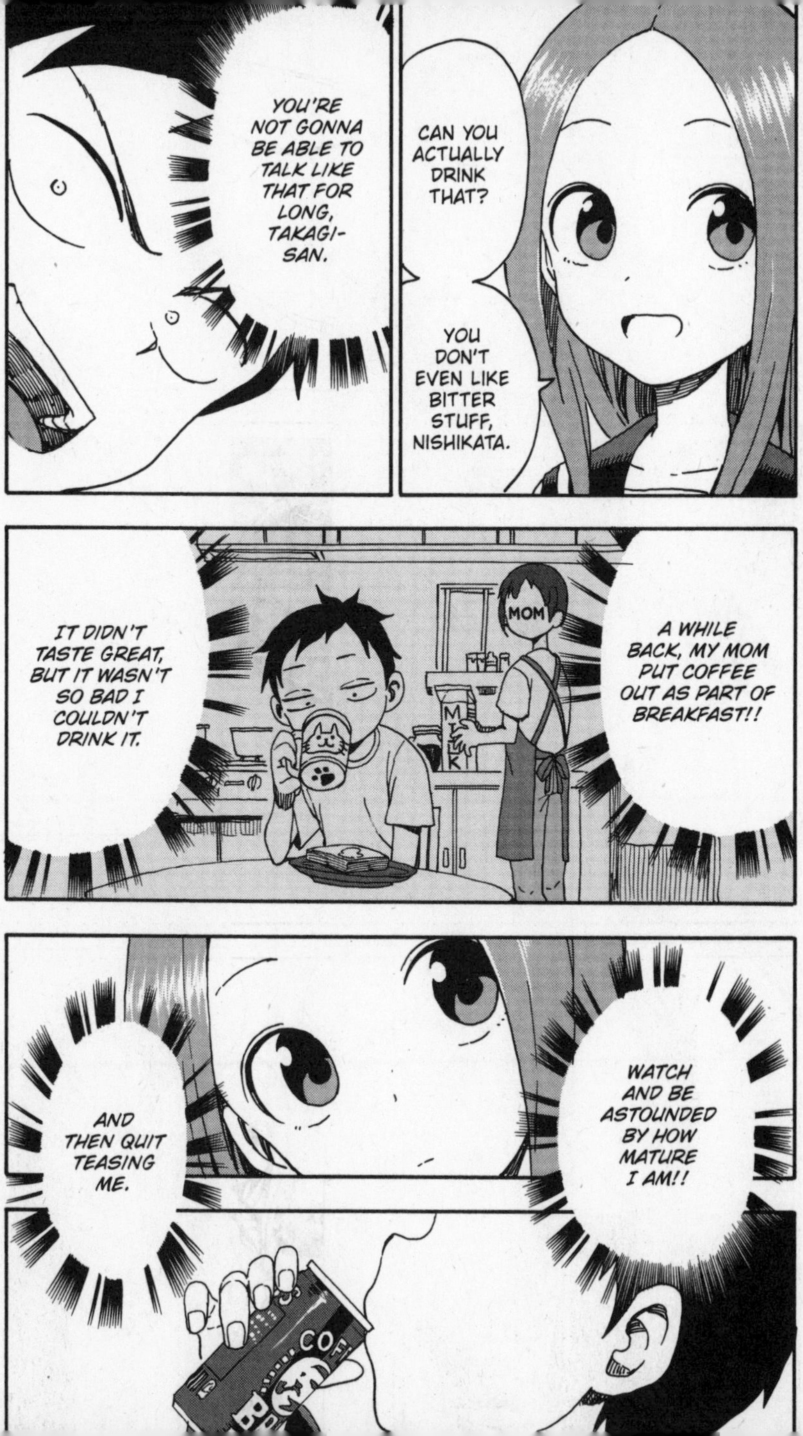
CAN YOU ACTUALLY DRINK THAT?
YOU DON'T EVEN LIKE BITTER STUFF, NISHIKATA.
YOU'RE NOT GONNA BE ABLE TO TALK LIKE THAT FOR LONG, TAKAGI-SAN.
A WHILE BACK, MY MOM PUT COFFEE OUT AS PART OF BREAKFAST!!
MOM
MILK
IT DIDN'T TASTE GREAT, BUT IT WASN'T SO BAD I COULDN'T DRINK IT.
WATCH AND BE ASTOUNDED BY HOW MATURE I AM!!
AND THEN QUIT TEASING ME.

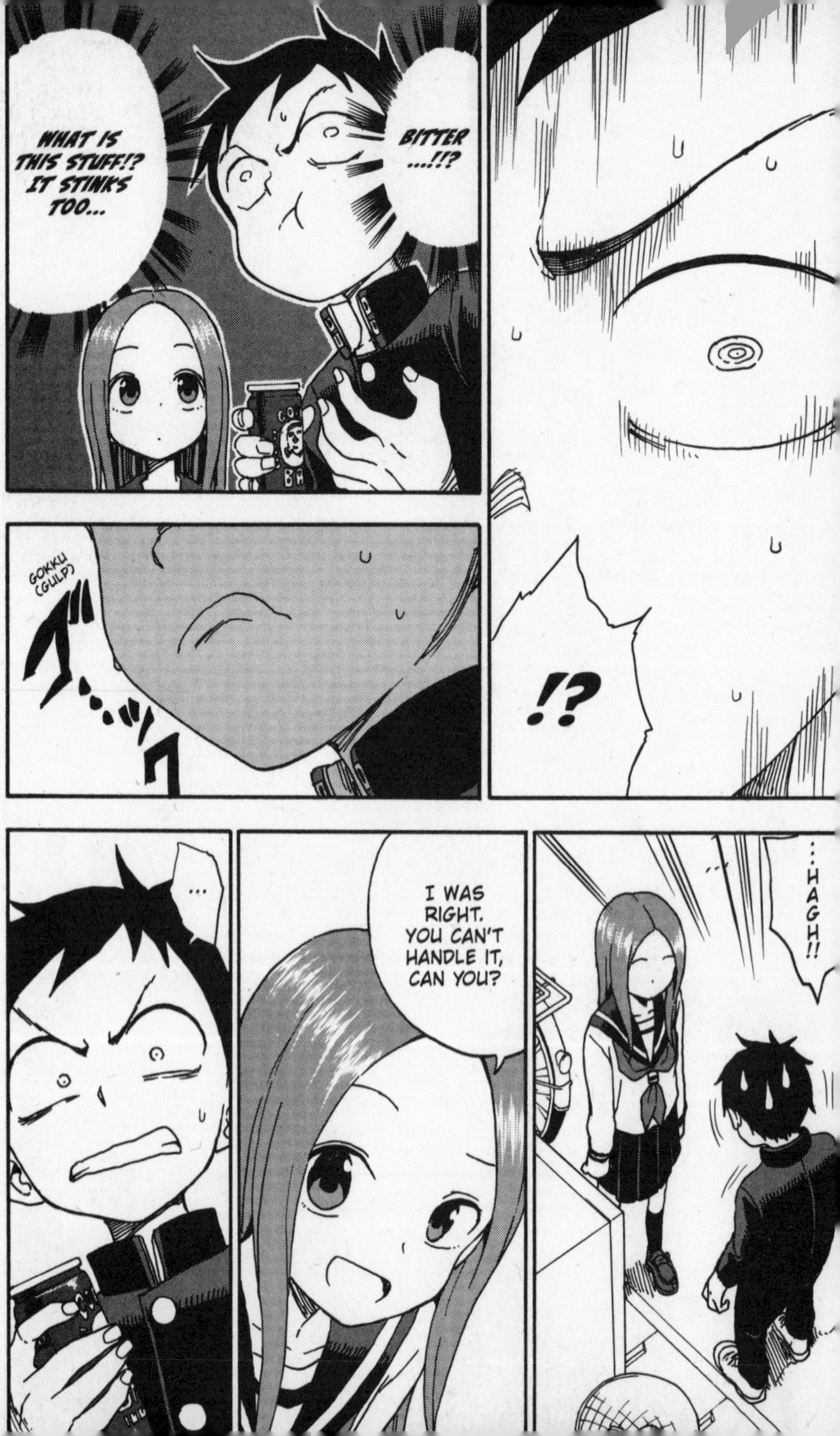
!?
BITTER ...!!?
WHAT IS THIS STUFF!? IT STINKS TOO...
GOKKU (GULP)
...HAGH!!
I WAS RIGHT. YOU CAN'T HANDLE IT, CAN YOU?
...

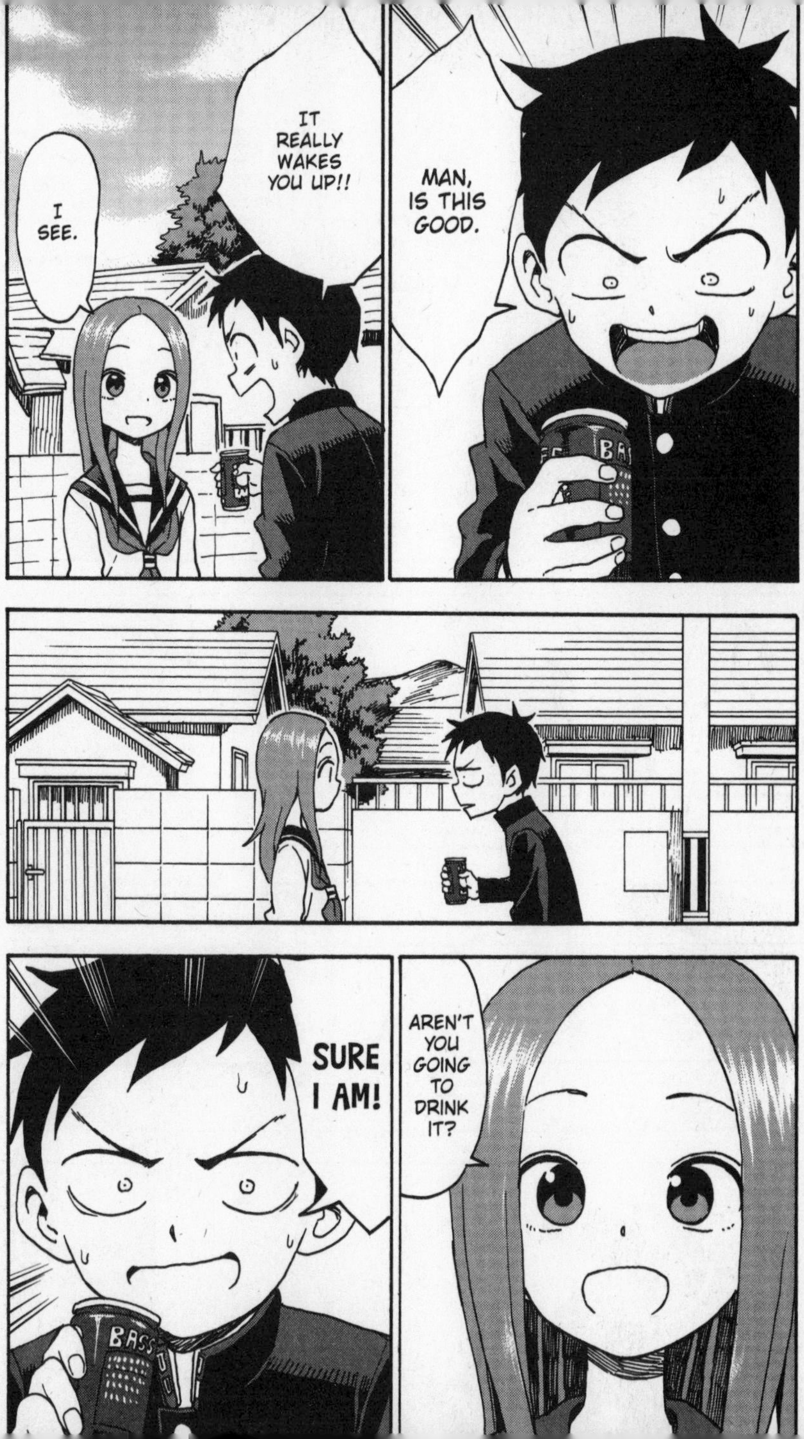
MAN, IS THIS GOOD.
IT REALLY WAKES YOU UP!!
I SEE.
AREN'T YOU GOING TO DRINK IT?
SURE I AM!

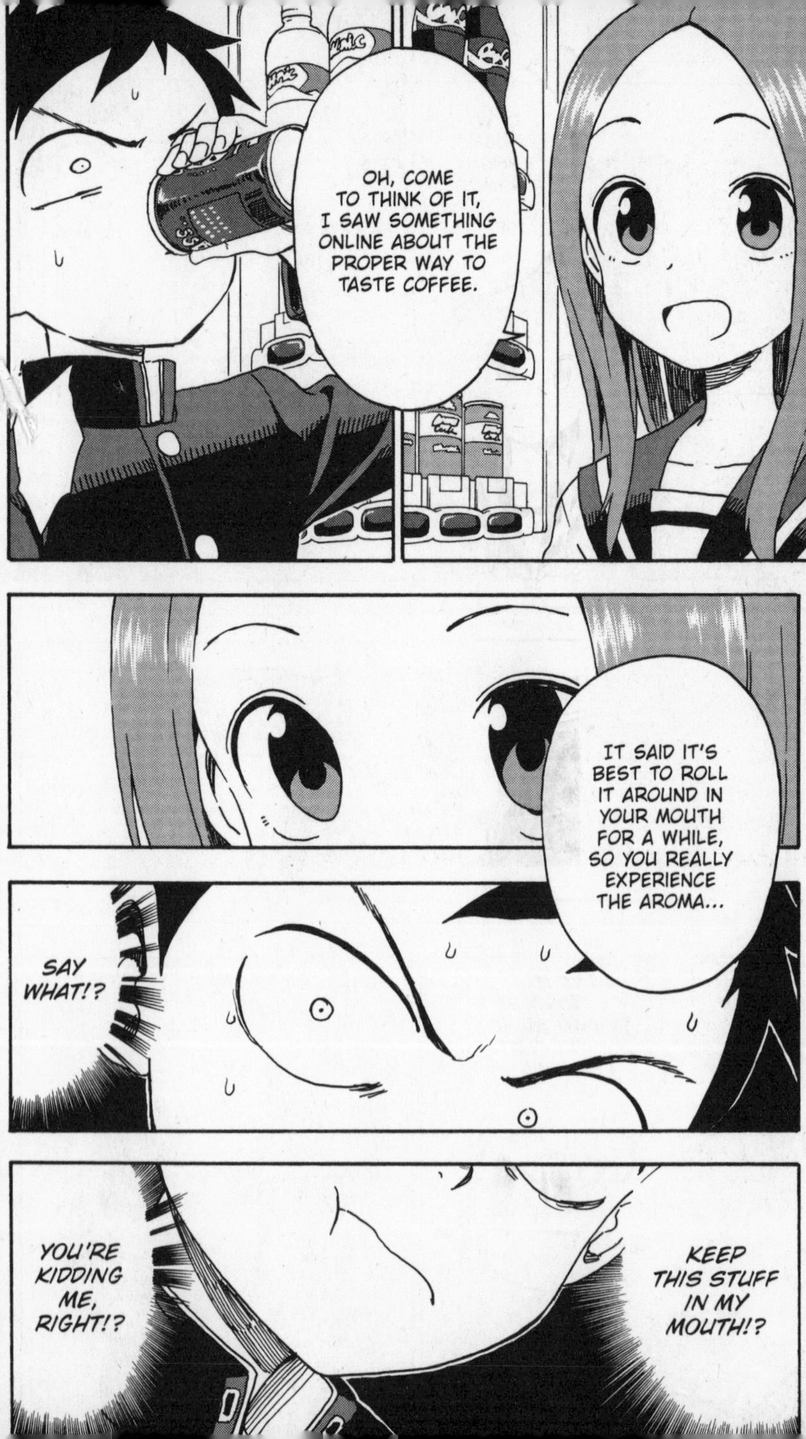
OH, COME TO THINK OF IT, I SAW SOMETHING ONLINE ABOUT THE PROPER WAY TO TASTE COFFEE.
IT SAID IT'S BEST TO ROLL IT AROUND IN YOUR MOUTH FOR A WHILE, SO YOU REALLY EXPERIENCE THE AROMA...
SAY WHAT!?
KEEP THIS STUFF IN MY MOUTH!?
YOU'RE KIDDING ME, RIGHT!?

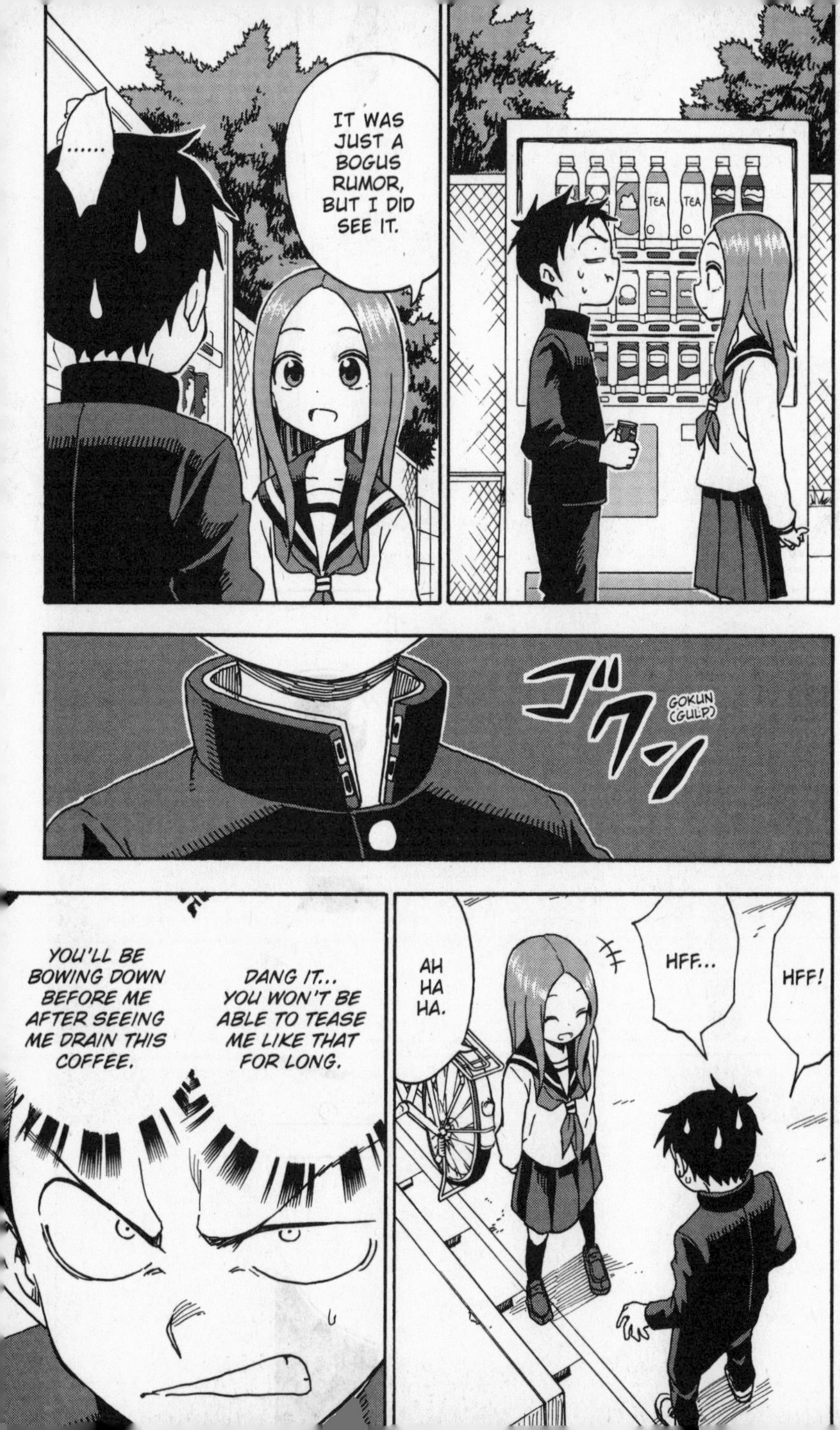
TEA
TEA
IT WAS JUST A BOGUS RUMOR, BUT I DID SEE IT.
......
GOKUN (GULP)
HFF!
HFF...
AH HA HA.
DANG IT... YOU WON'T BE ABLE TO TEASE ME LIKE THAT FOR LONG.
YOU'LL BE BOWING DOWN BEFORE ME AFTER SEEING ME DRAIN THIS COFFEE.

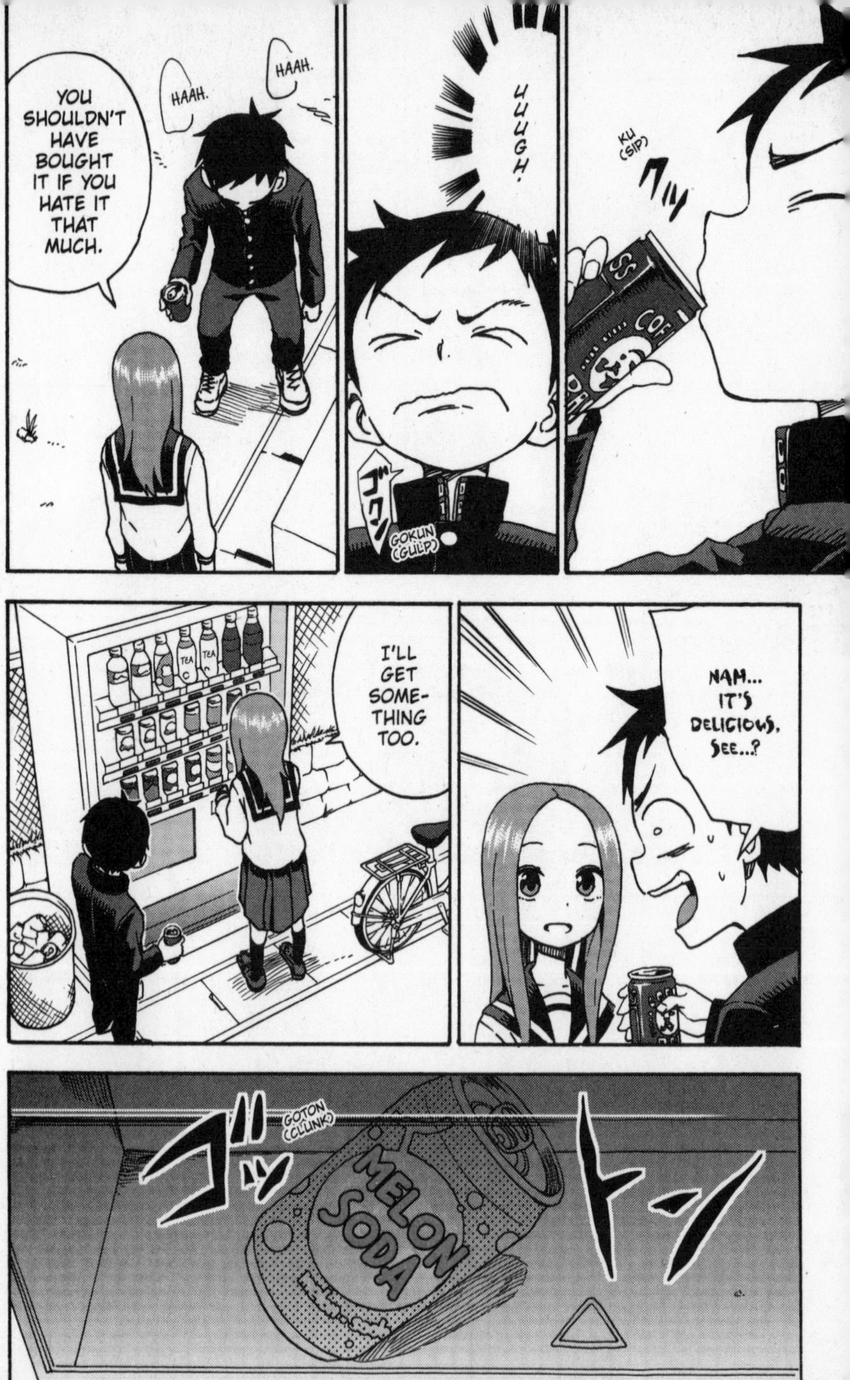
KU
(SIP)
UUUGH!
GOKUN
(GULP)
HAAH.
HAAH.
YOU SHOULDN'T HAVE BOUGHT IT IF YOU HATE IT THAT MUCH.
NAM... IT'S DELICIOUS, SEE...?
I'LL GET SOME-THING TOO.
GOTON
(CLUNK)
MELON SODA

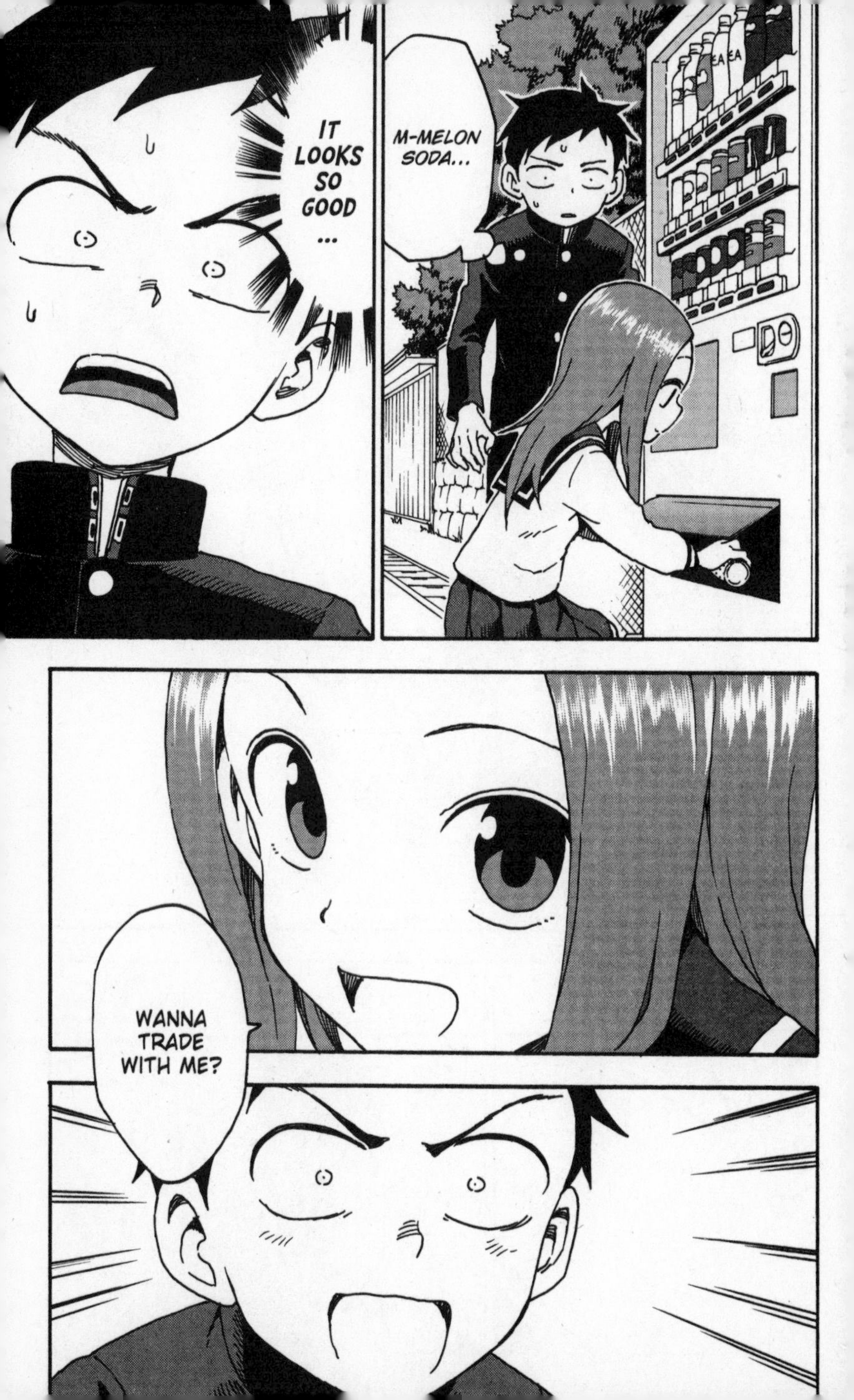
M-MELON SODA...
IT LOOKS SO GOOD ...
WANNA TRADE WITH ME?

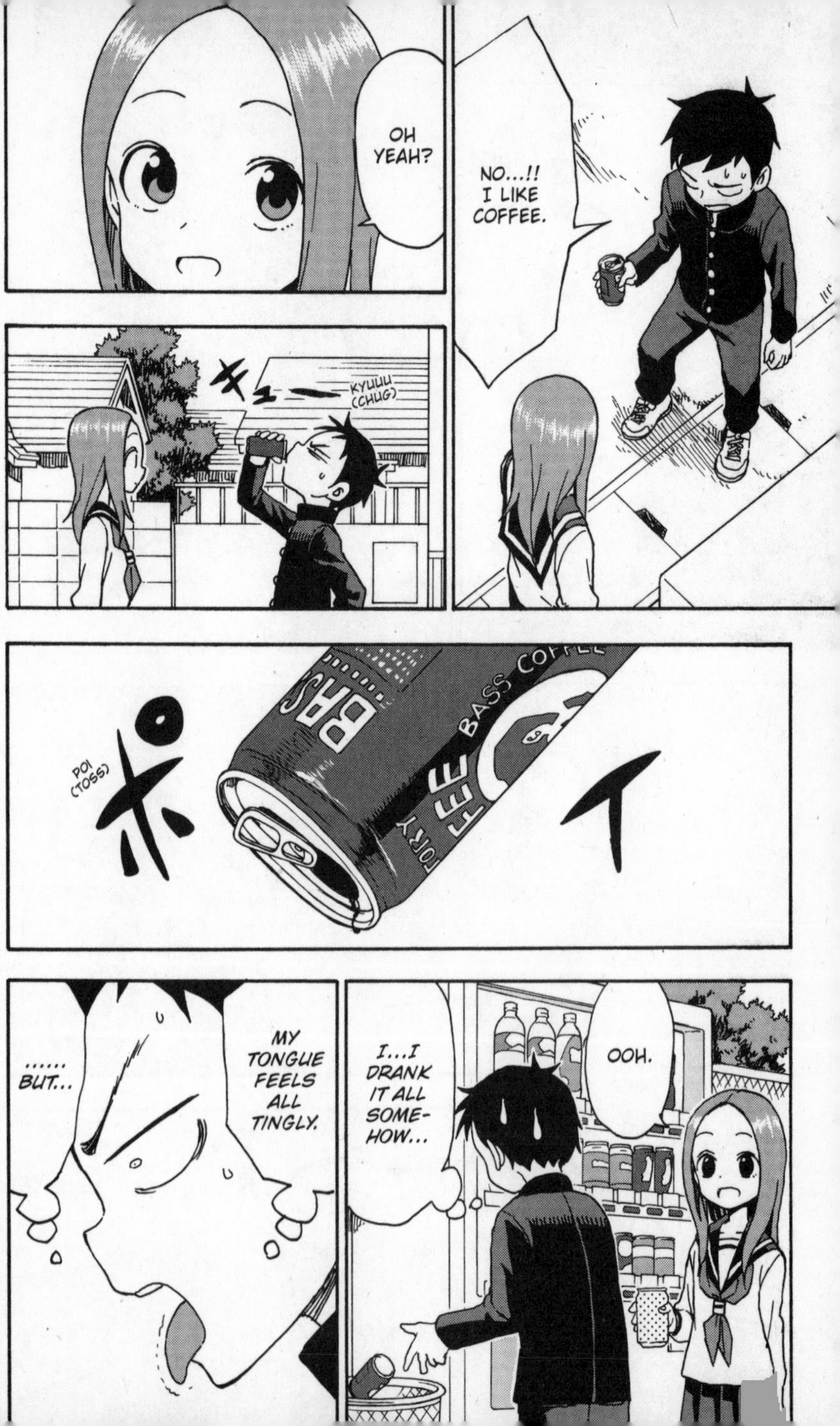
NO...!! I LIKE COFFEE.
OH YEAH?
KYUUU (CHUG)
POI (TOSS)
BASS COFFEE
OOH.
I...I DRANK IT ALL SOME-HOW...
MY TONGUE FEELS ALL TINGLY.
...... BUT...

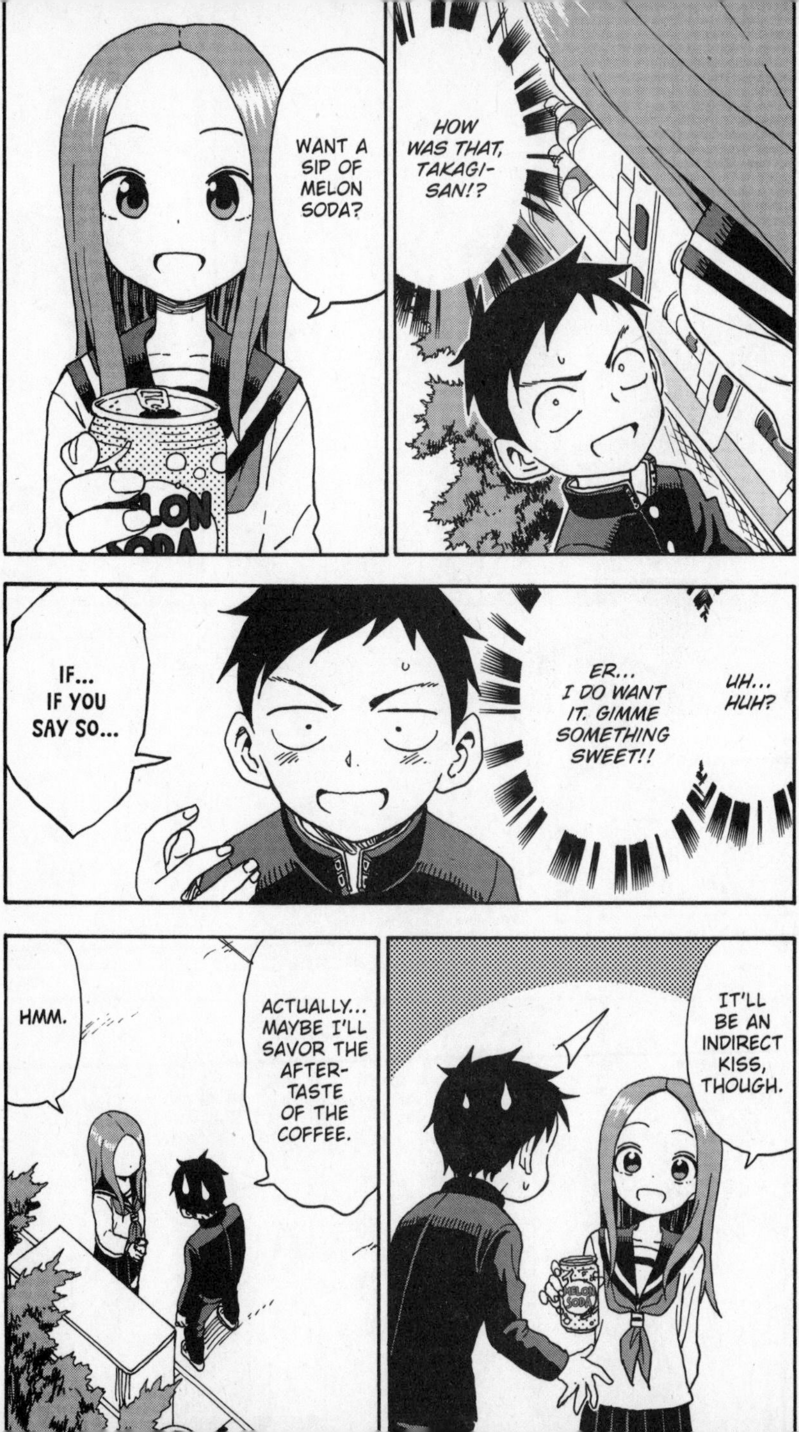
HOW WAS THAT, TAKAGI-SAN!?
WANT A SIP OF MELON SODA?
UH... HUH?
ER... I DO WANT IT. GIMME SOMETHING SWEET!!
IF... IF YOU SAY SO...
IT'LL BE AN INDIRECT KISS, THOUGH.
MELON SODA
ACTUALLY... MAYBE I'LL SAVOR THE AFTER-TASTE OF THE COFFEE.
HMM.

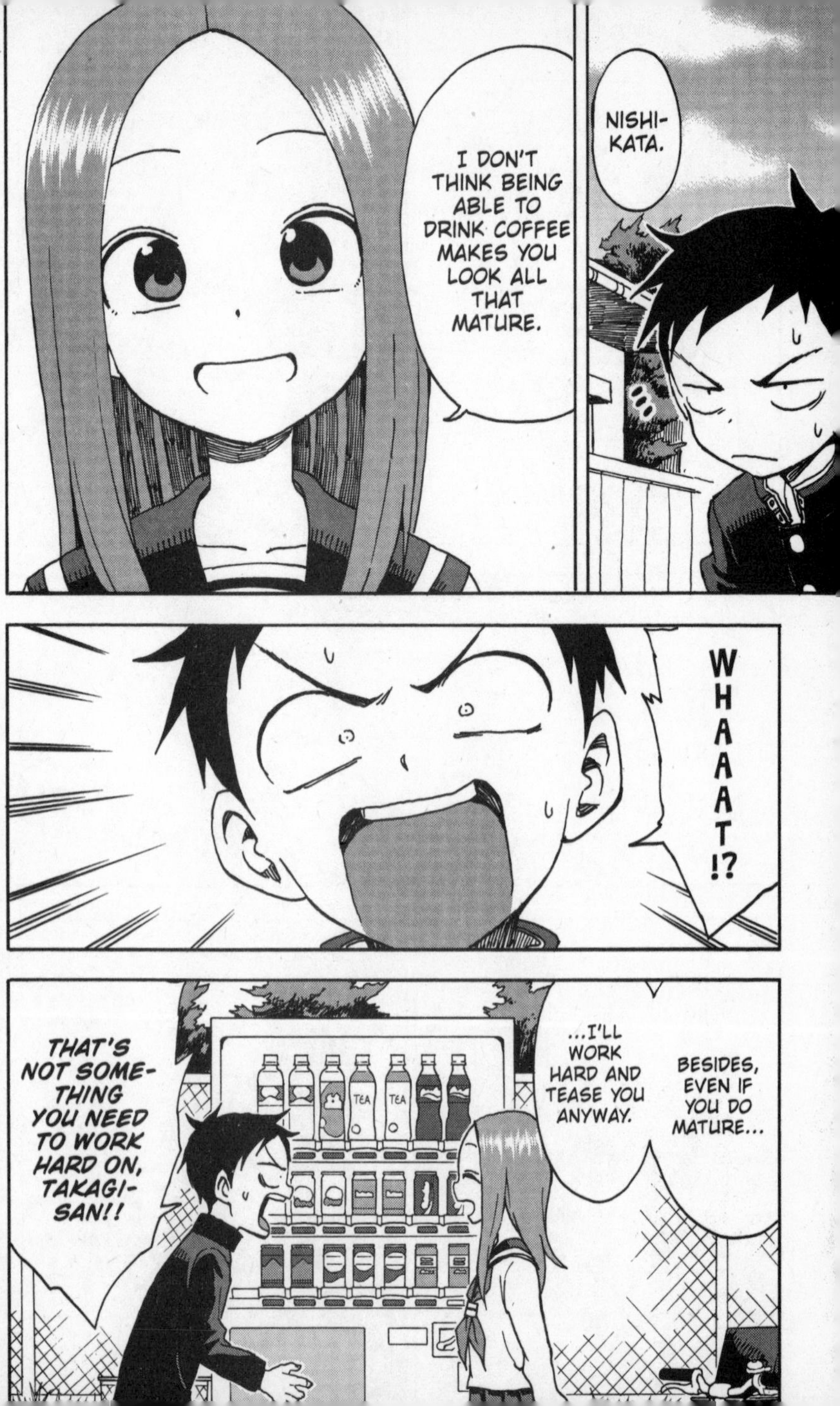
NISHI-KATA.
I DON'T THINK BEING ABLE TO DRINK COFFEE MAKES YOU LOOK ALL THAT MATURE.
WHAAAAT!?
BESIDES, EVEN IF YOU DO MATURE...
...I'LL WORK HARD AND TEASE YOU ANYWAY.
THAT'S NOT SOME-THING YOU NEED TO WORK HARD ON, TAKAGI-SAN!!

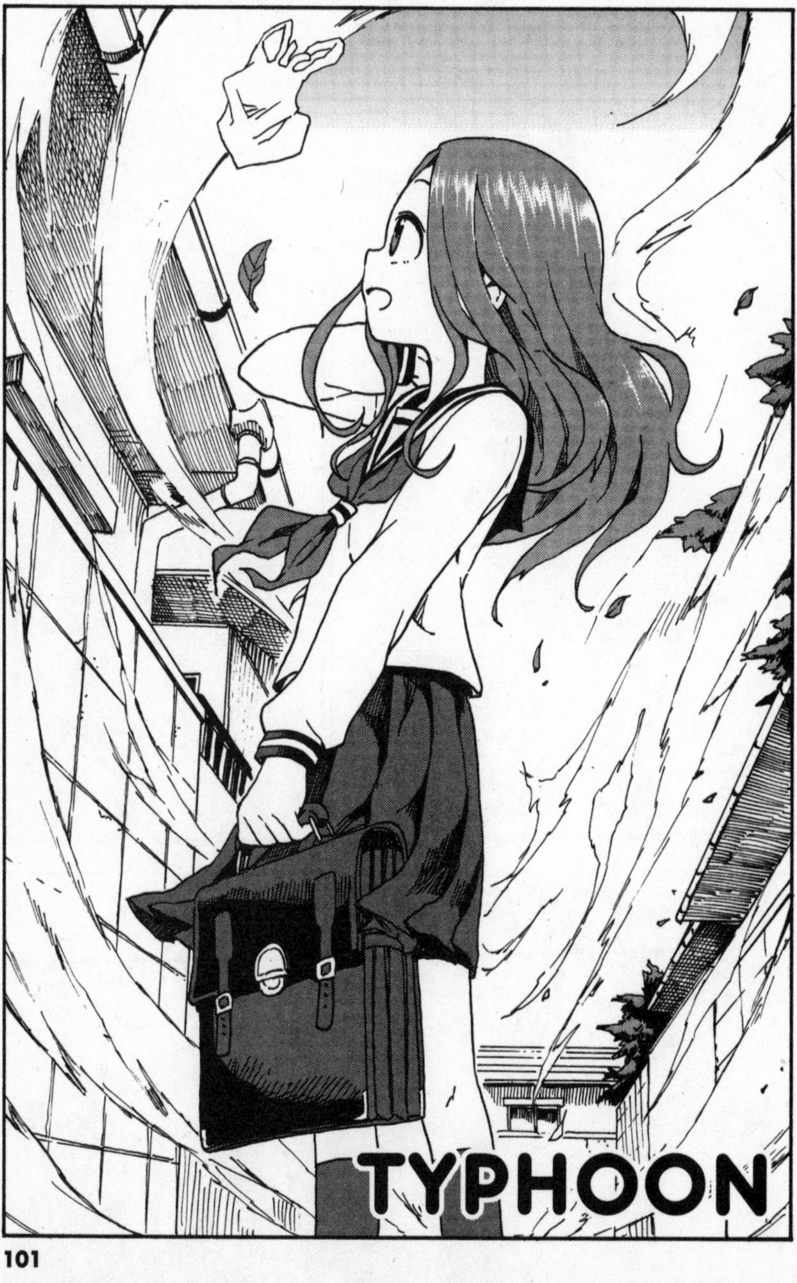
TYPHOON

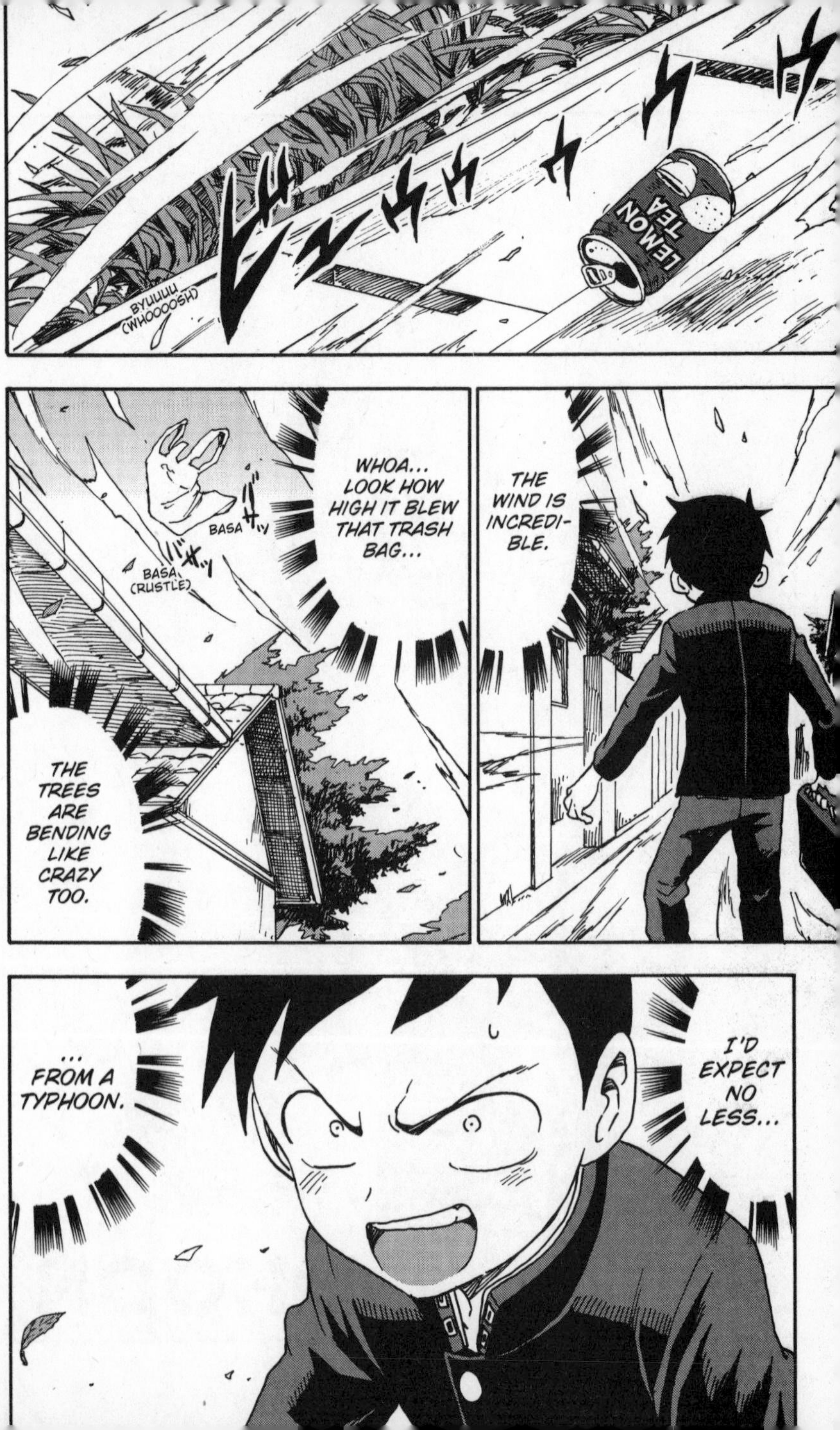
LEMON TEA
BYUUUU (WHOOOOSH)
THE WIND IS INCREDI-BLE.
WHOA... LOOK HOW HIGH IT BLEW THAT TRASH BAG...
BASA
BASA (RUSTLE)
THE TREES ARE BENDING LIKE CRAZY TOO.
I'D EXPECT NO LESS...
... FROM A TYPHOON.

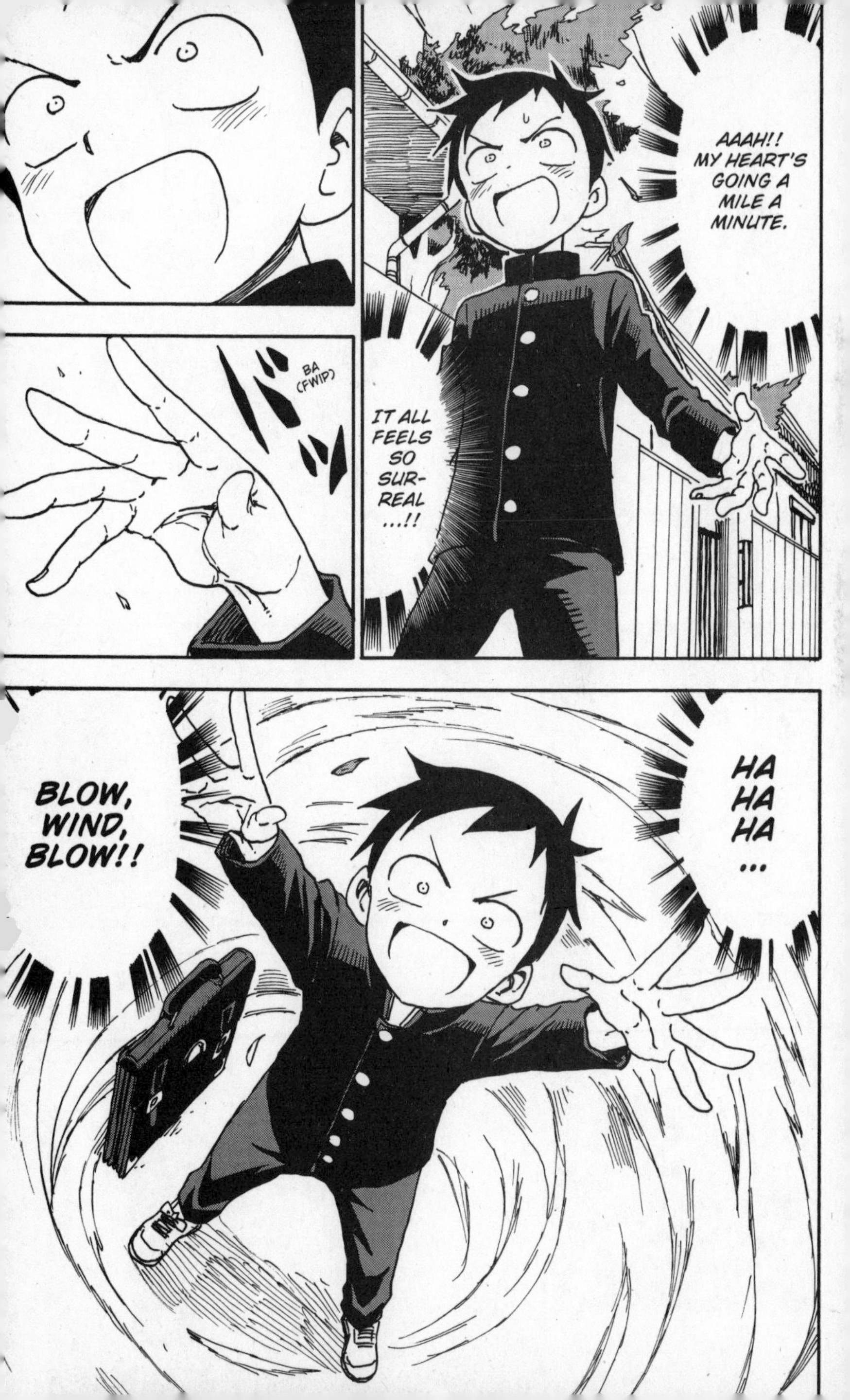
AAAH!! MY HEART'S GOING A MILE A MINUTE.
IT ALL FEELS SO SURREAL...!!
BA (FWIP)
HA HA HA ...
BLOW, WIND, BLOW!!

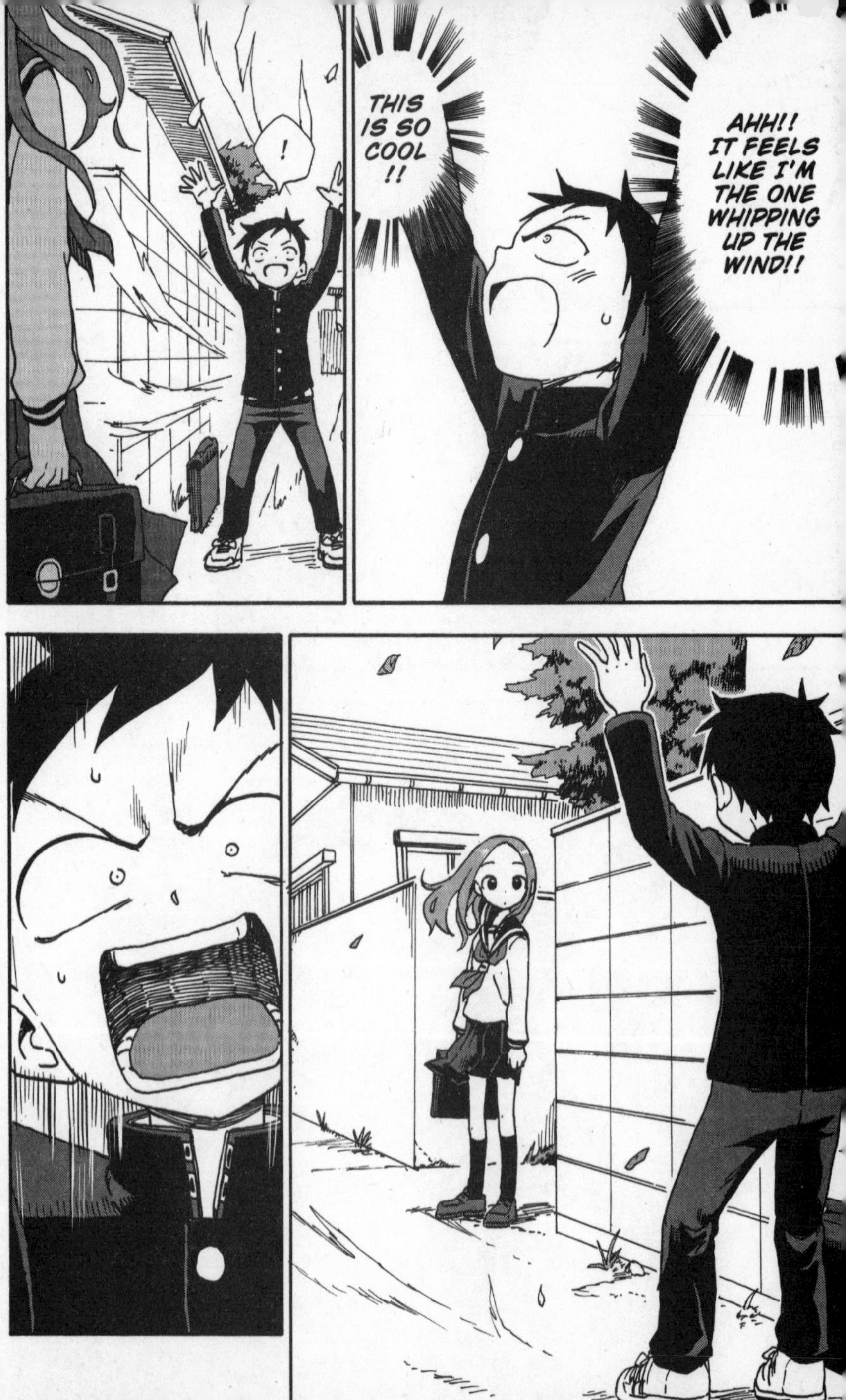
AHH!! IT FEELS LIKE I'M THE ONE WHIPPING UP THE WIND!!
THIS IS SO COOL !!
!

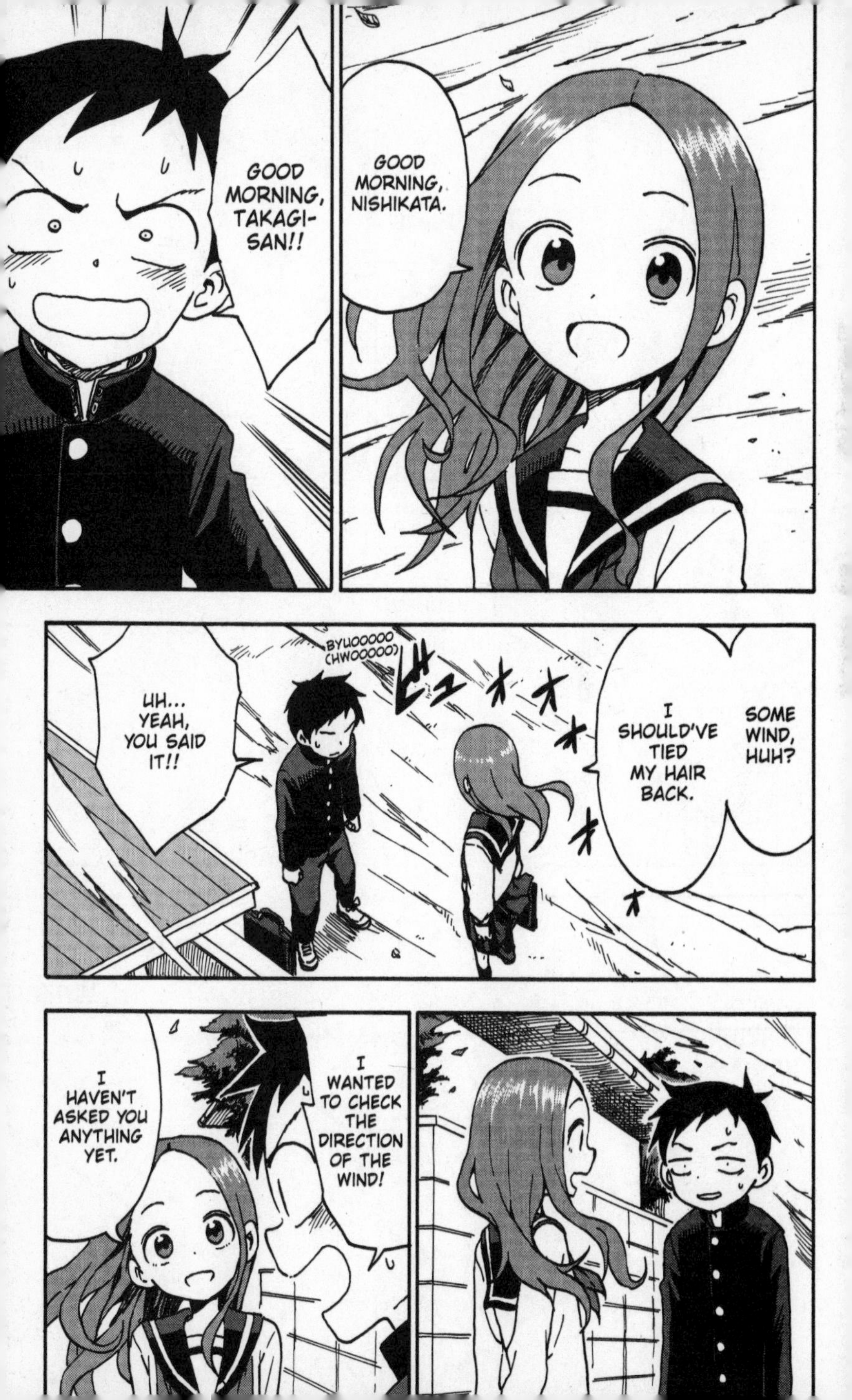
GOOD MORNING, NISHIKATA.
GOOD MORNING, TAKAGI-SAN!!
SOME WIND, HUH?
I SHOULD'VE TIED MY HAIR BACK.
BYUOOOOO (HWOOOOO)
UH... YEAH, YOU SAID IT!!
I WANTED TO CHECK THE DIRECTION OF THE WIND!
I HAVEN'T ASKED YOU ANYTHING YET.

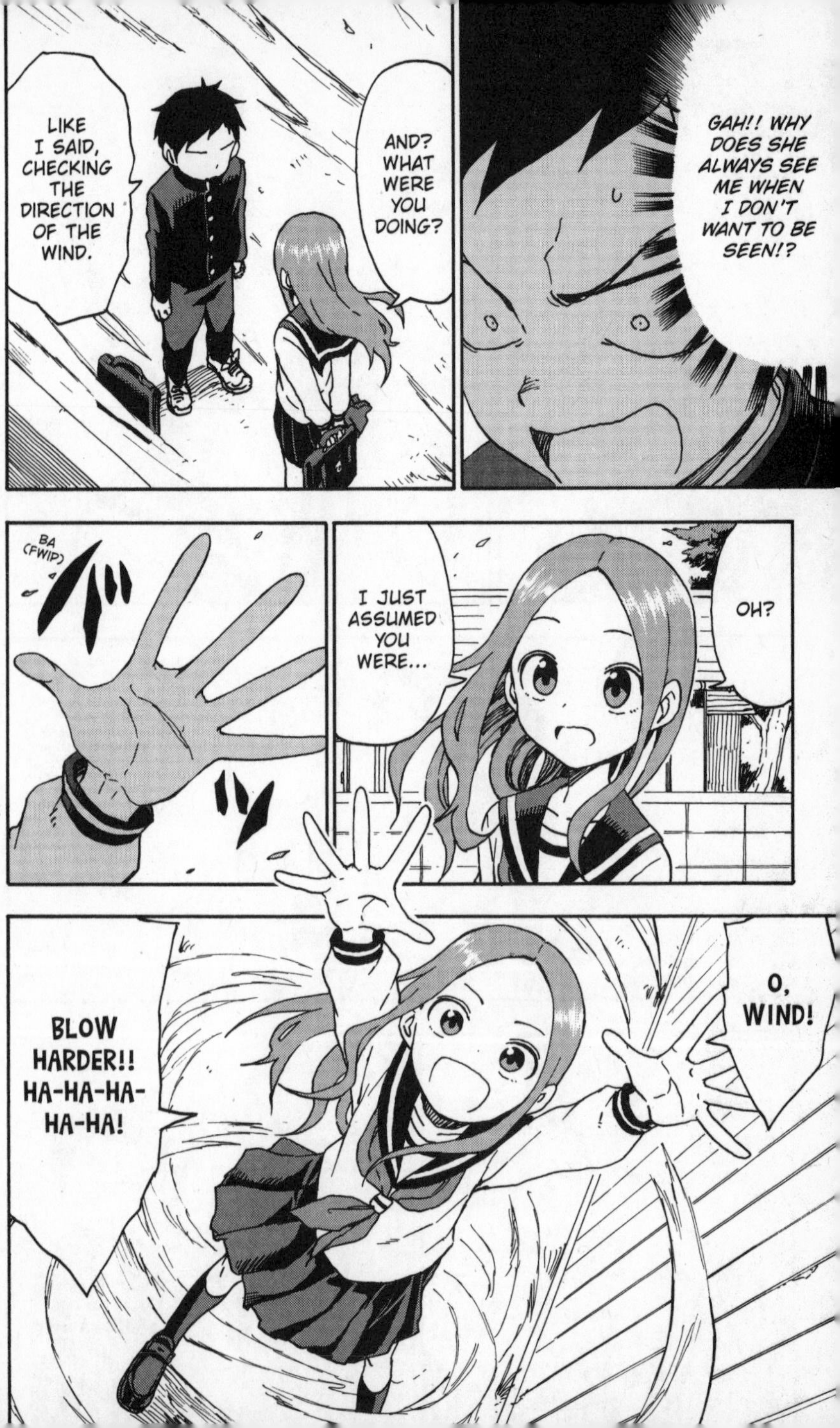
GAH!! WHY DOES SHE ALWAYS SEE ME WHEN I DON'T WANT TO BE SEEN!?
AND? WHAT WERE YOU DOING?
LIKE I SAID, CHECKING THE DIRECTION OF THE WIND.
OH?
I JUST ASSUMED YOU WERE...
BA (FWIP)
O, WIND!
BLOW HARDER!! HA-HA-HA-HA-HA!

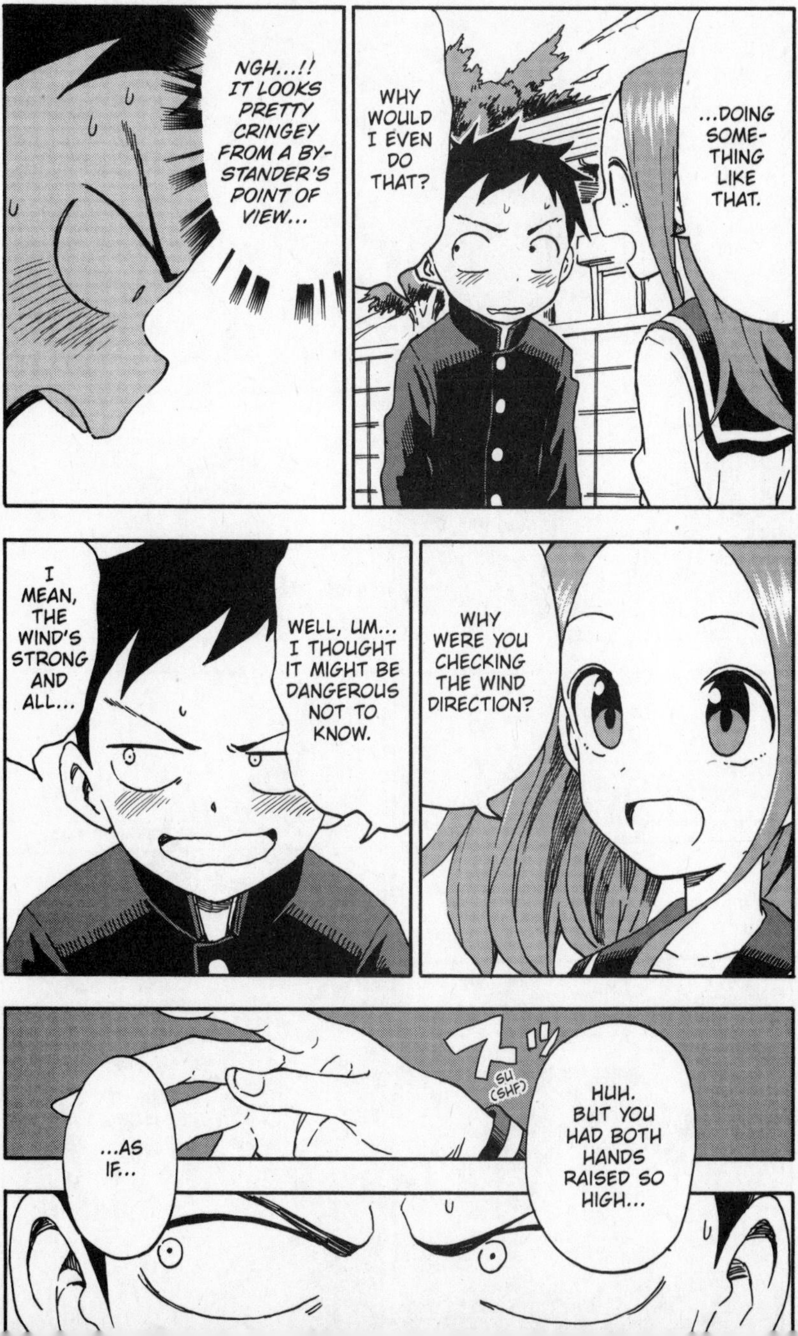
...DOING SOMETHING LIKE THAT.
WHY WOULD I EVEN DO THAT?
NGH...!! IT LOOKS PRETTY CRINGEY FROM A BYSTANDER'S POINT OF VIEW...
WHY WERE YOU CHECKING THE WIND DIRECTION?
WELL, UM... I THOUGHT IT MIGHT BE DANGEROUS NOT TO KNOW.
I MEAN, THE WIND'S STRONG AND ALL...
SU (SHF)
HUH. BUT YOU HAD BOTH HANDS RAISED SO HIGH...
...AS IF...

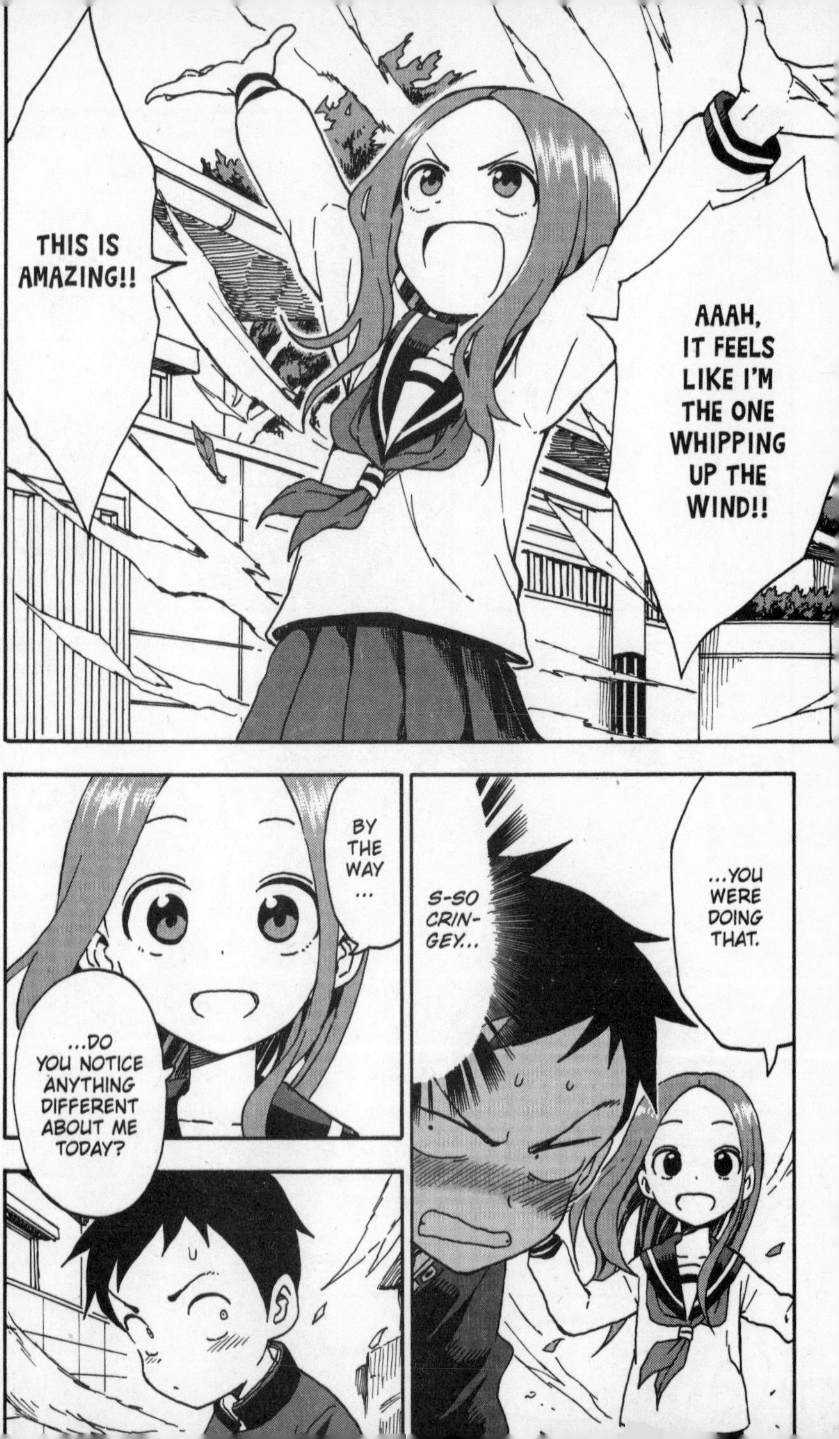
AAAH, IT FEELS LIKE I'M THE ONE WHIPPING UP THE WIND!!
THIS IS AMAZING!!
...YOU WERE DOING THAT.
S-SO CRIN-GEY...
BY THE WAY...
...DO YOU NOTICE ANYTHING DIFFERENT ABOUT ME TODAY?

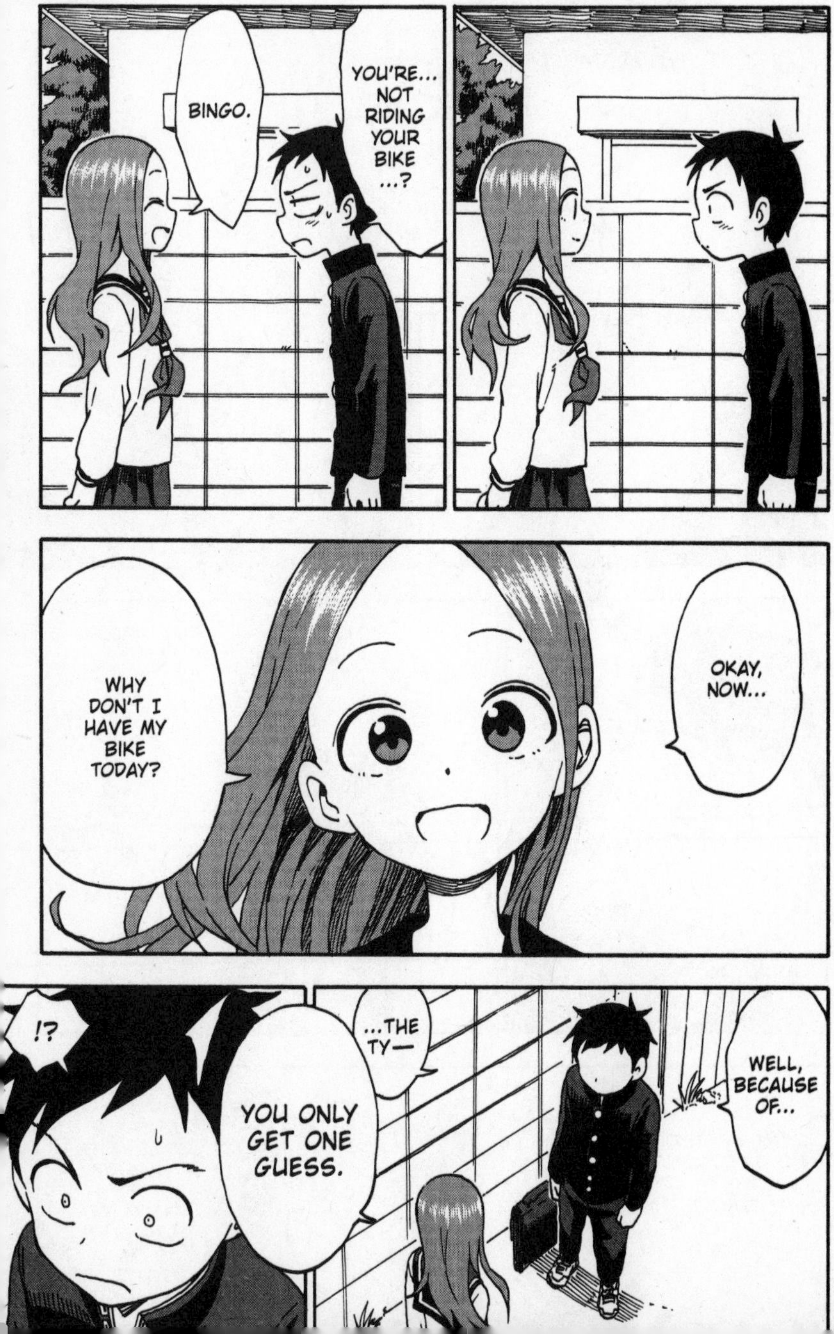
YOU'RE... NOT RIDING YOUR BIKE ...?
BINGO.
OKAY, NOW...
WHY DON'T I HAVE MY BIKE TODAY?
WELL, BECAUSE OF...
...THE TY—
YOU ONLY GET ONE GUESS.
!?

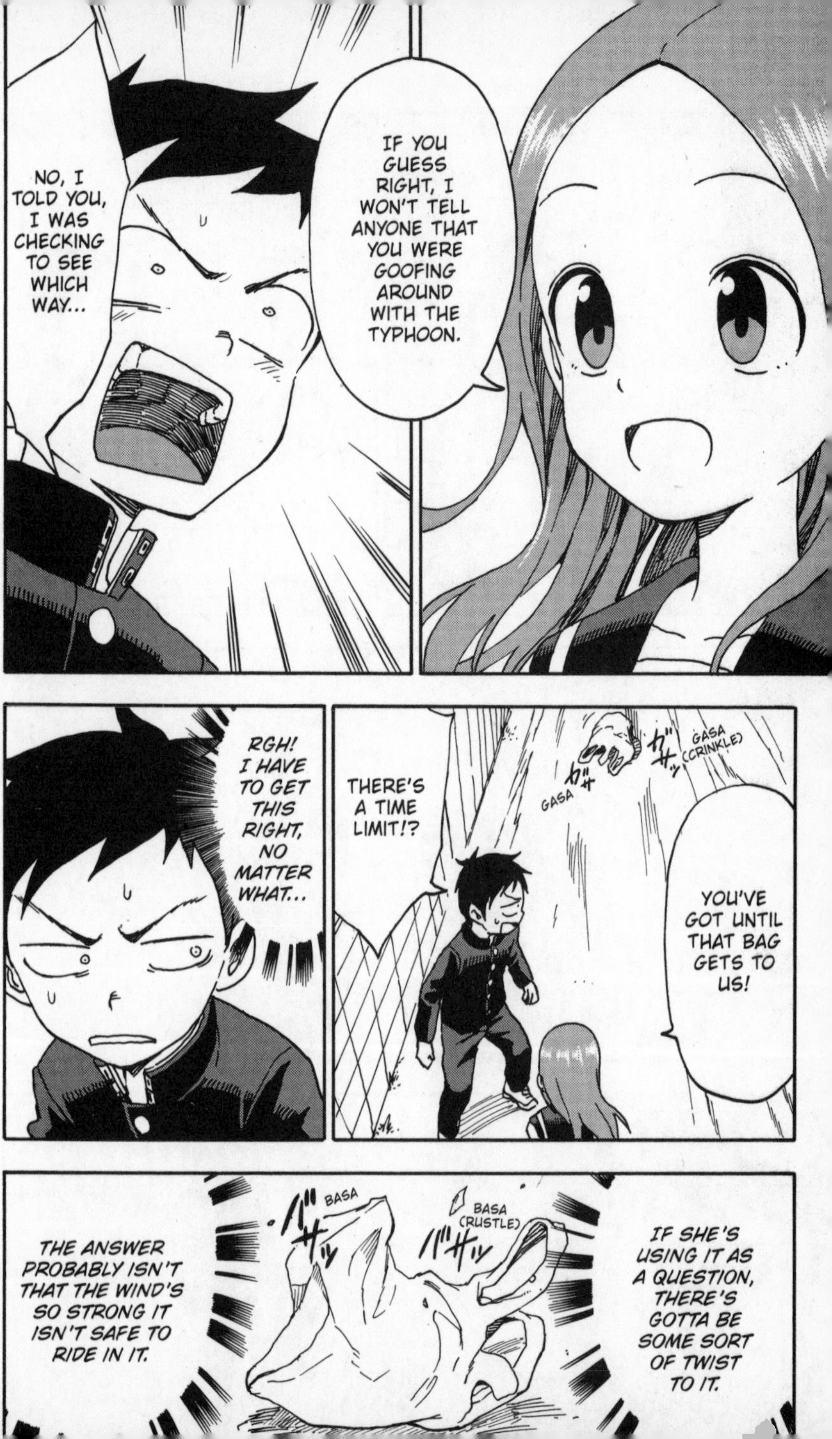
IF YOU GUESS RIGHT, I WON'T TELL ANYONE THAT YOU WERE GOOFING AROUND WITH THE TYPHOON.
NO, I TOLD YOU, I WAS CHECKING TO SEE WHICH WAY...
GASA (CRINKLE)
GASA
YOU'VE GOT UNTIL THAT BAG GETS TO US!
THERE'S A TIME LIMIT!?
RGH! I HAVE TO GET THIS RIGHT, NO MATTER WHAT...
BASA (RUSTLE)
IF SHE'S USING IT AS A QUESTION, THERE'S GOTTA BE SOME SORT OF TWIST TO IT.
BASA
THE ANSWER PROBABLY ISN'T THAT THE WIND'S SO STRONG IT ISN'T SAFE TO RIDE IN IT.

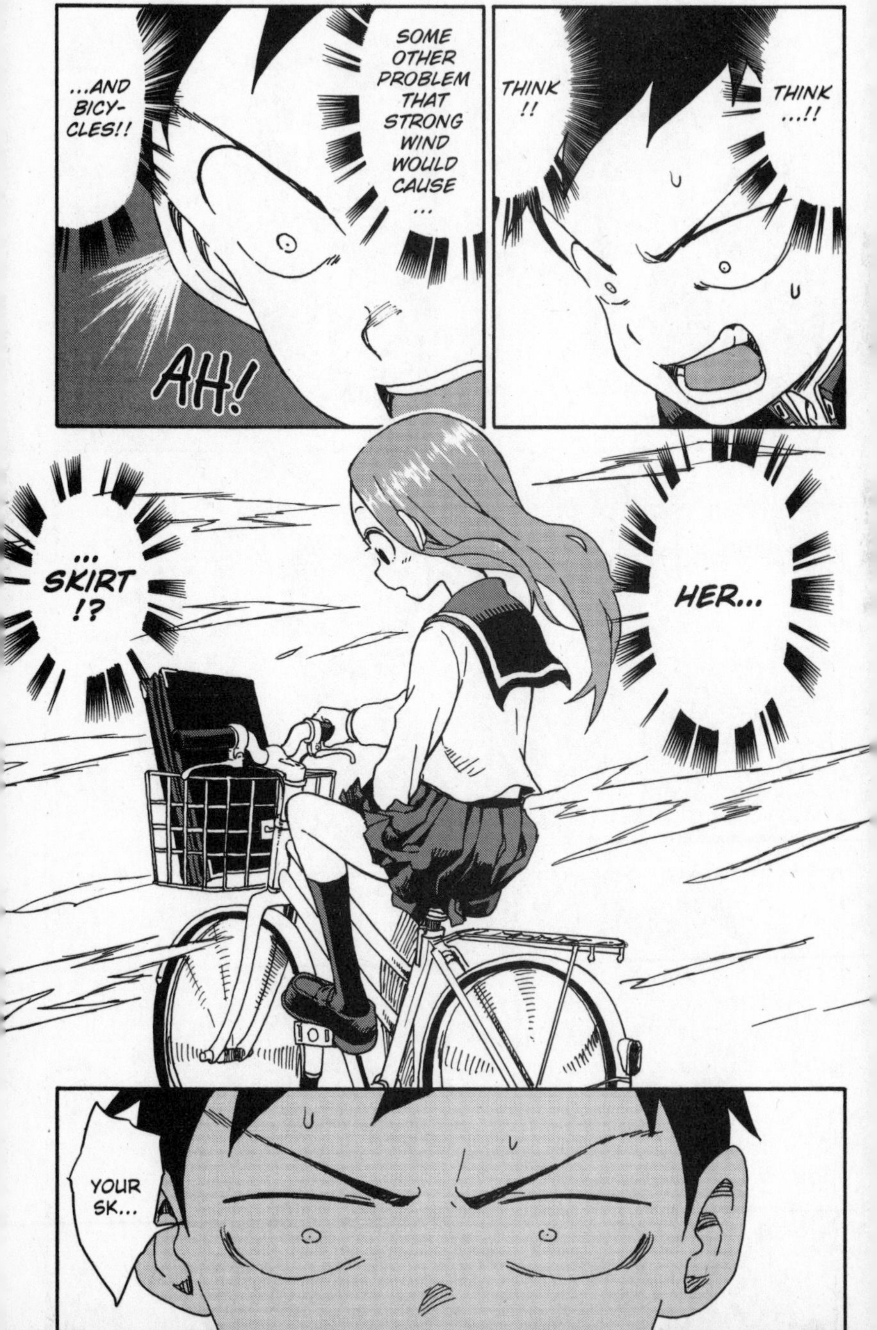
THINK ...!!
THINK !!
SOME OTHER PROBLEM THAT STRONG WIND WOULD CAUSE ...
...AND BICY- CLES!!
AH!
HER...
... SKIRT !?
YOUR SK...

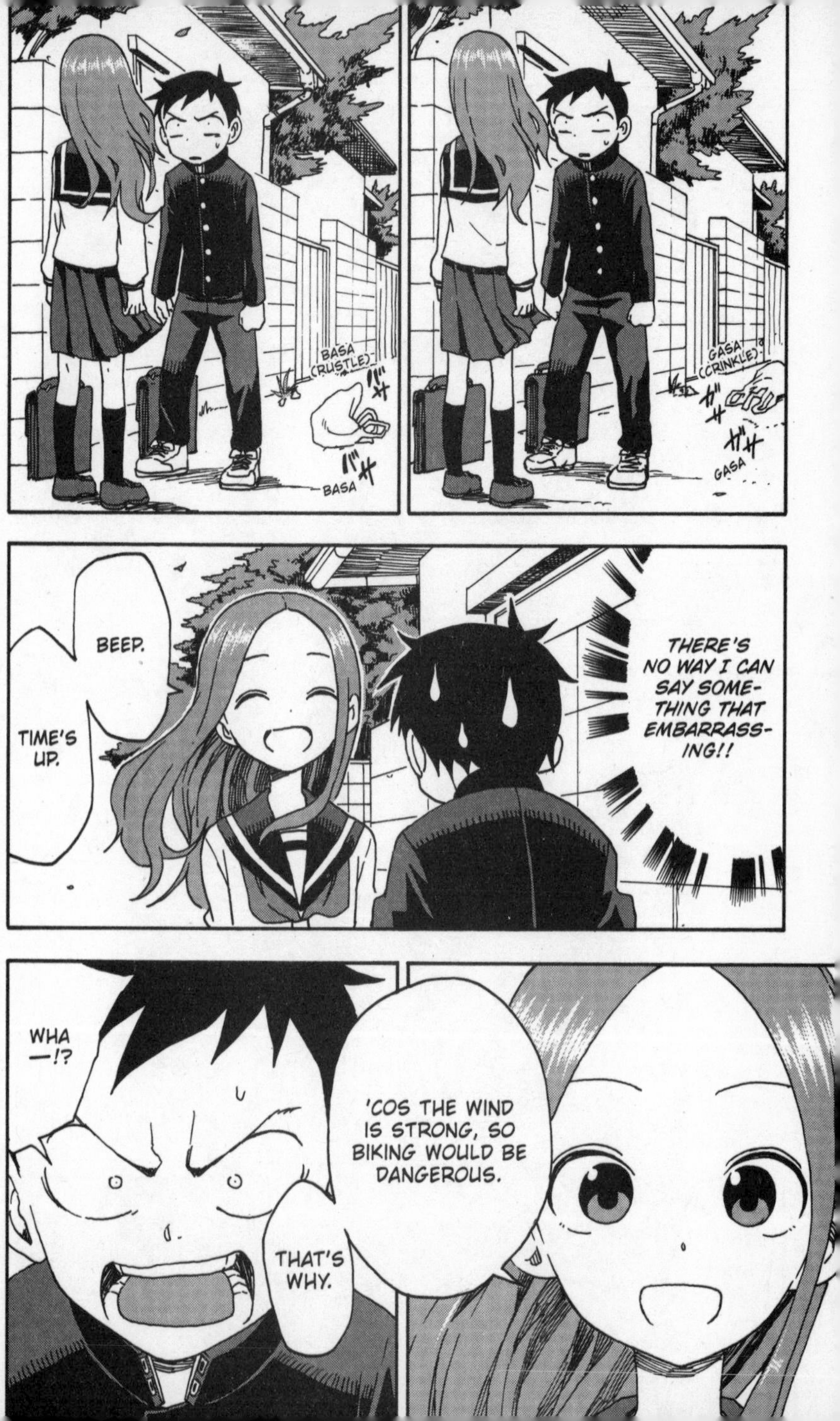
GASA (CRINKLE)
GASA
BASA (RUSTLE)
BASA
THERE'S NO WAY I CAN SAY SOME-THING THAT EMBARRASS-ING!!
BEEP.
TIME'S UP.
'COS THE WIND IS STRONG, SO BIKING WOULD BE DANGEROUS.
THAT'S WHY.
WHA—!?

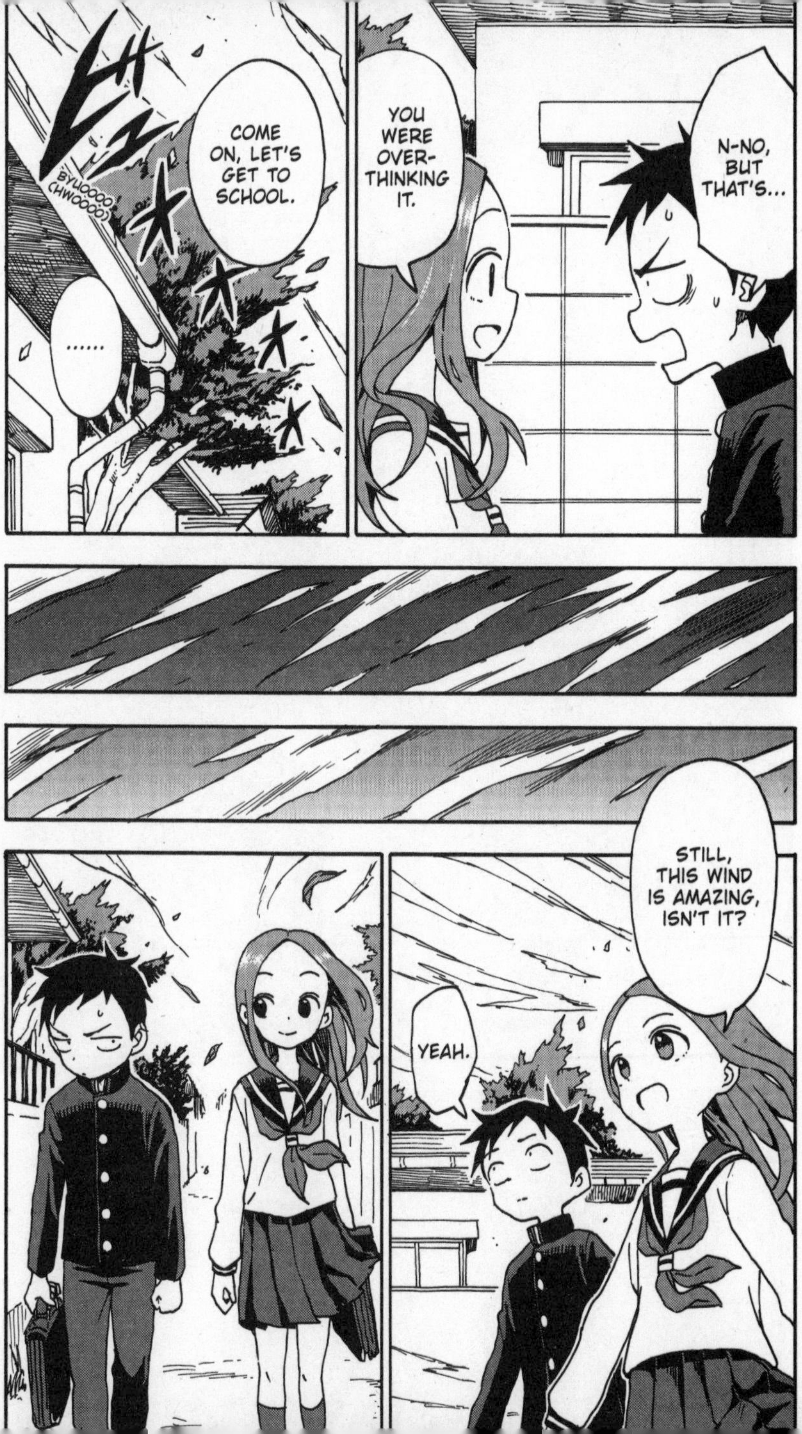
N-NO, BUT THAT'S...
YOU WERE OVER-THINKING IT.
COME ON, LET'S GET TO SCHOOL.
BYUOOOO (HWOOOO)
......
STILL, THIS WIND IS AMAZING, ISN'T IT?
YEAH.

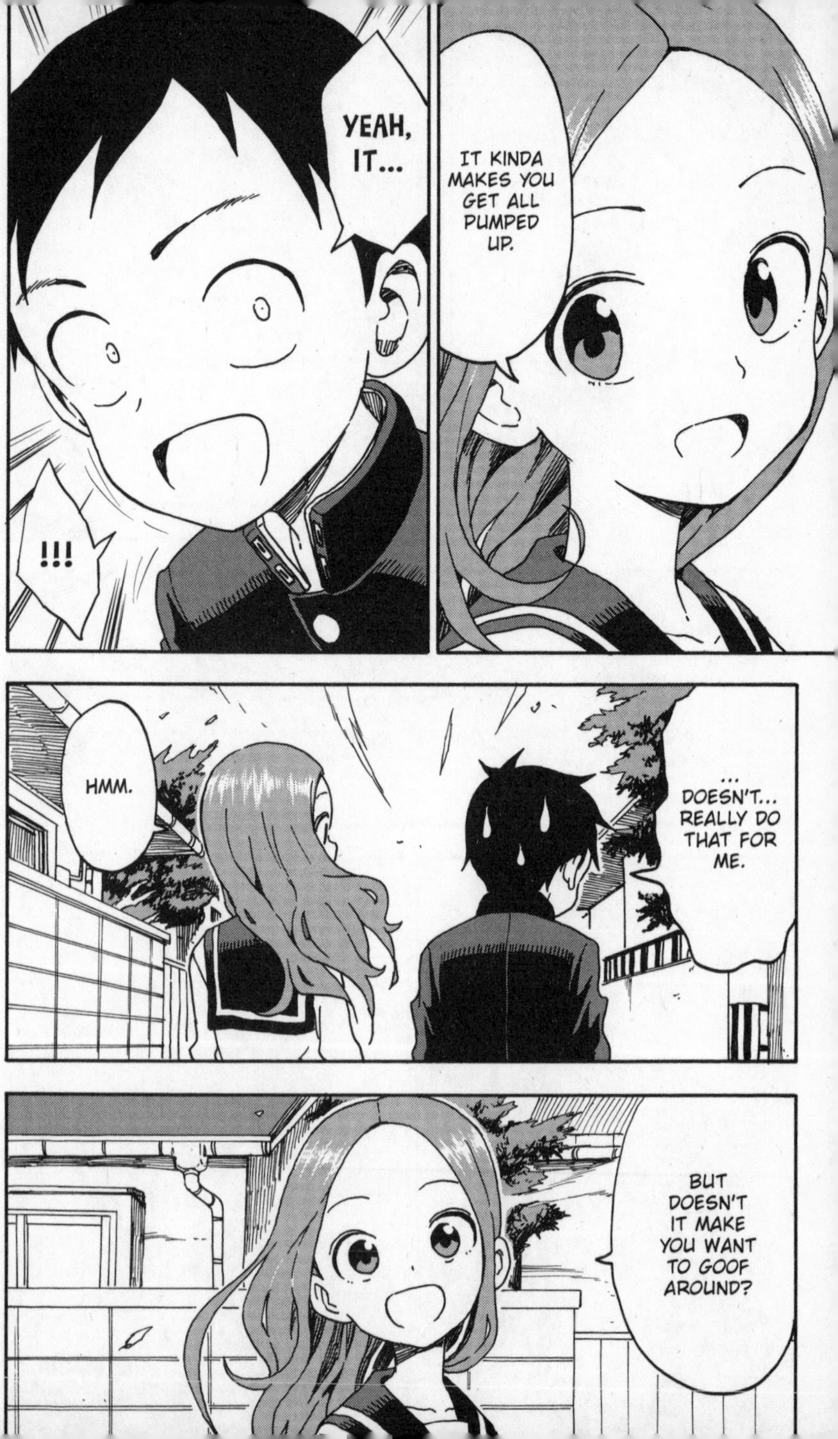
IT KINDA MAKES YOU GET ALL PUMPED UP.
YEAH, IT...
!!!
... DOESN'T... REALLY DO THAT FOR ME.
HMM.
BUT DOESN'T IT MAKE YOU WANT TO GOOF AROUND?

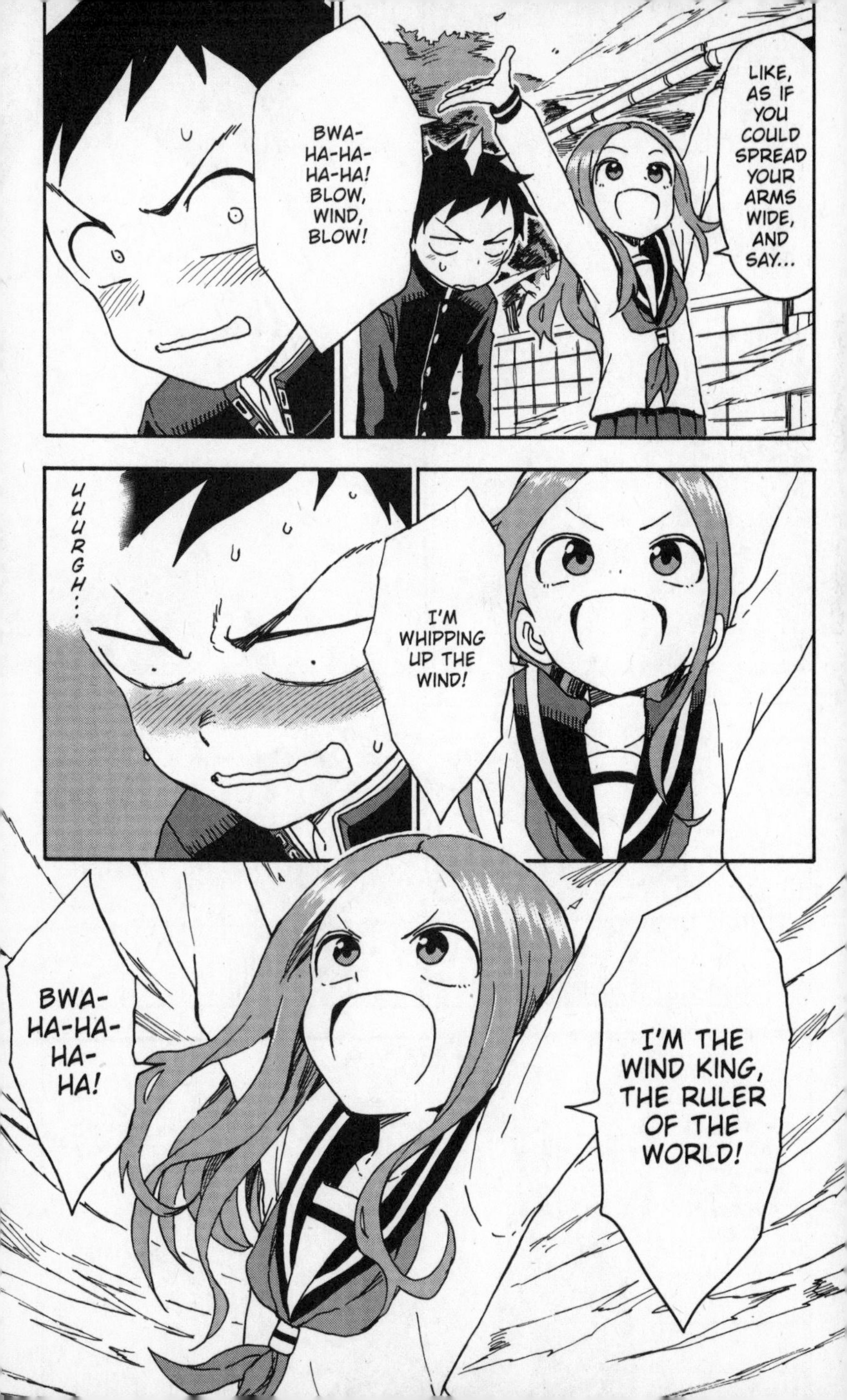
LIKE, AS IF YOU COULD SPREAD YOUR ARMS WIDE, AND SAY...
BWA-HA-HA-HA-HA! BLOW, WIND, BLOW!
I'M WHIPPING UP THE WIND!
UUURGH...
I'M THE WIND KING, THE RULER OF THE WORLD!
BWA-HA-HA-HA-HA!

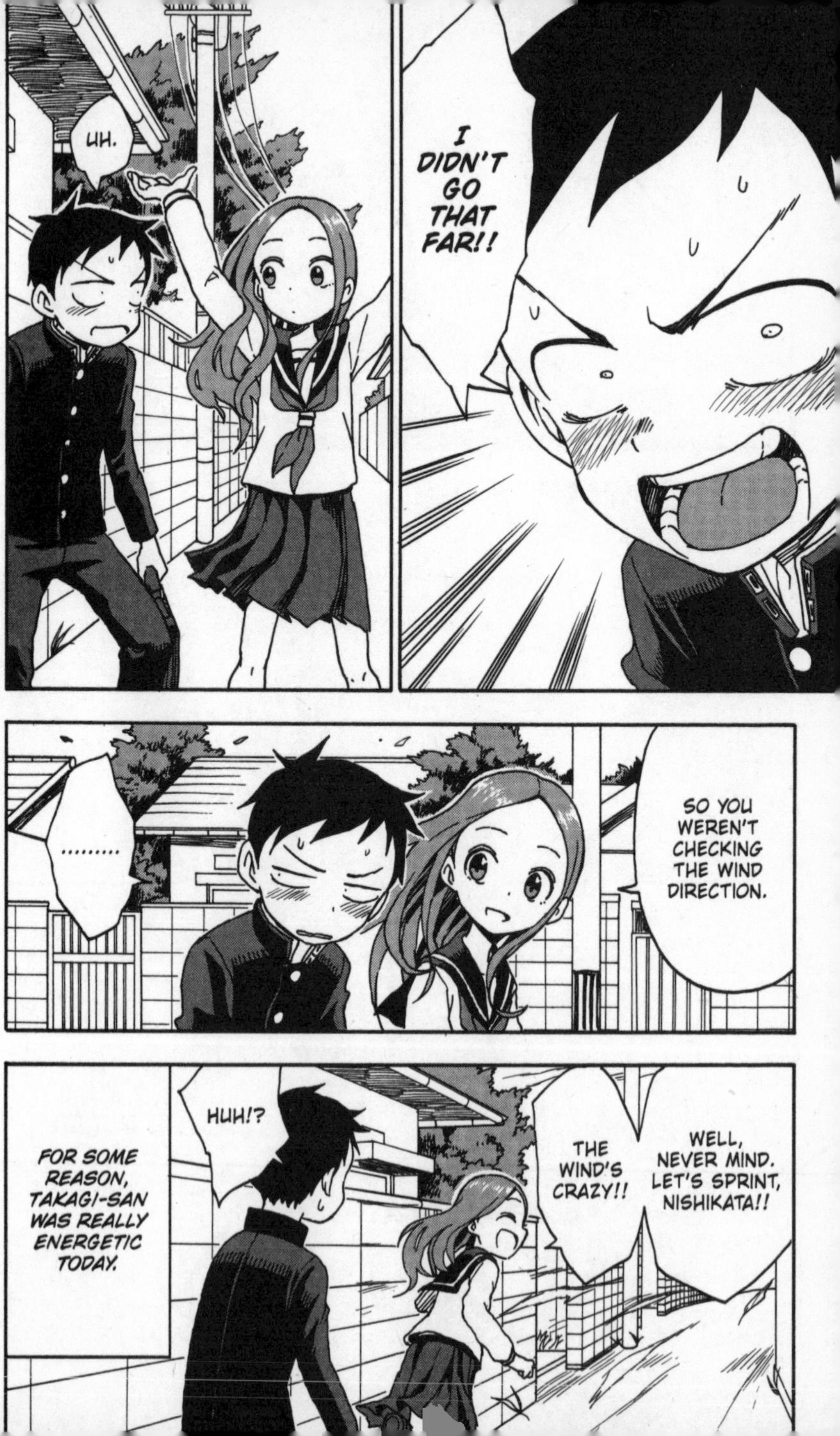
I DIDN'T GO THAT FAR!!
UH.
SO YOU WEREN'T CHECKING THE WIND DIRECTION.
....
WELL, NEVER MIND. LET'S SPRINT, NISHIKATA!!
THE WIND'S CRAZY!!
HUH!?
FOR SOME REASON, TAKAGI-SAN WAS REALLY ENERGETIC TODAY.

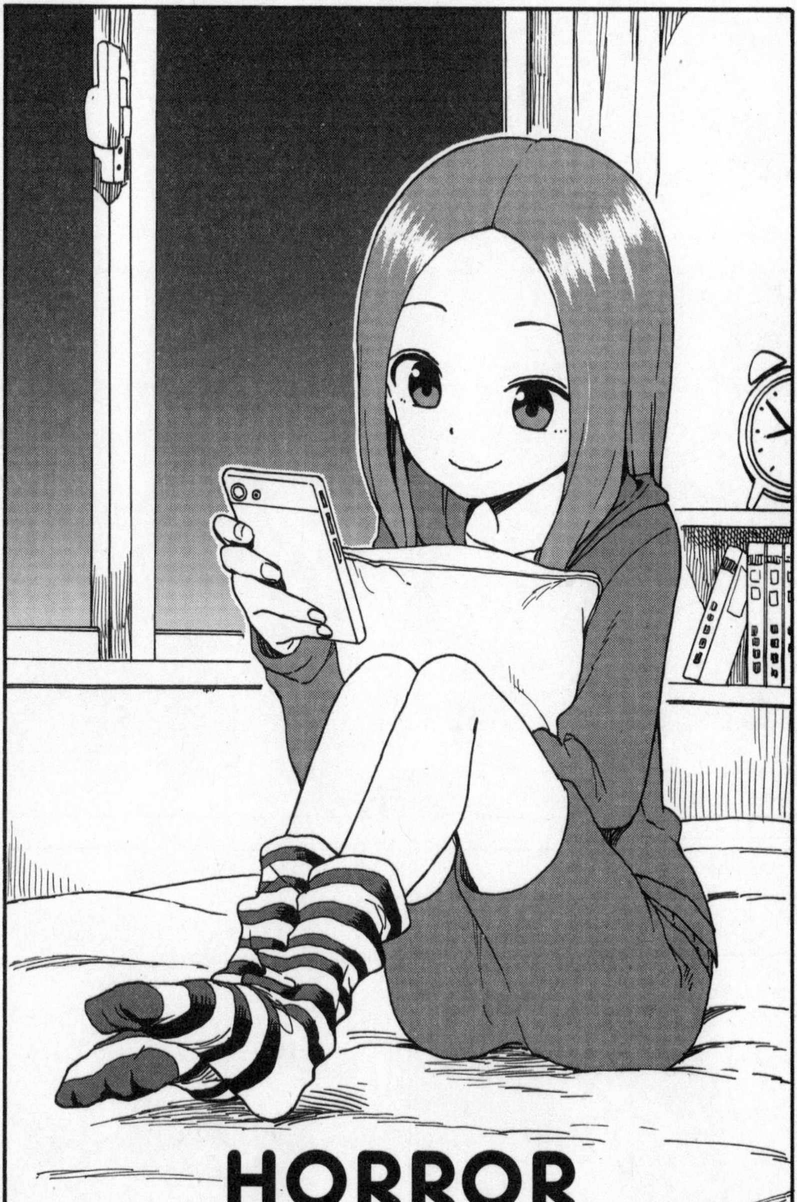
HORROR

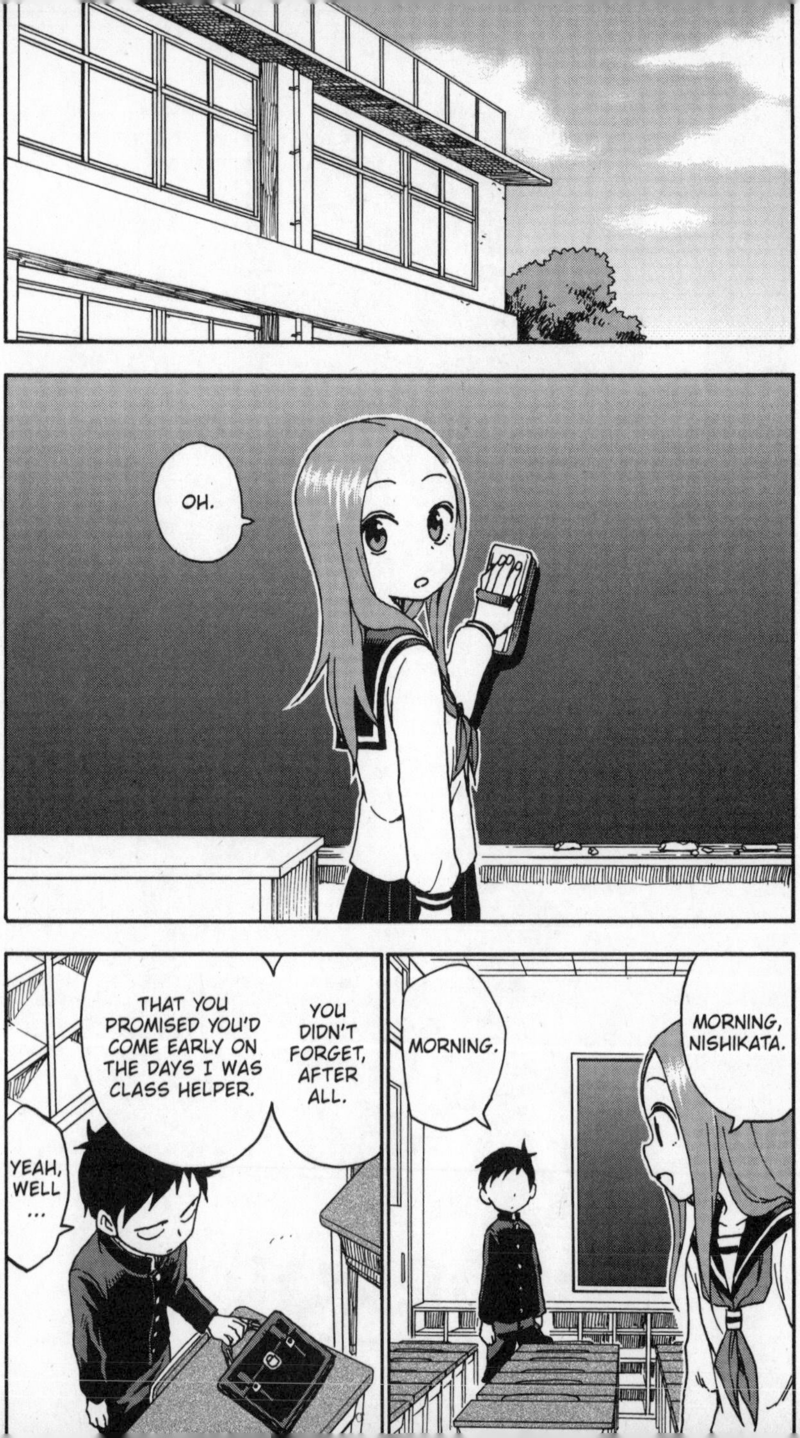
OH.
MORNING, NISHIKATA.
MORNING.
YOU DIDN'T FORGET, AFTER ALL.
THAT YOU PROMISED YOU'D COME EARLY ON THE DAYS I WAS CLASS HELPER.
...
YEAH, WELL ...

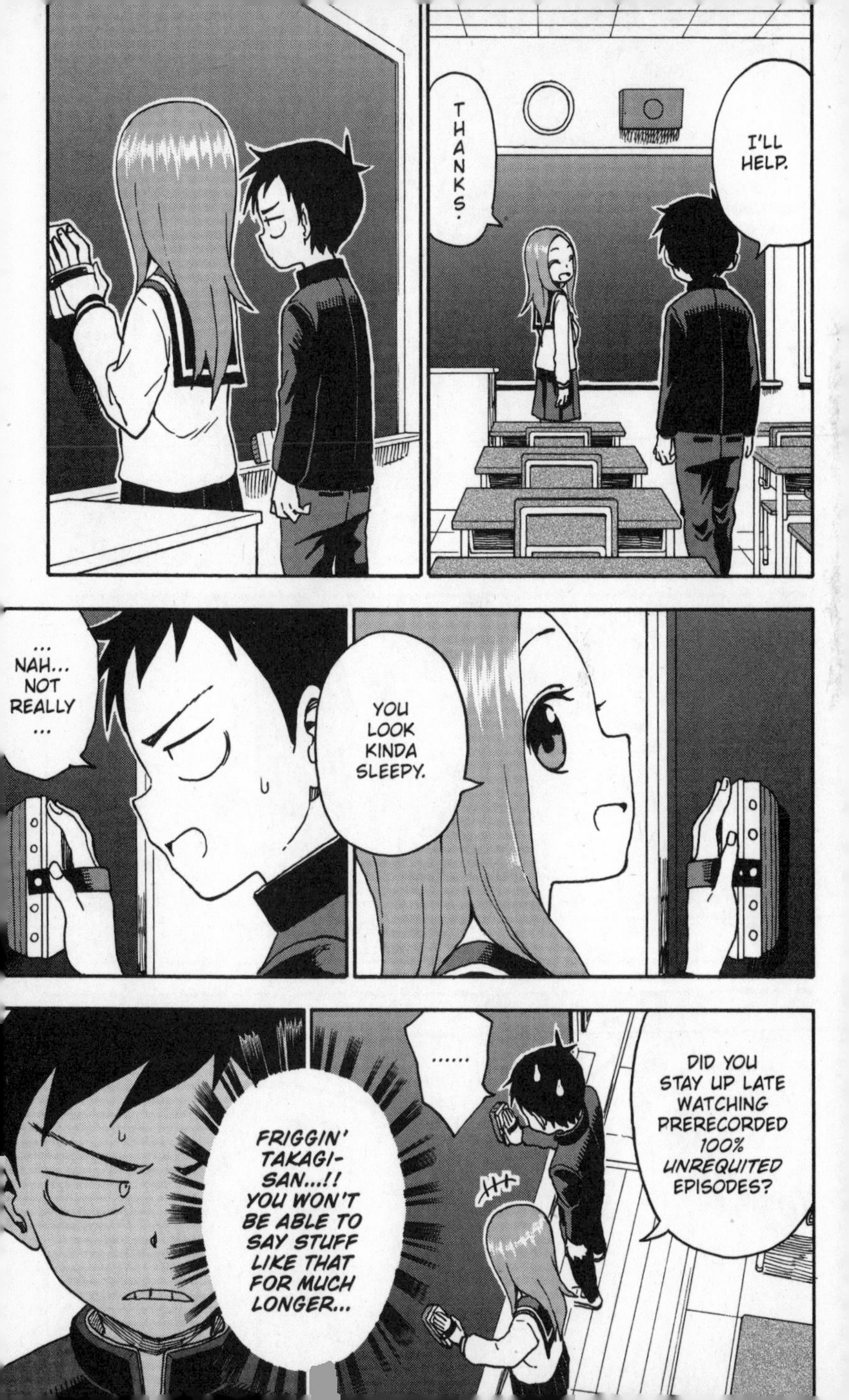
I'LL HELP.
THANKS.
YOU LOOK KINDA SLEEPY.
... NAH... NOT REALLY ...
DID YOU STAY UP LATE WATCHING PRERECORDED 100% UNREQUITED EPISODES?
......
FRIGGIN' TAKAGI-SAN...!! YOU WON'T BE ABLE TO SAY STUFF LIKE THAT FOR MUCH LONGER...

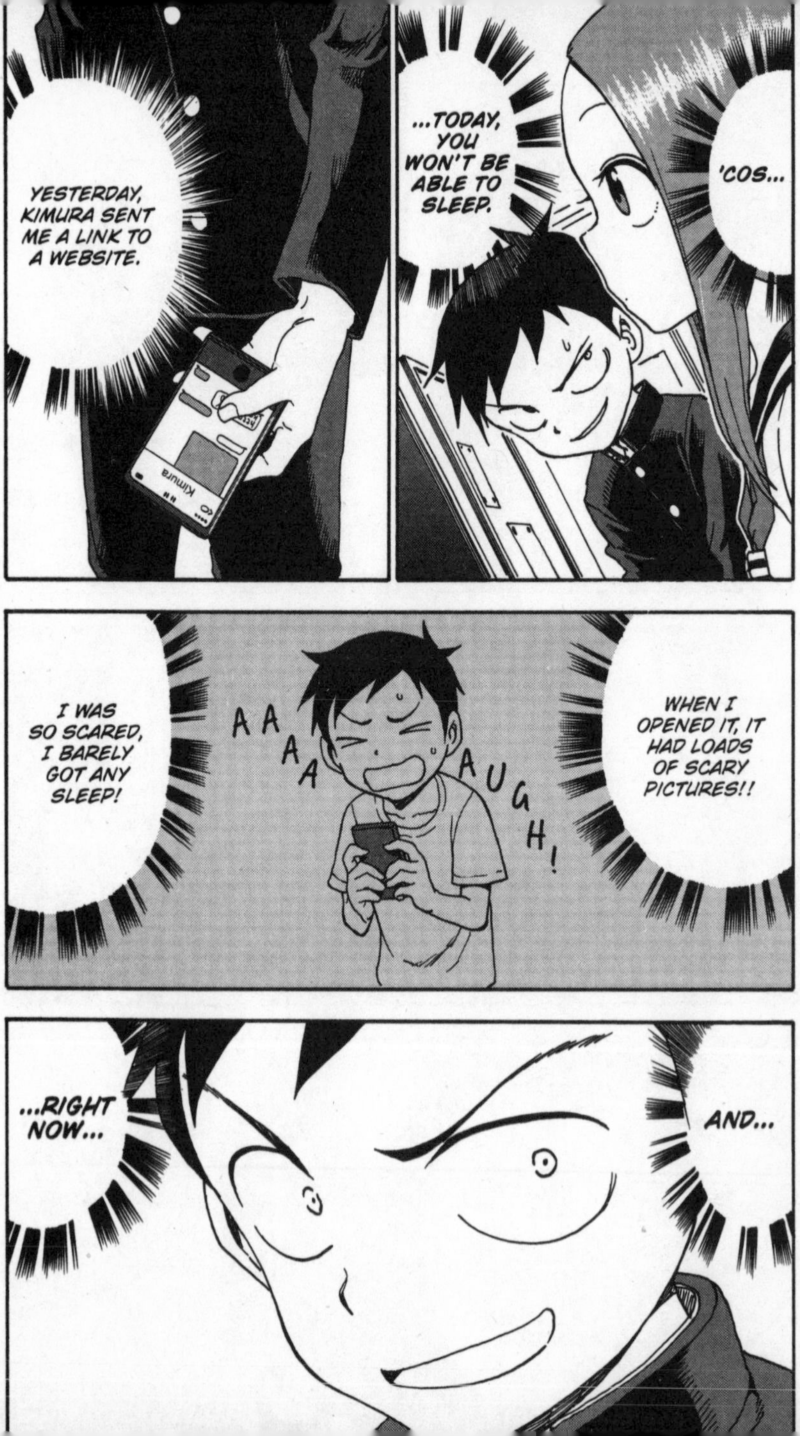
'COS...
...TODAY, YOU WON'T BE ABLE TO SLEEP.
YESTERDAY, KIMURA SENT ME A LINK TO A WEBSITE.
Kimura
WHEN I OPENED IT, IT HAD LOADS OF SCARY PICTURES!!
AAAAAUGH!
I WAS SO SCARED, I BARELY GOT ANY SLEEP!
AND...
...RIGHT NOW...

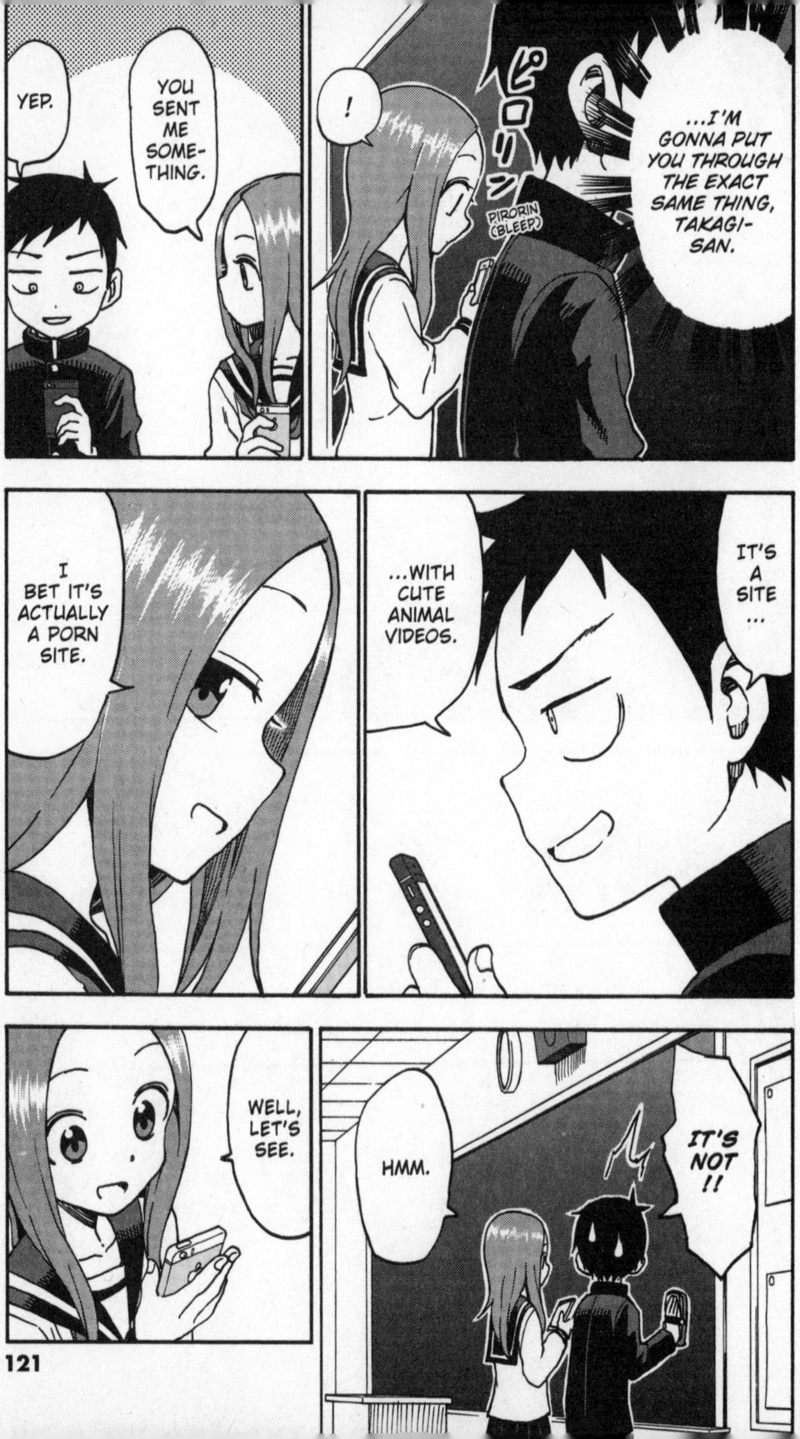
...I'M GONNA PUT YOU THROUGH THE EXACT SAME THING, TAKAGI-SAN.
PIRORIN (BLEEP)
!
YOU SENT ME SOMETHING.
YEP.
IT'S A SITE...
...WITH CUTE ANIMAL VIDEOS.
I BET IT'S ACTUALLY A PORN SITE.
IT'S NOT!!
HMM.
WELL, LET'S SEE.

HEH-HEH-HEH. AND? HOW IS IT? DID IT SCARE YOU SPEECHLESS, TAKAGI-SAN...?

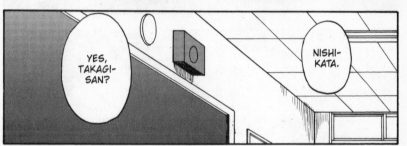

YES, TAKAGI-SAN?

NISHI-KATA.

HUH?

DO YOU ALWAYS LOOK AT THIS SORT OF THING?

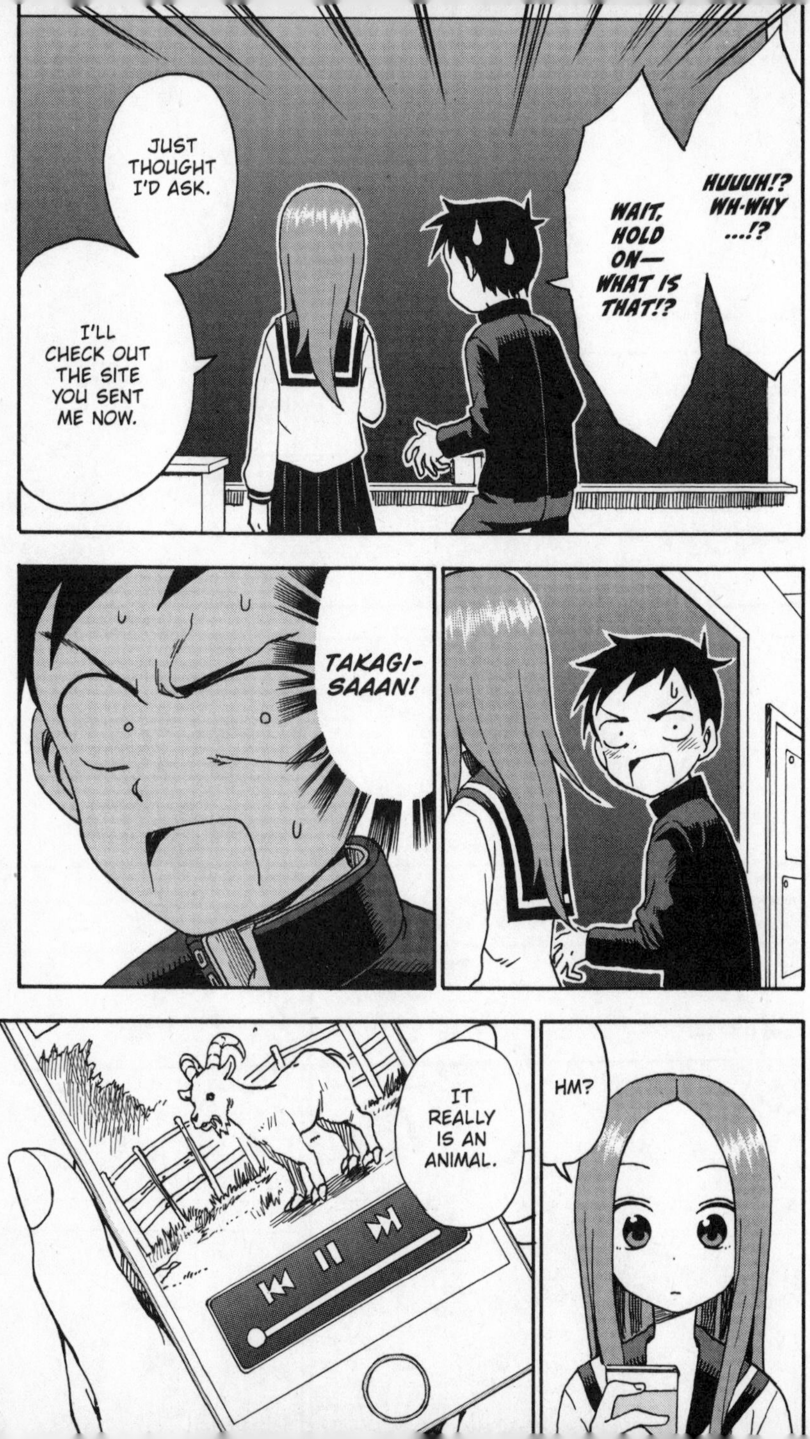
HUUUH!? WH-WHY ...!?
WAIT, HOLD ON— WHAT IS THAT!?
JUST THOUGHT I'D ASK.
I'LL CHECK OUT THE SITE YOU SENT ME NOW.
TAKAGI-SAAAN!
HM?
IT REALLY IS AN ANIMAL.

YOU LET YOUR GUARD DOWN, TAKAGI-SAN.

OH! IT'S SO CUTE.

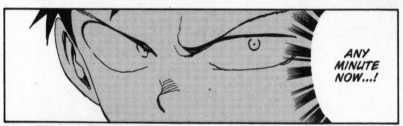

ANY MINUTE NOW...!

YES... GO!!

BURU (SHUDDER)

BURU

GOKI (CRACK)

GOKI

PI

PIKU (FLINCH)

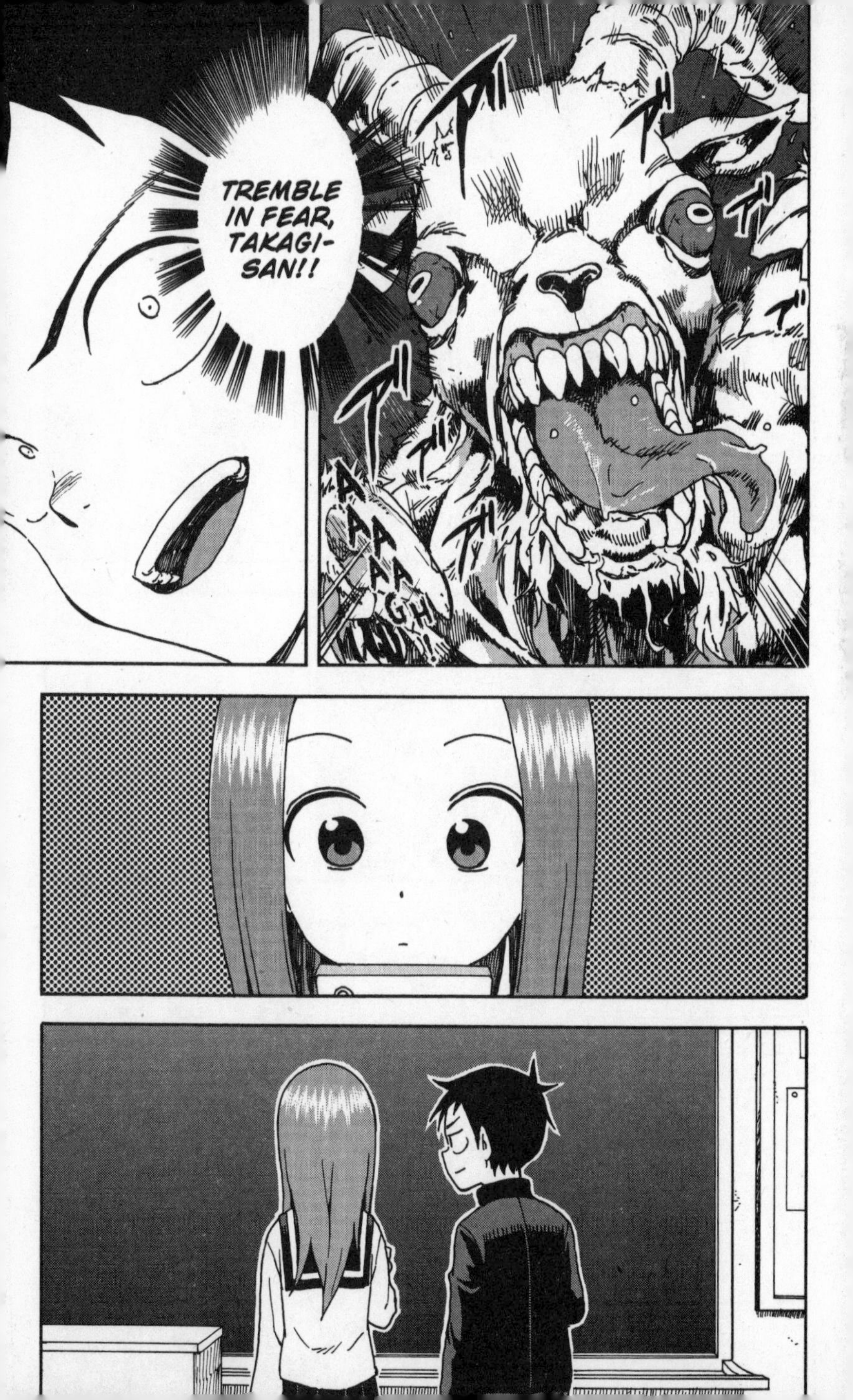
AAAAAGH!!
TREMBLE IN FEAR, TAKAGI-SAN!!

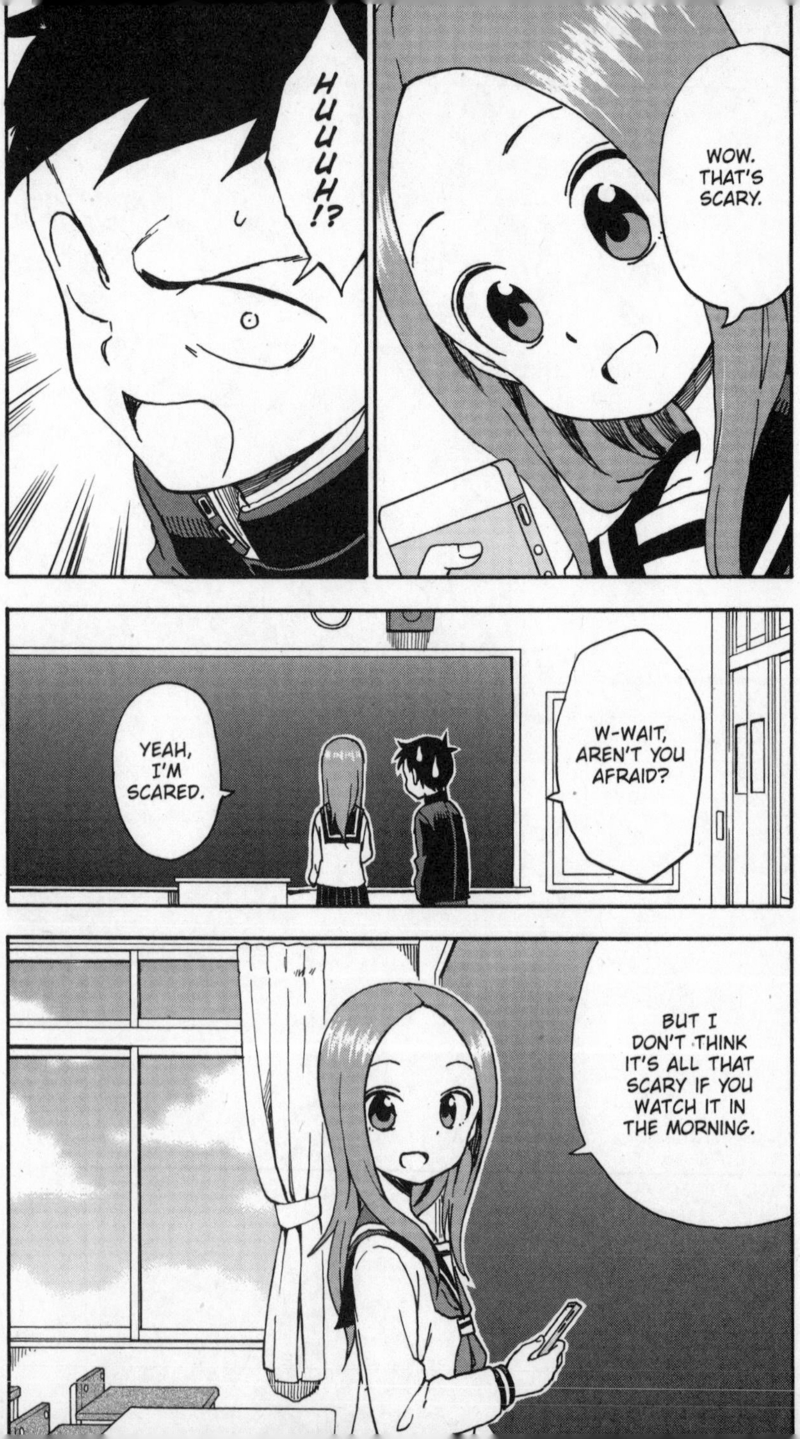
WOW. THAT'S SCARY.
HUUUUH!?
W-WAIT, AREN'T YOU AFRAID?
YEAH, I'M SCARED.
BUT I DON'T THINK IT'S ALL THAT SCARY IF YOU WATCH IT IN THE MORNING.

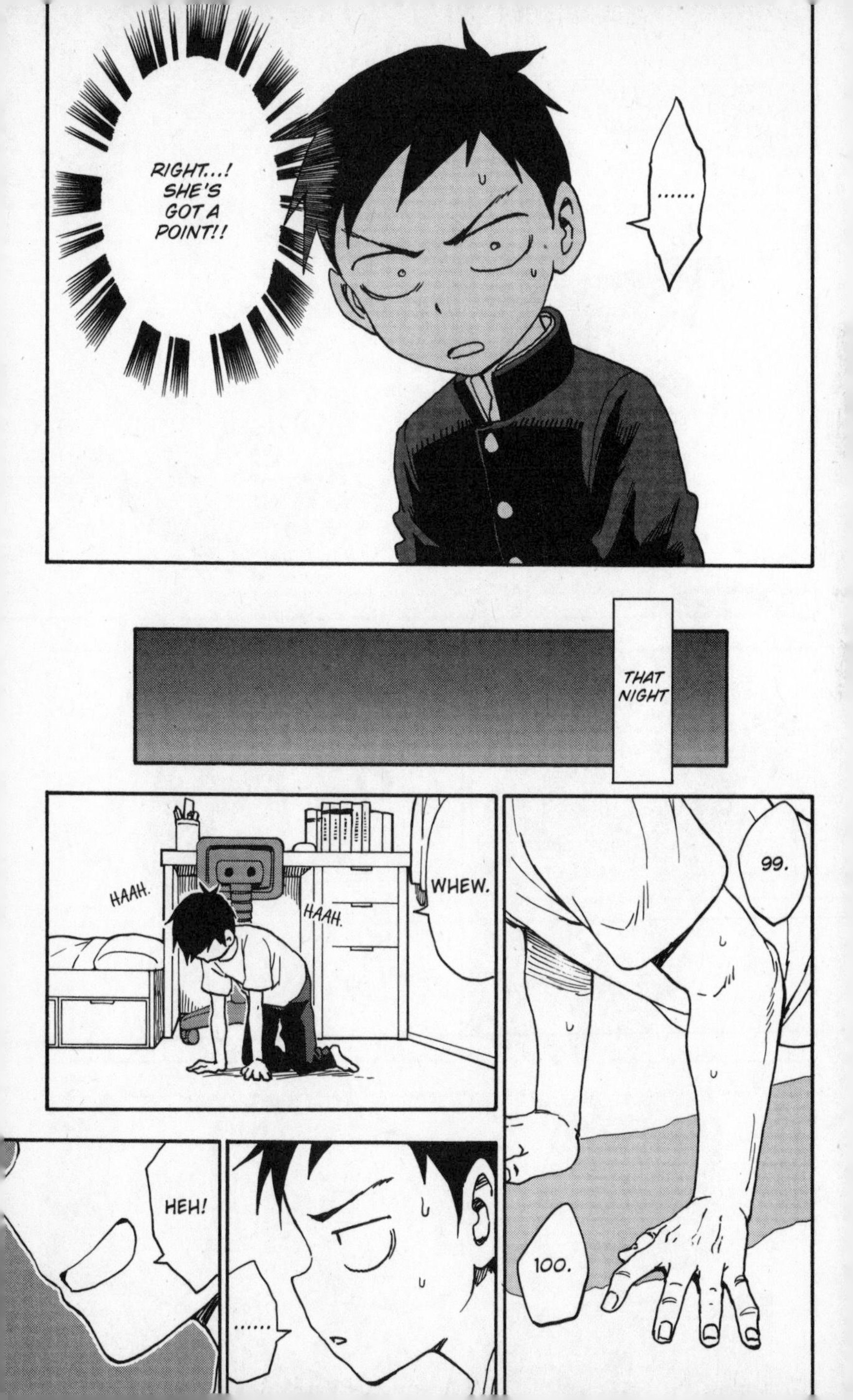
......
RIGHT...! SHE'S GOT A POINT!!
THAT NIGHT
99.
100.
WHEW.
HAAH.
HAAH.
......
HEH!

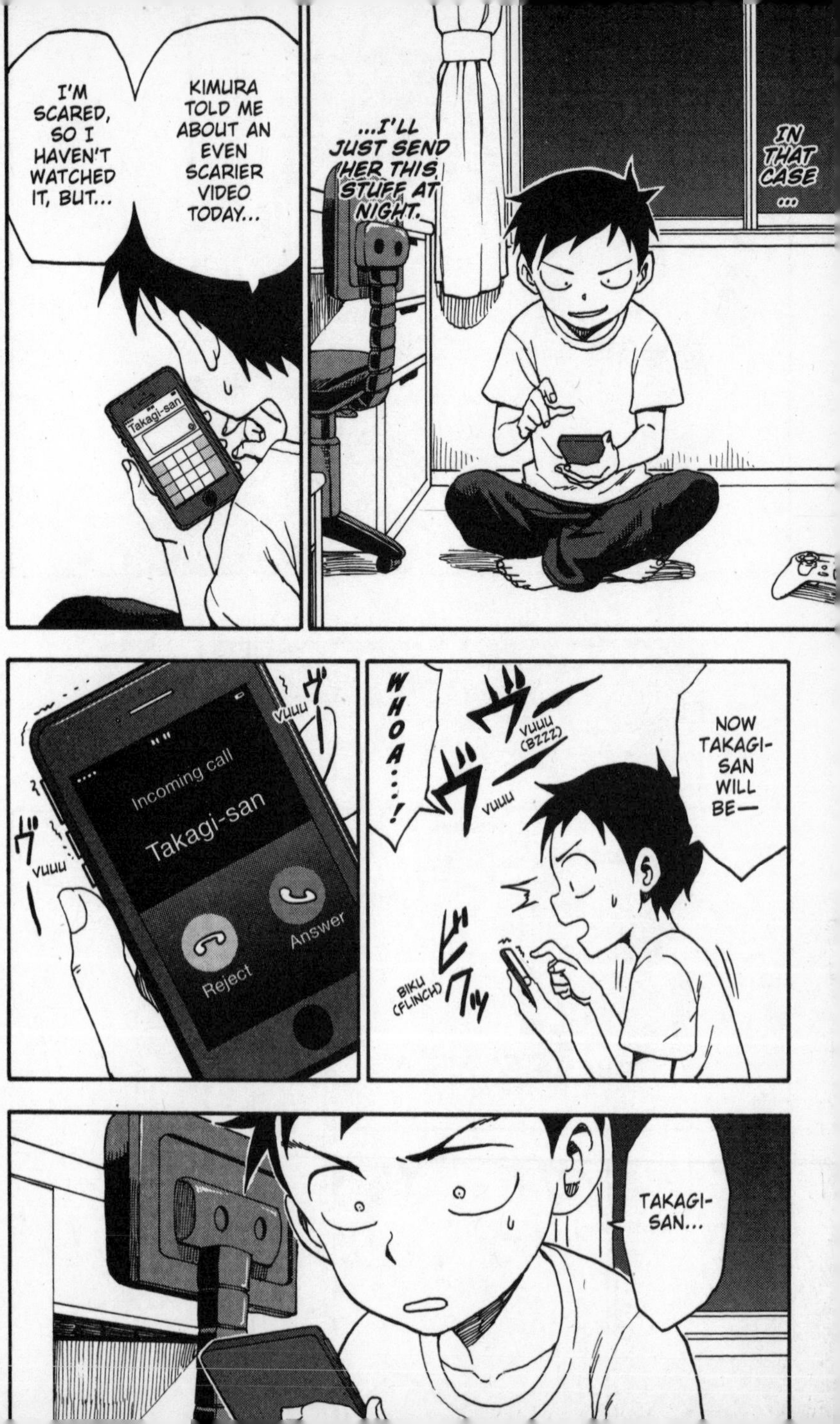
IN THAT CASE...
...I'LL JUST SEND HER THIS STUFF AT NIGHT.
KIMURA TOLD ME ABOUT AN EVEN SCARIER VIDEO TODAY...
I'M SCARED, SO I HAVEN'T WATCHED IT, BUT...
Takagi-san
NOW TAKAGI-SAN WILL BE—
VUUU (BZZZ)
WHOA...!
VUUU
BIKU (FLINCH)
VUUU
Incoming call
Takagi-san
Answer
Reject
VUUU
TAKAGI-SAN...

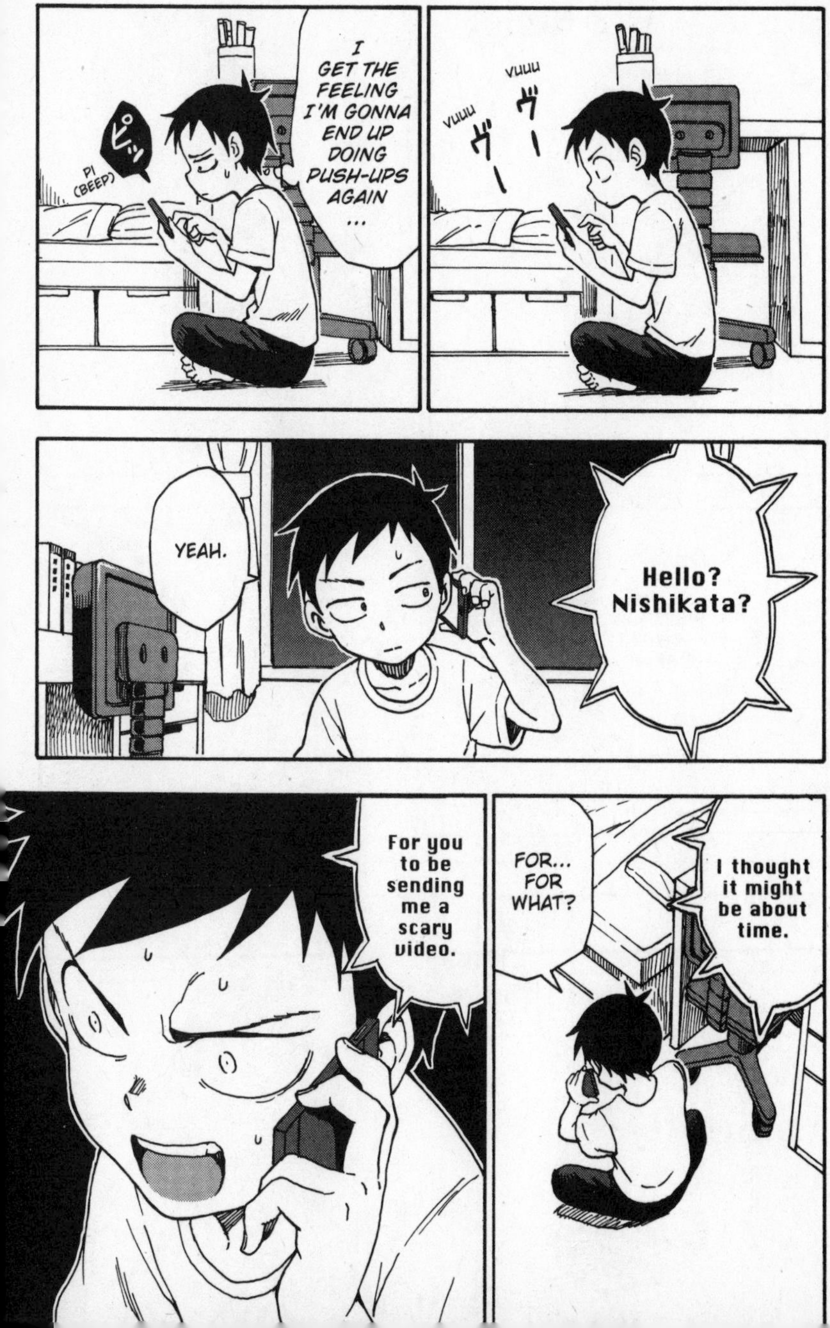

VUUU
ヴー
VUUU
ヴー
ピッ
PI (BEEP)
I GET THE FEELING I'M GONNA END UP DOING PUSH-UPS AGAIN ...
Hello? Nishikata?
YEAH.
I thought it might be about time.
FOR... FOR WHAT?
For you to be sending me a scary video.

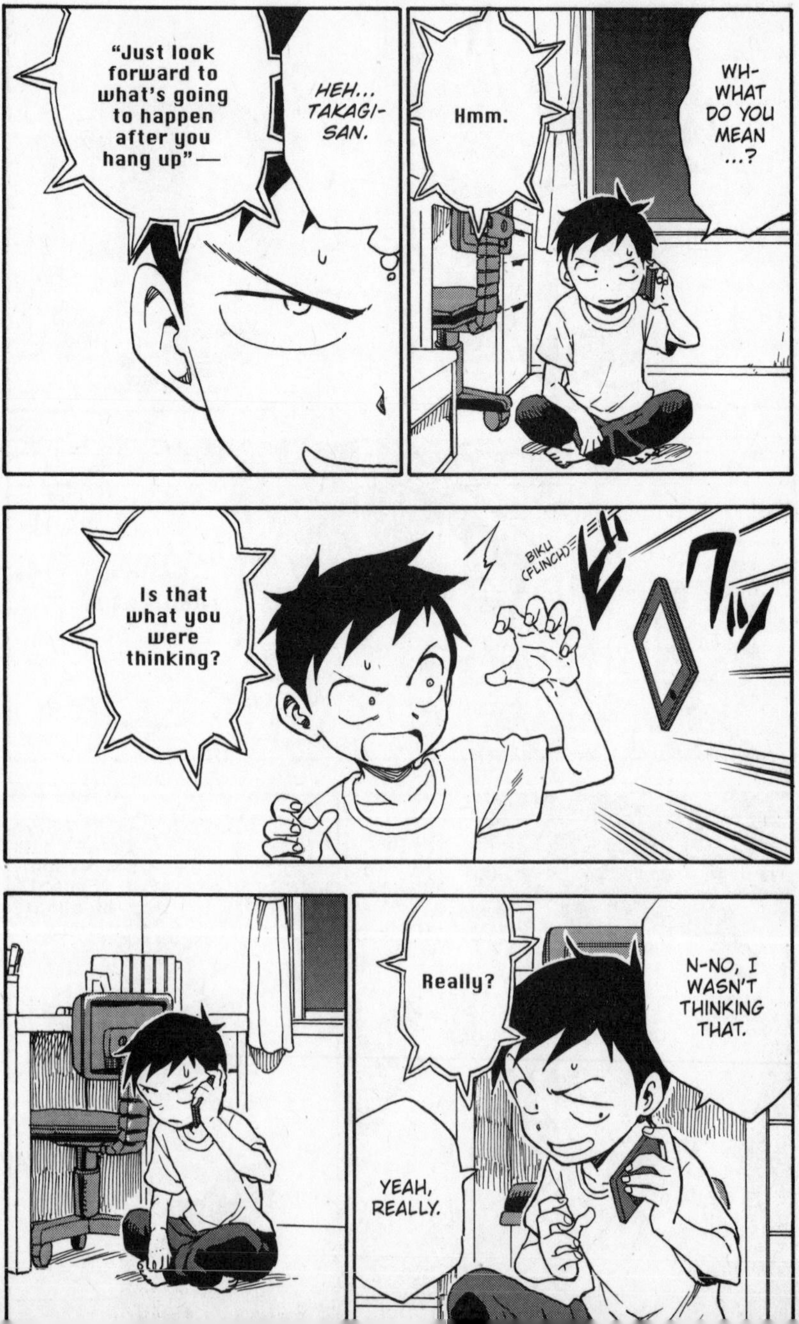
WH-WHAT DO YOU MEAN ...?
Hmm.
HEH... TAKAGI-SAN.
"Just look forward to what's going to happen after you hang up"—
BIKU (FLINCH)
Is that what you were thinking?
N-NO, I WASN'T THINKING THAT.
Really?
YEAH, REALLY.

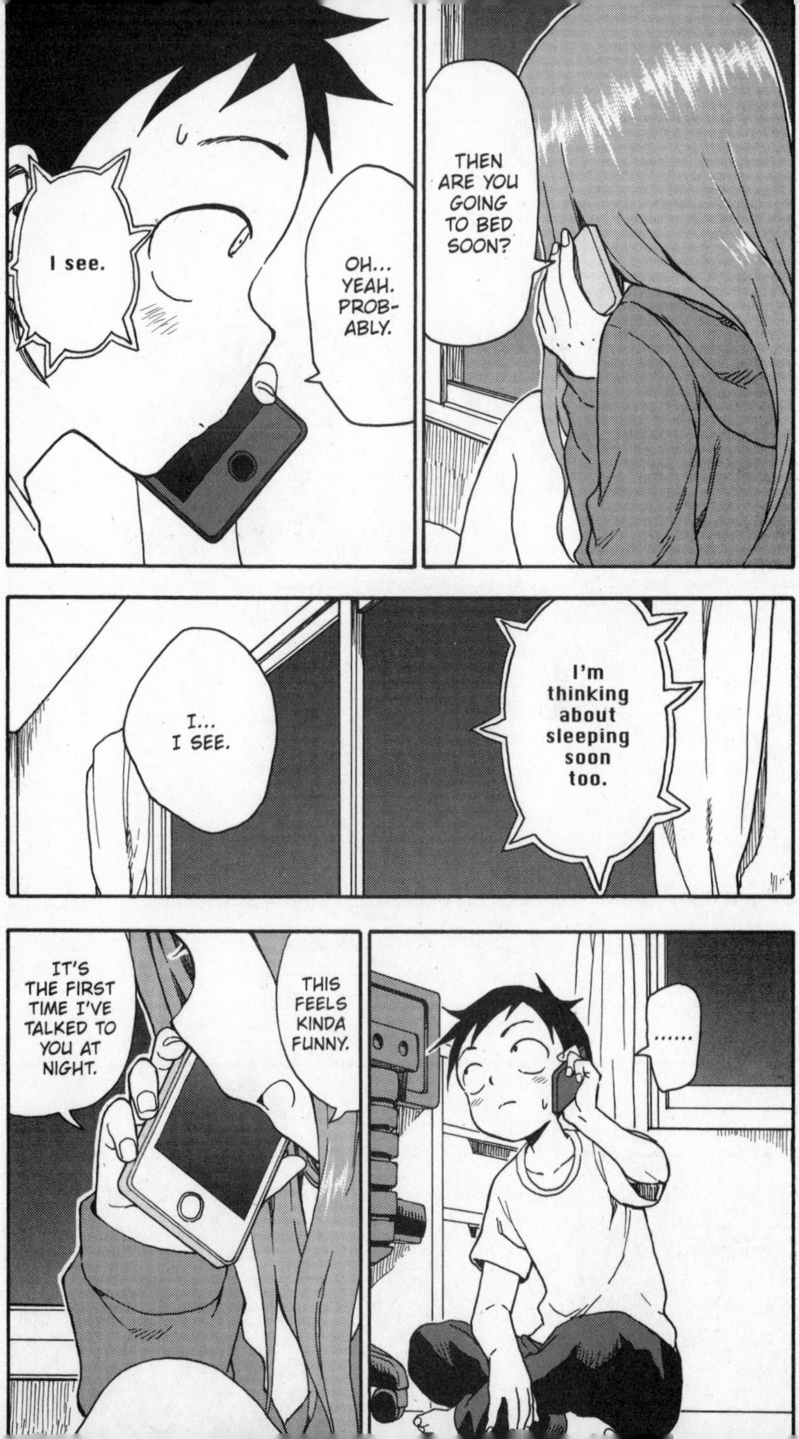
THEN ARE YOU GOING TO BED SOON?
OH... YEAH. PROBABLY.
I see.
I'm thinking about sleeping soon too.
I... I SEE.
......
THIS FEELS KINDA FUNNY.
IT'S THE FIRST TIME I'VE TALKED TO YOU AT NIGHT.

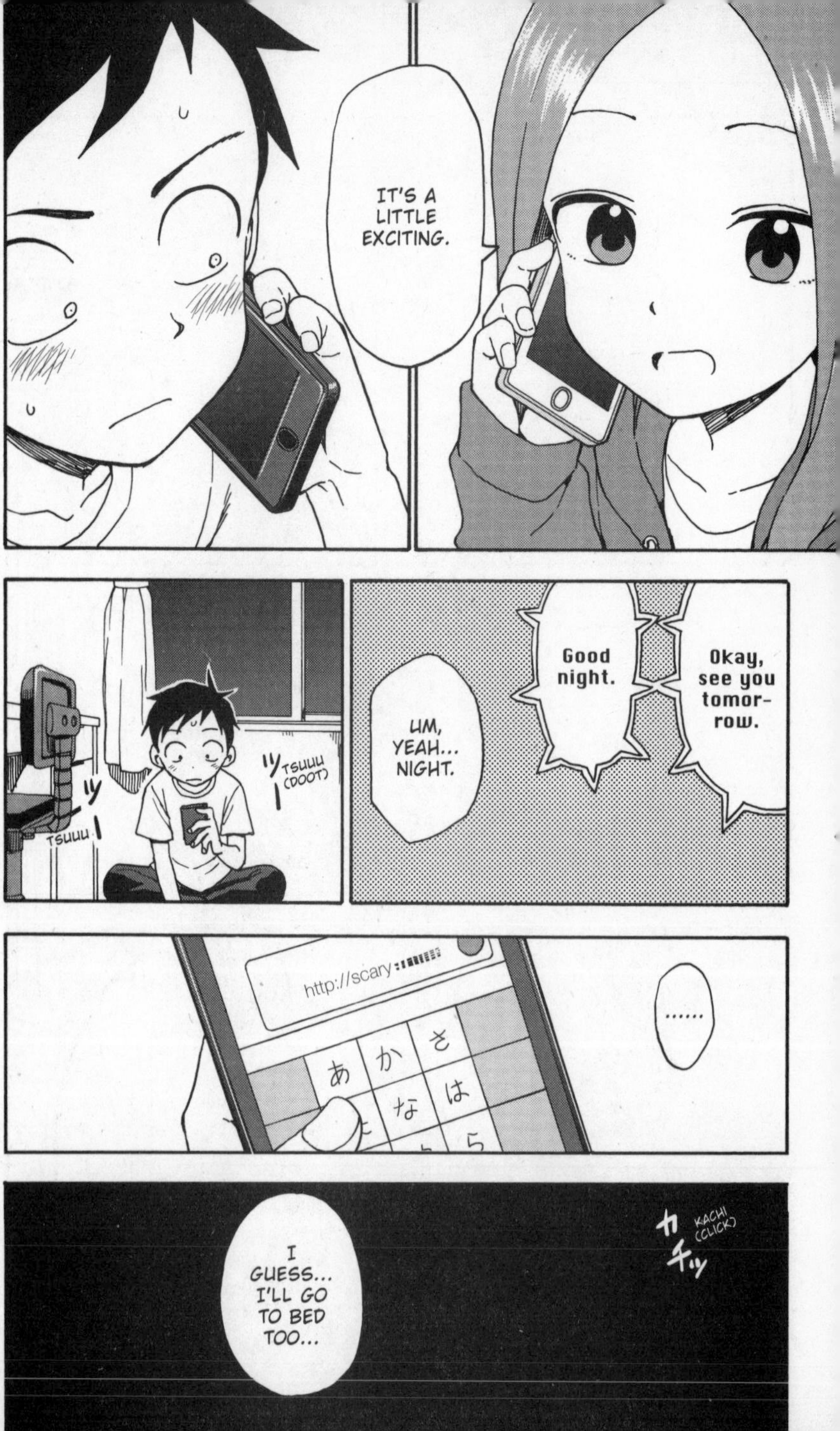

IT'S A LITTLE EXCITING.
Okay, see you tomor-row.
Good night.
UM, YEAH... NIGHT.
ツー TSUUU (DOOT)
ツー TSUUU
http://scary
......
KACHI (CLICK)
I GUESS... I'LL GO TO BED TOO...

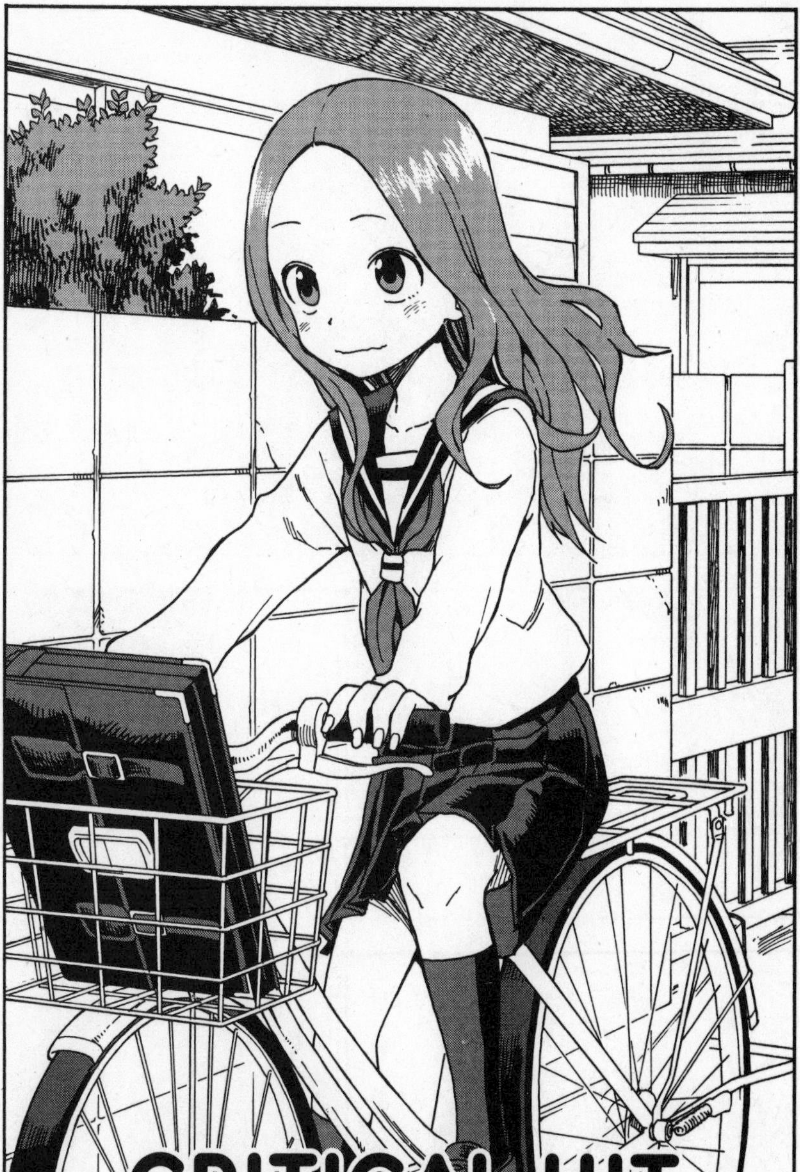
CRITICAL HIT

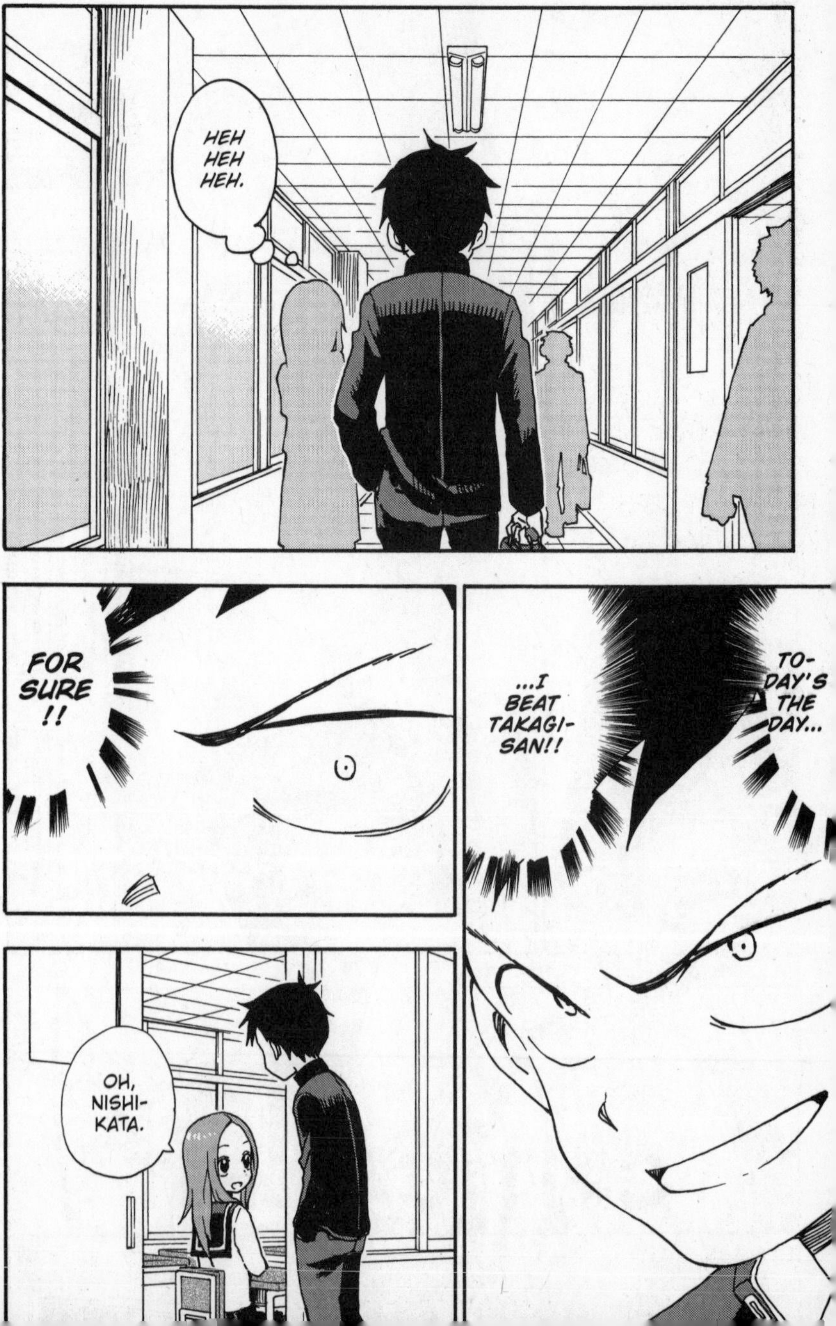
HEH HEH HEH.
TO-DAY'S THE DAY...
...I BEAT TAKAGI-SAN!!
FOR SURE!!
OH, NISHI-KATA.

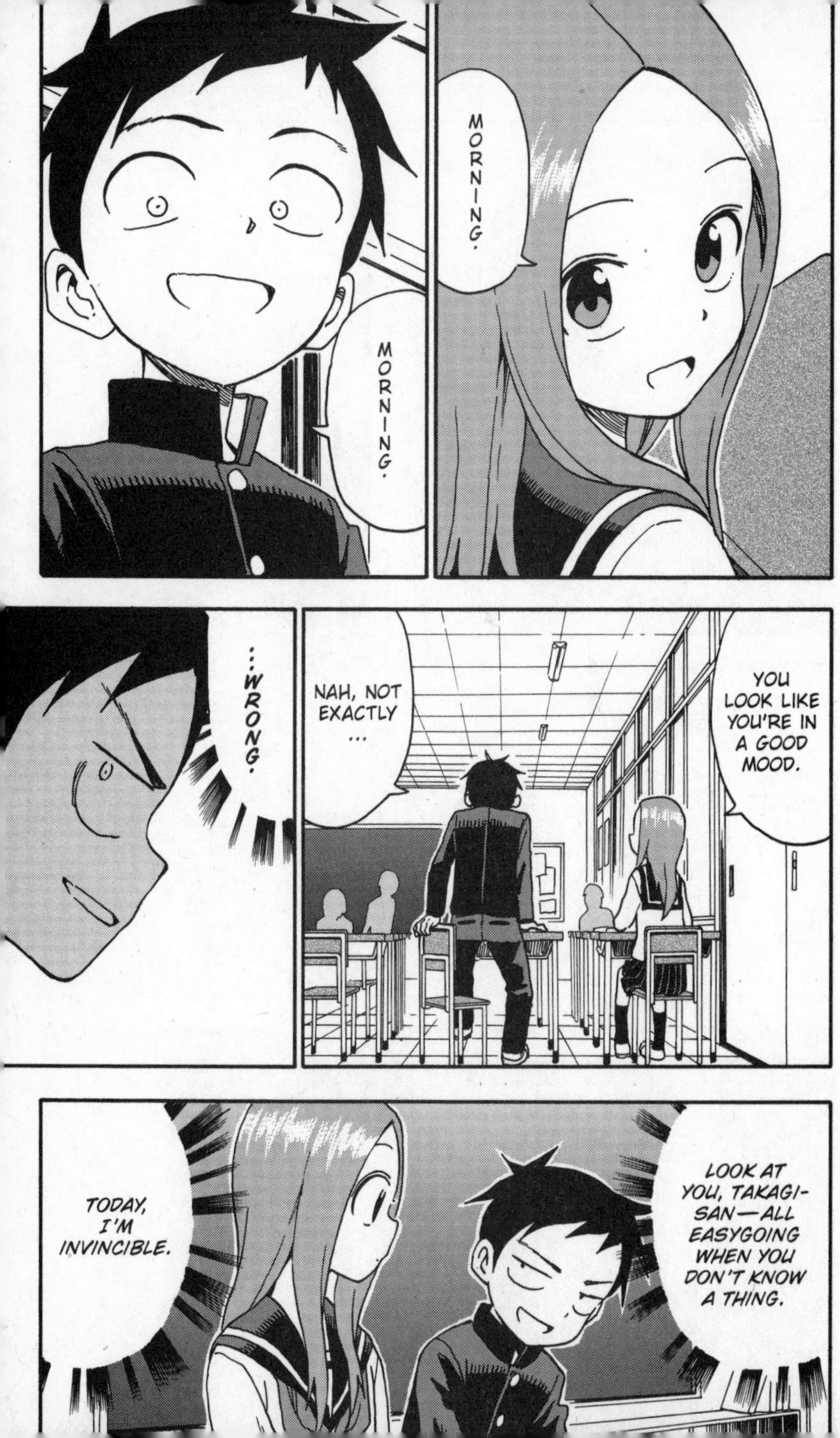
MORNING.
MORNING.
YOU LOOK LIKE YOU'RE IN A GOOD MOOD.
NAH, NOT EXACTLY ...
...WRONG.
LOOK AT YOU, TAKAGI-SAN—ALL EASYGOING WHEN YOU DON'T KNOW A THING.
TODAY, I'M INVINCIBLE.

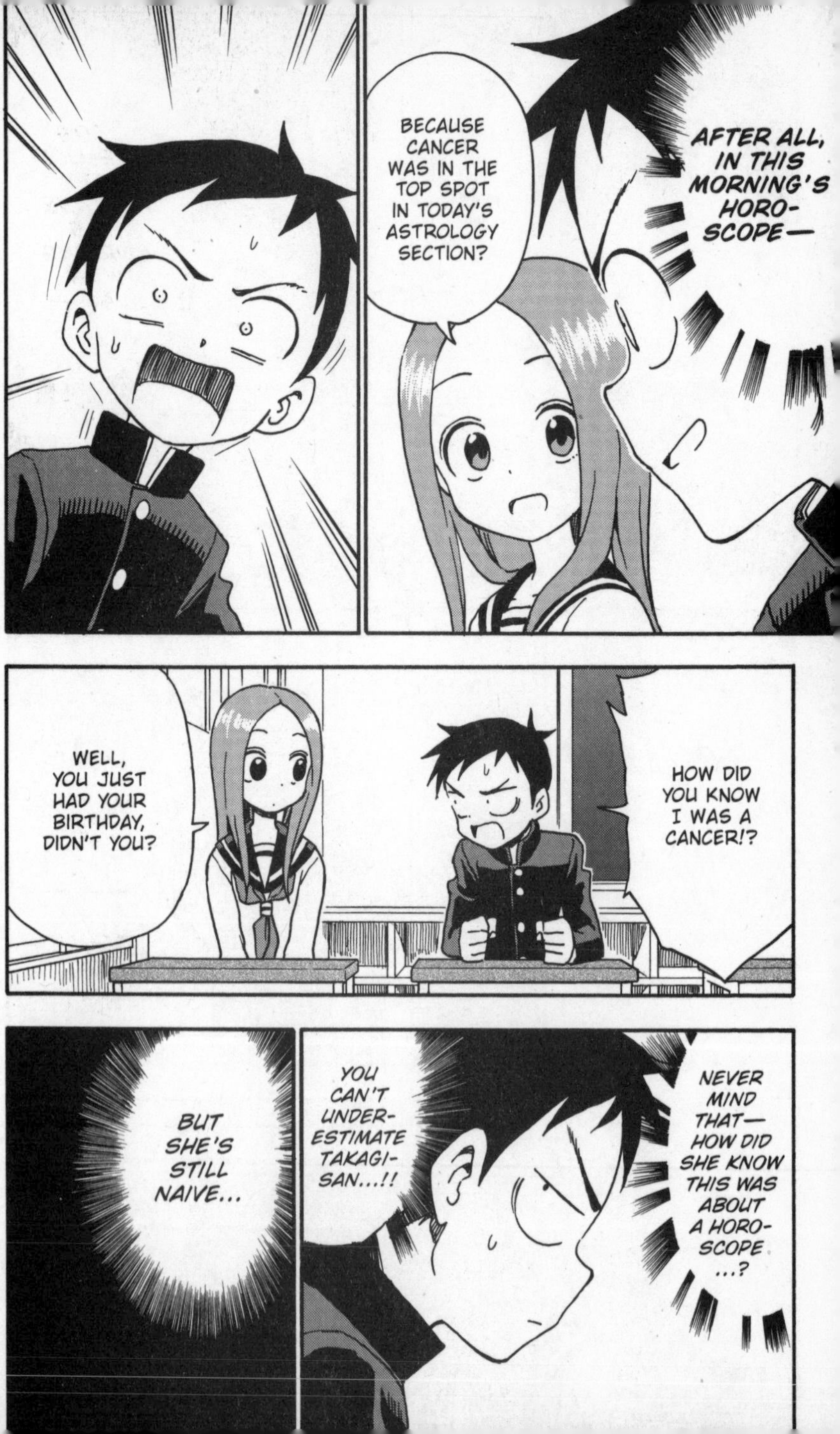
AFTER ALL, IN THIS MORNING'S HORO-SCOPE—
BECAUSE CANCER WAS IN THE TOP SPOT IN TODAY'S ASTROLOGY SECTION?
HOW DID YOU KNOW I WAS A CANCER!?
WELL, YOU JUST HAD YOUR BIRTHDAY, DIDN'T YOU?
NEVER MIND THAT—HOW DID SHE KNOW THIS WAS ABOUT A HORO-SCOPE ...?
YOU CAN'T UNDER-ESTIMATE TAKAGI-SAN...!!
BUT SHE'S STILL NAIVE...

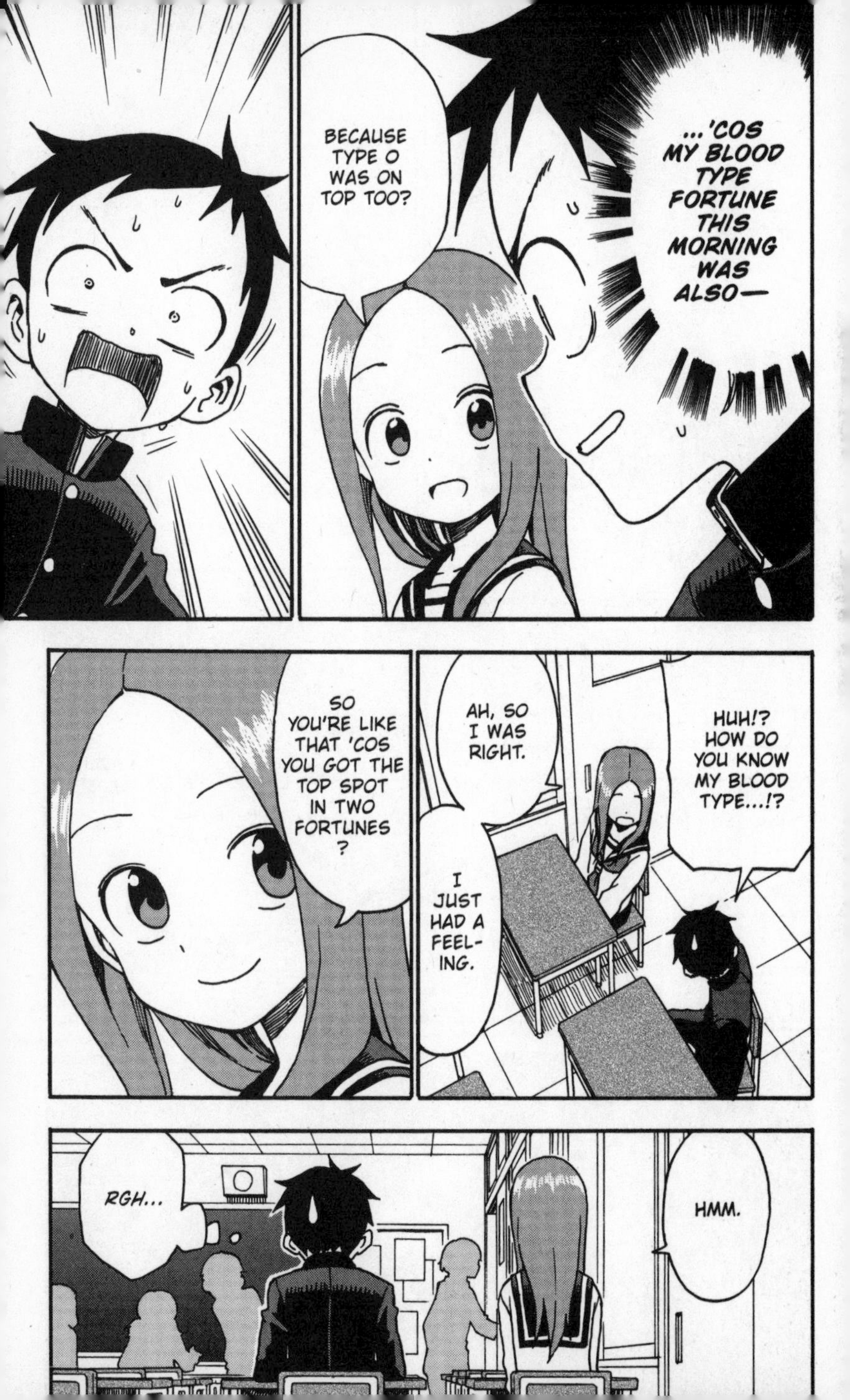
...'COS MY BLOOD TYPE FORTUNE THIS MORNING WAS ALSO—
BECAUSE TYPE O WAS ON TOP TOO?
HUH!? HOW DO YOU KNOW MY BLOOD TYPE...!?
AH, SO I WAS RIGHT.
I JUST HAD A FEEL-ING.
SO YOU'RE LIKE THAT 'COS YOU GOT THE TOP SPOT IN TWO FORTUNES?
HMM.
RGH...

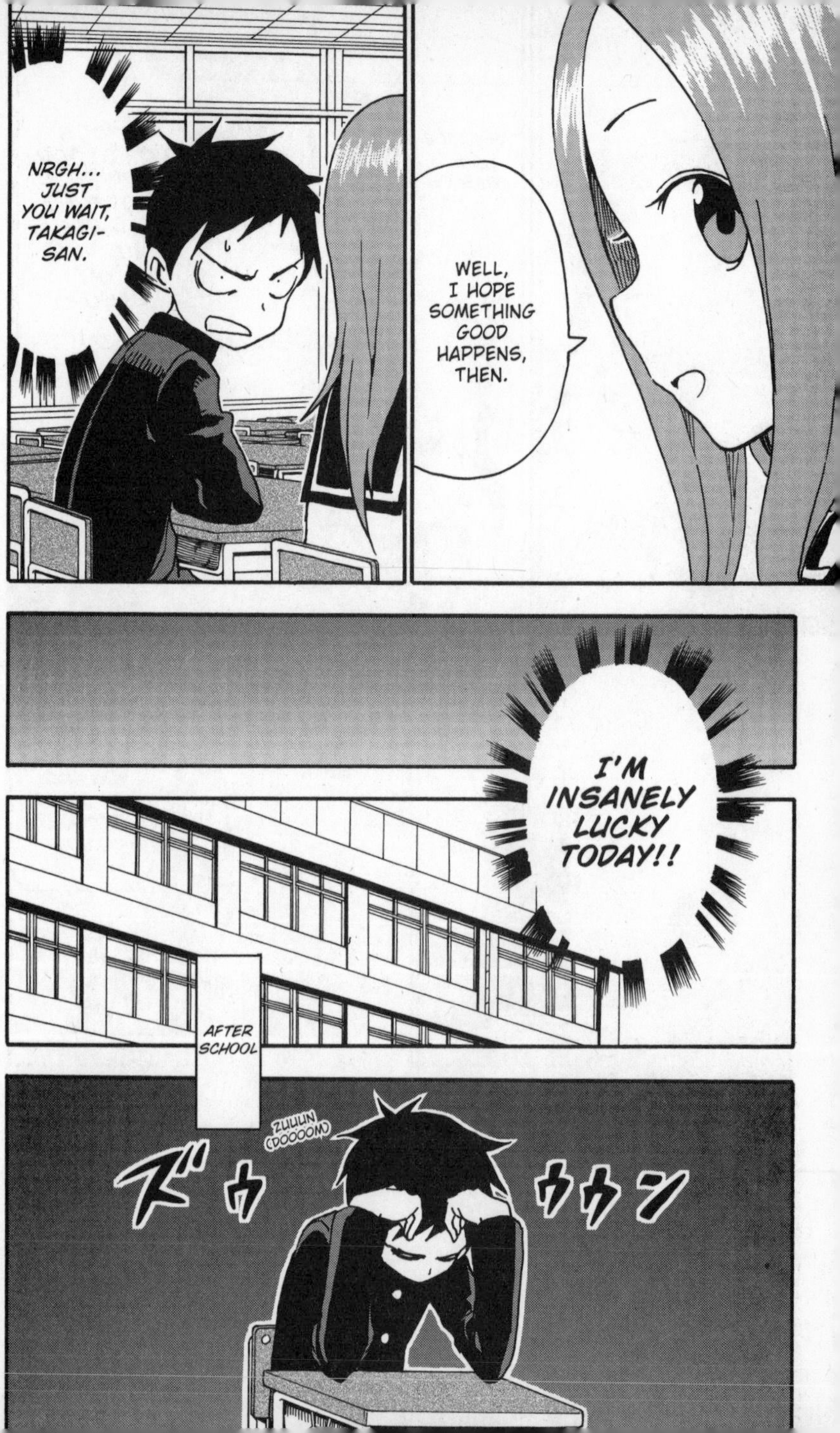
WELL, I HOPE SOMETHING GOOD HAPPENS, THEN.
NRGH... JUST YOU WAIT, TAKAGI-SAN.
I'M INSANELY LUCKY TODAY!!
AFTER SCHOOL
ZUUUN (DOOOOM)

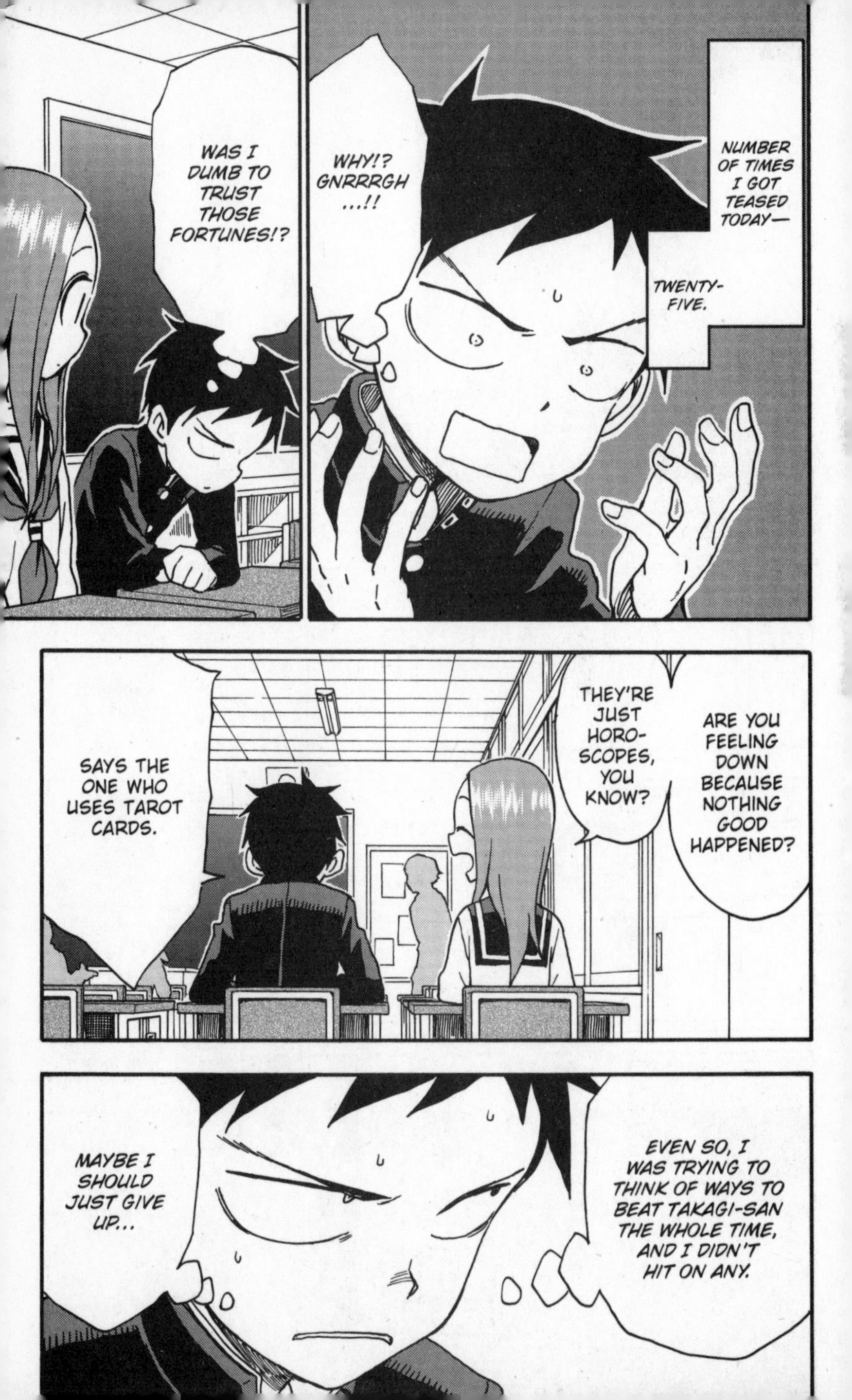
NUMBER OF TIMES I GOT TEASED TODAY—
TWENTY-FIVE.
WHY!? GNRRRGH ...!!
WAS I DUMB TO TRUST THOSE FORTUNES!?
ARE YOU FEELING DOWN BECAUSE NOTHING GOOD HAPPENED?
THEY'RE JUST HORO-SCOPES, YOU KNOW?
SAYS THE ONE WHO USES TAROT CARDS.
EVEN SO, I WAS TRYING TO THINK OF WAYS TO BEAT TAKAGI-SAN THE WHOLE TIME, AND I DIDN'T HIT ON ANY.
MAYBE I SHOULD JUST GIVE UP...

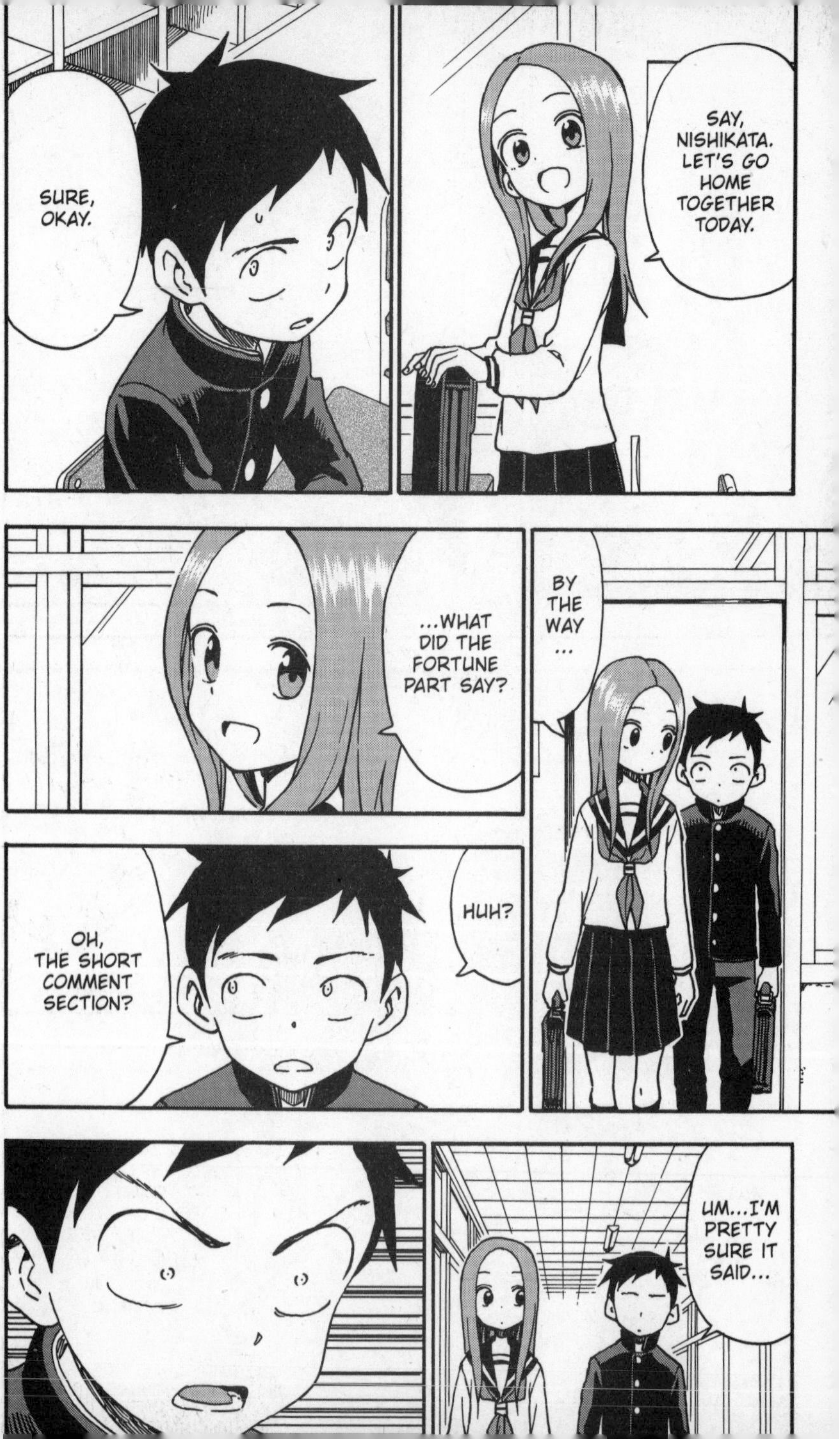
SAY, NISHIKATA. LET'S GO HOME TOGETHER TODAY.
SURE, OKAY.
BY THE WAY...
...WHAT DID THE FORTUNE PART SAY?
HUH?
OH, THE SHORT COMMENT SECTION?
UM...I'M PRETTY SURE IT SAID...

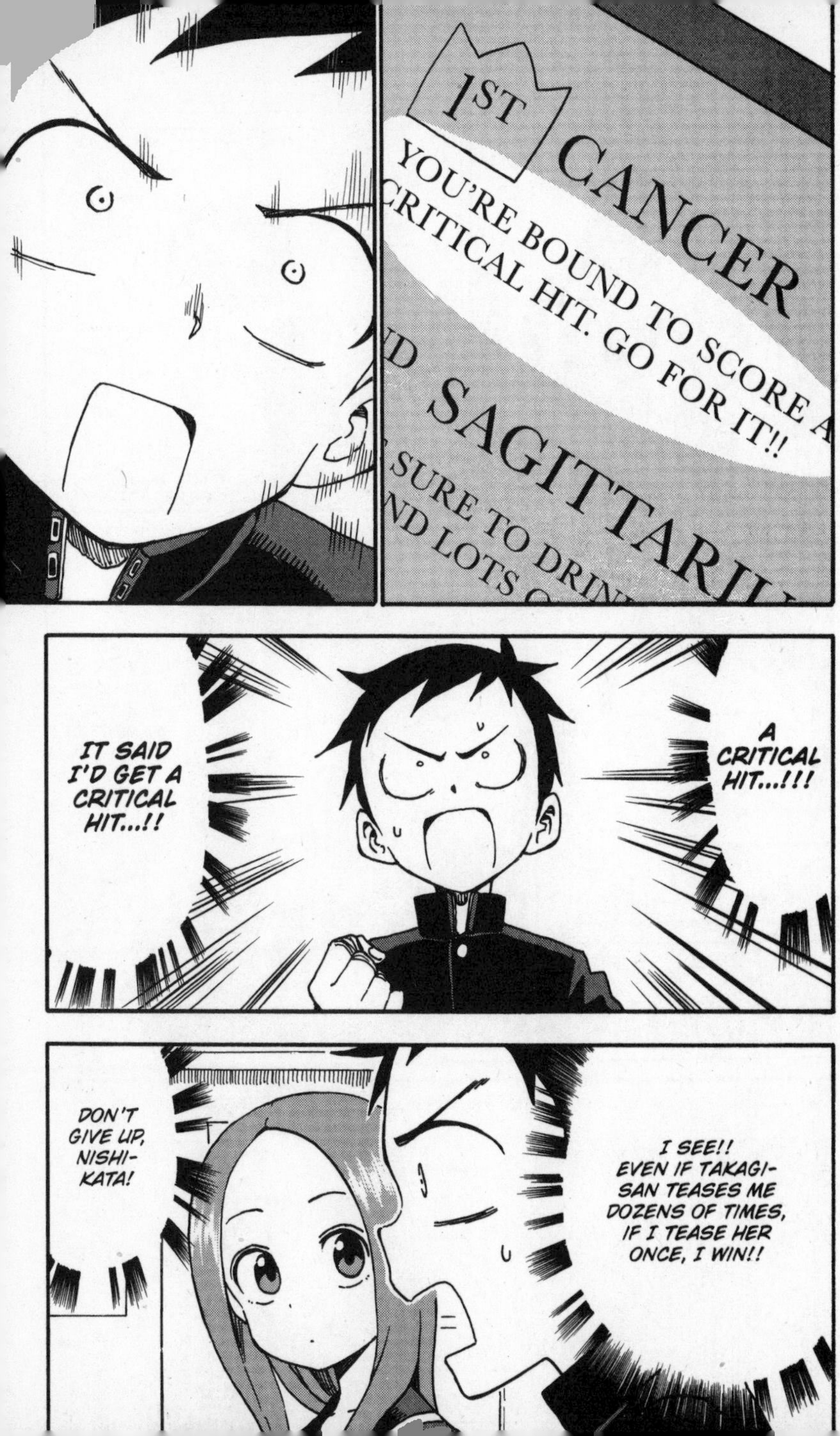
1ST
CANCER
YOU'RE BOUND TO SCORE A CRITICAL HIT. GO FOR IT!!
A CRITICAL HIT...!!!
IT SAID I'D GET A CRITICAL HIT...!!
I SEE!! EVEN IF TAKAGI-SAN TEASES ME DOZENS OF TIMES, IF I TEASE HER ONCE, I WIN!!
DON'T GIVE UP, NISHI-KATA!

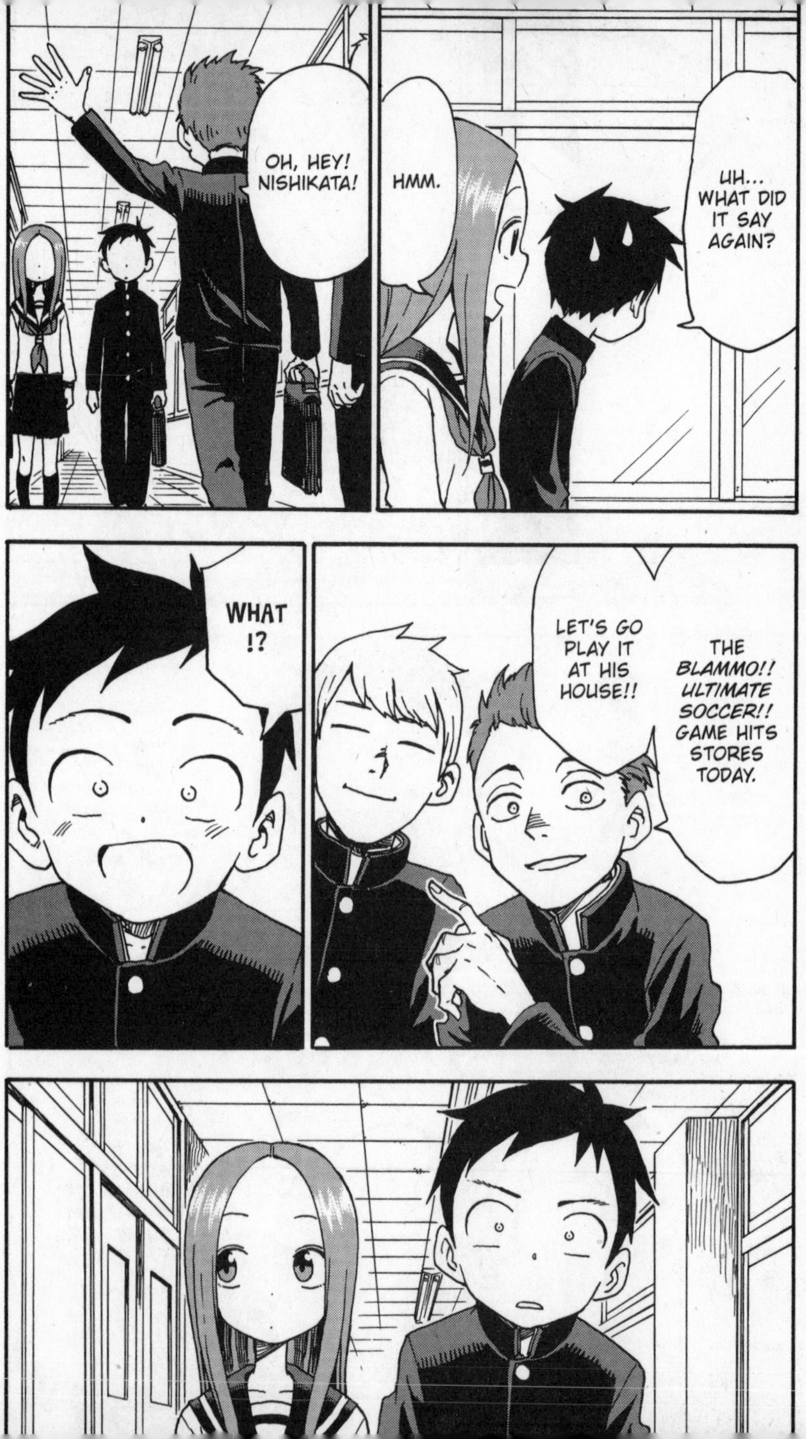
UH... WHAT DID IT SAY AGAIN?
HMM.
OH, HEY! NISHIKATA!
THE *BLAMMO!! ULTIMATE SOCCER!!* GAME HITS STORES TODAY.
LET'S GO PLAY IT AT HIS HOUSE!!
WHAT !?

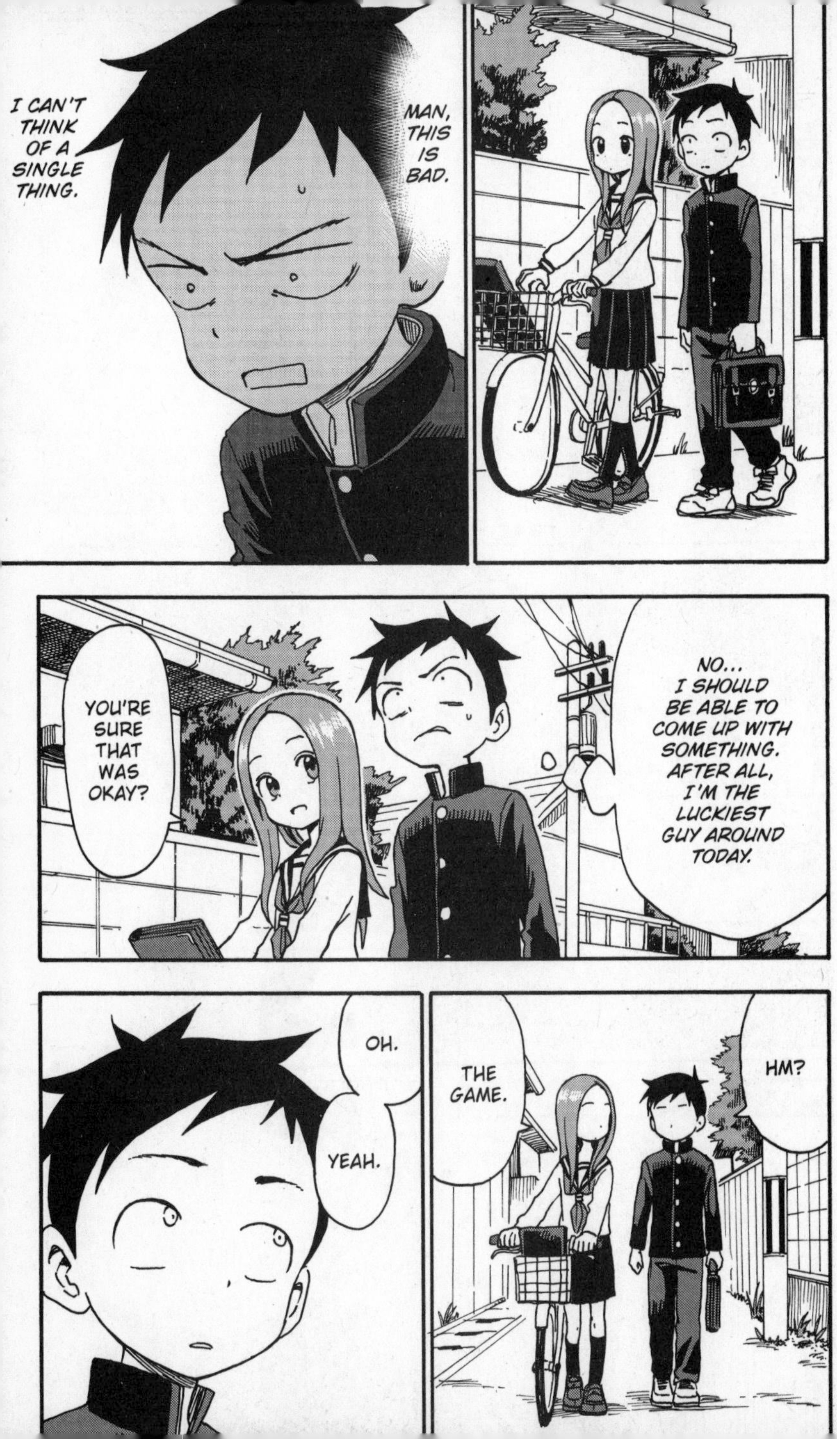
MAN, THIS IS BAD.
I CAN'T THINK OF A SINGLE THING.
NO... I SHOULD BE ABLE TO COME UP WITH SOMETHING. AFTER ALL, I'M THE LUCKIEST GUY AROUND TODAY.
YOU'RE SURE THAT WAS OKAY?
HM?
THE GAME.
OH.
YEAH.

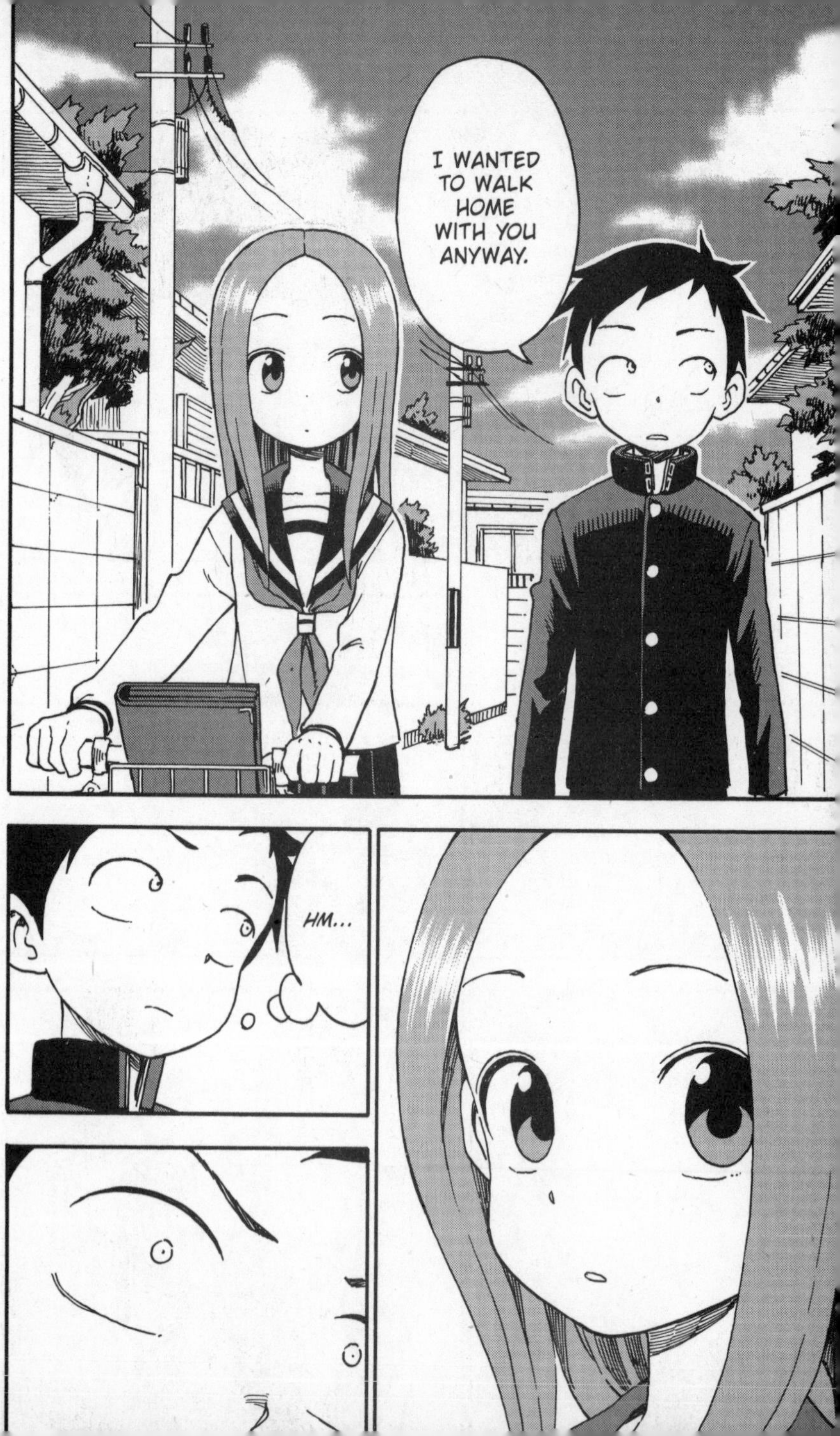
I WANTED TO WALK HOME WITH YOU ANYWAY.
HM...

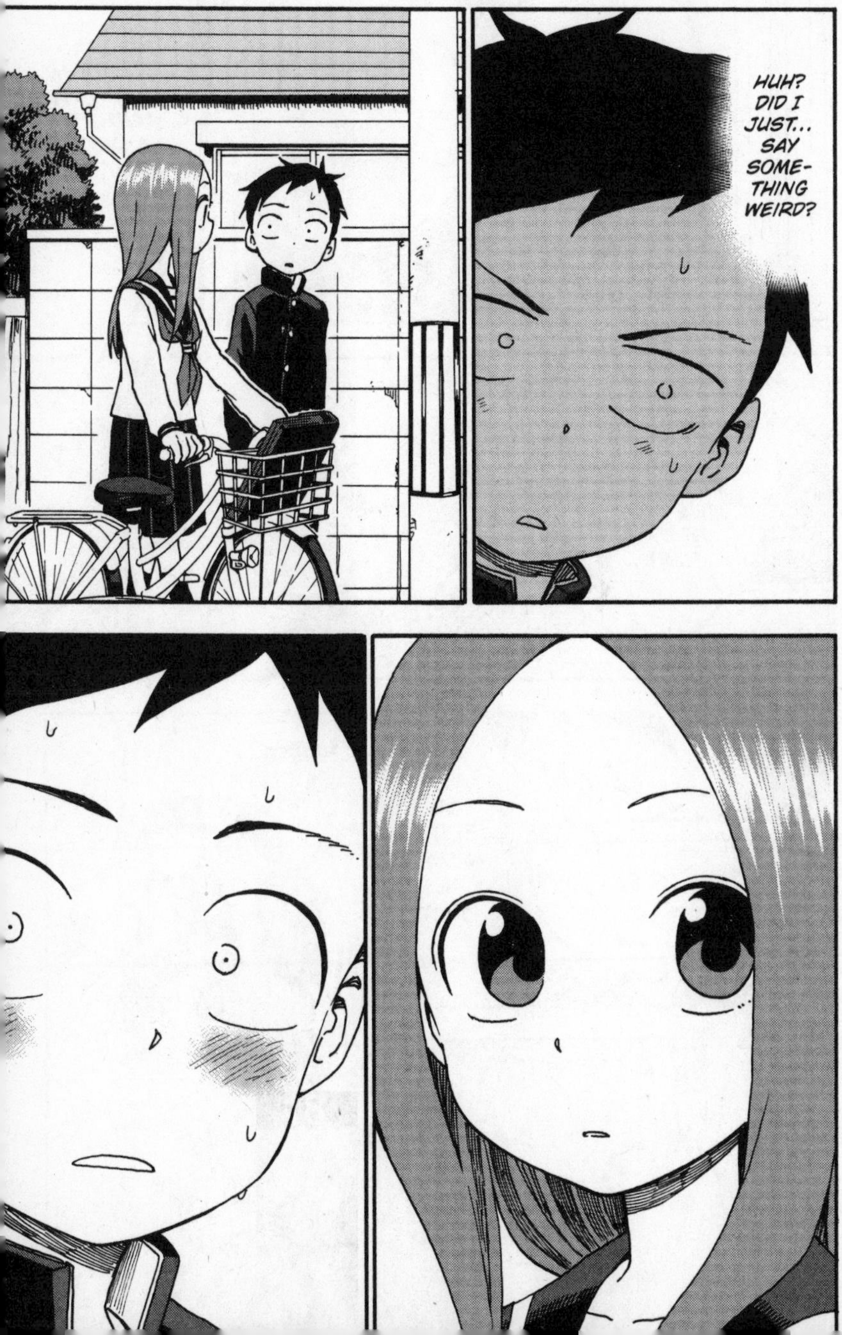
HUH? DID I JUST... SAY SOME-THING WEIRD?

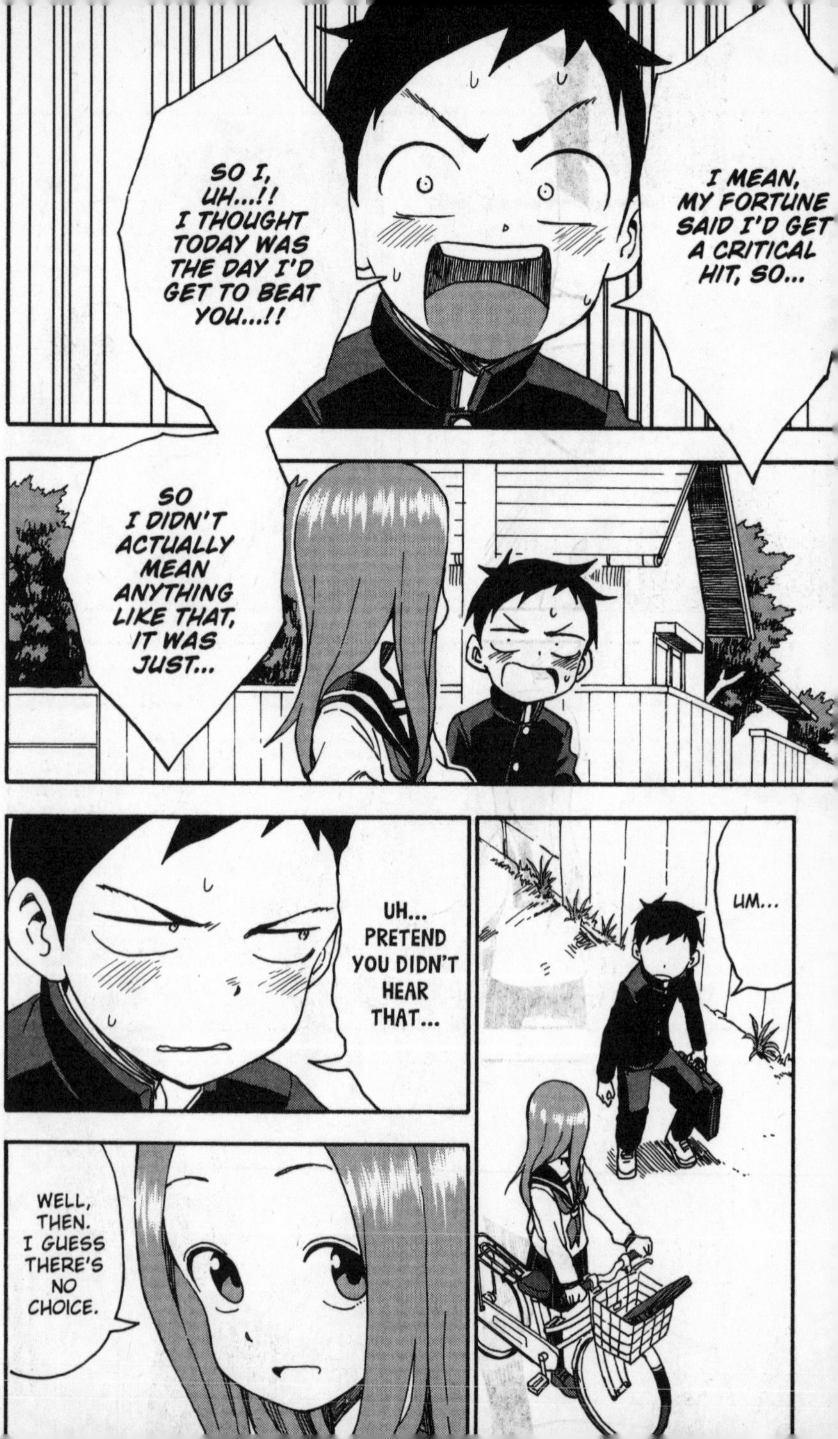
I MEAN, MY FORTUNE SAID I'D GET A CRITICAL HIT, SO...
SO I, UH...!! I THOUGHT TODAY WAS THE DAY I'D GET TO BEAT YOU...!!
SO I DIDN'T ACTUALLY MEAN ANYTHING LIKE THAT, IT WAS JUST...
UM...
UH... PRETEND YOU DIDN'T HEAR THAT...
WELL, THEN. I GUESS THERE'S NO CHOICE.

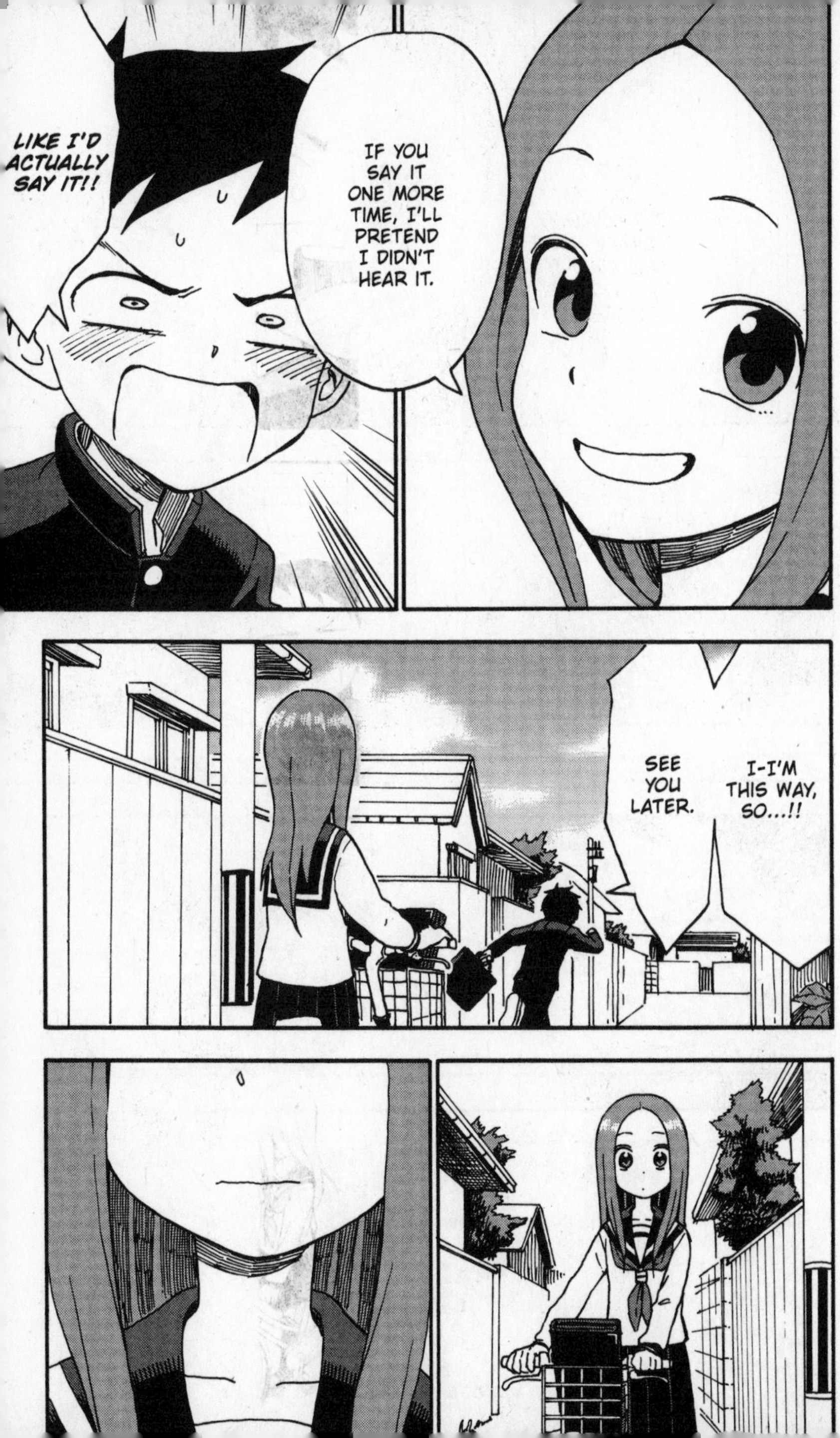
IF YOU SAY IT ONE MORE TIME, I'LL PRETEND I DIDN'T HEAR IT.
LIKE I'D ACTUALLY SAY IT!!
I-I'M THIS WAY, SO...!!
SEE YOU LATER.

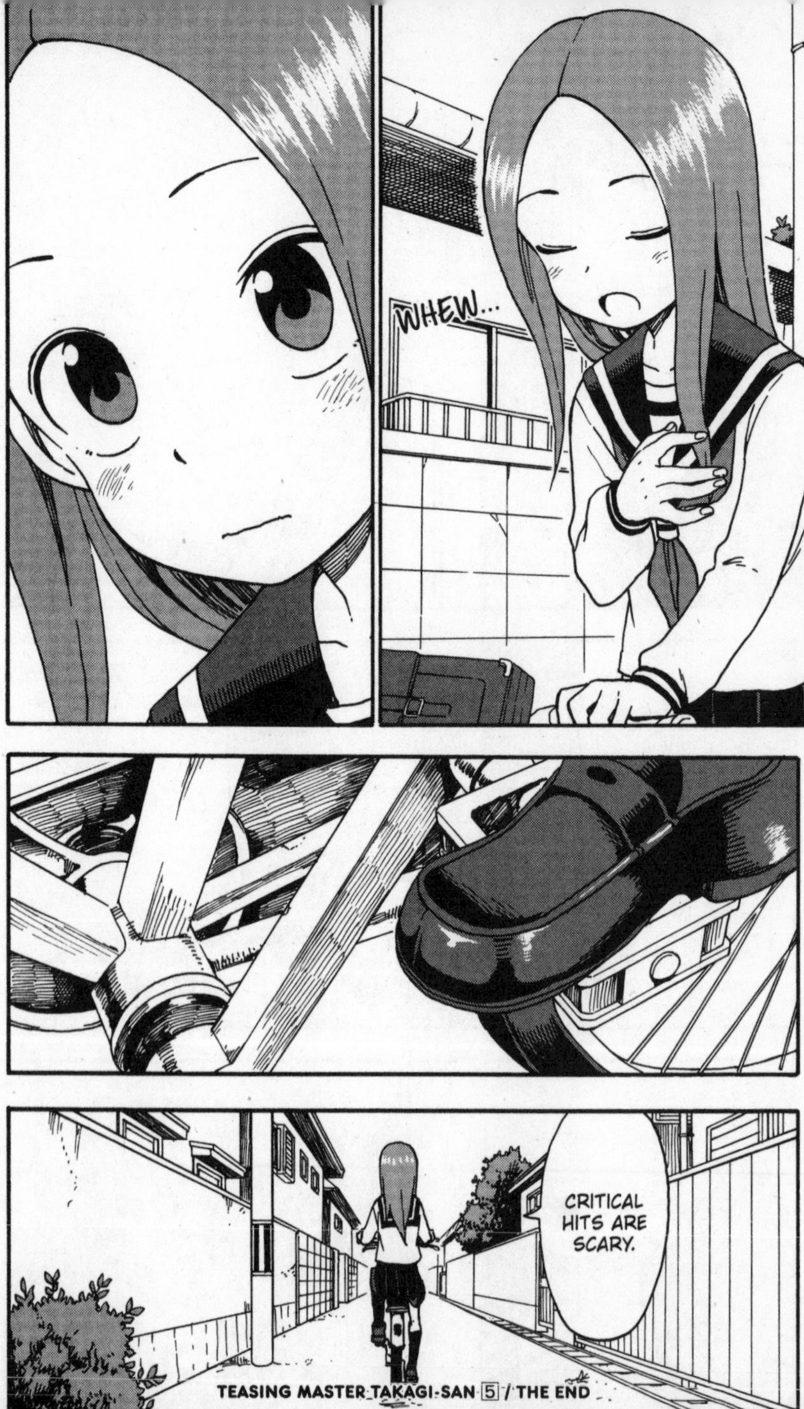
WHEW...
CRITICAL HITS ARE SCARY.
TEASING MASTER TAKAGI-SAN 5 / THE END

BONUS

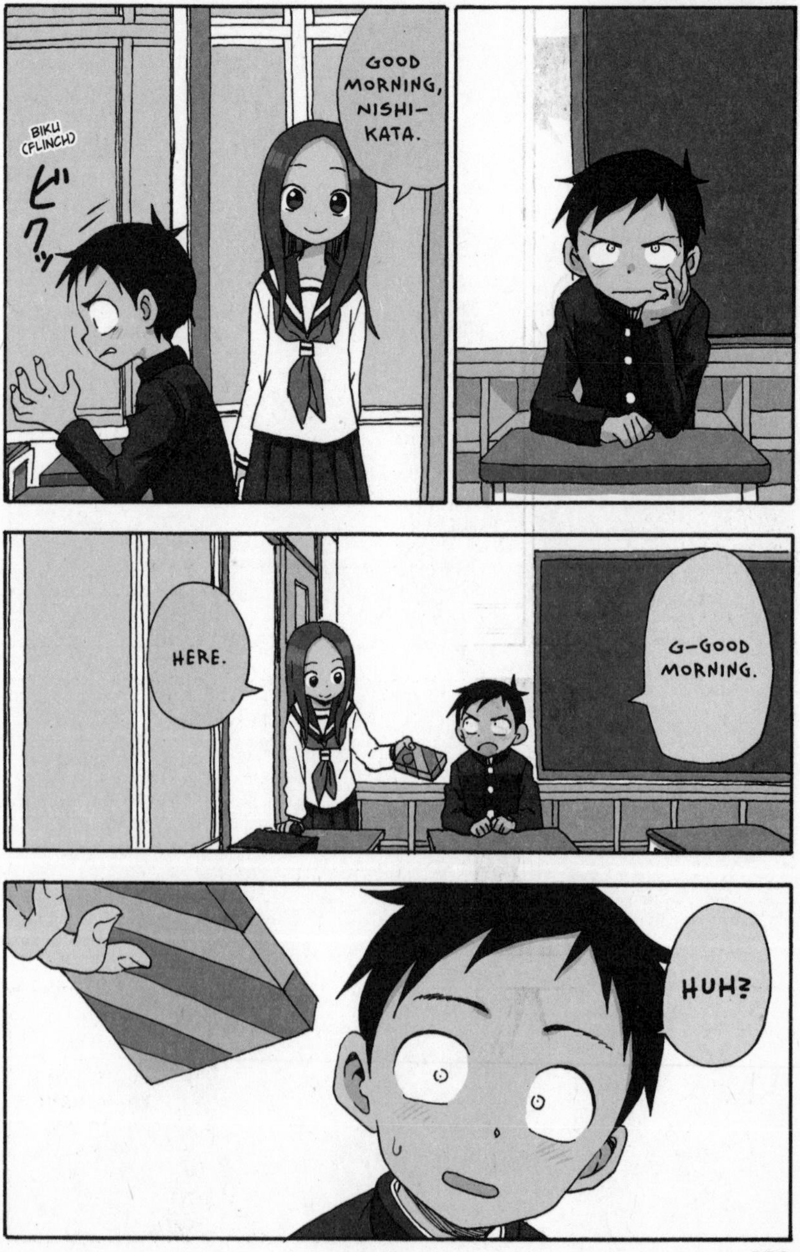
GOOD MORNING, NISHI-KATA.
BIKU (FLINCH)
ビクッ
G-GOOD MORNING.
HERE.
HUH?

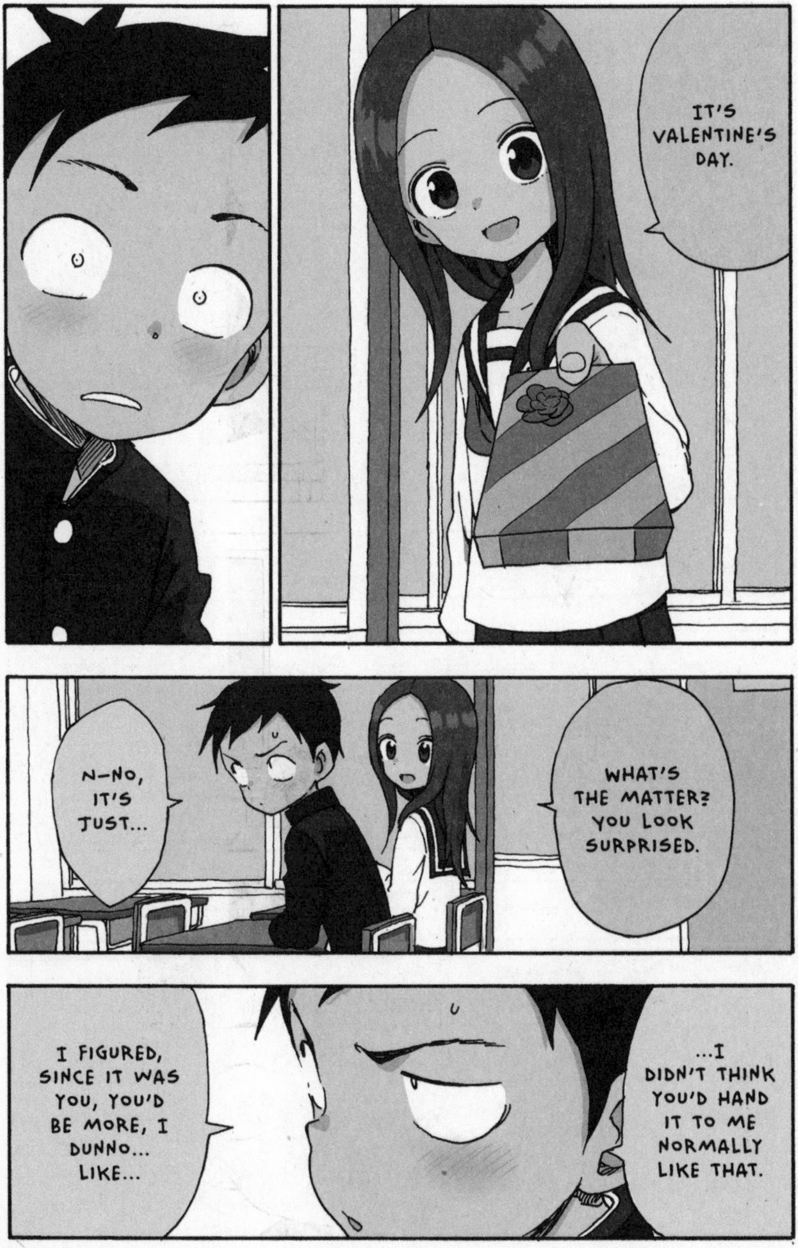
IT'S VALENTINE'S DAY.
WHAT'S THE MATTER? YOU LOOK SURPRISED.
N-NO, IT'S JUST...
...I DIDN'T THINK YOU'D HAND IT TO ME NORMALLY LIKE THAT.
I FIGURED, SINCE IT WAS YOU, YOU'D BE MORE, I DUNNO... LIKE...

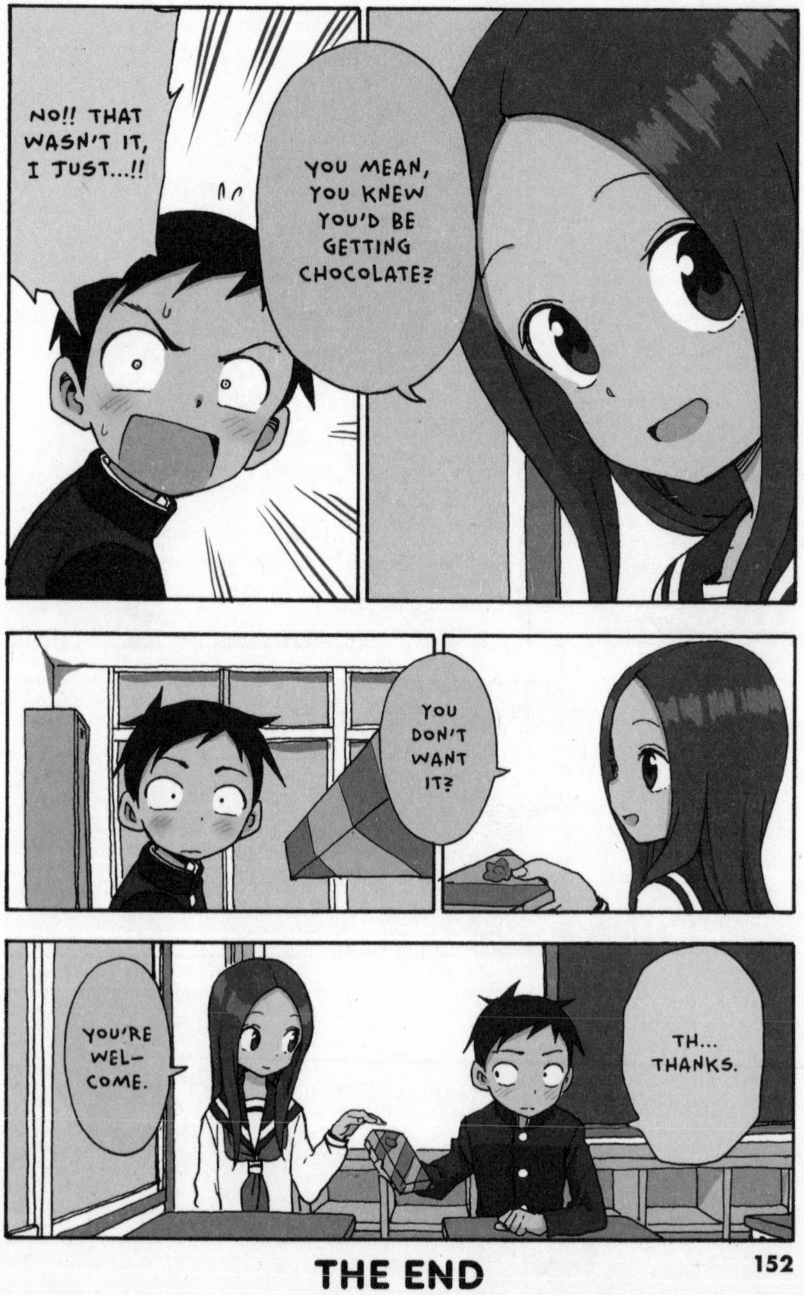
YOU MEAN, YOU KNEW YOU'D BE GETTING CHOCOLATE?
NO!! THAT WASN'T IT, I JUST...!!
YOU DON'T WANT IT?
TH... THANKS.
YOU'RE WEL-COME.

THE END

Teasing Master
Takagi-san

Translation Notes

COMMON HONORIFICS

no honorific: Indicates familiarity or closeness; if used without permission or reason, addressing someone in this manner would constitute an insult.

-san: The Japanese equivalent of Mr./Mrs./Miss. If a situation calls for politeness, this is the fail-safe honorific.

-kun: Used most often when referring to boys, this indicates affection or familiarity. Occasionally used by older men among their peers, but it may also be used by anyone referring to a person of lower standing.

-chan: An affectionate honorific indicating familiarity used mostly in reference to girls; also used in reference to cute persons or animals of either gender.

-senpai: A suffix used to address upperclassmen or more experienced coworkers.

-sensei: A respectful term for teachers, artists, or high-level professionals.

Page 52
This is a long-distance run for P.E. class, not an actual marathon.

Page 70
The sweet red bean drink, or *oshiruko*, is a thin soup made of sweetened red bean paste that can be served hot or cold. The ones in vending machines are usually hot. As with peanut butter, there are two styles: one that's blended until it's perfectly smooth, and another that's only partially blended, so that the unmashed bean fragments add extra texture. The one shown here is the latter type.

Page 76
Children are traditionally given money at New Year's by their parents and older relatives.

Page 137
Similar to horoscopes, in Japan, people use blood types to get a general sense of a person's personality and love compatibility.

Author's Note

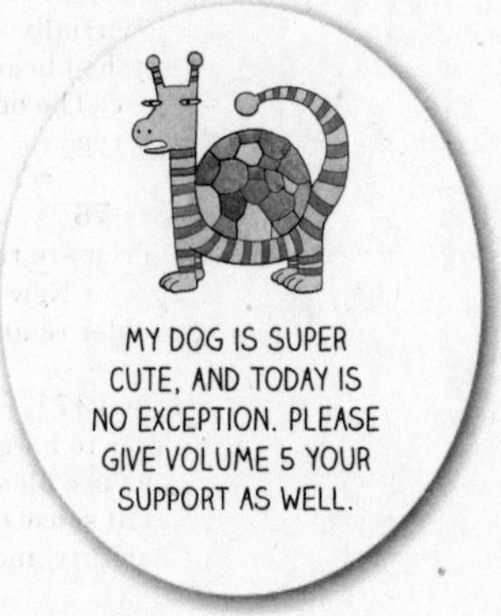
MY DOG IS SUPER CUTE, AND TODAY IS NO EXCEPTION. PLEASE GIVE VOLUME 5 YOUR SUPPORT AS WELL.

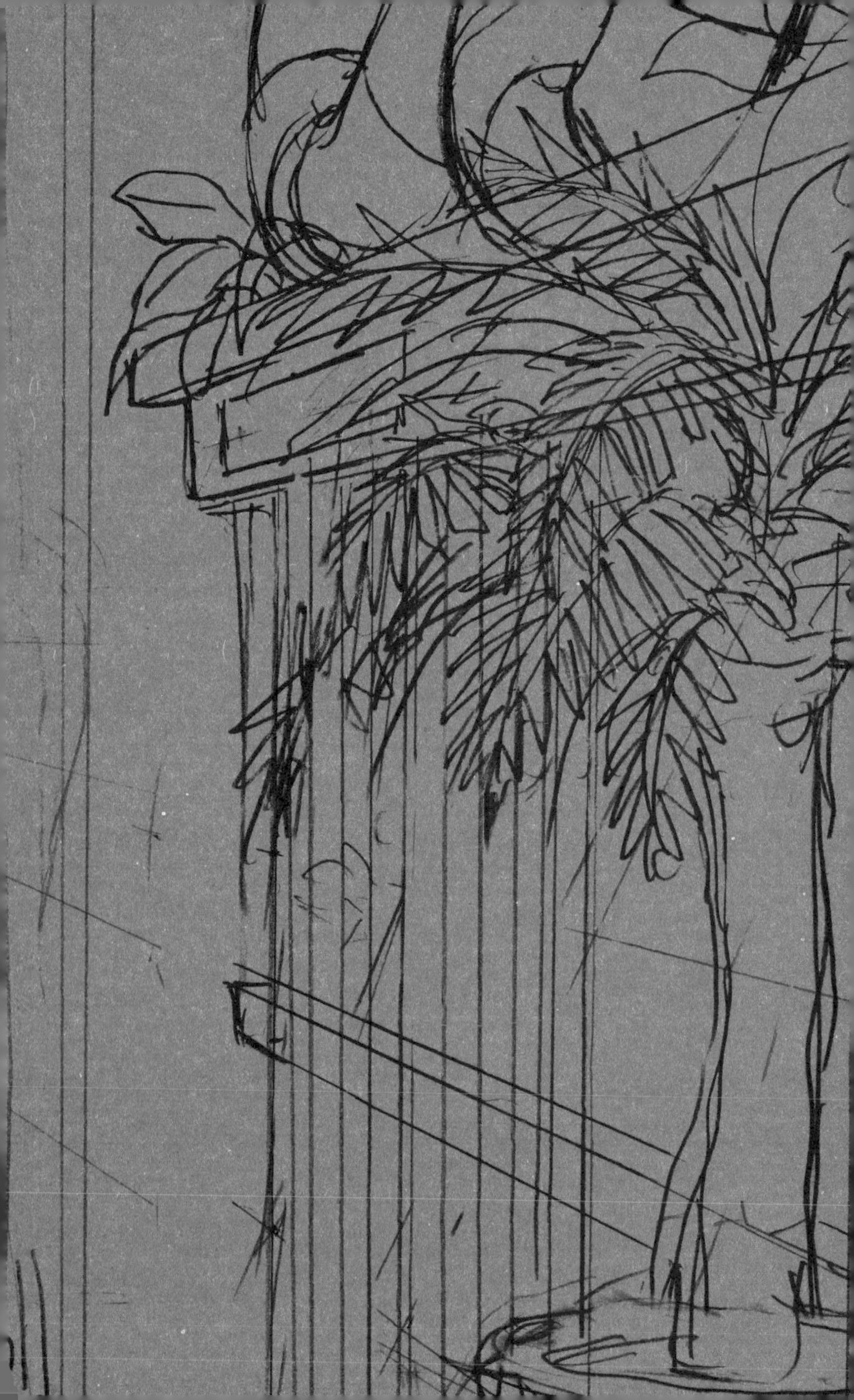

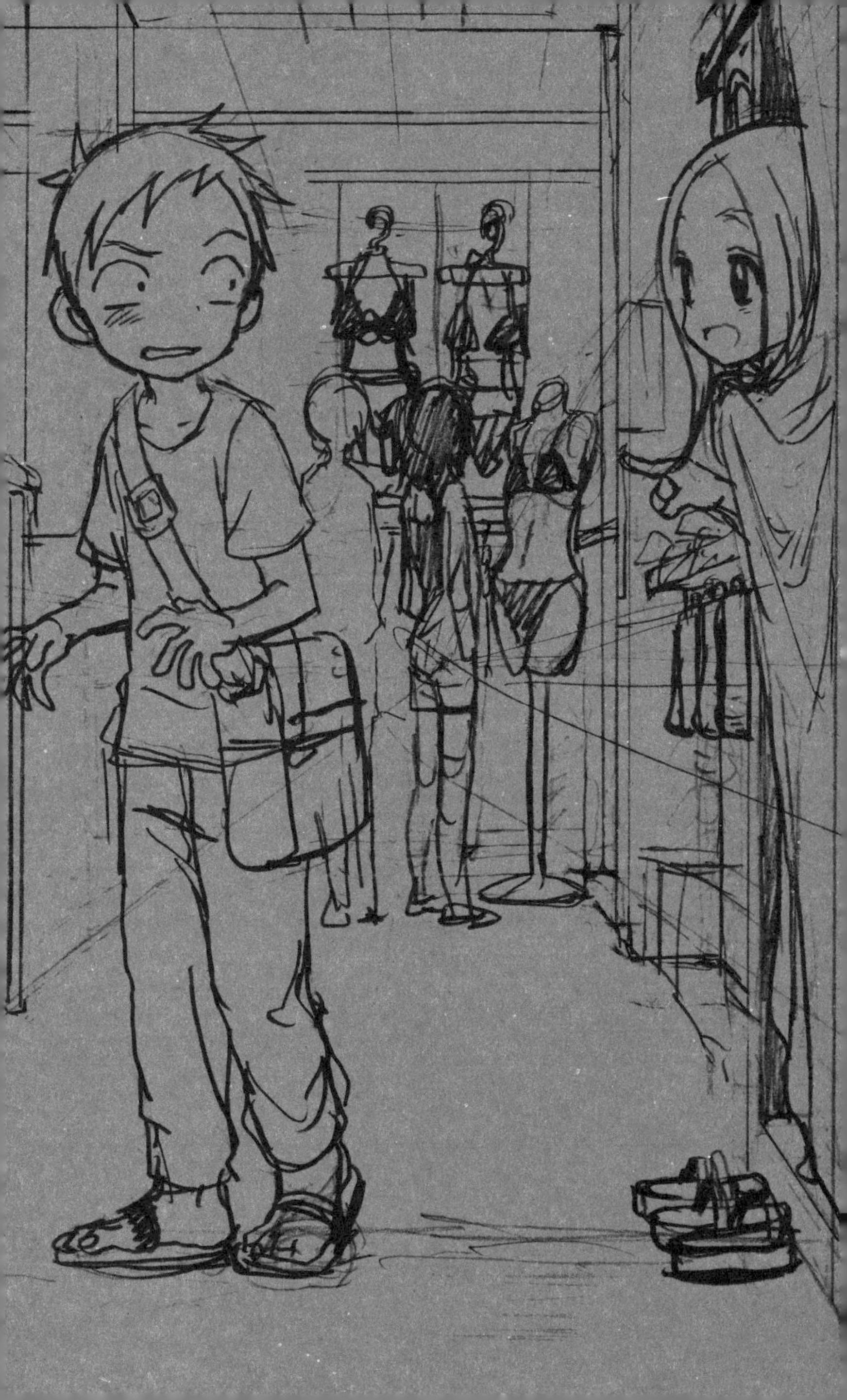

A Loner's Worth Nightmare: Human Interaction!

MY YOUTH R♥MANTIC COMEDY iS WRØNG, AS I EXPECTED

Hachiman Hikigaya is a cynic. He believes "youth" is a crock—a sucker's game, an illusion woven from failure and hypocrisy. But when he turns in an essay for a school assignment espousing this view, he's sentenced to work in the Service Club, an organization dedicated to helping students with problems! Worse, the only other member of the club is the haughty Yukino Yukinoshita, a girl with beauty, brains, and the personality of a garbage fire. How will Hachiman the Cynic cope with a job that requires—*gasp!*—social skills?